THE COST OF KNOWING

ALLAN N. PACKER

LUMINANT PUBLICATIONS

The Cost of Knowing

The Stone Cycle Book Two

Copyright © 2019 by Allan N. Packer

First edition (v1.3) published in 2019
by Luminant Publications

All rights reserved. Without limiting the rights under copyright reserved above, no part of this publication may be reproduced, distributed, transmitted, stored in, or introduced into a database or retrieval system, in any form, or by any means, without the prior written permission of both the copyright owner and the above publisher of this book.

The characters and events portrayed in this book are fictitious. Any similarity to real persons, living or dead, is coincidental and not intended by the author.

ISBN 978-1-925898-01-9

Luminant Publications
PO Box 201
Burnside, South Australia 5066

http://www.allanpacker.com

Cover Design by Karri Klawiter
Map illustration by Brian Plush

'The Cost of Knowing' is dedicated to Marc and Ray. I am grateful that they welcome me into their lives so willingly and unstintingly. And they keep presenting me with such delightful grandchildren!

PART I

VOLUME 1—THE FORMING

1

King Steffan the Second of Arvenon stood at the entrance to the royal tent, staring moodily out across a sea of smaller tents. A new frown creased his brow as the view was obscured by the latest downpour. The rain, apparently untroubled by royal displeasure, had been sheeting down fitfully since midmorning.

He closed the flap and stepped inside, banishing the showers. If only his frustrations could be dealt with so easily.

"What can we do, Bottren?" he asked irritably. "We're in the field with an army—finally—and going nowhere."

Bottren didn't respond, and Steffan didn't expect him to. Their central problem had not changed in the last three weeks. They could not find a way south through Deadman's Pass into Arvenon.

The pass was proving to be aptly named. A group of Rogandan soldiers had occupied the pass immediately after Steffan's wedding, and completely blocked a narrow section of it with large rocks. Access between Castel and Arvenon was no longer possible. The nature of the terrain and the determination of the defenders meant that every effort to dislodge them had failed.

Steffan's army, with the help of Castelan forces under King Istel and his commander, Lord Eisgold, had tried everything. A frontal assault had been disastrous—Steffan lost so many men that three weeks later he was still berating himself for ever agreeing to it. Steffan's and Istel's best archers had rained arrows on the position; they stopped when they discovered that the Rogandans were simply retrieving the fallen arrows and shooting them back. Agile mountain men volunteered to scale the walls of the pass, but the rain had made the rocks slippery, and every one of the climbers eventually plunged to their deaths.

Without this pass, they would have to head northwest all the way to the sea and take ship to Erestor. Then they would be forced to march east across much of Arvenon before they could reach the same point. Even if the ships were available, they simply didn't have time. If only there was a way to break through.

The Rogandans had chosen to defend a section of the pass where the walls narrowed to a thin neck. It was located almost all the way to the Arvenian side. From the summit of the pass the rolling hills of Arvenon could be glimpsed in the distance, over the heads of the defenders. Having the goal so close only increased Steffan's frustration.

No doubt Rogandans were roaming freely throughout Arvenon. The longer Steffan's army delayed breaking through, the sooner winter would creep upon them. Then it would be too late to do anything. The Arvenian capital, Arnost, might even fall if he was unable to break the Rogandan siege.

Steffan wondered what had become of Will Prentis. No doubt the defenders at Arnost were benefiting from his leadership, but once again Steffan wished he had brought Will to Castel with him instead of old Olaf. The deputy captain of the King's Guard might have been young, but he was energetic and effective. He would have forced his way through the pass somehow.

As Steffan's mind wandered, his thoughts found their way back to Essanda. He pictured her as he had seen her in their apartments in Castel Citadel, a smile playing across her young lips as she gazed intently at her new husband. She seemed to think highly of him for some reason he couldn't fathom. Lately he had taken to writing to her regularly. Young though she was, he could safely vent his frustrations with her, and having an outlet brought him some consolation. The letters she wrote back were thoughtful and sympathetic, and—he struggled for a moment trying to put his finger on it—artless. Yes, that was it. It wasn't that she was childish, or simplistic. She was actually very intelligent, and clearly trying to put herself into the role of a responsible queen. But somehow her carefree girlishness always managed to leak out. Steffan found it endearing.

The strangeness of his own thinking suddenly struck him. He was already forgetting that he had been maneuvered into this marriage. And somehow it had apparently become settled in his mind that years must pass before his bride could become his wife in full measure.

He sighed deeply, and dragged his mind back to the problem before him. He decided to try to think like Will. To find a solution that no one else had thought of, yet seemed so obvious after the event.

STEFFAN'S SOLDIERS moved into position just below the summit of Deadman's Pass, lining up behind a newly constructed siege engine. The engine resembled a tall tower on wheels. Thin metal shielding covered the front and sides of the monstrous wooden structure, and the platform at the top was broad enough to accommodate a dozen men and tall enough to overshadow the mound of rocks that blocked the pass.

At a signal from their commander, the soldiers began to push with all their might, even as horses at the front took up the strain and pulled. Slowly, reluctantly, the wheels began to turn, and the huge structure groaned as it inched forward up the pass. As it slowly crested the summit the horses were moved aside. The soldiers continued to push, and the siege engine gradually gained momentum as the road sloped downward. Soldiers inside the structure soon began to apply massive brakes to ensure it did not move too fast.

The best engineers of Castel had spent the previous week building the engine on the Castelan side of the summit, just out of sight of the Rogandans. Thankfully the rains had eased off, and construction had gone according to plan. But it had cost them another week.

Down the pass lumbered the engine, slowly and inexorably. Soldiers massed behind it, protected by its vast bulk. Harsh cries could now be heard from the Rogandans at the end of the pass. Arrows soon appeared, but the engine was barely in range, and most fell short. The remaining arrows bounced harmlessly off its protective shielding. Soldiers atop the structure now began firing back, their arrows easily reaching the defenders.

As the engine rolled closer, arrows from behind the barrier occasionally found their mark, and figures could be seen falling from the top of the engine.

Rogandan soldiers appeared, bearing large rocks which they attempted to place in front of their defenses. As soon as they left their protection they were met by a deadly hail of arrows. None made it back alive. A few achieved their purpose, though—some of the rocks would now prevent the engine from rolling all the way to the barrier.

As the siege engine approached the defenses Arvenian soldiers ran in front of it to remove the rocks, protected by a stream of arrows from the tower of the engine. Rogandan archers recklessly exposed themselves to prevent the attackers from reaching the rocks. One Arvenian went down, another, and then another. The rocks were removed, but not before seven of Steffan's soldiers lay unmoving before the barrier.

Now the attackers threw down jars of boiling oil from the tower. Cries of alarm could be heard as the jars shattered, spewing bubbling liquid over the defenders. Burning torches followed the jars and flames sprang up everywhere. The whole scene quickly descended into chaos. Few arrows now reached the top of the engine. Another signal was given and Arvenian and Castelan troops rushed from behind the engine and scrambled over the barrier. Within minutes loud cheering could be heard from the top of the siege tower. The defenses had been overwhelmed.

The battle for Deadman's Pass was over. The entire operation had taken less than an hour.

Steffan sat in his tent, eager with anticipation. He had just received word that the last rocks from the barrier had been cleared from the pass. Dusk was upon them now, and his soldiers were resting. Tomorrow he would re-enter his kingdom, and with an army at his back.

The king had just sent off a note to his young queen, informing her of the good news and warning her that before long he rode to war and to an uncertain future.

Some would undoubtedly think him foolish for investing time and emotional energy communicating with someone barely older than a child. But it was important to him, and he didn't care if others thought it strange.

It brought to mind something his father had told him soon after the death of Steffan's mother. He had just turned eighteen. While he greatly missed his mother, the world lay before him bright with hope and promise. His father, though, had borne the burdens of kingship for too many years, and he never recovered from the loss of his wisest counselor and most loyal supporter. He didn't openly show his grief, but it was barely four years before they buried him beside his wife, reuniting him in death with the one who had been his truest friend in life.

One day he had told Steffan that it was her companionship he missed the most. Recalling it, Steffan began to understand why his relationship with his young wife had already assumed such importance to him. He had no siblings, and he had essentially been alone since his parents died. Now he, too, had a companion.

There was nothing sexual in his response to Essanda—he had assigned that part of himself to a long hibernation. But he cared about her, and he was certain that she, too, had come to care about him. There was someone apart from himself in the world to whom his thoughts and feelings and concerns really mattered. He understood for the first time the significance of his father's words. A king, no less than any other man, needed to walk through life with a companion.

His thoughts were interrupted by the arrival of a messenger. "Our watchmen have seen riders approaching the pass, Sire. From Arvenon. Four of them."

"Friend or foe, bring them to me as soon as they arrive," the king instructed. "I need to know what's been going on in my kingdom."

The man bowed and left.

It was dark before the messenger returned. Four men entered the tent behind him, and the king's mouth opened wide with astonishment when he saw them.

"Will! Rufe! I thought you were shut up in Arnost. Has the city fallen, then?" he asked in dismay.

"No, Your Majesty," Will assured him. "Not as far as we know, anyway. The city was secure in the hands of the duke when we left it several weeks ago. They were well provisioned and well defended. I am confident they have been able to keep the Rogandans out."

His immediate concerns allayed, the king paused long enough to call for refreshments. He also sent to King Istel, asking him to join them at his convenience.

"King Istel will join us shortly. Who are your companions, Will?"

"This is Ander, and this is Nestor, Sire. They have traveled with us since we left Arnost."

"You are welcome," the king returned, as the men bowed.

King Istel arrived and was introduced to the men.

After satisfying himself that his father-in-law was comfortable, King Steffan addressed his attention to the new arrivals. "I am very glad to see you, Will! And you, too, Rufe. I will have great need of your skills in the days ahead."

Will bowed in response. "We are at your service, Your Majesty."

"So you left Arnost with only these companions?"

"No, Sire. Our party was larger at first."

"So where have you been and what have you been doing in the weeks since you left Arnost?"

"That is a long story," Will replied calmly.

"We can spare a little time," the king replied with a smile. "And I enjoy stories," he added, waving them to some empty seats.

2

The royal city of Varacellan, the many towered capital of the Kingdom of Varas, lay glittering like an elegant jewel in the afternoon sunlight. A stiff breeze whipped the flags on the lofty battlements of the royal castle, dispersing the fresh smell of salty air throughout the city. Tall ships lay at anchor in the harbor, sheltering from the heavy seas that pounded the coast beyond the inlet.

Varas was a small but prosperous kingdom encircled by Castel, Rogand, Arvenon, and the sea. A rugged and inaccessible coastline formed the northern border of Varas, but Varacellan, with its fine harbor, offered a haven that attracted ships from every corner of the continent and beyond. The capital had become the hub of a prosperous trade network, and goods flowed in abundance between the harbor and the main trade route south to Arvenon.

The broad River Aron formed much of the southern boundary of Varas, marking its border with Arvenon. Varas also shared a short and mountainous border with Castel to the west; otherwise the sea formed the longest stretch of the western fringe of the kingdom. To the east lay Rogand, across an impenetrable section of the Blue Mountains that extended along the entire eastern border of Varas.

Small as it was, Varas had somehow managed to retain a precarious independence over the years. That independence now appeared threatened as rarely before.

Within the audience chamber of the royal palace, a group of men waited restlessly, illuminated by the bright sunlight that flooded in through the broad windows. The faces of the men were grim.

"The Rogandan Ambassador is here, Sire."

"Show him in."

King Delmar of Varas sat in state flanked by four of his most senior advisors. The ambassador stepped into the room and bowed low. Delmar found the gesture more mocking than deferential. Was it because the Rogandan held his bow for slightly too long, or was it the poorly concealed smirk that flashed across his face as he returned to a standing position? Whatever the reason, his manner reeked of insincerity.

"Why are Rogandan soldiers massing at our southern border, Lord Grunsetz?" Delmar demanded.

"A mere misunderstanding, Sire," the ambassador replied with an oily smile. "Lord Drettroth simply wishes to ensure that Varas is not disturbed by any armed troublemakers fleeing Arvenon."

"We can secure our borders without your help," Delmar replied curtly. "And we are well able to manage our own relationship with King Steffan, too."

"I understand, Your Majesty. I trust you appreciate that Rogand would not want to see Varas drawn into Arvenon's quarrel with Rogand."

"I presume the 'quarrel' to which you refer is Rogand's unprovoked invasion of Arvenon."

Grunsetz frowned. "Your concern for Arvenon surprises me, Sire. Is there an alliance that Rogand is unaware of?"

"I said nothing about an alliance. But I would be a fool indeed if I ignored what was going on around me."

"Of course, Your Majesty. Rogand's concern is very simple. Castel has allowed itself to be aligned with the Arvenians, a decision that I fear their king may come to regret before long. Rogand simply wishes to avoid any similar...ah...misunderstandings with Varas."

"If Rogand wishes to avoid misunderstandings with Varas, you will withdraw your forces from our border."

"I regret that I can make no commitments on behalf of King Agon, Sire. But I will certainly convey your wishes to His Majesty."

"I am counting on you to do so," Delmar replied.

Lord Grunsetz bowed once again. "There is another matter I wished to raise," he said. "With your permission, of course."

"You may speak," Delmar replied.

"King Agon wishes to establish a treaty with Varas," said the ambassador.

Delmar eyed the man warily. What game was Agon playing? "What kind of a treaty?" he asked.

"A security pact. King Agon has learned that Rogandan traders are being attacked in Varas. He is concerned about the security of his people, especially now that they are being targeted."

"Rogandan traders are not being targeted. One trader was robbed here in Varacellan, and I believe he was injured. Investigations are being pursued vigorously. There are reports, though, that he contributed to the incident by cheating local merchants."

"King Agon views it differently. He wishes to establish a treaty that would allow Rogand to place soldiers in Varas to protect Rogandan traders."

"What?! So you are proposing to invade Varas, too?"

"Please, Your Majesty! Rogand has no such intention. King Agon's desire is to resolve this issue by means of a treaty."

"Varas will regard any intrusion by Rogandan forces as an act of war!"

"I implore you, Sire! What is to be gained by making an enemy of Rogand?"

"Let me return the question to you. What does Rogand gain by making an enemy of Varas?"

"May I speak frankly, Your Majesty? Rogand has little to fear from Varas. But King Agon wishes to offer Varas an opportunity to avoid any possibility of unnecessary strife."

"This audience is at an end, Lord Grunsetz. Your proposal will be considered. I will offer no more than that."

The Rogandan bowed once again and was ushered from the room.

THE DOOR HAD BARELY CLOSED on the ambassador before a heated debate broke out among Delmar's advisors.

"It's an outrage!" stormed Lord Radesen. "Grunsetz should be thrown out of Varas without ceremony!"

"We cannot fight the Rogandans and expect to win," Lord Lunevag countered. "Their army is simply too large."

"Is it possible that the Rogandans will invade?"

"Surely not. Why would they ask for a treaty if they were planning to invade?"

"Why demand the right to place troops inside our borders, then?"

"That is nothing more than a bargaining ploy. They are beginning negotiations with an unreasonable demand that can be withdrawn later as a gesture of goodwill."

"We must ally ourselves with Arvenon."

"What use would that be? The Arvenians cannot even defend themselves effectively—how could they aid us?"

"Rogand has not yet subdued Arvenon, for all Grunsetz's posturing. Their armies have been unable to take Arnost, if the reports are to be believed."

A new voice cut across the argument. "Varas should accept this treaty." Lord Tarestel spoke quietly, but all eyes turned to him at his words. "There is no other way we can avoid war. If we fight Rogand, our armies will be quickly overwhelmed. If we enter into a treaty we will at least retain some ability to determine our own destiny."

King Delmar frowned. He wasn't at all sure he wanted to encourage this particular line of thinking. "Your counsel is valued as always, My Lords," he said. "You are dismissed for now; please make yourselves available to meet again tomorrow. Lord Radesen, remain here for a moment."

Lord Radesen inclined his head in acknowledgment. The other advisors bowed and departed.

The king turned to the head of his judiciary, not attempting to hide his displeasure. "This matter of the Rogandan trader needs to be resolved decisively, Radesen! See that justice is done, and be prompt about it. And make sure that Grunsetz—and anyone else with even the vaguest interest in the affair—hears about the outcome and understands it fully. We don't need to give Agon a pretext for picking a quarrel with us."

Lord Radesen bowed deeply and hurried away.

Delmar watched him go with a heavy heart. Tarestel was right about one thing—Varas simply was not strong enough militarily to defeat Rogand. Should he have allied himself with Steffan? He had hoped that a neutral stance might allow him to avoid conflict with Rogand. But such hopes might be proving illusory.

Arvenon was a natural ally. The two countries shared a great deal in common, in language, culture, and religion. By contrast, the very thought of a treaty with Rogand stuck in his throat. And he was not at all convinced by Tarestel's argument that signing a treaty with Rogand gave Varas more influence over its own destiny. How could it be safer to invite a poisonous reptile into your home, when you could try to deal with it while it was still outside?

He had so little experience to draw upon. Why couldn't this crisis have waited a few more years? Throughout his brief adult years his course had never seemed smooth. For as long as he had been king, he had been forced to navigate a road filled with ruts and pitfalls. And it was abundantly clear that the path before him was about to become very bumpy indeed.

"You didn't share your own views after Grunsetz left the Council, Karevis," said King Delmar, "and I'd like to know what you think. I still cannot bring myself to believe that Agon wants to pick a fight with Varas. He's already fighting two kingdoms as it is. Maybe I'm just deluding myself, though. What do you think I should do?"

The two of them stood together on a palace balcony that overlooked one of the broad tree-lined streets of Varacellan. The breeze might have been fresh, but the weather was unseasonably mild. Locals and foreigners mingled freely, enjoying the late afternoon sunshine as they strolled happily along the street and browsed among the hawkers' stalls that offered tasty portions of food, bolts of colored cloth, cut flowers, and much else besides. Delmar wondered how many more such afternoons they would enjoy together in peace.

Lord Karevis had been leaning on the balcony gazing down at the sights below. He turned his attention away from the tranquil scene and faced Delmar.

"My heart says to fight," he replied. He paused for a long moment before adding, "I'm not sure that we can win, though."

Delmar sighed. "We have an army, but we're not sure we can take the risk of using it."

"Our soldiers are better trained and better disciplined than the Rogandans," Karevis asserted. "I have complete confidence in them. They will give a good account of themselves whenever it comes to a battle. My only uncertainty is how we can contrive to outmaneuver an adversary with such a significant advantage in numbers."

Delmar fell silent. Karevis had been born the same year as him and had remained his closest friend since childhood. They had played together, studied together, and trained together. They'd also quarreled and fought at times, but they'd never fallen out for long. Karevis was the brother Delmar never had.

Yet Karevis had never traded on this special relationship. Delmar routinely sought out his friend, sometimes to consult with him and sometimes just to enjoy his company. If other nobles ever found out, though, it wasn't because Karevis told them. Delmar had learned to trust his friend's discretion implicitly.

Though still a young man, Karevis now commanded the Varasan army, a role he had earned by dint of hard work combined with his very considerable abilities.

Delmar had always been impressed by his friend's strategic sense. And the commander had honed the skills of his soldiers to exacting standards. There was little doubt in Delmar's mind that the Varasan army could achieve more than any other army of equivalent size. He had no desire to throw away any of the lives of his soldiers to put his belief to the test, though.

In spite of the looming crisis with Rogand, Delmar still held out hopes that a settlement could be negotiated. He feared that his hopes may be nothing more than wishful thinking, though. Either way, he wouldn't need to wait long to find out.

KING DELMAR OF VARAS stood to receive his advisors as they filed into the room. Lord Karevis had already arrived.

He waited until they were all seated. "I've just received some very grave news, My Lords," he said. "The Rogandans have crossed the border. They have forded the River Aron and occupied the main pass into the lowlands."

This report was greeted with loud expressions of dismay.

"Are we at war with them, then?" asked Lord Lunevag.

"There hasn't been any real fighting," Karevis replied. "Our border guards were taken by surprise and overwhelmed. The army units stationed near the border have withdrawn and are awaiting orders."

"So much for Agon's interest in a treaty," said Lunevag.

Lord Radesen had thrust back his chair and was pacing around the room. "That means they've already overrun my estates!"

Delmar could smell the scent of fear among his advisors. It wouldn't take much for them to descend into panic.

"I intend to handle this situation personally, My Lords," he told them calmly, projecting a confidence he didn't feel.

"What do you plan to do, Sire?" asked Lord Tarestel.

"The difficulty of containing the Rogandan army has just increased significantly," he replied. "The Aron and the mountain pass have always been our strongest lines of defense. The loss of the pass in particular is a significant misfortune. I will contact Grunsetz and see if it is still possible to negotiate. I fear that our bargaining position is greatly diminished, though."

Some of the lords had a lot to say, and Delmar let them speak. Although many words were spoken, he heard little of any value. Lunevag and Radesen were still in denial, hoping irrationally that somehow life could return to normal. They were in for a rude shock. Privately, Delmar held out little hope that Varas would still exist as an independent kingdom by the end of another week. Whether they decided to fight or negotiate, the outcome would most likely be the same before long.

Tarestel largely kept his own counsel. The noble's wealth had always exceeded his power, and Delmar had long sensed that the discrepancy irked him greatly. The man had become craftier as he aged, if not wiser, and Delmar found himself wondering uneasily if Tarestel had his own agenda in this situation.

ONCE AGAIN KAREVIS had held his peace, and Delmar sought him out after dismissing the Council.

"Is the situation retrievable?" Delmar asked.

"While we held the pass we had a chance. It's hard to see how we can keep them out for long now, though." Karevis hung his head. "I strengthened the guard at the border, but I should have issued orders to expect an invasion, and to defend the river crossings and the pass at all costs."

"The fault does not lie with you," Delmar told him firmly. "I'm the one who failed to act decisively while I still had the chance. We've always had strong natural barriers on three sides, and our southern border has been secure thanks to good relations with Arvenon. It's become painfully clear to me that I've taken that far too much for granted." He shook his head, struggling to come to terms with his own blindness, and with the magnitude of the disaster that had been visited on his kingdom as a result.

"Until they invaded Arvenon, the Rogandans never had ready

access to our borders. Once they did, though, they didn't waste much time. Before long they'll control the entire continent."

Delmar placed his hands on his friend's shoulders and looked him in the eye. "Whatever happens now, do everything you can to protect our people. Don't fail me in this!"

Karevis looked downcast. But he nodded his agreement. "Should I join my men?" he asked.

"No. Send orders to resist further encroachments by the Rogandans, but not to actively initiate fighting before I've attempted negotiations."

Karevis bowed, and left to relay the orders.

Delmar knew he couldn't afford to delay. He had to act swiftly, not just because time was short, but because he needed to be actively doing something. He was frightened that if he allowed himself the luxury of thinking, he would quickly lose any hope of preserving his own self control.

There was so much he had planned to do. He wanted to enrich and strengthen the kingdom he had inherited, and broaden its alliances. He had expected to marry and have a family, and to one day grow old enjoying his grandchildren.

It was all too late now, though. The very best he could hope for was to fulfill his duty as king, and try to retrieve whatever he could from the wreckage.

KING DELMAR WAS bone weary by the time he arrived under a flag of truce with his aides at Rogandan army headquarters near the border with Arvenon. Having finally reached his destination, though, he found that his entire body was throbbing with nervous energy.

"Come in, Your Majesty." Grunsetz offered his usual oily smile as he ushered the king into his tent and pointed him to a seat. No refreshments or other courtesies were on offer. Delmar was not surprised.

"What brings you to my humble quarters?" the Rogandan asked.

"I'm here to negotiate," Delmar replied simply.

"Ah. Well advised, I'm sure. Perhaps I could have offered better terms at our earlier meeting. But no matter. Since your army has avoided bloodshed thus far, there is still an opportunity to reach a peaceful solution to the current disagreements. I know that Lord Drettroth is eager to meet with you."

Delmar did not like the implications of Grunsetz's comment. "Surely we can discuss details here, right now."

"That would also be my clear preference, Sire. Please understand that. But I am under strict instructions. Lord Drettroth is only willing to discuss details of an accord in person."

"What does he propose if I accept?"

"You will be escorted to his headquarters for the negotiations, protected by a special Guard of Honor in recognition of your rank. Your aides will be allowed to return to your capital to report on your behalf."

"You cannot be proposing that I go alone!"

"Those are my explicit instructions, Your Majesty. Lord Drettroth was most specific."

"And if I refuse?"

"You will be allowed to return to your army. Hostilities will commence immediately. Fighting has been delayed only out of respect for your stated desire to meet to discuss terms."

Delmar frowned. Discussing terms sounded a lot like surrender, and he had never made any such proposal. This situation was even worse than he had feared.

What choice did he have, though? He had been brought to Grunsetz by a roundabout route that gave him plenty of opportunity to review the size of the Rogandan army. He was sure that the detours had been entirely intentional. However good the Varasan soldiers might be, it was clear that the Rogandans had brought a large enough force to overwhelm Delmar's army, especially now that they controlled the pass and enjoyed ready access to the Varasan lowlands.

But going alone to meet Drettroth? Was it safe? Delmar glanced across at his aides. He hadn't brought them for protection—they were advisors, not soldiers. And even if they had been soldiers, he knew they wouldn't be able to safeguard him for long if Drettroth wanted him dead. By coming here, he had already placed his safety entirely in the hands of the Rogandans.

As for advice, he would just have to manage without his aides. He was more than capable of deciding for himself at the negotiating table anyway. The main implication of going alone would be the total lack of support. No doubt Drettroth would believe himself to be in a stronger bargaining position as a result. The Rogandan lord might be in for a surprise.

"I accept Lord Drettroth's conditions."

Another oily smile crossed the face of the Rogandan ambassador. "A wise decision, Sire," he said. "I am confident that you will be able to save your subjects much pain and suffering."

"Please excuse me while I instruct my aides," Delmar said.

The Rogandan bowed an acknowledgment, and Delmar turned to his chief aide and swiftly gave him messages for his noblemen back in the capital, and special instructions for Karevis and the army. He dismissed his aides and watched them ride away.

"If you please, Sire?"

Grunsetz ushered him toward a group of soldiers who were already mounted. Delmar's horse was led over to the group. He mounted it, and they rode away.

Grunsetz watched them go with a self-satisfied smirk. Everything was proceeding exactly to plan.

He summoned another soldier and pointed away in the direction taken by Delmar's aides.

"Take a squad and follow that group of Varasans. They are heading for their capital, Varacellan. Stay out of sight until you find a suitable location, then kill them all! Not one of them must be allowed to reach the capital alive.

"Dispose of their bodies when you're finished. There must be no evidence left behind. And I want no mistakes! Do you understand?"

The soldier nodded.

"Report back to me when you have completed your mission."

Soon a large body of Rogandan soldiers set off after Delmar's aides.

Grunsetz was now free to carry out the next phase of his plans. With King Delmar out of the way, someone else must rule Varas. The ideal candidate would be a Varasan nobleman—someone very compliant. Grunsetz was confident he had found the perfect person.

He could barely contain his glee. Varas had as good as fallen, and with little more effort than plucking an apple from a tree.

Lord Drettroth would be pleased. Very pleased indeed.

3

The never-ending staircase finally came to an abrupt end. Brother Vangellis halted, having reached its lowest extremity. Thomas descended the few steps that separated them and found himself standing in a tiny room fashioned roughly from the surrounding rock. A small wooden door in the opposite wall provided the only way out.

The monk began tugging at a large iron ring set into the door, and Thomas quickly lent his weight to the task. Thomas strained until he thought the veins in his face would burst. At last, with a loud creak of protest from the iron hinges, the stout wooden door moved slowly inward. A steady stream of soil from outside poured into the widening crack.

As soon as the opening became wide enough, Thomas slid through the gap. He stood quietly for a moment and gazed around him. Nothing unusual caught his attention in the dim light provided by the moon, so he turned once again to the door.

The entrance was almost covered by bushes and soil, and Thomas began to pull energetically at the branches and roots that blocked it. Then he threw his weight against the door from the outside while the monk continued to pull on the iron ring from inside. Soon the opening had visibly increased in size. Brother Vangellis extinguished the torches and left them inside the small room. He joined Thomas outside, and the two of them shoveled away dirt with their hands until they were able to pull the door shut once more. Finally, they did their best to restore the vegetation that Thomas had removed.

Thomas moved away from the opening and paused to catch his breath. After the long journey in the confined atmosphere of the enclosed stairwell, followed by the exertion of his recent labors, the crispness of the evening air felt very refreshing. He glanced back toward the door, and to his surprise found himself peering about for a moment before he found it. Its location had been cleverly chosen. Even standing immediately before it, the lie of the land concealed it so effectively that it could not easily be recognized as a man-made opening.

Brother Vangellis had turned away toward the river. "Let's find this coracle," he whispered. Thomas could sense the urgency in his voice.

The ground sloped sharply downward, every inch of it covered with trees, bushes, and lush grass. They began crisscrossing their way methodically down the slope, fully alert for any sign of the hidden vessel.

Before long, Thomas heard a soft call through the gloom. "I've found it!"

Thomas followed the monk's voice down almost to the river bank. The coracle lay upside down beneath a large bush. They lifted it together and carried it to a clear patch of grass, flipping it over so that it sat on its base. It was small and light, but surprisingly capacious. It was most likely intended for one occupant, but the two of them would easily be able to squeeze into it. A single wooden board bisected the inside of the vessel, providing both stability for the frame and a crude seat for passengers to sit on. A couple of paddles had been secured under the wooden board.

Thomas looked at it doubtfully. The river was wide and fast flowing, and the vessel seemed small and frail. Brother Vangellis, however, was clearly delighted with it.

"This brings back happy memories, Thomas," he said.

The look of incredulity on Thomas's face must have been obvious even in the moonlight, because the monk hastened to add, "But I haven't forgotten that we'll be navigating in the dark. And fleeing from the Rogandans."

While speaking, he reached into the coracle for the paddles and placed them on the seat within easy reach. Thomas picked one up and examined it. A relatively short shaft led down to a pair of broad wooden blades. He practiced dipping it in and out of an imaginary river.

"You'd best leave the paddling to me, Thomas. For a while, at least. Can you help me carry the coracle to the water?"

As soon as they placed it in the river, the little craft threatened to spin away with the current. Brother Vangellis held onto it tightly, and motioned for Thomas to get in. The boat wobbled precariously as he climbed aboard, and he sat down in a hurry to avoid being pitched into the water. The monk wasted no time. In one fluid motion, he pushed off from the bank, stepped nimbly into the boat, and took a seat. Planting his paddle confidently into the water, he angled the blade into the current and steered the coracle out into the middle of the river.

The moon provided just enough light for Brother Vangellis to keep the coracle away from the banks and avoid protruding branches and rocks. He clearly knew what he was doing.

Thomas, nervous and uncomfortable, tried not to move more than he needed to. As time passed, though, and the water seemed to be mostly staying in the river where it belonged, his anxiety about Drettroth overwhelmed his uncertainties about the coracle.

"It was Harald, wasn't it?" he finally asked.

"I fear so, Thomas," the monk replied. "It seems he was more than just a wandering thief. I don't doubt that many other such 'travelers' were sent throughout Arvenon with instructions to watch out for you."

Thomas shook his head, totally overwhelmed as he grasped for the first time the scale of the manhunt mounted against him. So much deadly strife lay behind him. Apparently there was to be no end to it.

His thoughts churned restlessly as he struggled to absorb this new reality. The broader implications slowly began to dawn on him, too. He was not the only person affected by this development.

"The Rogandans seem to know I'm traveling with a monk," he said. "I'm sorry that you're involved as well now."

Thomas knew that the monk had already experienced more than enough trouble of his own. He was nevertheless relieved beyond words that he wasn't fleeing for his life alone. Brother Vangellis had confidently taken charge of the coracle, and Thomas was entirely willing to follow his lead whenever they decided to leave the river.

The trouble wasn't limited to them, either. He was painfully aware that many others had been drawn into his problems as well.

"What will become of the monks?" he asked.

"I don't know. They are in God's hands."

Thomas didn't find the monk's answer reassuring. But God would have to take care of his own in this case. No one else was in a position to do it.

The dark outline of the plateau slowly diminished as the current swept them further downriver. Brother Vangellis leaned forward, peering intently into the darkness ahead. After some time he broke the silence.

"We've put some distance between ourselves and the monastery now, Thomas, and it's difficult to navigate in the dark. I think we can afford to stop and rest for the rest of the night. We can continue our journey in the morning."

Thomas wasted no time in agreeing. The monk steered the coracle toward an inlet where the water flowed less swiftly, and with a few powerful strokes he guided them to the bank.

They had no food and no blankets to wrap themselves in, and they couldn't risk lighting a fire. So they simply lay down on the river bank and tried to sleep. Thomas failed miserably—he spent most of the night cold, hungry, and restless. Worst of all, anxiety about the future threatened to overwhelm him.

Just before dawn he fell into a restless sleep, filled with nightmares. When he woke, he couldn't remember any of the details. His dreams hovered just out of the reach of his conscious mind, although the feelings of dread lingered.

Brother Vangellis was nowhere to be seen. He had gone to sleep long before Thomas—gentle snores had begun to sound not long after they lay down—and he must have woken before Thomas, too. The figure of the monk soon reappeared in the pre-dawn half light, though.

"Follow this little stream for a short distance, Thomas. The water upstream tastes fresh, and you might benefit from splashing some of it on your face, too."

Thomas followed his advice. Filling his belly with water was better than leaving it entirely empty, but his stomach still grumbled, and he came back feeling wretched. He was starting the new day as he had ended the previous one—cold, hungry, and anxious.

As soon as it was light they set off again. Once the current had them in its grip, Brother Vangellis turned to Thomas. "I'm sure you're feeling as hollow as I am," he said. "Let's travel for a couple more hours, then we can pull in and find something to eat. In the meantime, let me give you a chance to control the boat yourself."

The monk demonstrated how to steer and handle the craft. At first, whenever Thomas tried to paddle, the coracle simply spun around in a circle. Brother Vangellis showed him how to angle the blade with his wrist while sweeping the paddle through the water to move the vessel forward.

After some practice, Thomas began to grow in confidence. He successfully directed the boat from one side of the river to the other and back again. Then he tried a bit too hard, and nearly pitched both of them into the water.

His teacher waved off his embarrassment with a laugh. "Don't worry, Thomas. The world isn't likely to end if we capsize. If it does happen, though, don't try to climb back in while we're in the water. It won't work. We'll need to swim for the bank, and tow the coracle along with us."

"Won't it sink?"

"No, it should float. Some air will get trapped underneath a coracle if it flips over cleanly."

The sun had risen above the trees before they landed the craft again. Thomas found his spirits rising with the sun. Having something to do had improved his state of mind considerably, and the anticipation of food helped even more.

"How do you know if mushrooms are good to eat?" Thomas asked. They had been wandering inland for a couple of hours, and had already collected a small pile of mushrooms that promised to take the edge off their hunger.

"Experience, Thomas. Bitter experience at times," his companion replied, offering him a wry smile. "I have been very sick indeed after eating mushrooms that looked and tasted delicious. After a while you get to know what's safe and what isn't."

"That's good to know," said Thomas. "But I'm left with the same question."

The monk smiled. "You're right. Next time we find mushrooms, I'll try to point out what to look for. A tip for beginners, though—stay away from mushrooms with white gills."

In the end, they added a few berries to their collection, and, best of all, a young wild turkey. The turkey was unlucky. If they'd been less famished and the bird less plump and self-satisfied when they stumbled upon it, the outcome might have been different. But the turkey would now be joining them for dinner, notwithstanding its noisy objections. They finally headed back to the boat with arms laden and bellies rumbling loudly.

The turkey needed to be cooked, so lighting a fire had become a necessity. It was difficult to imagine that any Rogandan soldiers could be close enough to observe the smoke. Nevertheless the monk carefully chose a small natural clearing surrounded by tall trees, and sent Thomas off looking for dry timber to feed the fire. After what seemed an interminable delay waiting for the food to cook, they finally found themselves feasting heartily.

By the time they lay down to sleep, the fire had burned down to glowing coals. For Thomas, soaking up the warmth with a satisfyingly full belly, the trials and worries of the previous night seemed far away.

THOMAS WAS startled awake by a hand shaking him. "We need to go!" Brother Vangellis whispered urgently into his ear. Thomas sat up and squinted around him in the half light. Dawn was close. A thin line of smoke rose high into the air from the remains of the fire. Nothing else unusual could be seen, but he could faintly hear rough voices calling in the distance. They didn't sound near, but they couldn't have been too far off, either.

Clouds of dust rose as the monk hurriedly scooped dirt over the ashes of the fire, ending the telltale line of smoke. Observing that Thomas was fully awake, he motioned toward the river. They hurried to the coracle and launched it, praying that they would make it past the Rogandans before being discovered.

The monk steered them out into the current. In the semi-darkness they saw no one, and after a while they dared to hope that they had made a clean escape.

The light grew steadily brighter as they drifted silently downstream. Looking ahead, Thomas noticed a disturbance in the river off in the distance. He turned to Brother Vangellis. "What's that?" he asked, pointing ahead nervously.

"White water," the monk replied. "There are rapids ahead. Crouch down and hang on tight—I'll try to steer us through them."

The noise of the river grew ever louder as they approached the rapids. Thomas gripped the sides of the coracle and bent down as low as he could. He peered over the top of the boat, trying hard to convince himself that the monk knew what he was doing. The boat picked up speed as the current swept them into the roiling waters. The little craft bucked and swayed violently, and for a few anxious moments it seemed that they must surely capsize. But then the rapids spat them out the other side, and they were through the worst of it. The monk deftly swept his paddle in and out, guiding them to calmer water.

Thomas sat up again and stretched, trying to relieve the tension in his muscles.

"That was fun," said Brother Vangellis with a grin.

Thomas didn't respond, but his opinion must have been obvious, because the monk laughed when he saw the look on his face.

Ahead of them the river swung right in a broad sweeping curve. A wide beach covered with yellow sand lay on the inside of the bend. Brother Vangellis began guiding the boat into the slower current near the beach. Then Thomas noticed a man sitting on a log on the far side of the beach. Spotting the coracle, the man leaped to his feet and called out a single word of warning. Thomas didn't need to be told that the man was Rogandan.

A number of other men appeared on the beach. One approached the water's edge and called out to them, in their own language but with a heavy accent.

"BRING THE BOAT IN TO THE BEACH NOW, MONK!" he shouted. "WE WANT THE BOY."

He spread his hands in a gesture of appeal. "Turn him over to us," he called. "I guarantee that he will not be hurt, and you can go on your way. Disobey, and both of you will die!" The man fell silent and stood with arms folded, waiting to see what they would do.

Brother Vangellis did not hesitate even for a moment. He vigorously paddled the boat away from the beach and back into the swifter current.

Thomas looked fearfully toward the gradually diminishing figure of the Rogandan on the beach. The man had begun waving his arms and pointing emphatically toward them. Thomas watched with increasing alarm as four horsemen galloped across the beach and splashed their horses into the river. They surged out into the strongest part of the current and set their horses swimming after the coracle.

It could not be doubted that they would reach the boat before many minutes had passed.

It was obvious to Thomas that the pursuit on the river had reached a critical stage. Two of the riders had quickly given up the chase when their horses struggled to keep up and fell behind. But the other two continued in hot pursuit, and one had now swum almost to within a stone's throw of the coracle.

Both riders had long since slipped off the backs of their horses into the water. They glided along beside them, firmly gripping the manes of their mounts in one hand.

Thomas was finding it difficult to breathe. A tight knot had been twisting inside his stomach, and his heart was racing. He forced out an agitated question. "Should we have done what the Rogandan said?"

The monk's face was set in a firm line. He was too busy paddling to do more than spit out words between strokes.

"His guarantees...mean nothing...Only Drettroth...can offer guarantees...And Drettroth cares...for no one...just his own...interests...You've seen that."

Thomas could only nod mutely.

"We're not...that desperate...It's not over...Not yet, Thomas."

Thomas knew that the horses could not keep swimming like this for much longer. And the water was cold. The soldiers must surely be suffering. The monk was visibly tiring, too, although he had refused an offer of help. The chase was coming to a head, and soon.

The nearest soldier had urged his mount to a final effort. With the prize seemingly almost within his grasp, he began to stretch out a hand to grab the side of the coracle.

"Thomas! The nostrils."

Thomas understood. He grabbed the spare paddle and began scooping sheets of water at the horse. The creature snorted and tossed its head. Seeing the rider straining harder to reach the boat, Thomas redoubled his efforts, directing an almost continuous stream of water at the face of the horse. Unable to breathe freely, the animal began to panic. It jerked away from the coracle, and the rider lost his grip on its mane. He quickly kicked out toward the boat on his own.

As the soldier approached, Thomas lifted the paddle free of the water, and began swinging it down hard at the swimmer's arms. The soldier dodged the paddle while still attempting to swim closer. As he strained forward to grasp the coracle, Thomas finally landed a heavy blow on his arm. The blade of the paddle split in two with a loud crack and broke away from the shaft. The soldier cried out in pain and pulled away. Nursing his injured arm, which was almost certainly broken, he struck out weakly for the shore.

During the confusion the other horse had drawn closer. His rider approached more cautiously.

Thomas tried to splash water toward the horse with his hands. Without a paddle he was forced to scoop much more vigorously, and the coracle began to rock dangerously. Then Brother Vangellis cried out a sudden warning. They had been swinging around another bend in the river, and Thomas looked up to see a new set of rapids foaming white almost immediately before them.

As they approached the turbulence an arrow fell into the water near the coracle. Startled, Thomas looked across the river and saw the right bank lined with soldiers. Even before they reached the white water, arrows began falling around them. Then they were into the rapids. The last rider and both horses were swept in after them, and Thomas caught a brief glimpse of heads dipping in and out of the foam.

Brother Vangellis suddenly leaned violently to one side. Thomas turned to him, thinking he had been hit by an arrow. But then the coracle capsized, and all was chaos. Somehow Thomas sucked in air before the waves covered his head. Then the current took him. The turbulent waters tossed him around unmercifully, and he barely managed to thrust his head above the surface for an occasional breath. Miraculously, he had not been smashed into any rocks, but the rapids still battered him relentlessly.

The turbulence ceased abruptly. Before he could clear the water for another breath, he was grabbed firmly from behind. Reacting instinctively he tried to fight against the arm that held him, but the grip was too strong. He was pulled under the coracle and thrust upward into a vacant space beside the seat plank. Gasping, he filled his lungs with air.

The arm had belonged to the monk. Both of them clung to the upended seat, craning their necks upward into the life-giving pocket of trapped air, and let the current carry them. Occasional arrows rattled off the hull of the boat, and others sliced into the water around them. But the coracle hid and protected them.

Once again it seemed that the Rogandans had no access to a boat. The rain of arrows soon ended but many more minutes passed before the monk dived under the boat and disappeared. Thomas heard a slow series of taps on the hull and guessed that the monk was letting him know that it was safe to emerge. He dived clear himself and surfaced to a river empty of enemies.

The monk began to tow the coracle to the riverbank. Thomas tried to help as best he could. The rapids had exhausted him, though, and he spent more time hanging onto the boat than towing it.

Brother Vangellis was almost spent, too, and it felt like an eternity before they finally reached the bank. They dragged the boat out of the river, then both collapsed onto the grass that grew almost down to the water's edge.

They lay there without moving for many minutes. Then the monk sat up, wincing as he stretched his limbs. "We need to keep moving, Thomas. Even if they think we're dead, they'll still look for us. They'll try to get you to Drettroth, whatever state you're in."

Thomas groaned, then slowly sat up himself.

"We've lost both of our paddles," said the monk. "I will see if I can find something we can use instead."

He headed for the trees near the river's edge and disappeared into them. Before long he returned with a couple of branches, and a bundle of thick reeds tucked firmly under one arm. The largest branch was a thick limb that would probably only be useful to push them off from the bank. The other branch was shorter with a sturdy fork splitting the main limb halfway down its length.

The monk sat down and began tightly winding the reeds across and around the fork to create a crude blade. "You'll find a stream over there, Thomas," he said, pointing downriver a short distance. "We have nothing to carry water in, so take a long drink while you have the chance."

Thomas took his advice and headed to the stream. He returned to find the monk examining his makeshift paddle critically. "This might work, at least for a while," he said, waving it through the air.

Brother Vangellis wasted no further time, heading straight for the coracle. He examined the hull briefly. "It doesn't look like the arrows have done any real damage," he said. With an effort he flipped the coracle over. "Are you ready, Thomas?"

The youth nodded and joined him. They lifted the boat into the water, and Thomas clambered in stiffly. The monk put the two branches into the boat and climbed in himself, more gingerly this time. He used the thick limb to push off from the bank and slowly they began to move forward as the current caught them.

Brother Vangellis used his new paddle sparingly, mostly angling it like a rudder to steer them into the faster-moving water.

Once they were underway he turned to Thomas. "I think we should just drift for as long as we can. We'll have to pray that there are no more Rogandans—and no more rapids—waiting for us."

Thomas felt too weary to offer more than a nod in response.

"There's something else I need to say, too." The monk paused, apparently choosing his words. "It was no accident when the coracle capsized in the rapids. I did it intentionally. I knew I was taking a big risk; we could have drowned. But I decided that the risk from the Rogandans was greater. I owe you an apology for putting your life in danger in that way, especially since I offered you no choice."

Thomas shrugged. "We're alive. And we're still free," he said. Finding nothing else worth saying, he fell into a brooding silence.

The immediate danger appeared to have passed, but Thomas could not relax. He had long since recognized just how much trouble the stone had brought him. But it was becoming clear that his real troubles were only beginning. The stone was unreliable, and largely closed to him. All it brought him now was deadly peril, and for so little return. And yet, although he could not clearly articulate the reasons, he was not willing to even consider giving it up.

Perhaps the stone had some kind of hold over him. If so, he had undoubtedly brought it on himself; he remembered the scroll saying something about fearful risks resulting from overuse. Even the writer of the scroll had been ensnared—he said that the stones haunted his dreams—and he had never as much as seen them.

"Have you been thinking about the scroll?" asked Thomas.

Brother Vangellis returned a tired smile before shaking his head. "I'm sorry, Thomas. After all the excitement I haven't had the energy to think about anything much at all."

Thomas was not deterred. "I've been wondering about the writer of the scroll. Randolf of Clerbon, wasn't it? How did he find out so much about the stones?"

"I don't know. It must have been frustrating for the poor fellow, though—always searching for the stones, but never finding them, and constantly acquiring knowledge that he couldn't use."

"Maybe he wasn't able to use the knowledge himself, but he answered some questions for me."

"Which questions?"

"I always wondered why the stone behaved so strangely with the two rabid animals; all it showed me each time was a wolf. But according to the scroll, the stone doesn't reveal as much about animals. And I never understood why the stone revealed nothing about Will's thoughts when I first met him. It changed his appearance, but that was all. But I'd broken my arm."

"And the scroll suggested that pain diminishes the power of the stone." The monk finished the thought for him.

"Yes. At the time I had very little experience with the stone, too, so maybe that was another reason. The scroll said that the power of the stone increases with familiarity. That certainly matched my experience."

Thomas fell silent again, and Brother Vangellis apparently had nothing further to say, either.

The scroll had explained so much, but there were questions it hadn't answered, too. Why was the stone largely ineffective now? He felt sure that Randolf of Clerbon could have given him a reason. If only Brother Erastus had found the entire scroll, and not just the first part of it.

He also didn't understand why he had seen wolf eyes in his own face when he looked in the mirror. After his fight with Simon, the stone hadn't been working at all, so why did it work then? And why wolf eyes? The scroll talked about afflictions of the spirit affecting the stone, and he had certainly been in turmoil since the fight. Did that have something to do with it?

Maybe it had been about his future. He had sensed at the time that the wolf eyes pointed to a possible destiny, one that he had been desperate to avoid. Thankfully, the scroll had indicated that the stone's glimpses into what lay ahead should not be taken as certain. And yet the stone's vision of Will's future had come so close to the mark. It was mystifying.

Thomas tried to recall everything the scroll had said, but his attention wandered. His fears about the future began to rise up again and press in on him. He couldn't think straight, and he soon found it impossible to concentrate. As the boat continued to drift peacefully along with the current, his thoughts churned and boiled like the rapids.

The afternoon wore on as they floated downstream, allowing the river to take them wherever it would. The coracle was too small to allow them to lie down or stretch out, and Thomas felt increasingly uncomfortable. It was also now many hours since he had eaten, and hunger began to gnaw away at him. After a time he began to feel thirsty, too, but he knew enough not to drink from the river. Eventually, his weariness overshadowed everything, and he found himself drifting in and out of sleep sitting up, in spite of the discomfort.

The countryside that slid by them was untamed and apparently unsettled. The sun set, and still they floated on.

Just after sunset they passed a scene that caused them to shrink down fearfully in their little craft. Many small fires burned brightly in a huge clearing, and armed Rogandan soldiers sat around the fires feasting noisily. The smell of cooked food wafted tantalizingly across the water. They drifted by undetected, but long after the fear had faded Thomas still struggled to rid his mind of images of warm fires and hot food.

By the time day was about to break, Thomas could bear it no longer. His aching muscles, empty stomach and growing thirst had reinforced the fear that dragged at his will and sapped his energy. "If we don't stop soon, I'll go mad!" he finally exclaimed.

"If you can wait just a little longer, Thomas, I think we will soon be able to leave the river for good." The monk's voice was calm, although Thomas could sense his concern.

Now that the silence had been broken, Thomas's anxieties burst forth. "Why did the Rogandans try to kill us? Doesn't Drettroth know what will happen if he tries to take the stone by force? I don't understand it."

"Even if Drettroth knows, his soldiers may not," Brother Vangellis replied. "His men clearly know that he is searching for you, and they may know you have something he wants. But I doubt that he has told anyone about the stone. I doubt that he could trust even his own commanders if they knew what it was capable of."

Thomas peered uncertainly at the monk in the gloom. "Do you want the stone?" He couldn't help blurting it out.

The monk laughed, but there was no mirth in it. "You need not fear me, Thomas," he replied. "I don't envy you the burden of this gift, if I can borrow from the words in the scroll."

Thomas shamefacedly recalled everything that the monk had done to help him, and the huge risks he had taken for his sake. He suddenly felt very contrite. "I'm sorry. I shouldn't have said that."

Brother Vangellis laughed again, more cheerfully this time. "Forget it," he said. "I've promised to help you in any way I can, and I mean to make good on that promise."

Thomas didn't know what to say. Perhaps sensing that, the monk quickly changed the subject. "As soon as there's enough light, we can find a suitable landing place. We have two options. We can hide the coracle so we can use it again. The risk is that the Rogandans might find it. They're certain to search the riverbank for any trace of us. The alternative is to let it drift on without us. They may eventually find it, but they won't know for certain where we abandoned it."

The choice was an easy one for Thomas. "I don't care if I never see a coracle again!" he said.

"It's decided, then," the monk replied. "We need to look for a large stream that empties into the river. That's where we'll land. A fast flowing stream will remove our footprints."

Thomas didn't respond. His mind drifted off, away from the coracle, the river, and even the Rogandans. For the first time in what seemed like an age, he found himself thinking of Arnost, and wondering if the siege still continued. Somewhat guiltily, he spared a thought for his father in the city, and his mother away at her brother's farm. Then he realized that in his preoccupation it hadn't occurred to him to wonder what had become of Will and Rufe and their other companions. He would have expected Will to have an army behind him now, and to be fighting the Rogandans. But Drettroth didn't seem interested in battles. He was too busy chasing the stone.

As his thoughts continued to wander, he reluctantly faced the fact that Elbruhe no longer constantly inhabited the back of his mind. Even in the extremity of his present circumstances, he still felt guilty about allowing her to be pushed so far from his conscious awareness.

Everything was changing. He tried to remember what his life had been like back in Arnost before the stone and before the Rogandans came. But he couldn't recapture it. Everything he had cared about was now beyond his reach. His old life, like the old Thomas, was gone.

Some measure of tranquility eventually came to him as the sky began to lighten in the east. He fixed his gaze into the heavens, watching the last of the stars disappear as the strengthening light swallowed them up.

After a while he turned his attention to the monk. "They'll never stop chasing me, will they?" It was a statement more than a question.

Brother Vangellis regarded him silently for a long moment. Then slowly he shook his head.

A COUPLE more hours passed before the monk spotted a suitable stream in the right terrain.

"This is it, Thomas. We might as well leave the coracle in the river and swim for the bank. Jump in quickly before we're carried beyond the stream."

Thomas launched himself into the river, struggling to reawaken cramped muscles. The monk followed him in, flipping the coracle over before swimming away from it. "If the Rogandans find it capsized, they might decide that we drowned in the rapids," he said. "If we're fortunate."

The little craft had disappeared from sight before they reached dry land.

Stepping ashore into the mouth of the stream, they allowed it to lead them away from the river. The monk did not halt until the stream had begun to narrow noticeably. After drinking deeply from its cool waters they clambered out onto some rocks.

They sat there for a while soaking up the sun. Then, putting the river and the stream behind them, the two fugitives disappeared into the wilderness.

4

"How many soldiers did you see?" Kuper asked.

"Hundreds, at least. We'll need to find a way around them." Rellan lifted his good arm and pointed vaguely toward the tree line off to the south.

"Hold the horses while I take a closer look."

Kuper clambered up almost to the top of the ridge, then bent low as he approached the summit. He knelt down and peered over the top. Dozens of tents stretched out before him on either side of a large stream. Groups of horses were tethered around the outer boundaries of the camp. A large number of small fires could be seen dotted around the site. A cluster of men had gathered around each of the fires. Kuper lay downwind of the camp, and the smells wafting toward him suggested that a good few of the soldiers were preparing food. It was the smoke that had first betrayed the location of the camp.

Between the camp and the ridge, flocks of sheep huddled together in fenced pens made of rough timbers. A few milking cows had been tied to posts nearby. Kuper wondered what had become of the shepherds and farmers and their families.

He climbed back down and rejoined his brother. "The Rogandans don't seem to be expecting trouble—they haven't posted sentries.

There are plenty of soldiers coming and going, though, so we can't stay here."

They remounted and set off hastily toward the distant forest.

Not for the first time, Kuper found himself battling with frustration. Will had entrusted them with the responsibility of reaching Lord Burtelen in Erestor and returning to Castel with the army that the nobleman had been raising. It had seemed like a straightforward assignment. But their journey had not been going smoothly. At first they made good time after leaving Will and the others in the village. But in the last few days they had spent far too much time avoiding Rogandans, with the result that they were much further south than they should have been. Steffan's Citadel, the gateway to the Duchy of Erestor, now lay to the northwest through dense forests, rather than due west across rolling hills.

Halfway to the forest they paused to rest their horses.

"Too many Rogandans for my liking," said Rellan with mild understatement.

Kuper nodded. "There must be thousands of them roaming around Arvenon."

"I wonder if Lord Burtelen is going to be happy about leaving the Duchy undefended."

"I've been wondering about that, too."

They sat in silence for a few more minutes before resuming their journey. The sun had dipped below the tree line by the time they reached the outskirts of the forest. As the trees closed in around them, they crossed a well-worn path that ran southwest into the forest. The path seemed to be running at least partly in the right direction, and after a moment's hesitation they turned onto it.

Almost immediately, faint cries of alarm reached them from further along the track. Both of them reacted instinctively, digging their heels into their horses' ribs. They galloped along the path, keeping their heads down to avoid low hanging branches.

Ahead of them the path broadened into a clearing that held a cluster of houses. One of them sprouted roaring red flames, and a torch had just been thrown onto the thatched roof of another. A small band of Rogandans scurried around among the houses, grabbing pigs and chickens, and hunting down panicked villagers.

Kuper had his bow in hand even before he brought his horse to a halt. Three arrows flew and three Rogandan soldiers fell before the raiders even realized they were under attack. A fourth soldier, a big brute of a man, had just stood up with a triumphant shout, lifting high a squirming pig. Rellan rode him down, his sword swinging from his good arm. Three raiders remained, and they decided to run for it. Only one made it to his horse, leaping onto its back and urging it toward the forest. He never made it out of the clearing. An arrow took him in the neck, and he crashed to the ground dead.

A strange calm settled over the scene, disturbed only by the roar and crackle of the fires. A few distraught women knelt weeping beside the still forms of their loved ones. Some of the men stood grim-faced and trembling as they beheld the ruin of their village.

One man, bowed with age, came to the twins.

"I am the headman," he said. "My heartfelt thanks to you on behalf of all my people. We are extremely grateful for your intervention."

"You need to leave quickly," Kuper told him. "These soldiers were just a foraging party. More Rogandans will come when they don't return. An entire army is camped in the fields north of here."

"Do we have time to bury our dead?" the man asked.

"You'll be taking a big risk," Kuper replied. "We can't defend you. We can't even stay to help you. Are any of you able to ride a horse?"

The man nodded. "Some of the men have ridden before."

"Then tell your women and children, and any men who can't ride, to leave at once with whatever they can carry. Send riders to watch all the entrances to the village. You can use the raiders' horses. The rest of the men can do what is necessary for your fallen. They can follow the others on horseback as soon as they have finished here. They can also flee if the need arises."

The man nodded once more. "I will do as you say." He called a number of men by name and gave them instructions. They left immediately to do his bidding.

When he was finished, Kuper took the opportunity to ask for directions. The headman was able to give them detailed instructions, kneeling down and drawing in the dirt as he talked.

Kuper thanked him in his turn. Then the twins mounted their horses and bade him farewell.

"Thank you again for your kindness," the headman said, bowing his head in gratitude.

"May better fortune smile on you in the days to come," said Rellan.

They turned their horses back onto the path and rode away. They soon passed a group of fugitives, mostly women with small children, who had already left the village and were heading deeper into the forest. Most of the women carried heavy burdens, but they set down their loads as the twins rode by and waved to them, calling out their thanks.

Rellan and Kuper stayed on the main path until it crossed a wide stream. Then, following the headman's instructions, they turned onto a smaller path that headed due west. The path was barely visible at first, but it soon became wider and better established. They pressed on until it was almost dark, then turned aside from the path to find a suitable place to sleep.

The next day they rose at first light and continued their journey westward within the boundaries of the forest. They saw no further sign of the Rogandans. And, even though they mostly traveled on established paths, they saw no signs of human habitation. At times they felt as though eyes were upon them, but they never caught as much as a glimpse of another person. Deer sometimes crossed the path off in the distance, but never close enough for Kuper to take a shot.

When they camped that night they took turns to watch. It was not necessary for them to discuss the arrangements—they simply came to an unspoken understanding, just as they had so often done from the time they were children.

In the half light before dawn Kuper found himself on duty. He sat with his back to a tree, his head drooping low. Even to a careful observer he would have appeared to be fast asleep. But he was awake, with senses fully alert.

The horses, standing off to the side of the twins, were unusually skittish. Kuper's bow lay within easy reach, and he was ready for trouble. But he did not move a muscle. As the minutes passed, the horses gradually settled. All appeared to be calm.

Then the stillness was shattered. The horses exploded into action with squeals of protest. A small figure sprang onto the back of one of the animals, urging it forward. He was hanging on to the halter of the other horse.

Kuper was on his feet in an instant, his bow stretched taut with an arrow ready to release. The diminutive thief looked back as he raced away, and Kuper hesitated. Then he lowered his bow, and the horses disappeared into the forest.

Rellan, now fully awake, looked at his brother questioningly.

"He was just a boy," Kuper told him. "I couldn't do it."

Rellan acknowledged this decision with a shrug. "I would have let him go, too," he said.

Without the horses, their task had become much more difficult. With no better options on offer, they shouldered their bows and began following the path on foot.

The fading light of late afternoon found them further west than most men could have traveled in a single day. But they were lithe and fit and on a mission. Apart from occasional brief stops to fill their water skins in a stream, they had walked or jogged almost continuously.

With dusk approaching they slowed their pace and began looking around for a place to spend the night. Then Rellan straightened, closing his eyes and lifting his nostrils to the breeze. "I smell smoke," he said, turning his gaze upwind into the spreading gloom. "It's faint, but it's unmistakable."

"I can't smell a thing," Kuper replied. "But then your sense of smell has always been uncanny."

"Shall we find out what's going on?" Rellan asked.

Kuper nodded. "Getting horses is our biggest priority. Where we find people we're likely to find horses. With any luck, they might be willing to help us once they find out what we're doing."

"We don't know who they are, of course."

"No, we don't. There's always a risk. But they're not likely to be Rogandans. And the fact that we're not, either, will probably be enough to earn us a welcome. Anyway, we don't have to reveal ourselves before we take a look at them."

"Agreed," said Rellan. "I'm willing to chance it. And where we find a fire, we're likely to find food," he added with a grin. "I'm hungry!"

Kuper set off after his brother as he began picking his way among the trees.

They had to walk for several minutes before Kuper also began to smell the smoke. Not for the first time, he marveled at the sensitivity of his brother's nose.

With the fire close nearby, they began to move more cautiously through the trees. Before long they could hear the crackle of the flames and catch glimpses of the glow. Not knowing if sentries were posted, they separated and approached independently.

Kuper moved forward until a single tree separated him from the small clearing that boasted the fire. A group of cloaked figures sat around it, feasting on the remains of a deer. There was nothing especially alarming about them. Kuper and Rellan had sat around many such fires themselves.

Bows and quivers of arrows lay beside some of the feasters. And the occasional glint of metal at their sides told him that all of them were armed. None of that was surprising, though—these were dangerous times.

As Kuper watched, his brother stepped out from the shadows into the firelight. "Greetings, friends, and well met," said Rellan, stretching out his good hand and allowing them to see his other arm in a sling.

All of them leaped to their feet, drawing swords or knives. "Who are you, and what are you doing here?" one of them demanded. They spread out to surround the intruder.

"I'm just a weary traveler, attracted by the warmth of your fire and the smell of your food," Rellan replied brightly. "My brother and I thought we might join you in the hope of sharing your hospitality."

At the mention of a brother, Kuper also stepped forward into the firelight, hands empty and palms outward. "My greetings to you, as well," he said cheerfully as they spun around to face him. He moved slowly and deliberately to the fire and sat himself down in front of it, sighing loudly and contentedly. Rellan joined him.

The others watched them warily for a while. One of their number, a tall bearded man with a prominent scar across one eye, finally nodded to the others, and they came and joined them at the fire. All of them remained watchful.

"May we share your deer?" Rellan asked.

The others looked to the man with the scar. "Help yourselves," he replied.

Kuper hadn't realized how famished he was until they started eating. Everything went quiet for a while as they hungrily devoured slice after juicy slice of venison.

Eventually Kuper wiped his mouth with his sleeve and sat back, smiling and contented. Rellan, limited by his one good arm, had been making slower progress. But he, too, eventually managed to satisfy his hunger.

Their hosts still hadn't relaxed, so Kuper decided to take the initiative. "Our sincere thanks to you all," he said, nodding politely in acknowledgment of their hospitality. "My name is Kuper, and this is my brother, Rellan. We are traveling to Erestor on the king's business, and lost our horses this morning to a thief."

At the mention of horses and a thief, a couple of the men started noticeably. Their leader, however, remained unmoved. "I am known as Scar," he said evenly. "Anyone who trespasses in this domain must give an account of themselves to our leader. We will treat you with respect if you come with us willingly. We would prefer to avoid trouble."

Kuper assessed them calmly. His instincts told him that Scar could be trusted. "We will come willingly," he promised.

Scar issued brief instructions to the other men, who immediately began clearing up the site. They sliced the remaining strips of meat from the deer, disposed of the carcass, and covered the fire.

Scar turned to the twins. "Please remove your weapons," he said. "We will take good care of them, and they will be returned to you as soon as our leader permits it. Later in our journey it will be necessary to blindfold you briefly. But for now please walk with us."

After the twins had handed over their bows, arrows, and swords, the group set off, heading east along the path. They traveled at a brisk pace for over two hours, and Kuper found it galling to be retracing so many of their steps from earlier in the day. Then Scar and one of the other men blindfolded them, spun them around a few times, and led them into the forest. Their guides proved to be skillful and effective; Kuper rarely stumbled. After traveling for what must have been another hour, they finally came to a stop, and Kuper's blindfold was removed. Rellan stood close by, gazing around curiously.

Kuper was standing in a huge natural clearing. In the moonlight he could see a large number of rough dwellings around the outer edges of the clearing. A giant bonfire burned brightly in the center of it. Men and women came and went from the dwellings, going about their business. If children also lived there they must have been indoors, most likely asleep, because none were visible, and none appeared as he watched.

A hooded figure stood before the fire, facing away from the newly arrived party. Scar led the twins forward, other men flanking them watchfully. The figure turned as they approached, and they found themselves facing a woman, her long dark hair flowing forward over her right shoulder. She was dressed like a man, and the firelight revealed a face both proud and stern. Sharp and intelligent eyes studied them critically.

"These men found their way to our fire, Anneka," said Scar after a respectful bow. "They call themselves Kuper and Rellan," he said, nodding to each of them in turn as he spoke.

"Where were your sentries?" Anneka demanded curtly.

"I hadn't posted sentries," he replied. "It will not happen again."

She glowered at him for a moment, then turned her attention to the twins. "Your arm," she said to Rellan, "is it broken?"

"It is," he confirmed.

"How did you break it?"

"In a fight."

"With the Rogandans?"

"No, with the retainers of a minor baron."

She considered that for a moment, frowning. "Why are you here?"

"We are on our way to Erestor," Kuper said, breaking into the conversation. "We would have been far away by now, but our horses were stolen this morning."

"Who stole them?"

"A boy."

"You couldn't prevent a boy from stealing your horses?" she asked, a mocking edge to her tone.

"I could have stopped him," Kuper replied calmly. "But putting an arrow into the back of a child is not my way."

"Perhaps a small moving target is beyond your skill level," she suggested.

Kuper did not reply.

She sighed. "I will decide about you in the morning." She turned to Scar. "Find them a hut to sleep in. And guard them well. No more surprises."

Scar bowed, then led them away.

"She's a cheerful one," Rellan ventured.

Scar frowned at him. "Don't presume to pass judgment on your betters," he said. "We owe our lives and our well-being to her."

"No insult intended," he replied with a smile.

Scar and a couple of other men led them to a small hut that held nothing apart from four straw mattresses covered with blankets. The other men positioned themselves outside the hut. The brothers went inside, and the door closed behind them. Kuper heard a bar drop into position across the door.

Rellan moved straight to a mattress and stretched himself out on it.

Kuper did likewise. He lay on his bed trying to relax. After the frustration of their roundabout journey toward Erestor, their forward progress had now come to a sudden and complete halt. Nothing could be done about it tonight, though. Tomorrow was a new day, and they would have to face its challenges then.

He closed his eyes and almost immediately fell into a deep slumber.

5

"Is it wise to give Will Prentis command of the entire army, Sire?" Lord Bottren's face was impassive, but his concern showed in his voice. "Most of Istel's nobles are strongly opposed, and even some of our own people are less than enthusiastic."

Not for the first time that week Steffan struggled to master his growing irritability with this topic. "The decision belongs to me and Istel, Bottren. We've made it, and it's final!"

The two of them sat astride their horses on a rise, surveying a plain before them bustling with purposeful activity. Importantly, the plain was on Arvenian soil, a few miles beyond Deadman's Pass. To one side lay the main army camp, situated between the plain and a river that flowed down from the mountains near the pass. The camp had borrowed its name—Hazelwood Ford—from the nearby river crossing.

Soldiers drilled in companies, mounted troops galloped back and forth, and off to one side bowmen fired volleys of arrows into the air. Everything Steffan could see told him the troops were ready for action. Thanks to effective initiatives on the part of Will in the days since his arrival, their skills had been honed and their morale greatly boosted. Further, Steffan saw evident signs that the soldiers were becoming increasingly enthusiastic about their new commander. That was no surprise to him.

The soldiers might be in good condition, but the leadership was another matter. A constant undercurrent of intrigue and infighting among the nobles had been annoying Steffan immensely for weeks. Since the appointment of Will, though, the discontent had found a new focus and risen to a crescendo.

Coordinating the forces of two independent kingdoms was always going to be a challenge, and Steffan had felt embattled from the beginning. Thankfully, Istel supported him—on most occasions, anyway. Nevertheless, the squabbling and backbiting never showed any signs of relenting. At times the nobles around him seemed to have forgotten entirely who the real enemy was.

More than ever, Steffan was convinced that the army needed to be on the move, confronting the Rogandans. It wouldn't take long for Will to silence his detractors once the fighting started.

He turned to Bottren. "Find Will," he commanded, "and send him to me."

Bottren bowed his head in acknowledgment. Turning his horse, he kicked it into a gallop and disappeared over the rise.

"We now have an army of seven thousand men encamped in Arvenon with more expected to join them. What is our commander planning to do with them?"

'Our commander' had become the label of choice for the Castelan nobles when referring to Will. It was invariably delivered with a condescending sneer. At first the sneer had been subtle, at least to his face. Never subtle enough to hide it completely, but enough to avoid the appearance of a direct challenge. Of late, any pretense at veiling the insult had been abandoned, occasionally even in the presence of one of the kings.

Will ignored it. He answered to King Steffan, not to any of these men. His king had given him a job to do, and he meant to carry it out to the best of his ability.

Usually both kings sat in the daily Council of War, but on this occasion neither one of them was present. Their absence gave the nobles full freedom to vent their feelings.

"Is it true that you deliberately destroyed one of your own towns? Don't imagine you can do the same here in Castel!"

"Some of your soldiers are asking why you abandoned your capital to its fate. What do you have to say about that?"

Will held his peace in the face of their hostility. Reasonable answers never satisfied people asking unreasonable questions.

He wasn't surprised by their opposition. He'd faced similar challenges from a number of the nobles at Arnost. Even saving their capital had not softened the attitude of some of them.

They had been born to rule over commoners like him. The two kings had flouted every convention the nobles held dear by placing Will in charge of the army. The kings themselves were not affected, of course, because Will was still subject to them. But the appointment was a slap in the face for every one of the noblemen. It said more clearly than words that neither King Steffan nor King Istel had any regard for the ability of their nobles. They preferred to place the fate of their kingdoms in the hands of a commoner.

Defeating the Rogandans wouldn't help Will—it would surely only deepen the insult. The nobles would always believe they could have done better.

BOTTREN QUICKLY LOCATED Will and arrived to find him still in council with the other lords. The sun might have been shining brightly out in the wide world, but storm clouds gathered in the council room at Hazelwood Ford. In spite of his own reservations about Will's new role, Bottren had no desire to see him fed to the baying hounds around the table. When delivering the summons from King Steffan, he added a note of urgency to the message.

Will responded immediately. Standing, he bowed stiffly, and left with his rescuer.

Bottren knew that once he was gone, the other lords would vent their spleen without restraint. At least Will wouldn't have to listen to it, though.

The two of them rode for a time without speaking.

"The mood looked ugly in there, Will," Bottren finally ventured.

Will simply shrugged.

Bottren studied the man riding calmly beside him. For a commoner his poise was nothing short of remarkable. He didn't seem at all overawed by the nobility with whom he now spent so much of his time. Scarred and stern of face, he looked every inch a soldier. The permanent limp he carried from his battle wounds only reinforced the aura that surrounded him. Will Prentis was almost certainly a veteran of as many clashes as any other person in the king's army. It was easy to forget entirely how young he was.

In a moment of sudden honesty, Bottren owned that he, no less than Istel's nobles, had been blinded by his prejudices. Yet he had seen how the Arvenian soldiers stood taller in Will's presence, and witnessed the growing enthusiasm in their cheers whenever their commander rode by.

Will's usefulness was not limited to the battlefield, either. Every Council of War benefited from his insights, and no practical matter seemed to escape his attention. Bottren himself had not fully grasped the importance of logistics until Will's careful probing had exposed a number of serious inadequacies in the planning around equipping and feeding the soldiers.

Even the Castelan soldiers increasingly deferred to Will. That was appropriate, of course, given his role as commander of the combined armies. The Castelan nobles, though, were well aware of this growing respect and vigorously sought to undermine it.

Bottren glanced at Will again, allowing himself to see the young commander with new eyes. For the first time he acknowledged what he knew his king had long since recognized: this grave young man was a vastly more capable leader than any of the nobles, and offered the best hope—maybe the only hope—of defeating the Rogandans.

"Don't let them get to you, Will—you're a better man than any of them." The acknowledgment was long overdue, but Bottren knew there was never a wrong time to begin giving credit where it was due.

"Thank you, My Lord," the commander returned simply. "It would seem that your confidence is not shared universally, though," he added with masterful understatement.

"Perhaps not," the lord replied. "But the king sees it the same way, and his opinion is the one that matters."

They rode on in silence.

A single concern troubled Bottren. He succeeded in pushing it down for a time, but finally it would not be denied.

"Is the Rogandan army really as big as our scouts report, Will?" he finally asked.

"Yes, My Lord, it is immense. Almost beyond counting."

"How will we defeat them?"

"I don't know," Will replied candidly. "But somehow we must find a way."

WILL, currently in the final stages of preparing for conflict, had been fully absorbed for several days. The looming battle would be his first as commander of the allied forces.

Rogandan forces had increasingly been concentrating near the small village of Pinder's Flat. It was uncomfortably close to Steffan and Istel's main camp at Hazelwood Ford, and the constant presence of Rogandans in the area had become a growing irritant. The two kings were determined to drive them away. The encounter would not decide the outcome of the war, but it would be an important test for the new allied army.

Planning was proceeding smoothly, at least on the surface, but nevertheless Will was troubled. He turned away from the maps spread out before him and faced King Steffan.

"I would prefer to fight this next battle with your own soldiers, Your Majesty."

"I understand, Will," the king returned. The request clearly exasperated him, but he was visibly working hard at remaining calm and reasonable. "I must remind you, though, that defeating the Rogandans is not the only objective in this action. We need victories, but we also need to build an effective fighting force that includes both Arvenian and Castelan armies. Victories can help us establish that, but only if we win them together."

"May I speak frankly, Sire?"

"Of course, Will."

The king's words suggested he was open to hear whatever Will had to say. The firm line of his jaw said something entirely different. Will decided to voice his concerns anyway.

"Your goal of a unified force might be better achieved with someone other than me as commander, Your Majesty. Perhaps you would be better served if one of your noblemen took command."

King Steffan stiffened. "I never expected this from you, Will," he growled. "I don't need you going soft on me."

The king's response stung, but Will remained silent.

"I've appointed the person best equipped to lead this army, and that person is you," the king insisted, jabbing a finger at him emphatically. "I'm not entering into discussion on this. My very kingdom is at stake!" Brows bristling, he frowned across at Will, who maintained his silence.

"I know the cooperation from some of Istel's people might be a bit half-hearted at times," he conceded, "but you simply need to find a way to work with them."

It seemed clear that the king had little understanding of the extent of the hostility of the Castelan nobles toward the upstart commoner. But Will knew he could not expose the true situation without openly criticizing the lords, and that was simply out of the question. And besides, the king was right. It was his responsibility as commander to resolve any problems that affected the army, including this one.

"May I request, then, Your Majesty, that you appoint a liaison to coordinate the Arvenian and Castelan forces on my behalf?"

King Steffan frowned. "Who did you have in mind?" he asked.

"Lord Bottren," Will suggested. It was a risk, but he had the feeling that Bottren would be willing to work with him. And it might help ease tensions if the Castelans could interact with another nobleman instead of him.

"Consider it done," the king replied, reaching for parchment, his quill, and the royal seal.

A VAST CLOUD of dust drifted slowly into the sky ahead. The ring of metal on metal sounded above the cries of men and the scream of horses.

Will and Bottren skidded their horses to a halt at the top of a rise. The village of Pinder's Flat lay behind them. Below them, the placement of the rival armies could be clearly seen, even though men were fighting and dying little more than an arrow's flight away. The extreme vulnerability of the Arvenian left flank was immediately obvious.

Bottren stared in horror at the conflict raging below. "What are we going to do, Will?" The look on his face bordered on panic.

Will rapidly scrutinized the scene before him, witnessing the growing confusion spreading from the hard-pressed left wing of the Arvenian ranks. The battle hung on a knife edge. If he didn't respond decisively the struggle below him could quickly degenerate into a rout.

"Archers, My Lord, NOW! Bring up the Castelan bowmen! We drive off the Rogandan reserves, or our left flank collapses."

Even as the wide eyed Bottren galloped away, Will spurred his horse frantically down toward the heaviest of the fighting.

"To me, men! For the king and for Arvenon!"

Will crashed into the seething mass of men, his sword weaving a skillful web of destruction. Others took up the cry, "For the king and for Arvenon!", and pushed through the press to reach him.

Seeing their commander fighting on the field of battle gave new heart to Steffan's harried soldiers. The cluster of men gathering around him gradually grew in size. Rufe appeared from the Arvenian center and charged into the fray at the head of a grim band of horsemen. For the first time the Rogandan momentum was halted. Outnumbered five to one, Will's soldiers nevertheless began to surge forward.

Then a Rogandan horseman, clumsily avoiding the stroke of an opponent's sword, crashed into Will and almost knocked him from his horse. Rufe, witnessing it close at hand, was powerless to help in the melee. His face registered alarm, then slowly the alarm was replaced with rage. His face glowed red, and his whole body shook. Raising himself high in the saddle and roaring ferociously, he broke upon his enemies like a wave.

The Rogandans fled in terror from the madman, some throwing away their weapons in their haste. A gap opened up in their front line, and it quickly widened as Will's men began to push vigorously into it.

At this critical moment Bottren arrived with the archers. A steady shower of arrows flew over the heads of the combatants and fell among the soldiers gathered in the Rogandan rear. Some turned and fled. Others pressed forward to escape the deadly rain, and collided with those fleeing Rufe's berserker fury. The chaos spread, and soon the entire Rogandan front line began to disintegrate.

The Arvenian army, so close to collapse only minutes before, instead began to visit ruin upon the Rogandan forces. Superior numbers did nothing to help the invaders as men became trapped and helpless in the middle of the Rogandan lines. Foot soldiers were crushed and trampled in the press without ever facing an Arvenian soldier.

The eager embrace of Malzakh awaited many Rogandans that day. But more than enough escaped to whisper abroad a rumor of the wrath of Arvenon and the terror that awaited its enemies.

At Pinder's Flat, Will became commander of the combined army in more than just name. Steffan's soldiers embraced him with the same enthusiasm as their countrymen at Arnost. They were willing to go anywhere with him, and said so openly.

The small detachment of Castelan archers were also quick to adopt him. Will had assigned them a crucial role in the battle, and when it was over he swiftly acknowledged that they had carried out their task flawlessly. He also openly accounted to them a generous portion of the credit for the victory. It soon became clear that the Castelan soldiers were glimpsing for the first time a leader they might follow without hesitation into the valley of the shadow of death.

The Castelan nobles were another matter entirely. The battle was not even over before the recriminations started. When the leaders finally met to review the battle the atmosphere in the room almost crackled with tension.

"What madness led us to Pinder's Flat?" one of Istel's nobles demanded with a sneer. "The terrain favored no one but the Rogandans!"

The speaker, Lord Eisgold, had bitterly opposed Will's leadership from the beginning. Will held his peace. He glanced across at Bottren and saw his second-in-command pale with anger.

"The conditions were so appalling it left me no choice, Sire," Eisgold spat, turning to King Istel. "Your soldiers would have been massacred if I'd left them exposed in the position *he* assigned them." His thumb jerked toward Will. "It was only thanks to my considerable experience that they were extracted without a catastrophe."

Will smiled grimly to himself. It was true that the extraction had been well executed. If the soldiers had been led into battle with the same enthusiasm, the outcome would never have been in doubt.

"This looming massacre you speak of, Eisgold," Bottren interjected. "How many men did you lose?" His voice trembled with suppressed rage. "What was your death toll before you decided to abandon your post? I heard it was as many as four or five!" he sneered.

Eisgold rose from his chair in a rage. "Are you accusing me of cowardice?" he bellowed.

Everyone began shouting at once. Many of the nobles leaped to their feet, gesticulating wildly.

"SILENCE!"

The word came almost simultaneously from the lips of both sovereigns. One by one the nobles fell silent, and resumed their seats. Istel's face glowed red with anger, but Steffan's revealed an icy calm. The two kings exchanged glances, and Istel nodded, deferring to his younger ally.

"None of you will speak until invited to do so," King Steffan commanded emphatically. He paused to allow them to recover themselves.

"In *my* assessment," he asserted, "Pinder's Flat was indeed a near calamity. Disaster was averted only by the quick action of our commander. At considerable risk to himself!"

Istel's noblemen glowered, but said nothing.

"Will, do you have anything you wish to say?" King Steffan offered.

Will paused, his mind racing. How should he respond? What could he possibly say that would make any difference?

It was obvious that Eisgold's action was intended to finish him. Some of his supposed allies were determined to see him fail, whatever the cost to their own cause.

Will's plan of battle had been simple. He had chosen a position to the south of Pinder's Flat. The site was protected by marshland on the left, preventing any flanking movement from that direction. The left wing he entrusted to King Istel's men under Lord Eisgold. The best of King Steffan's troops took the center with Rufe at their head. A lightly wooded slope climbed away to the right of the site. The wood prevented any rapid deployment of soldiers, but it was not impenetrable. Will accordingly assigned a sizable contingent of Arvenian troops to the right wing to guard against any attempt by the Rogandans to turn his right flank. Castelan archers stood close by in reserve to be quickly deployed wherever they might be needed.

The Rogandans vastly outnumbered his force. But that would

probably always be the case in this war. And victory should have been readily within their grasp, if Eisgold had not removed his soldiers as soon as the fighting started. If the Rogandans had exploited the gaping hole on his left wing more quickly and effectively, the battle would have been over, and decisively so, in a couple of hours.

He knew that Eisgold's soldiers were not to blame. In fact he had heard that they were seething. They had been ready to fight, and were bewildered at being withdrawn so quickly from the battle. Now, with a victory won and praise and honors distributed freely elsewhere, they resented having being sidelined.

The perverse obstinacy behind Eisgold's behavior was maddening. Facing the Rogandans on the battlefield seemed straightforward compared to battling the Castelan nobles. Will could summon little enthusiasm for a campaign of this type. But he could not afford to retreat. The stakes had risen significantly, and Will wondered if the king fully realized the gravity of the situation. If he stumbled, the king would not long be able to continue to support him. And given the absence of an obvious successor, along with the disunity and lack of combat experience of the nobility, his removal had the potential to deal a fatal blow to the Arvenian cause.

He pushed down the sinking feeling in his gut. There was no room for weakness or self pity. He was now fighting for his life on two fronts, and he had to win both wars. There simply was no other option.

The king was still waiting patiently for his response.

"I have a question, Sire."

"Ask it," King Steffan replied.

"How would you respond if one of your soldiers withdrew from the heat of battle without orders?"

The sovereign did not hesitate. "I would have the man executed. There is no room in my army for deserters or cowards." He glanced across at Istel, who nodded his acquiescence.

"And if one of your noblemen withdrew?" Will continued.

Eisgold bristled, but did not speak.

"I would have the man immediately relieved of command. *If* I was in a good mood," King Steffan growled.

Again Steffan glanced across at Istel. A deep frown creased the Castelan's face. After a moment's hesitation he nodded again, firmly.

"You asked if I wished to speak, Your Majesty," Will offered calmly. "I do have something to say," he continued, getting to his feet.

"There are times when decisive action on the part of a leader can mean the difference between victory and defeat in a battle. Occasionally the situation demands such a rapid response that there is no time to seek confirmation from the commander.

"Today's battle at Pinder's Flat was *not* such an occasion," he asserted bluntly. He paused to let his meaning fully sink in. "Nevertheless, I would suggest that we choose to view today's action as a learning experience."

Will bowed in deference to the two sovereigns and waited for them to respond. King Istel nodded his assent at once. King Steffan glared darkly at the nobles for a moment, then nodded as well.

"As long as I am commander, though," Will continued, a hard edge in his voice, "if any leader orders a troop withdrawal again without my authority I will not hesitate to request that Your Majesties take the strongest possible action against that leader."

He gazed slowly around the table, locking glances briefly with any of the nobles willing to meet his eye. Then he sat down.

Lord Eisgold was one who boldly met his stare. He glared back at Will with an undisguised look of pure hatred.

6

The fire sizzled and spat as fatty juices dripped down onto it. Thomas turned the makeshift spit one last time, confident that the hare was finally ready to eat. He examined the meat carefully, searching for the most evenly cooked portion. Having selected a leg, he tugged at it hopefully. To his delight it came away readily in his hand—surely the meat would be tender. Then he carefully handed the prize to Brother Vangellis.

The monk, his brow furrowed in concentration, took a bite and chewed it critically. Then he delicately pulled away pieces of meat with his teeth until only bone remained. Finally he licked his fingers clean.

Thomas, anxious and impatient, could restrain himself no longer. "Well?" he demanded.

The monk frowned a moment more, then beamed him a broad smile. "Wonderful, Thomas. Beautifully cooked! And a fine piece of meat."

Thomas exhaled in relief and grinned back at him proudly.

Life in the wilderness had been harsh. With the weather gradually becoming colder, he rarely felt warm enough during the long nights. And he nearly always ended the day hungry, even though they spent many of their waking hours searching for food. But he knew he had toughened up a lot. He might be lean, but his muscles had firmed up visibly and he'd developed physical strength he never had before. He was a different person from the awkward youth who had ridden away from Arnost.

For the first time in his life he was learning to fend for himself. He knew how to use available materials to start a fire, he knew which berries to pick, and he could now identify mushrooms that were safe to eat.

Today had been his crowning achievement. He had fashioned a trap, caught a hare, made a spit, lit the fire, and skinned, cleaned, and cooked his catch. Every action had been carried out by him entirely on his own.

The monk's approval was immensely gratifying. With the verdict behind him, though, there was no further reason to hold back himself, and Thomas attacked the hare without further ceremony. Brother Vangellis looked on with a smile for a moment before joining in the feast.

After the food was gone Thomas sat back with a sigh of satisfaction, gazing at the fire flickering at the entrance of the cave. The surrounding terrain hid the entrance very effectively, and they had not hesitated to select the cave as their dwelling place almost as soon as they discovered it. It was small, but dry and sheltered from the prevailing winds. And it was adjacent to a reliable spring, an important consideration since they had no containers suitable for storing water.

Their new home was serviceable, if somewhat primitive. They made whatever improvements they could. They built a fire pit just inside the mouth of the cave. They gathered quantities of firewood and stored them at the back of the cave. They searched out suitable vegetation to soften the ground they slept on. And they had almost finished constructing a large covering made of wood to shield the entrance of the cave from the elements during bad weather.

They had not seen a single person in the weeks since they left the river, nor any signs of habitation. If there were villages in the vicinity, they had not been able to discover them. Isolated as they were, Thomas was not exactly lonely. Brother Vangellis was an ideal companion; he was knowledgeable, even-tempered, and easy to get along with. But Thomas missed other company more than he was willing to say. He would have given a great deal to see Will and Rufe again, and another day or two with Brother Hann would have been worth twenty tasty hares.

He could hardly complain, though. Disappearing from sight was exactly what they had been trying to do. And he himself—or rather his stone—was the reason for their exile.

"I don't understand it," Thomas said. "Why does the stone only work occasionally now? The scroll said nothing about the stones behaving this way."

"A large portion of the scroll seems to have been lost," Brother Vangellis replied. "Perhaps your questions would have been answered in the missing sections. It's also possible that the scroll's author didn't know everything about the stones."

"But it's almost as if the stone wanted to save Arvenon."

"What do you mean?" the monk asked.

"Since I found it again, that's all it's done. It exposed the Rogandan soldiers at the gates of Arnost, and also revealed the man who had betrayed Will and planned to hand the city to the Rogandans."

"What about the time when it showed you something about Will?"

"I may have got that wrong. I don't really know."

"But Will only believed your story about the stone after that happened. I suspect you did see something that really took place."

"Perhaps you're right. Maybe that needed to happen for Will to believe in the stone. Otherwise, I may not have been able to convince him about the Rogandans at the gates."

"So you're saying that the stone doesn't want the Rogandans to take over Arvenon?"

"I don't really know," said Thomas. "If the scroll is right, that isn't at all how it works. It doesn't seem to have a will of its own. It would be nice to think that the stone doesn't want Lord Drettroth to get it, though."

"It's hard to believe he really has any claim on it."

"How could he have a claim on it?" Thomas asked, bewildered.

"You first found the stone near Arnost. But how did it get there? Was Drettroth aware of it then? Was he involved in some way? There's a lot we don't know."

Both of them had many more questions than answers. When Thomas lay down to sleep, he couldn't get the stone out of his mind. Was there a pattern they were missing? Why did it work the way it did? Would it only come to life in a crisis now? The scroll didn't give that impression. If Randolf of Clerbon was to be believed, the stones —like the rock before them—were simply there to be used. Wisely or foolishly. There was no hint of anything more than that.

And what about Lord Drettroth? If the scroll was right, he couldn't take the stone by force and expect to be able to use it. Was he aware of that?

Or did the Rogandan leader have some reason to believe that he could induce Thomas to give him the stone? Perhaps Drettroth had access to the entire scroll. Had it given him ideas about how he might make use of fear and intimidation? Thomas tried to imagine how far Drettroth might go and what he might do to persuade him to hand it over. He soon decided not to think about that anymore.

When Thomas did eventually get to sleep, his dreams were troubled.

THOMAS WOKE to the patter of rain outside the cave. He opened his eyes and glanced around. The dull light showed him the figure of Brother Vangellis, still sleeping soundly.

He looked up, squinting at the sky outside the cave, and cried out in alarm. A small figure stood framed in the gray morning light. It was a boy, scantily dressed, and dripping wet from the rain. He stood in the entrance, staring in at them.

The minute Thomas's cry rang out, the boy disappeared.

Brother Vangellis sat up, startled. "What's the matter?" he asked, peering around groggily.

Thomas was on his feet, just inside the cave, staring out into the rain. "Someone was here! Right here, at the entrance to the cave."

His companion got up and joined him. "Who was it?"

"It was a boy. He was looking at us!"

"So we're not alone after all," the monk said quietly.

Thomas found it difficult to hide his agitation. Even here, hidden in the wilderness, they had been discovered. "I thought we were safe here!" he said in dismay.

"I don't think there's much reason to worry, Thomas. It was just a boy. We don't seem to have any Rogandan soldiers here yet."

As they stood gazing out, the boy reappeared. He came from the direction of the stream, and stood in the rain, looking pitiful.

"Hello," said Brother Vangellis.

The boy did not respond.

"Do you live near here?" the monk asked. With still no reply, he tried again. "Do you need our help?"

The boy betrayed no sign of understanding him.

Brother Vangellis then spoke a few words in another language. Still no response. He tried again, apparently in a different tongue, and the boy came to life, speaking rapidly and urgently.

The monk turned to Thomas. "Well, that's a surprise. I wondered if he was a nomad. But not so. He speaks Rogandan."

"Rogandan?!" Thomas became more alarmed than ever.

"Please, Thomas—you'll frighten him away!"

The boy was indeed on the brink of running away and hiding again. Brother Vangellis spoke to him again, and he calmed down.

"I don't care if he runs away! I'd be happy if he left and never came back."

"That wouldn't help us. He knows we're here now. But he isn't a threat. His mother is sick, and he's scared."

"What are we going to do?"

"Go with him, and see if we can help his mother," the monk said calmly.

Thomas shook his head in disbelief. "You can't be serious! We could be captured."

"There's a risk, it's true." Brother Vangellis paused for a moment, thinking. "Why don't you stay here?" he finally asked. "I'll go with him, and come back as soon as I can. If something goes wrong, you'll still be safe."

Thomas made no attempt to hide his dismay. "What if you're taken? How will I be able to keep the stone safe on my own?"

"You are more capable than you realize, Thomas," he replied, "and you're stronger than you were as well. But if you should come to be alone, I don't believe you will ever find yourself entirely abandoned. Help can come from unexpected quarters."

His words failed utterly to comfort Thomas.

Brother Vangellis tried to reassure him. "You needn't be concerned. I'm sure I will be back very soon. If these people meant to harm us, we would have had Rogandan soldiers in our cave this morning instead of the boy."

It was obvious that Brother Vangellis would go, whatever Thomas said. So he said nothing. But he didn't try to hide his anxiety. His obvious agitation clearly troubled the monk, but he left anyway.

In the end, Thomas had an entire day to wrestle with his discomfort. He wavered between feeling alarmed about the future and worried about the safety of his friend and protector. He felt too agitated to follow his normal routines, so he ate nothing all day apart from a few nuts that had been left in the cave.

By the time the sun set, with still no sign of the monk, his anxiety had become unbearable. He couldn't decide whether to risk sleeping in the cave, or to hide nearby where he could watch the cave in safety. A part of him was tempted to assume the worst and conclude that his friend had been captured. But it would have meant fleeing on his own, and that notion was simply unthinkable. In the end he found a vantage point up a nearby tree, and sat down to watch.

His hunger kept him awake at first, along with the discomfort of his perch. But eventually weariness overtook him. At one point he snapped awake to find himself starting to fall. After it happened a second time, he climbed down from the tree and lay down at the base of the trunk.

HE WOKE to the sound of someone calling his name. Bright daylight shone around him—he appeared to have slept through half the morning. Stiff and uncomfortable, he picked himself up and glanced around. Brother Vangellis was standing outside the cave, looking tired and worried. No one else was in sight.

Thomas headed for the monk, peering warily about him as he stepped out from the cover of the trees. As far as he could tell, they were entirely alone.

"I was concerned about you, Thomas. It's good to see you safe."

"Where were you? I thought something had happened to you!" Thomas couldn't keep the distress from his voice.

"I was caring for the boy's mother. She has a serious injury and she'd lost a lot of blood. I stayed with her all night, and I'm hopeful she will recover. I promised to visit her again tomorrow."

Thomas looked at him wide eyed. "Surely we need to flee! We're not safe now that we've been discovered!"

"I can't do that, Thomas. Not until she's out of danger."

"But she's Rogandan. They're the ones trying to capture us—the ones who've invaded our country! Why is her health more important than anything else?"

"She's a person, just like us. And I imagine that her life is as precious to her—and to her family—as my life is to me," Brother Vangellis replied quietly.

"But you never even met her until yesterday."

The monk sighed. "No, but I have met her now. And her family."

He paused and looked Thomas in the eye. "I could stay away. But what if she died as a result, and Lord Drettroth's soldiers never appeared? She would have died for nothing."

"And what if Drettroth's soldiers appear when you're at her house? You might end up dying instead," Thomas exclaimed.

The monk smiled sadly. "Life doesn't always offer us sunny days and simple choices. Sometimes you have to do what needs to be done, and let the future worry about itself."

"But what if more than one thing needs to be done? How do we decide between them? Healing a sick person might be important, but it isn't the only thing that matters. Lord Drettroth and the whole Rogandan army are chasing us. We can't let him get the stone!"

Brother Vangellis didn't answer.

Thomas couldn't think straight. He didn't have the monk's certainty when it came to making hard choices and taking risks in the name of doing what needed to be done. He needed time to master his disordered thoughts, so he set off aimlessly, heading away from the cave. Brother Vangellis didn't follow him. His friend had apparently decided he needed time to himself.

As he wandered, Thomas found himself wrestling with competing thoughts and feelings. One part of him wanted to flee, and to do so immediately. He couldn't do it without Brother Vangellis, though. He was only beginning to realize how much he'd come to rely on his mentor.

Another part of him, though, could not begrudge his companion's unquestioning care for this nameless Rogandan family. Deep down he knew that the monk was right.

Will hadn't hesitated to help Baron Rudungen's villagers, even at risk to himself and his men. He had clearly decided that it would be callous to deny assistance to the vulnerable when in a position to offer it. This situation was no different. The fact that the woman was Rogandan didn't change anything.

His biggest struggle was in deciding what he should do himself. Visiting the woman seemed pointless—he couldn't speak her language, and he wasn't at all sure he could make any kind of useful contribution. And the responsibility for the stone weighed heavily on him.

His mind was still churning when evening fell. He joined Brother Vangellis in the cave as usual.

Thomas asked a question that had been nagging him all day. "What's a Rogandan family doing living in Arvenon?" he said.

"Apparently a few families fled Rogand some years ago. They've been hiding out in the wilderness ever since. They didn't tell me why they left."

They conversed a little more, but Thomas didn't offer to accompany the monk the next day.

He woke once again to full daylight. His companion was nowhere to be seen; he was clearly fulfilling his promise to visit the sick woman again.

For a time Thomas busied himself looking for food, trying to convince himself that he was where he needed to be. The truth was, though, that he was miserable and lonely. More than once, as the day wore on, he would gladly have gathered his courage and set off after his friend. But he had no idea where to go. In the end he gave up any pretense at being usefully occupied, and sat down in sight of the cave, waiting for the monk to return.

Life had changed beyond recognition since the arrival of the boy. Nothing felt straightforward anymore. And yet, although Thomas never openly acknowledged it, he had always known that hiding away in the wilderness couldn't last forever. He hadn't wanted to think about the future. Now the future had arrived.

Brother Vangellis hadn't returned by nightfall, and Thomas fell asleep at the base of the tree again.

He woke around dawn with someone calling his name strangely.

"Toomaz!"

He peered out suspiciously into the half light. The boy was standing outside the cave. His shoulders were stooped, and he looked downcast.

"Toomaz!"

When there was no response, the boy turned and stared into the trees behind him. He appeared to be receiving instructions from someone hiding out of sight.

Fully alerted now, Thomas didn't move. After several minutes had passed, a Rogandan soldier stepped out from the trees, then another. Soon half a dozen men stood in the open, looking around them.

Last of all, another person was dragged into the open, his hands bound before him. It was Brother Vangellis.

The monk looked around him, then his voice rang out. "Flee, Thomas!"

He paid for his warning. A heavy blow from one of his captors felled him, and he went down hard. He didn't get up.

Thomas looked on in horror. His first instinct was to turn tail and bolt. Knowing he hadn't yet been spotted, though, he forced himself to pause and take stock so he could plan his next move sensibly.

The unthinkable had happened—his guide and companion had been captured. Will or Rufe would try to dream up a way of freeing the monk. But Thomas wasn't a soldier, and he didn't doubt that any attempt on his part at heroics would be sure to end in disaster. The monk was right; he had to flee.

The Rogandans almost certainly had trackers among them. If he ran blindly, they would hunt him down sooner or later, and probably sooner. It was abundantly clear to him what he needed to do.

The Rogandans were already spreading out, beginning their search. Thomas slipped away through the trees, heading for a nearby stream. After a few minutes he reached it. Stepping into the middle of the flow, he began to follow it downstream, heading away from the Rogandans.

He knew it was important to step out of the stream onto rocky ground to hide his footprints. After many minutes, though, he still hadn't found a suitable place. The stream was getting wider, and he guessed that the river could not be far away now.

He paused to take a long drink, then trudged on until the river came into view. Crouching down low, he moved stealthily forward. No other person was in sight. Very slowly and carefully he approached the mouth of the stream. Still seeing no one, he slipped into the river and surrendered himself to the current. He stayed close to the bank and swam slowly downriver, shivering in the cold water. He left the river when he came upon a suitable place to land.

Climbing out, he moved away from the water. He searched among the trees until he found a fallen limb that promised to be large enough to support his weight. He dragged it close to the water's edge and left it there.

Then he hid himself among the trees. As soon as night fell, he would once again take to the river.

He sat down on the ground and considered his situation. He had very few options. His first instinct had been to head deeper into the wilderness, although with no plan beyond avoiding capture. But the river had now become his only alternative. If he went with the current, he had no idea where it would take him.

He had to get away from the Rogandans—that much was clear. Lord Drettroth could not be allowed to take possession of the stone. But where would he be safe? Even in the wilderness the Rogandans had somehow managed to track him down. He could try to find a place that was not controlled by the invaders. But some of his own countrymen—men like Pisander—might betray him if they learned about the stone and gained the tiniest inkling of what it could do. Even Will might not be able to protect him.

He no longer had a guide to follow. But what use was a guide, anyway, when there was nowhere safe to go?

Utterly miserable, he buried his head in his hands and did battle with self pity.

When the daylight eventually failed, he made his way back to the river and dragged the tree limb into the water. He eased himself in and slowly guided it to the middle of the river. The water was cold, and he knew he wouldn't be able to stay there for long.

He drifted with the current, supported by the branch. The sounds of the river filled his ears, and he could see nothing except the stars above him peeking through thick clouds.

He fell to thinking of Brother Vangellis. What would his captors do to him? He remembered the blow that had felled the monk, and hoped he was not seriously injured.

It was clear that his own fears about visiting the sick woman had been well founded. The two of them almost certainly could have avoided capture by running away. But he knew that Brother Vangellis would never have been able to live with himself if they'd done that. And Thomas could not have retained his own self respect if he'd tried to force the issue.

He had been right about the risks. But in spite of the dire consequences, he knew that Brother Vangellis had been right, too, and in ways that mattered more.

The monk had done his best to respond to the needs of those around him, and ended up paying the price himself. Others might think that such behavior was stupid. Thomas, having personally benefited so much from the monk's assistance, could never see it that way. If he had the opportunity to say anything to Brother Vangellis at that moment, it wouldn't be words of reproach. He would instead apologize for failing to offer his unqualified support when the monk had simply set out to do what compassion told him needed to be done.

What would become of Brother Vangellis now? He didn't like to think about it.

What would become of him, for that matter? He might still be free, but his own future felt no less uncertain.

He would have given a great deal to have his friend with him again. Thomas never had more reason to appreciate the cheerful hopefulness and steady companionship of the monk.

But Brother Vangellis was gone, and he was truly alone.

7

Kuper woke at dawn, disoriented and not immediately sure where he was. Thin shafts of sunlight peeked through small cracks in the walls around him, revealing his brother on a straw mattress surrounded by blankets. It all came flooding back. He sat up and stretched. He had woken to a dawn that, like so many before it, promised many more risks than certainties. They would need to keep their wits about them.

Rellan was already awake and using his good hand to gingerly massage the muscles of his other arm in the sling. Seeing that Kuper had woken, Rellan turned to him with a crooked grin. "I can't wait to gaze once again upon the gracious countenance of our hostess," he said.

"Don't push her," Kuper replied firmly. "We're going to need her help."

Rellan winced with pain as he continued his massage.

Kuper looked at him in concern. "Is something wrong with your arm?"

"It's very sore this morning. I'm not sure if it's because of all the action yesterday, or the way I slept on it last night."

Kuper had him remove the sling and gently pull up his sleeve.

The flesh of his forearm was discolored and covered with angry-looking bruises.

"That looks bad! Maybe they have someone here who can help."

"It's nothing," Rellan protested.

Kuper shook his head stubbornly. "It isn't nothing. I need you back to full strength, Rellan. You'll be of no use to anyone until those bruises heal. You have to rest, and that's an end to it."

The morning was well advanced before Anneka called for them again. As they left the hut, Kuper nodded toward his brother's arm, raising his eyebrows inquiringly.

"Don't worry about me," Rellan replied. "We can think about my arm later."

Scar took them to a corner of the clearing where Anneka sat flanked by several men. In the afternoon light she appeared less mysterious, but equally stern. Scar pointed to a pair of rude chairs that faced the others, and Kuper and Rellan seated themselves. The woman nodded Scar to a seat, then turned her attention to the twins.

"My name is Anneka, and I lead this community. These are troubled times, and we live a precarious existence here. If my welcome was lacking last night, it is because we are not always sure whom we can trust." She pointed toward the children running noisily around the clearing, and to a small group of elderly men and women sitting together in the sun. "We have many mouths to feed. Even more since the Rogandans came. And there are never enough strong arms and capable hands to provide for them."

She paused, studying them silently for a moment. "In our world we meet foes more often than friends. Which are you?"

"We are merely soldiers of the king who wish to be on their way," Kuper replied. "Removing the Rogandans from Arvenon will ease your burden. You can help bring that day closer by aiding us now."

As they spoke, the quiet clip-clop of hooves reached them as a small group of horses were escorted across the clearing. They were led by a diminutive figure who hummed cheerfully to himself as he walked. Seeing the horses, Rellan pursed his lips and issued a piercing whistle that rose and fell melodically. One of the horses whinnied in response and pulled away toward him. The lad restrained it with difficulty.

"I'm delighted to see that my horse has found its way to a good home," said Rellan, a cheeky grin spreading across his face.

"Mine, too, apparently," said Kuper, spotting his own horse in the group.

Anneka's face hardened. "Are you accusing us of stealing your horses?" she demanded.

"I can't speak for my brother," Rellan replied, "but such a thought certainly never crossed my mind! I am merely overwhelmed with joy that our lost mounts have been recovered and can now be restored to us."

Kuper's brow furrowed as he looked at his brother. Rellan had always been known for his impudent brashness, but choosing the right moment wasn't always his greatest strength.

Anneka was not amused. She frowned as she looked back and forth between the twins and the horses now disappearing from the clearing. "Perhaps there is a simple way of settling this," she said. She turned to Kuper. "You claim to be a bowman. How good a bowman?"

"I am not entirely without skill," he acknowledged modestly.

"Then let us put your skills to the test," she said. "Yours against those of our best archer. If you win, take two horses of your choice and go. If you lose, you will abandon any claim on our horses, and remain here to work for us until I release you. Do you agree?"

Kuper looked at Rellan, who winked at him. Kuper frowned back at his brother in frustration. Their horses had been stolen from them, and now he was expected to win them back. They should have been well on their way to Erestor right now. No one except the Rogandans would benefit from this foolishness.

The harsh truth, though, was that he couldn't see that he had another option. "I agree," he said reluctantly.

"It's a pity I can't use my arm," Rellan told her. "I'm the better archer."

She glared at him, not impressed.

"He isn't boasting," Kuper admitted. "It's the truth."

Anneka sent away one of her men, and he returned with a young man who carried a bow slung over his shoulder. The new arrival greeted the two strangers warmly. "I am Hender. I understand we will be competing for some horses," he said to Kuper with a grin.

"We're competing for much more than that," Kuper replied testily. His brother might find this situation amusing, but he saw very little to smile about.

At that moment two men rode slowly into the clearing. They approached the group, and the first man dismounted, offering a quiet greeting to the leader. Seeing his arrival, others wandered over to greet him. A small crowd of men, women, and children had soon gathered.

The other man looked harried. Riding was clearly uncomfortable for him, and he dismounted awkwardly. His companion led him to Anneka and introduced him.

"All of us are very grateful to you!" the newcomer exclaimed. "My people could not have managed without the food you sent us. We have been traveling much more slowly than we hoped; we have so many children with us. Even with your help, the first group will not arrive here much before sundown tomorrow."

Looking around him, he caught sight of Kuper and Rellan. "You are here, too!" he cried out joyfully. "Our rescuers!" He rushed to Kuper and took his hand, shaking it vigorously.

"These men were there when you were attacked?" Anneka asked. She looked skeptical.

"No," he replied, "but they arrived very soon after." He pointed to Kuper. "I've never seen such a bowman," he said enthusiastically. "Six arrows, and six Rogandans went down. And his friend here killed their leader. With his sword."

Anneka looked back and forth between them all. Finally she turned to Kuper. "Why did you help them?"

"We were passing by," he said, "and saw that they were defenseless. We couldn't just leave them to be slaughtered."

"The odds were against you," she said.

Kuper shrugged. "There wasn't time to consider the odds."

She nodded to herself. "You can have two horses," she said decisively. "We should be aiding you, not hindering you. Please pardon my doubts." She looked up toward the sun. "If you set off soon, you should be well on your way before night falls. I will send someone to guide you."

Kuper nodded his agreement. "Thank you for your offer of a guide. We will accept it gratefully." He pointed to his brother. "May I ask a favor, though? Do you have anyone with healing skills? My brother's arm needs some attention."

"I am the healer in this community," Anneka replied. "I will take a look."

She drew closer, and Rellan presented his arm. She probed his forearm thoroughly. She didn't appear to be making much of an effort to be gentle, and Kuper winced more than once on behalf of his twin as he looked on. One or two of the other onlookers seemed a bit surprised at her roughness as well. It seemed clear to Kuper that his brother had managed to get under her skin, even in the short time they had been with her.

Rellan bore it all without comment.

"Who set the arm?" she asked.

"A monk who was traveling with us," Rellan replied.

"He seems to have done the job properly," she conceded, somewhat grudgingly.

"He was a capable healer. And almost as gentle as you," Rellan replied, regarding her with a straight face.

The look she gave him made it perfectly clear what she thought, both about him and his comment. Nevertheless, she carefully pulled down his sleeve and reapplied his splint. "It's badly bruised, but you haven't broken it again," she said. "Don't move the arm any more than is necessary. I suggest you delay your departure. I will examine it again in the morning."

He bowed in gratitude and beamed at her innocently, a smile lighting up his face.

She scowled at him in response, turning on her heel and walking away briskly.

Kuper steered his brother away from the crowd. "What were you thinking?" he asked. "Riling her won't help anyone!"

Rellan flashed him a grin. "What a magnificent woman," he said happily.

Kuper groaned. He knew his brother well enough to see the signs of a looming disaster, and he had no idea how to head it off.

It was clear that they were going to be stuck there for some time, so Kuper decided to make himself useful. He kept his eyes open for a while to learn where help was most needed. Eventually he ended up spending the afternoon assisting with the repair of a roof, in readiness for the coming winter.

There was little that Rellan could do to help with physical work, but he likewise wasted no time finding other ways of occupying his time. Soon after climbing onto the roof, Kuper looked down and saw his brother at the center of a noisy and enthusiastic group of children. Rellan was pretending to be a one-armed monster, lurching around slowly with an arm outstretched to grab them. Whenever he caught someone, they always quickly managed to escape. The children deliberately placed themselves almost within reach, then sprang away whenever he came too close, squealing with excitement. Later Kuper noticed the children sitting around his brother, hanging on his every word while he told them stories.

Most interesting of all, Kuper had spied Anneka shooting frequent glances toward his twin. From a distance he had the impression that more often than not she wore a frown. But there was no doubt that, for better or for worse, Rellan had managed to capture her attention.

The next morning Kuper rose early and set off into the forest with one of Scar's traveling companions to chop wood. Upon his return he found that Rellan had collected his bow and was giving some of the older boys tuition on archery.

When Anneka sent for Rellan late in the morning, his twin hurried along behind him. Kuper was unable to shake off the feeling that a disaster was imminent and that he was powerless to prevent it. He had tried to warn his brother the previous night, but at such times Rellan had a frustrating habit of giving every appearance of hearing him out, then doing exactly what he had been warned not to do.

When they arrived, Anneka avoided eye contact with Rellan, focusing her attention solely on his arm.

"Thank you very much for your thoughtful care for me," Rellan said brightly. "I didn't expect to find such gracious help hidden away in the wilderness."

Anneka pointedly ignored him. Kuper concluded that she probably thought he was mocking her.

She continued to examine Rellan's arm. She seemed a bit more careful this time, but Kuper still felt glad it wasn't his arm beneath her probing fingers.

"Your arm is improving. But you need to rest it properly if you want it to heal." As she spoke, she looked up into his eyes for the first time. What she saw there clearly disconcerted her. At first she colored, then she frowned in intense annoyance.

"I don't know what you think you've been doing with the children," she burst out angrily. "Many of them have been through a lot, and they don't need you talking nonsense to them."

His response was one of innocent bewilderment, which did not improve her mood.

"I was merely recounting some of my adventures," he said mildly, "and telling them how fortunate they are to live in such a place as this, with a wise and thoughtful leader who takes care of all their needs."

"It's true," one of the bystanders blurted out. "I overheard him."

Kuper noticed that a small crowd had quietly gathered, and that they were observing the interaction with keen interest.

"One of the young girls asked me what I do at bedtime when I'm feeling sad," Rellan continued. "I told her that I find a happy thought and think about that. She asked me, 'What kind of happy thought?'.

So I suggested she think about something nice that happened that day, and come up with ways of showing she was grateful the next morning."

"He did say that," another observer confirmed. Anneka frowned.

"She asked me what happy thought I was going to take to bed with me that night, and how I could show I'm grateful in the morning. I told her that I would go to sleep thinking about their kind leader who is mending my arm, and that I would specially thank her in the morning."

"I heard that, too," chipped in another person. Someone stifled a snort of laughter.

Anneka rounded on the bystanders crowding around them. "Don't you have anything else to do?" she snapped.

They scurried away. Kuper went with them, and Rellan followed after first thanking her gratefully once again.

The latest incident had clearly agitated Anneka. Later he heard her yelling at someone, which hadn't happened before in his hearing. He noticed others looking at each other with raised eyebrows.

Soon after that Rellan disappeared. Kuper kept an eye out for him. As the day wore on he had the impression that Anneka was doing the same.

Darkness fell without any sign of his brother. At one point Kuper was standing alone, leaning against a tree, when Anneka joined him.

"Thank you for all your help, Kuper," she said. "You've been working very hard, and all of us appreciate it."

"It's the least I can do," he replied.

They stood together in silence for a while. "Have you seen your brother?" she finally ventured.

"No, I have no idea where he has gone."

She sighed. "I wish he was more like you. I don't know what it is, but I find him extremely irritating. I've found myself wondering if he's setting out to vex me deliberately."

Kuper laughed. "It isn't just you," he said. "You're not the first person to find him annoying. There were times when he drove my mother crazy, much as she loved him."

Anneka smiled grimly. "Without having met her, I feel a strong sense of connection with the poor woman."

Kuper laughed again. "In his defense, though, I should say that not everyone finds him irritating—it's just a lucky few." He paused for a few moments. "I told you that he's my brother," he continued. "He's actually my twin, although we're not identical twins, as you can see, and we're very different in many ways. I know him well. He is strong willed, it's true, and can be provoking at times. But he's also loyal and courageous. And by nature he's kind and very generous."

"Perhaps I have been a bit too harsh with him," she said with another sigh. "I don't know what's come over me. I've been snapping at people all afternoon, and feeling very ashamed about it."

They talked about other matters for a few more minutes, then she excused herself and departed, leaving Kuper with much to think about.

Rellan finally appeared late that night. He slipped under his blankets without a word. Kuper looked at him questioningly, and he responded with nothing more than a wink. Then he rolled over and immediately went to sleep.

The next day Kuper noticed Rellan watching the comings and goings around Anneka closely. As soon as his brother saw her alone, he headed over to talk with her. Kuper watched anxiously. His brother pulled a large bunch of wildflowers from beneath his coat and handed it to her. She looked surprised. They exchanged words for a while, and she actually smiled. Then he said something else to her, and she stiffened. She threw the flowers on the ground, spun on her heel, and departed, white with anger. Rellan bent down and carefully picked up the flowers. He left them on a table and came over to Kuper.

"What just happened?" asked Kuper anxiously.

"Yesterday afternoon I went searching for flowers for Anneka," his brother told him. "When I gave them to her she thanked me and asked me what had prompted the gesture. I told her that I could see how hard she worked, and thought that she might enjoy something of beauty to take her mind off her many responsibilities.

She liked that. Then I also said that she'd seemed grumpy and unhappy yesterday, and that I hoped the flowers would cheer her up."

Kuper shook his head and covered his face.

"Well, she *was* grumpy!" Rellan retorted. "Everyone could see it. What good does it do to pretend to ignore something when it's so obvious?"

Kuper just groaned.

"Don't worry," Rellan said with a grin. "She'll get over it. She's too good a person to let such a small thing bother her for long. And they were very nice flowers."

Kuper shrugged. What else could he do?

Anneka reappeared after an absence of a couple of hours. She behaved normally, and even examined Rellan's arm again, managing to stay calm and detached while doing so. Before he left she apologized to him for her earlier outburst. Rellan apologized in his turn for having offended her. Having thus declared a truce they both went about their business.

Late in the day refugees began arriving from the destroyed village, and every adult in the community was soon very busy. That evening Kuper and Rellan found themselves sharing their small hut with several others.

On the afternoon of the next day Anneka called for Rellan once more and examined his arm. Kuper noticed that she was more gentle this time. She seemed relaxed, even with a crowd of people nearby.

"The swelling on your arm is finally going down," she said. She turned to Kuper. "You will be able to resume your journey again tomorrow."

"Then there's time for an archery contest this afternoon," said Rellan brightly.

People responded immediately, calling excitedly for Hender. He was close at hand and stepped forward with a smile. Loud cheers erupted around him.

Anneka tried to look severe. But then she shrugged. "Oh, very well," she said.

The people crowded around their champion, slapping him on the back and urging him on.

Kuper fetched his bow and moved to the center of the clearing with Hender. Rules were agreed upon, and the two men took their places. The onlookers stood back to give them space.

The first contest called for a single shot at a stationary target. Two pine cones were spotted high up in a tree across the clearing. They were so far away that Kuper could barely see them. He was given the first shot. He pulled the bowstring back to his ear and let fly. The arrow streaked away toward the target, and rattled the pine cone, dislodging it. Many people applauded politely, and some of the newly arrived refugees cheered.

Then Hender took aim. A hush came over the crowd. The onlookers exhaled as he released his arrow, and a collective sigh chased it on its way. The arrow flew straight to the pine cone, knocking it to the ground. Someone ran to the tree and held up the arrow. It had skewered the cone neatly. The entire crowd erupted in cheers.

Kuper applauded with them, a smile of appreciation on his face.

The second target was a pair of small rocks, one for each contestant. This time, Hender would shoot first. A volunteer threw the first rock high into the air, and Hender drew his bow and fired. The arrow flew to the rock and hit it squarely, sending it tumbling through the air. Once again the crowd erupted.

The second rock was thrown, and Kuper took his shot. As he released the arrow a bird flew past. The arrow barely missed the creature, and the crowd gasped. The arrowhead shaved the side of the rock, causing it to wobble a little on its way to the ground.

"Lucky bird!" shouted Rellan enthusiastically, prompting bursts of laughter from the crowd.

The final test required the contestants to land an arrow into the center of a round knot high up in the trunk of a large tree across the clearing.

Kuper took his time before releasing his arrow. It sailed across the clearing and embedded itself right in the middle of the knot.

"Hooray!" shouted Rellan, to more laughter.

Hender drew his bow and fired, then rapidly nocked another arrow and fired again. The first arrow landed right alongside Kuper's arrow, so close the two were touching. The second arrow split the two down the middle. Everyone in the crowd shouted themselves hoarse. Rellan shouted along with them.

Kuper congratulated Hender and shook his hand. "You bested me, fair and square," he said with a smile. The crowd cheered again, honoring both their champion and the gracious loser.

Anneka stepped forward and held up her hands for silence. She waited until the noise had subsided. "There's been little reason to celebrate in recent days," she called out. "But tonight we will hold a feast in honor of Hender, and in honor of a worthy contest. It will also be an opportunity to bid farewell to our new friends, who are leaving in the morning." Groans and sighs of disappointment greeted this latest news.

"Hunters will soon be off to bring us fresh meat," she called. "Prepare a bonfire!"

Another cheer went up at her words, and a buzz of excitement filled the air as the crowd dispersed. Dry wood was gathered in the center of the clearing and the fire built up once again. Spits were erected in anticipation of the spoils of the hunt.

The twins did not see Anneka again until later in the evening. The celebration was well underway, and they had been sitting with Hender enjoying fresh venison and quiet conversation. The bowman had just left them to join a group of revelers. Someone found a lute, and men and women jumped to their feet to dance. Hender was pulled into the circle by an attractive young woman who appeared to be on very friendly terms with him. The two of them were soon spinning and whirling with a sea of couples in time to a popular Erestorian folk dance.

The twins rose to their feet and nodded respectfully as the leader approached.

"It's a good thing our fate didn't depend on me defeating Hender," said Kuper.

"Your departure will be our loss. Your bow and your help would have been very welcome among us," she said. "And you, yourself, of course," she added with a smile.

"What about me?" Rellan asked, a wounded expression on his face.

She shot him a dark look, but didn't bother to answer.

"We haven't talked a great deal about what is going on in the rest of Arvenon," she said, changing the subject. "We hear so little news of the outside world."

"You know that the Rogandans are roaming freely throughout the countryside," Kuper replied. "I believe you're also aware that the king is in Castel with his new bride, and that Arnost is besieged. You may not have heard, though, that one of the lords was planning to betray the king. He has been imprisoned in Arnost. He came from Erestor," he added, "so you may know of him."

She reacted sharply. "Who was it?"

"The Earl of Pisander."

"Pisander?" She spat the name. "A dungeon is too good for him! I hope the rats gnaw his bones." She paused while she mastered her anger. "Please excuse me. Let us speak of something else," she said.

"Is the pass into Erestor open?" Kuper asked. "We need to get through as soon as possible."

"No, the Rogandans are besieging Steffan's Citadel, so the pass is closed. There is another way, though. It is difficult, and impractical for a large company. But a small party should be able to get through. I have promised to send a guide with you. He will help you find the way."

"We are grateful for your help," Kuper replied.

"It is the least I can do, if only to mend my sorry welcome when you first arrived."

Rellan had been listening quietly. But at this point he broke into the conversation, a serious expression on his face. "There is one other boon you could grant, if you were willing," he said.

She looked at him suspiciously. "What is it?" she asked.

"The honor of accompanying me in the dance," he said, bowing formally.

She was too shocked to respond. Without waiting for an answer he grabbed her hand and pulled her toward the dancers. Kuper could see the blood rising in her face and winced, waiting for an eruption. But the dancers raised a cheer as they saw their leader apparently joining their merriment, and she quickly mastered herself. Soon the whole company was hooting and hollering in delight as Rellan used his one good arm to deftly lead her through the dance in time with the music.

Kuper had no doubt that Anneka had yielded for the sake of her people, and he wasn't looking forward to her reaction once the dancing was over. His unease grew as the evening wore on.

Other men partnered her briefly on the dance floor, then Rellan claimed her once again for a lively jig.

As the dance ended it apparently became plain even to Rellan that she had reached her limit. He escorted her away from the dancers, to the cheers and applause of the crowd. She acknowledged them with a wave and a smile, but her smile seemed forced to Kuper.

She walked right past Kuper without pausing. Rellan trailed along in her wake. Soon they disappeared behind some trees, out of sight of everyone. Their raised voices ensured that Kuper was still able to hear them, though.

"How dare you humiliate me like that!"

"Where was the humiliation? You heartened your people enormously by joining in their fun."

"Don't throw that back in my face. You forced me to do it!"

"And you were going to force us to stay here to work for you. After stealing our horses!"

"Aargghh! You are the most insufferable, most arrogant, most presumptuous man I have EVER met!"

With that, she stormed off into the night.

Rellan joined him, kneading the muscles of his healing arm. "Well," he said with a tight smile, "this has been an evening I won't forget in a hurry."

. . .

THEY ROSE AT DAWN. As they readied themselves to leave they were joined by their promised guide, a wiry man who introduced himself as Yosef.

"Your leader has not come to bid us farewell," Rellan observed.

"Her movements are not always predictable," Yosef replied. "We may see her yet."

Other people were already about their business as they mounted up to ride out of the clearing. Seeing them leaving, a number of men, women, and children hurried over to speak with them.

"My children love you, Rellan! Thank you for spending time with them."

"Thank you for helping with my roof, Kuper."

"How will I learn to be a proper archer, Rellan? Please come back soon."

"Go get the Rogandans, Kuper!"

One little girl came up to Rellan, and said to him very seriously. "Our leader likes you."

He smiled back at her. "I like her, too."

Many of the recently arrived refugees also came to wish them well, and to offer again their heartfelt thanks.

Last of all, Hender came up to Rellan, looking a bit sheepish. "Where did you find the flowers?" he asked quietly. Rellan laughingly gave him directions.

Mostly for Rellan's sake, Kuper kept an eye out for Anneka. But she didn't come.

They finally managed to get away, with people calling farewells after them. They continued to wave back until the clearing was out of sight.

After they had been traveling for several minutes, their path took them past a giant fallen redwood. Once they were beyond it, Kuper looked back and saw a lone figure standing on the fallen trunk. It was Anneka.

Following his gaze, Rellan turned in his saddle. He raised his arm high in farewell.

She watched them silently, her face unreadable. She did not wave back.

Her figure slowly dwindled in size as they rode on, until the path turned, and they saw no more of her.

"That's curious," said Yosef, stealing a sideways glance at Rellan. "In all our years in the wilderness, that's the first time I've seen her with flowers in her hair."

Rellan visibly relaxed. His cheeky grin reappeared, and he winked at his brother. "Anneka and I will meet again," he said. "I feel it in my bones."

8

"You don't have to like it, Karevis. But if you're not willing to follow instructions you'll be replaced by someone who is."

Karevis glared at Lord Tarestel, making no attempt to conceal his contempt. He had never liked the man. Tarestel had always seemed a little too willing to sacrifice the greater good of the kingdom for the sake of his own advancement. He had never been too obvious about it, though. Karevis likened him to an eel—very slippery and with the potential for a nasty bite. Now he had far exceeded the worst expectations even of Karevis.

"So you're going to rule Varas as a puppet of the Rogandans?" Karevis asked him.

Tarestel answered slowly, with exaggerated patience. "I've explained it already. The Rogandans are holding the king, along with the aides who accompanied him. He has not been harmed, but that is certain to change if we choose not to cooperate. Grunsetz has given me an ultimatum—either I act as Lord Protector of the kingdom, or he will appoint a Rogandan to do it. Surely even you wouldn't want to see that happen!"

"What is being done to free the king?"

"You simply don't understand, do you? Your precious world is gone! Gone! And the king with it. Everything is changing around us. Soon Arvenon and Castel will be gone, too."

Tarestel was becoming excited. "The Arvenians and the Castelans resisted, so their *people* are going to pay." He began jabbing his finger at Karevis. "Their people will suffer because of the choices made by their leaders! We can't let that happen here. We have to work with the Rogandans. It's the only hope our people have!" Tarestel came to a halt, his passion abating.

Karevis frowned. He didn't like Tarestel, and he didn't trust his motives. But what he was saying seemed to make sense. Uncomfortable sense. Karevis remembered the words of the king, possibly the last words he would ever hear from his friend: *Do everything you can to protect our people. Don't fail me in this!*

The moment that Tarestel had echoed Delmar's directive, Karevis knew he had no choice. Much as he disliked it, he was going to have to work with the man.

He raised his hands in a gesture of surrender. "I understand. You will have my support." It was his turn to jab his finger at Tarestel. "But only for as long as it protects the people! Do you understand?"

GRUNSETZ HANDED Tarestel a parchment covered with numbers. "It has proven necessary to levy another tax," the Rogandan announced in a bored tone of voice.

Tarestel scanned the document, his alarm increasing every moment. "This is monstrous! You can't be serious!"

Grunsetz shrugged. "The cost of occupying and protecting Varas is proving to be significant."

"But there will be riots!"

"You need not fear for your safety. We now have our soldiers stationed in every city and throughout the countryside. Rioters will be dealt with ruthlessly."

"But this will beggar every family in the country!"

"Some of your countrymen are lazy. Perhaps you need to

encourage them to work harder," the Rogandan suggested. "Of course there are other ways of raising the money. Our previous levies don't seem to have troubled your coffers at all. If you are so concerned for your countrymen, perhaps you could help them out this time and pay your fair share." Grunsetz treated Tarestel to one of his nasty smiles.

Tarestel felt himself beginning to sweat. "I won't be able to govern effectively once this becomes known."

"That's your problem, Lord Protector. If I recall correctly, you volunteered for this position. You seemed to believe that your king had done an extremely poor job of ruling Varas, and that you could do so much better. If the task is no longer to your liking, I'm sure another of your countrymen can be found to take your place. Perhaps someone a little more pliable next time."

"But how could I—or anyone else for that matter—possibly come up with this much money?" Tarestel asked in despair.

"You must squeeze, my dear Lord Protector," Grunsetz replied. He raised his fists by way of illustration and tightened them slowly. "Squeeze! And if that doesn't do it," he added, "then squeeze some more!"

Lord Karevis headed to the tent of Zornath, the Rogandan liaison, in response to his latest summons. Karevis might be commander of the army in name, but the Rogandan held all the real power. Zornath allowed Karevis to continue to issue directives to the Varasan officers, but not before every word had been carefully vetted.

The Rogandan was like a terrier yapping at his heels, never leaving him alone for an instant. And Karevis wasn't alone in his suffering, either. A host of lesser Rogandan 'liaisons' had been sprinkled liberally throughout his army, and every one of his officers now shared his pain. Zornath had placed his men well—the Rogandan seemed to catch the faintest whisper from the Varasan ranks, often before Karevis himself became aware of it.

A few of the Varasans had even become informants, reporting on their fellow soldiers. Karevis could hardly bear the shame of it. He knew that most of his men shared his disgust, but there was little that any of them could do about it.

Many times Karevis had found himself thinking that his situation could not possibly get any worse. But he had been wrong, so very wrong. Every single day he seriously considered resigning his position. So far he had refrained from doing so. He stayed for one reason only—he knew that his men would suffer in a multitude of ways if he left. He still retained some ability to shield his subordinates from the most painful decisions of his new masters, and he would remain for as long as that continued to be true.

The guards stopped him when he arrived at Zornath's tent. He stood outside, like a fox at bay, waiting for the hounds.

"Ah. Come on in, Commander," called the Rogandan, finally noticing him. He stepped inside the tent, and Zornath pointed him to a stool. The liaison was himself seated in a large armchair. Karevis sat down, pretending he didn't notice the discrepancy.

"I have some wonderful news," Zornath said, flashing one of his toothy smiles.

Karevis braced himself. Thus far, the Rogandan's notion of good news had never matched his own. Not even vaguely.

"Lord Drettroth has ordered the Varasan army into the field," Zornath told him, beaming with delight. "Is that not splendid? There is nothing soldiers love more than being on campaign!"

Clearly it was wonderful news as far as Zornath was concerned. Karevis had rarely seen him so cheerful.

"What does Lord Drettroth have in mind?" Karevis asked, not expecting an answer.

Normally, Zornath loved to keep him in the dark. On this particular occasion, though, the liaison appeared to be in an expansive mood. "Our destination is Arvenon. Your soldiers have many fine qualities, Commander, I am sure. But in Arvenon they will have one particular advantage over our own men—they speak the same language as the Arvenians. This skill will undoubtedly prove very useful when dealing with the local people."

Karevis pondered the news. Using a common language to communicate with the Arvenians was all very well. But Drettroth didn't need an army for that. Going on campaign sounded much more to the point. More trouble was brewing, because nothing would ever induce him to fight alongside the Rogandans against the Arvenians. He was certain the vast majority of his men would feel the same way.

Sooner or later he was going to reach a breaking point. If things had been bad before, they were about to get a lot worse.

He wondered if Tarestel was aware of Drettroth's plans. "How does the Lord Protector view this development?" he asked the liaison.

Zornath flicked his fingers dismissively. "It is no concern of his. There are more than enough Rogandan soldiers stationed in Varas to ensure the security of his rule. He has no need for the Varasan army."

Karevis wondered how Tarestel was liking his role as Lord Protector. He wouldn't be surprised to learn that the ambitious nobleman was finding life as a Rogandan vassal every bit as distasteful as he was himself.

His musings were interrupted by the liaison.

"Efficiency will become of paramount importance once our army is on the march," Zornath told him. "Some of your men are not communicating effectively with their liaisons. Get me a list of names of all of your men who speak Rogandan. They will be assigned secondary roles as translators."

The Rogandan appeared to lose interest in the conversation. "Deliver the list by noon tomorrow, Commander. And do not be late!" he commanded. "You are dismissed," he added in an imperious tone, dropping his gaze to a document lying in front of him.

As the commander left Zornath's tent, he wracked his brains for the thousandth time, trying to conjure up a way of extracting his army from the clutches of the Rogandans. But as always, his mind was blank.

Why hadn't they fought while they still could? If the Rogandans had defeated them, as would have been likely, the outcome for the people of Varas could scarcely have been worse than it was now. And his men would have fought like tigers. The Rogandan army would have been left considerably weakened.

Instead, the Rogandans had been able to send their most feeble soldiers to Varas as occupiers, and use the Varasan army to swell their ranks in Arvenon.

He didn't doubt that King Delmar would have chosen differently if he'd had his time over again. But it was too late. And there was no point in blaming his friend; the king must surely have paid a heavy price of his own. Karevis had no way of knowing exactly what had become of Delmar, but by now he knew enough about the Rogandans to make some intelligent guesses.

He returned to his quarters in a gloomy mood, troubled by dark forebodings.

Essanda frowned up at Count Gordan. "Why is everyone so unhappy these days, Gordy?" she asked.

The noble was sculpting a tiny image of a horse from a piece of wood. He glanced up from the carving and gave her an affectionate look. "People are frightened, Your Majesty. They're worried that the Rogandans might defeat us," he replied. He bent his head again, returning to his labors.

He was refreshingly direct with her, as always. It was something she especially appreciated about him. Other people usually told her what they thought she needed to hear.

To most adults she was invisible. She had always been shown appropriate deference, of course, first as Princess of Castel, and now as Queen of Arvenon. But she was just a child to most of them. Sometimes they even said so out loud. And in her presence, too. To them she was a delicate doll—a bit fragile, and needing to be handled gently. She wasn't seen as an independent person in her own right.

Count Gordan treated her as if she was intelligent. She liked that.

"But Steffan—His Majesty, I mean—isn't going to let them win. I know he has great faith in his soldiers."

Count Gordan contented himself with a grunt of acknowledgment. She didn't quite know how to read it.

"Why don't people like Will?" she asked.

"Will Prentis?" He put down his knife. "You seem to know quite a lot about what people think," he said, raising an eyebrow.

She smiled innocently at him, but didn't reply. He was right, of course—she did know a lot. She heard things. She could probably thank her invisibility for that, at least in part. She could also thank her new husband. He had apparently decided that she was intelligent, too, and she suspected he told her much more than he should have.

"People don't like Will because he isn't a nobleman," Count Gordan said. He glanced around the room, apparently satisfying himself that they were alone. "And also because he's smarter than any of us nobles," he added with a grin.

"He can't be smarter than you!" she protested.

"Thank you, Your Majesty," he said, bowing his head low. "You honor me greatly."

He looked at her seriously. "I believe that I am a useful diplomat, Your Majesty. Your father seems to think so, anyway. But the truth is that when it comes to war, Will *is* more clever than me—more clever than any of us. Much more so. He seems able to outthink his opponents. And, just as important, men are willing—even eager—to follow him into battle. None of the nobles can make the same claims. And many of them can't forgive him for it."

"How do you know all this, Gordy?"

"I have my ways of finding out what people think, too," he said.

She looked at him questioningly. "Is there anything we can do to make it easier for the nobles?"

He shook his head, admiration in his eyes. "You never cease to amaze me, young Essie," he said, calling her by the affectionate name he had used since she was a small child. "You give the appearance of being so naive and unaware, but you quickly see to the heart of it, as always."

She looked at him quizzically. "What do you mean?" His familiarity did not offend her in the least—he had been almost like a second father to her, and she felt secure in the knowledge that he loved and admired her.

"I meant, Your Majesty, that most people sympathetic to Will would be thinking about ways of strengthening him at the expense of his critics. You turn your attention instead to the source of the problem."

He paused for a moment. "I have given the matter a great deal of thought," he admitted. "I'm sorry to say that I don't have any good answers, though." He sighed. "Everyone is proud and stubborn at times. For some strange reason, though, people with few accomplishments and abilities can be the proudest and most stubborn of all. The only real achievement some can claim is to have brought down people better than themselves. If you can call that an achievement."

A gong sounded, announcing dinner. He rose and took her hand, leading her from the room.

THAT NIGHT as she lay in bed, Essanda remembered a tale she had heard from one of her father's oldest advisors.

"A fool set a fire at the home of his rival," the advisor had said. "He looked on gleefully while the fire took hold, and he actively discouraged his neighbors from fighting the blaze. Soon the fire could not be contained. To the arsonist's delight, his rival lost everything.

"Meanwhile, though, the fire spread out of control and engulfed the whole town. Before long it consumed the home of the fool, too, along with all of his possessions.

"What did the fool learn from this disaster? He convinced himself that the fault lay with his rival, since the fire had spread from his house. He abused his victim publicly, demanding compensation. His victim had no compensation to offer, of course. Both men were ruined, along with the entire town.

"The fool lost everything except his folly. The greater fools, though, were the townsfolk, who stood by and did nothing when they could have saved their neighbor's home and prevented the destruction of their town."

Essanda didn't know what she could do to help against the Rogandans. But she drifted off to sleep determined not to stand by and watch her kingdom fall because she'd done nothing to save it.

9

Thomas had only been in the water a short time before he began to feel the cold acutely. He tucked his arms in to his body and began kicking his legs, but it didn't help. Soon he was shivering uncontrollably.

It was clear that he couldn't stay in the river. Releasing the branch that had supported him, he swam to the bank opposite from where he had started. He hoped there was at least a small chance that the Rogandans were only occupying one side of the river.

Locating a place to land, he dragged himself out onto the bank. Then he got up and began squeezing water from his clothes. The night air was cool, and he knew he needed to dry himself and find somewhere out of the wind as quickly as possible. Teeth chattering and arms hugged to his chest, he headed inland.

After picking his way through the foliage for a few minutes, he found a small animal track heading away from the river. He turned onto it instinctively, following it until it widened into a small clearing. An animal had been digging near the base of a tree, leaving loose soil scattered around. The soil had been exposed for long enough to have dried out thoroughly. After a moment's consideration, he stripped off most of his clothes—everything except his trousers and the pouch holding the stone—and put them to one side. Then he picked up handfuls of the dirt and began spreading it over his body. He kept at it until a thin coating of mud covered him. Finally he wrung out his clothing as best he could. Then he set off again, following the animal trail where it continued across the clearing.

It didn't take long before the mud began to dry on his body, leaving behind a clinging layer of dirt. He brushed at the dirt as he walked, managing to remove most of it. His clothes were still too wet to put back on, but his body was nearly dry, and he was no longer shivering quite so violently.

When the trail led him into an area of denser undergrowth, he turned off the path. Having found a piece of ground covered with soft grasses, he gathered together several fallen branches still covered with leaves and made a low shelter. He hung his clothes on the outside to dry, and crawled in. The grass was cold on his bare skin, but he was so tired he drifted off to sleep anyway.

He woke in the night to the haunting cry of an owl. Crawling out from beneath his shelter he hunted for his clothes. They had blown away in the breeze, and it took him a few minutes to find them. They were almost dry, so he put them on and climbed back under the branches.

He lay there thinking about his urgent need for food and better shelter, especially with the weather becoming cooler. Above all he knew he must remain truly hidden. The harsh reality of his isolation pressed in on him. Once again he wondered where Brother Vangellis was, hoping fervently that he was not badly hurt.

The loss of the monk's companionship was a heavy blow, and he wished they could have remained together. The monk was beyond his reach, though. He was alone in the wilderness with no hope of rescue.

It would have been easier than ever to lose control of his emotions, but he knew the time had come to toughen up. He simply could no longer afford to indulge in self pity. His mental toughness needed to match his newly developed physical strength. He had to survive on his own.

. . .

THE MORNING WAS HALF SPENT when Thomas first heard the horse. He had been checking his snares, and finding them empty had followed the animal trail back to the river. Arriving at the water's edge, he peered out cautiously, looking for boats or any other sign of the Rogandans. He had seen people on the river more than once, and had even spotted a soldier on the opposite bank on one occasion. But up to now there had been no sign of pursuers on his side of the river. No one had come anywhere near where he had been hiding for the past few days.

He left the river when he heard loud whinnies from further along the path. His heart beat a frantic rhythm as he hurried off the path and hid himself. Was he about to be discovered at last?

After a few minutes a horse and rider came into view, heading along the path. He guessed that the horse must have propelled its rider into some of the low hanging tree branches that overhung the path, because the man had both blood and bruises on his face. The rider was cursing the animal roundly. Thomas could not understand a word he was saying, but his meaning was very clear.

As he drew nearer to the river, the rider dismounted. He roughly wrapped the reins around a branch, then picked up a stick from the ground and laid into his horse with it. The terrified animal drew back and reared up, screaming in fright.

Muttering loudly, the man set off on foot toward the river.

As he disappeared from sight, Thomas peered back along the way he had come. No other riders were in sight—this soldier was apparently traveling alone. Thomas looked first at the animal and then ahead to where the rider had disappeared.

Could he dare to steal the horse?

He looked on anxiously—the soldier could return at any minute. If he was going to do it, he needed to move quickly, but still he hesitated. What if the man reappeared at the very instant he stepped into the open?

He stood rooted to the ground in an agony of indecision, breaking out into a cold sweat as the moments fled away. Finally, his heart pounding in his chest, he acted. Full of apprehension, he approached the horse. It watched his approach with eyes bulging, and began to pull away. He spoke to it quietly, drawing upon all his experience with the animals. The horse calmed down, and he loosened the reins and led it away. Incredibly, the soldier still did not appear.

The moment he was out of sight of the place where he had found the horse, Thomas climbed into the saddle and rode away, bending low to speak soothingly into the animal's ear.

Once well clear of the area, he drew in a deep breath and exhaled loudly. He couldn't believe it. By now the Rogandan would have returned to find his horse gone. With luck, the soldier would assume that it had broken free and wandered off. The way he had treated the animal could only make that outcome seem more likely.

Thomas twisted around in the saddle and checked the saddlebags. The soldier had thoughtfully bequeathed him dried meat, a large chunk of cheese, and some stale bread, along with a water skin. Thomas even found a warm coat crammed into one of the saddlebags.

His situation had improved dramatically, beyond his wildest imagining. Having started with nothing, he all of a sudden found himself with a horse, a water skin, food, and warm clothing. He still had one problem, though. He had no idea where he was, and even less idea which way to go. After pondering the situation for a while, he decided to head east, away from the river. He would keep away from roads and travel mainly at night. Most of all, he would stay as far as possible from any Rogandans.

THE HORSE PICKED its way through the undergrowth between towering trees. Paths were almost non-existent here in the deep forest, suggesting that it might be an excellent place to remain hidden. Assuming Thomas could cope with the loneliness. He decided not to think about that.

The ground sloped steadily downward, and the sounds of a

stream somewhere ahead penetrated through the trees. The horse made for the water, and Thomas let it have its head. The trees parted to reveal a narrow path, with a small stream bubbling away merrily beside it.

The horse stepped into the stream and lowered its head to drink. As it did so, Thomas gulped down the last mouthfuls from his water skin. When the animal had finished he dismounted and refilled the skin from the stream.

Thomas felt like stretching his legs, so he set off down the path, leading the horse. He walked on for about half an hour. Then, around a bend in the path, he spotted something that stopped him dead in his tracks. Further down the stream sat an old and misshapen crone, dressed in black, facing away from him. She was rocking backward and forward, making a peculiar keening noise.

Thomas had never seen a witch before, but he had heard people talk about them, and she seemed to match the description perfectly. Everything about her suggested menace and extreme danger. He stood there transfixed, his skin crawling and his eyes almost popping out of his head. His horse, unconcerned, began grazing on some grass beside the stream.

In the improbable hope of exposing her character, Thomas reached down and untied the pouch at his waist. He thrust his fingers in for the stone, and clutched it in his hand. To his surprise the crone suddenly appeared harmless. She seemed more frightened than frightening. He released the stone, and the impression went away. He grasped it again and caught a glimpse of grief and pain. The stone did not permit him to read her fully, but it was evident that there was nothing evil about her. In spite of her appearance, he sensed an air of quiet dignity and decency about her. The overwhelming impression, though, was one of great distress.

More curious than alarmed now, he put away the stone, and approached her cautiously. As he drew near it became obvious that the strange sound he had heard was a dismal combination of sobbing and wailing. Sensing the depth of her anguish, his heart went out to her, unappealing though she was.

He tried to imagine what Brother Vangellis might do if he was here. He stopped a little distance from her. "Hello," he called. "Is there anything I can do to help you?"

At the sound of his voice she leaped into the air with a startled cry and spun around toward him. Her face was hidden within a large hood, but her reaction plainly revealed her terror.

He showed her his empty hands. "I won't hurt you."

Her body shook as she faced him. She seemed completely dismayed to have been discovered. Having spent so long hiding himself, Thomas felt considerable sympathy for her reaction.

"Can I help you?" he repeated.

She faced him without speaking, no doubt entirely unwilling to trust him.

He sat down on the path, wanting to demonstrate that he had no intention of harming her. He tried to study her without seeming to stare. Why was she hiding away in this remote place? And who was she? She might have been ugly, but an old crone she was not. The nimbleness of her movements made it plain that she was anything but old.

He tried again. "Are you in pain?"

She remained silent, so he decided to wait.

Eventually she must have decided to take a risk. "My...my father. He is very sick." Her voice sounded strange—unnaturally husky.

Once more Thomas found himself wishing that the monk was with him. He himself was no healer, and he guessed there was little he could do to help. "What's wrong with him?" he asked.

"He has a high fever."

Thomas looked at her with surprise. "A high fever?"

"Yes. I am afraid...that he will die." Her head was bowed and her face hidden, but a teardrop appeared from within her cowl and fell to the ground.

"Do you have any feverwort?"

"What is that?" she asked tremulously. Her hand disappeared into her hood, and she appeared to be busy brushing at the tears that now flowed freely.

"It's a herb that can be used to bring down fever."

"What does it look like?" The dullness of her tone conveyed no expectation that any herb could make a difference.

He described it to her briefly, then began searching around the banks of the stream. She also looked, but only half heartedly.

Thomas found it first. He called her over and showed her the plant's broad green leaf and pale flower.

She bent her head to look at it. "We can try," she said, sounding resigned. She seemed thoroughly dispirited. "I will take you to him."

He followed her shuffling steps away from the stream and into the trees. He studied her from behind as they walked. Her back was disfigured with a prominent hump at the top of it, and her right shoulder stood higher than her left. She looked hideous, and he quickly found himself looking anywhere but toward her back. Had it not been for the reassurance provided by the stone that she was harmless, he would never have dreamed of approaching her, much less going anywhere with her. But he'd also heard the monk say that beauty or ugliness on the outside of a person was not a reliable guide to what they were like on the inside. He promised himself he would try to remember that.

They soon came to a small cabin, and she disappeared inside, holding the door ajar for him. He followed her in. The light inside the single room of the cabin was dim, but he was able to make out the figure of an older man on a bed. The man was tossing and turning and moaning. Thomas approached him and felt his forehead. It was burning up.

"Do you have any warm water?" he asked.

She shook her head, but went to a fire that had burned low and stirred it up. Then she threw on a piece of wood. A metal pot hung over the fire, and she added water to it.

Thomas tried hard to remember what Brother Vangellis had done in such cases. He knew that the monk had used the feverwort to make a broth. But did he use the stem, the leaf, the flower, or all of them? How much water should he use? He simply didn't know.

Then a vague memory stirred in his mind. He recalled the monk talking about berries and mushrooms and what was safe to eat. He had pointed out some flowers that were good to eat and others that were poisonous. Then he had used feverwort as an example of a plant with an edible flower. At least that's what Thomas thought he had said.

The woman came to him with a bowl filled with warm water. Thomas hesitated until he began to sense her uneasiness. He took a snap decision and threw in the entire plant—stem, flowers and all. He sincerely hoped he was doing the right thing. Something needed to be attempted, though—it appeared that the man would be in serious trouble if he didn't receive help of some kind soon.

Thomas stirred the water and quickly noticed a pleasant aroma filling the little room. The man continued to toss and turn, calling out in his delirium. He said something incoherent, then began groaning. Twice he mumbled, "Elena," before resuming his groaning. Thomas guessed that the woman's name was Elena, because more tears emerged from within her hood as soon as she heard the name.

The color of the water had now changed with the addition of the feverwort. Thomas knew he was taking a risk feeding it to the man, but the soothing aroma gave him hope, and the man's condition added a sense of urgency. He asked for a spoon and used it to begin feeding drops of liquid into the man's mouth. He remembered that the monk usually prayed while he was doing this. Just in case it made any difference, he mumbled something under his breath that he hoped was suitable. He had no confidence that God had even heard him, but he'd done the best he knew how.

After continuing to spoon in the broth for a while, he handed the task to the woman. She was eager to help, and it was better than having her standing anxiously beside him wringing her hands as she had been doing.

"I'm going to attend to my horse," he told her, and slipped out of the cabin, heading for the stream.

The horse nickered a greeting as he approached. The two of them had quickly come to an understanding—Thomas was delighted with the freedom of being on horseback once more, and the horse seemed very contented with its change of master. He led the animal to the hut and removed its bridle, saddle bags, and saddle. The man's condition was uppermost in his mind, and he couldn't face the idea of entering the cabin and finding him worse. So he put off his return and gave his horse a thorough rub down instead.

Eventually the inevitable could be delayed no longer. He opened the door and went inside. To his surprise the woman looked almost relaxed. He bent low to examine the patient. The man was still unconscious, but he no longer appeared quite so restless. He had stopped moaning, too.

The bowl was almost empty of water, so the woman went to the fire and refilled it.

"Would you like me to feed him again?" Thomas asked.

She nodded and handed him the bowl. Thomas wasn't at all sure that he warranted the confidence she was apparently placing in him. If his treatment proved effective, the credit rightly belonged to the monk. Nevertheless, she seemed content to trust her father to his care. He resumed the task of patiently feeding drops of fluid to the man.

It soon became apparent that the woman had another reason for allowing him to take over from her. She was busying herself preparing food. The smells that began to fill the room reminded Thomas just how long it had been since he last enjoyed a good meal.

When the food was ready she pointed him to a stool and handed him a bowl. The food was simple—a stew with vegetables and some kind of meat—but it tasted very good. As he ate he glanced across at the cook. He could not see her face, but from the movement of her head she seemed to be alternating her gaze between her father and him. She appeared to be observing him particularly closely. He was enjoying the food far too much to be distracted by her scrutiny, though.

When he finished he closed his eyes and let out a long sigh of contentment. The woman had returned to her father and had resumed feeding him the fluid. She glanced at him briefly, then ignored him in favor of her patient.

Thomas began to feel restless. He wasn't needed at the moment, and he didn't know what to do with himself. "I think I will look for more feverwort," he told her.

She nodded, but said nothing.

He left the cabin and headed off into the forest on foot.

Several hours passed before he finally returned. He had been busy. As well as searching for feverwort, he had made and set a couple of rabbit snares. It wasn't clear even to him why he had decided to set snares. He told himself that he wanted to repay the woman for the meal. Setting snares was an odd way of thanking her, though, considering he was nothing more than a visitor. He was behaving as though he had settled there.

By now the light was fading. He checked on his horse, then approached the cabin. In the act of opening the door, he hesitated, and eventually knocked softly instead. The woman came to the door and opened it. Although he couldn't see her face, he had the impression that she was surprised at his timidity. She waved him in.

"I've found more feverwort," he said, handing her a large bundle of plants.

She nodded her thanks and laid them out to dry near the fire.

He headed over to her father. The man had not woken, but he did seem more settled.

With the light in the cabin almost gone, the woman lit a couple of candles, placing one of them near the head of her father. Then she laid some blankets on the floor beside him.

"Please," she said to Thomas, indicating a simple mattress across the room. Then she lay down on the blankets. Thomas had the feeling that she had given him her own bed, but he didn't like to argue. He lay down himself.

DAYLIGHT GREETED him when he woke. Two small windows were set into opposite walls of the cabin, and the shutters had been opened. Dim light was shining through them determinedly. He sat up and looked around. The woman was awake and tending to her father. He was still lying down but had clearly regained consciousness. The man spoke to her softly, and Thomas could not hear what he was saying. Noticing that his visitor was awake, the man turned to him and regarded him silently.

After a couple of minutes of this scrutiny, Thomas began to feel uncomfortable. Apparently sensing his unease, the woman turned to her father and spoke quietly to him. The older man gazed at her thoughtfully for a moment, then turned back to Thomas.

"I understand it is you I have to thank for my recovery," he said.

"Please don't mention it," Thomas replied awkwardly. "I may not have done anything much at all—it's possible you would have recovered on your own."

The man seemed to soften a little. "From what my daughter, Elena, has told me, I very much doubt it," he replied. "I am Rubin," he continued. "What is your name? And how do you come to be here?"

"My name is Thomas Stablehand. I have been traveling with a friend—a monk. He taught me about feverwort. He was taken by the Rogandans a few days ago." To his own embarrassment, he was unable to keep a quaver out of his voice. He steadied himself. "I am trying to hide from them."

"You will be safe here," the woman said. She sounded eager.

Rubin frowned for a moment. Then he seemed to relent. "You are welcome to stay with us," he said, "at least for a while. Other people do not seem to find us here." He looked significantly at his daughter. "Not often, anyway."

She looked back at her father without speaking.

"Thank you for your kindness," Thomas replied. "I do not wish to impose on you."

Rubin nodded his acknowledgment but did not speak.

Thomas again began to feel uncomfortable. "Please excuse me," he said. "I must see to my horse." He got up and left the cabin.

As he led the horse to the stream, he thought about both the woman's eagerness and the man's apparent reluctance to host him. The daughter's motives were easy to understand—she credited him with her father's recovery. As for her father, he didn't blame him for his hesitation. The simple truth was that the man knew nothing about him.

And there was indeed one thing of great consequence they did not know about him. He knew that the Rogandans would never stop searching for him. His hosts had no idea that by allowing him to stay with them, they would sooner or later be putting themselves at great risk. But could he bring himself to abandon human companionship once again, and set off alone into the unknown? Where would he go? How could he bear it?

As he wrestled with his conscience it occurred to him to wonder why they were hiding away, so far from the rest of the world. What secrets did they have of their own? The more Thomas thought about it, the more uneasy he began to feel. Would he be safe if he remained with them?

Then a memory came to him of the woman wailing at the stream. The stone had shown him that she was no threat. It was hard to imagine her encouraging him to stay if she knew it would put him in danger.

Even without the stone, he suspected that in time he would have come to recognize the gentle spirit hidden behind the woman's deformity. She was an object of pity rather than fear. He had never seen her face, concealed as it was beneath her expansive hood, but once or twice he had caught fleeting glimpses of her chin or her cheek. She appeared to have unsightly red splotches across her skin. He had the clear impression that she was surpassingly ugly, and he was grateful that she thoughtfully hid her face from sight.

He came to a decision. He would stay, at least for now. But he would be truthful with his hosts, and tell them that he was being hunted relentlessly by the Rogandans. Then they could decide for themselves whether they wanted to ask him to leave.

The challenge would be to explain why the Rogandans wanted him so badly. How could he do that without exposing the secret of the stone?

10

Kuper stared absently at the flickering flames as his brother threw another branch onto the fire. After several days away from the saddle, a long day of riding had left him feeling weary. They had finally stopped as the sun was setting.

Given their remote location they had no qualms about building a fire to banish the evening chill. He glanced across at his brother once again. Rellan seemed uncharacteristically withdrawn since leaving the community in the clearing. At that moment he sat gazing into the fire, apparently lost in his thoughts.

The afternoon had seen them climbing the slopes of a mountain after emerging from the forest in late morning. With daylight fading, they had reached the shores of a vast natural lake that stretched out before them like a small inland sea. The highest mountain peaks still towered above them, but they had reached their immediate destination.

"Tomorrow we will find a way around the lake and into Erestor," Yosef said. "Fortunately, we've had no rain in the past week. The path is dangerous at the best of times, but it can be extremely treacherous when it's wet."

"I had no idea there was any way across the mountains except through the main pass," said Kuper.

"The pass is certainly the simplest and most obvious way. It runs right through Steffan's Citadel. But the citadel gates are shut and barred right now. You can thank the Rogandans for that—they're camped in the fields below it. I've heard they're packed in so tight down there that a mouse couldn't sneeze without them knowing about it. There's no way past them to the citadel."

"A pity. I was looking forward to seeing the citadel again."

"You know it?"

"Yes. We grew up in a small village on the Erestorian side of the pass, and the citadel could be seen from our village. It was quite a sight."

"It's an impressive fortress," Yosef acknowledged.

Yosef unpacked and passed around some food from his saddlebags, and talking ceased for a while as they ate.

Rellan finally broke the silence. "When did you join the community in the forest?"

"I went there with Her Ladyship—Anneka, as she now insists on being called—six or seven years ago. Her husband owned large estates in northern Erestor, and she lived there with him and their two-year old son. He was a good man. A jealous nobleman falsely accused him of disloyalty to the king, and the lords were preparing to try him for treason. But fighting broke out when soldiers were sent to bring him in. He was killed along with his son."

Rellan's eyes narrowed. "The nobleman who brought down her husband—was he called Pisander?"

"Yes, it was the Earl of Pisander. He didn't get that title until later, though. He was known as Lord Dunnridge at the time."

Rellan got to his feet and began pacing around restlessly.

"Pisander has been brought down himself," said Kuper. "And because of disloyalty to the king, too."

Yosef shook his head.

Rellan paused, his arms spread wide in exasperation. "Punishing other people for his own weakness? Other *innocent* people?"

Unable to think of a useful response, Kuper held his peace.

Several minutes passed before Rellan was able to master his agitation. Finally he returned to the fire and sat down again. "What did Anneka do?" he asked.

"She fled with his surviving retainers. I was one of them. She led us into the wilderness.

"A lot of people would have been crushed by what happened, but not her. She's unusually capable—she'd never been content just to live in her husband's shadow. And she's caring and compassionate as well, which is why her people are so loyal.

"The crisis brought out her strengths more than ever. They were dark days, though, especially during the first couple of years. It was only the force of her will that kept us going."

"The community seems to be well established now," Kuper observed.

"Yes, although it's never been easy. The hunting is good, but the soil there is not well suited to farming, and we've never been able to grow enough crops. Anyone who's dispossessed—or even discontented—seeks us out, and we seem to have a never-ending number of mouths to feed. The Rogandans have made it much worse."

The conversation lapsed, and they decided to build up the fire and prepare for sleep. They lay down, wrapped in their blankets, but sleep proved elusive. Rellan tossed and turned restlessly, and Kuper also struggled to get to sleep on the hard ground. As he lay there, Kuper thought about Pisander and the perversity of human nature. He was grateful that his captain and his king lived according to much higher standards. Both of them were consistently honest and direct in their dealings with other people. He recognized, too, that he had always taken that entirely for granted. He drifted off wondering where Will was, and what he was doing.

THE NEXT DAY found them navigating around the southern edge of the huge lake. There were no paths, so they picked their way carefully across steep slopes that supported little vegetation. A sheer rock face just above them capped the top of the slope; there was no way across it. Yosef warned them that the lower slopes were unstable, so they traveled as near to the top as possible. Even so, the soil was loose and slid away freely under the hooves of their horses. Kuper had no difficulty understanding how the slopes could become treacherous after a soaking rain.

At about the halfway point they crossed a steep hillside strewn with large boulders. As they moved forward in single file with Yosef in front, the ground crumbled away beneath their guide's horse. The animal stumbled, throwing Yosef from its back. In a moment he was sliding helplessly down the slope. The others watched in horror, powerless to stop him. Yosef's horse, ears back and nervous, stamped its hooves restlessly, threatening to destabilize the slope even more.

Halfway down the slope Yosef landed hard against a boulder. It held firm.

At the same time, Kuper dismounted and gave his reins to his brother. He carefully moved to Yosef's horse and calmed it. The flow of soil down the slope gradually ceased.

Yosef lay still for so long that Kuper became alarmed. "Are you injured?" he called.

"I'm fine!" Yosef called back. "I'm just catching my breath."

After a few moments more, Yosef cautiously began climbing back up the steep bank, loose earth tumbling down around him as he went.

He was exhausted by the time he reached the others. He lay quietly for several minutes, trying to recover from his exertion. "This is the most difficult section," he told them. "The ground becomes firmer just beyond the next ridge."

"We can find our way from here," Rellan told him. "If you return now, you should be clear of the lake before nightfall."

Yosef didn't immediately reply, so Kuper decided that further encouragement was necessary. "Rellan's right, Yosef," he added. "Once we get past the lake and swing north, we'll be back in familiar territory. You need to head back before your horse becomes unmanageable."

Yosef considered the situation for a few moments. Then he slowly nodded. "You're right. You know where you need to go from here. I doubt that I can be of much use to you anymore."

After satisfying themselves that Yosef was able to make his way back safely on his own, they parted. Dismounting and leading their horses, they picked their way carefully across the hillside. Once they reached firmer ground, they looked back and saw that Yosef had also made it beyond the unstable section of the slope.

Several hours passed before they were finally clear of the lake. In open country at last, they gave the horses their heads. Many leagues still lay between them and Maranelle, the capital of the Duchy of Erestor.

As they rode, Rellan threw off his sling.

Kuper drew his horse closer to his brother's and slowed a little. "What are you doing?" he called.

"I've had enough of it," his brother called back. "I'm going to need both arms for what's coming next."

An image of his brother dancing, with Anneka in his arms, immediately came to Kuper's mind. He kept his face impassive, but inside he couldn't help grinning. Both of them kicked their heels into the flanks of their horses and sped away, heading for the sea.

After waiting with growing impatience for three hours, Kuper and Rellan finally found themselves confronted with a minor underling to Lord Burtelen.

"We need to see Lord Burtelen urgently. We have an important message to deliver to him."

"Who is the message from?" asked the official. His dismissive tone said more plainly than words how little importance he placed on them and their message.

"The commander of the king's armies."

"Captain Olaf?"

"No. The new commander. Will Prentis."

"Who is this Will Prentis? I've never heard of him."

Kuper forced himself to stay calm. "He is the person who saved Arnost from the Rogandans. He is the one who requested the duke to send Lord Burtelen back to Erestor."

"That fellow? He's just a commoner."

Not for the first time in his life, Kuper wondered why it was that the lower the ranking of a minor official, the more self-important he tended to become. This man was almost insufferable, which suggested he sat a long way down the pecking order.

"We're not here to discuss this with you," Rellan interjected. "We're here to see *your master*. If you continue to block us, you will answer to the king!" His pointed emphasis on 'your master' was not missed by the official, who simply became more obstructive.

"Give me the message, and I will pass it on to His Lordship," he sniffed.

"We were instructed to hand it to him personally," Kuper insisted, struggling to remain civil.

"Well, I will see what can be done. Perhaps he might be able to find time, sooner or later, in his busy schedule to attend to you. Come back next week, and I might have better news."

A nasty smile came over Rellan's face. "You're clearly a very busy man. You must have many important things to do. We're only soldiers. Life is very simple for us." He looked at his brother complacently. "How many people have we killed in the last two weeks, Kuper?"

"Probably more than I can count on the fingers of both hands," Kuper replied casually.

Rellan turned back to the underling. He slowly looked the man up and down, starting at his feet, and ending by staring insolently into his eyes.

The man began to sweat visibly. "I'll find someone else for you to talk to," he squeaked, and scurried away without looking back.

Before another hour had passed Kuper and Rellan found themselves ushered into a small but ornate reception room. The walls were covered with paintings, mostly depicting military actions. Kuper gazed at them admiringly until Lord Burtelen was announced. He entered the room almost immediately, looking harried and red in the face.

"What's this I hear about a message from Will Prentis?" he asked.

Kuper passed on the messages entrusted to him.

Lord Burtelen paused to absorb them. "Where is Will now? And where is the king?" he asked.

"We left Will some time ago, My Lord. We were forced to divert more than once because of the Rogandans, but he should have joined the king in Castel several days ago. We don't know any more than that."

"He asks me to bring an army to Castel at once. That's out of the question. I haven't been idle—I have a small army ready to march. Most of the men are camped this side of the Citadel. They're well led, and they've been training hard. But winter will be upon us before long. And—more significantly—the Rogandans have a much larger force waiting on the other side of the pass." He paused, narrowing his eyes. "How did you get through, for that matter?"

"A local guide showed us another way through the mountains."

The nobleman frowned. "It wouldn't be good at all for Erestor if word got out about an alternative route across the mountains."

"I don't think you need to be concerned, My Lord," Kuper replied. "The way we took was not an established path. Without detailed local knowledge I doubt that anyone would find it. And it's difficult to imagine a large party using it. The going was extremely challenging, and we attempted it only because our need was pressing. We almost lost our guide at one point."

Lord Burtelen nodded, apparently satisfied. "I can see that the two of you are unusually resourceful," he said. "For now, take some time to rest and refresh yourselves. I will meet with you again in the morning." He clapped his hands, and a retainer hurried in to do his bidding. He instructed the man to arrange food and accommodation for Kuper and Rellan, then dismissed them all.

THE TWO MEN found themselves ushered to a table laden with food—

freshly roasted venison with a wide range of cooked vegetables, along with seafood accompanied by leafy salads. A pile of tasty-looking pastries lay ready to hand, and goblets filled to the brim with rich red wine sat beside the plates.

Both of them stared wide eyed at the lavish spread for several minutes before daring to eat. Once they made a start, though, they attacked the food with energy. The servings were generous, but the plates were nevertheless carried away empty.

After the rich meal they were led to a room containing a bath filled with steaming water. After taking turns soaking in it, they dressed themselves in fresh clothes that had been laid out for them. They were finally shown to a bedroom that boasted a pair of comfortable beds.

The room also contained a pair of embroidered couches. They weren't yet ready to sleep, so each of them selected a couch of their own and stretched themselves out. Neither of the twins had ever experienced such luxury.

"I don't know how we're going to get Lord Burtelen's army past the Rogandans," Kuper said.

"We need to do a lot better than getting an army past them," Rellan replied. "We can't leave the Rogandans behind to attack us from the rear, and we can't leave Erestor undefended for them to pillage, either."

They talked into the night without resolving anything. Eventually they retired to their beds.

Kuper went to sleep surrounded by unaccustomed opulence, but he didn't sleep well. He lay on the bed restless and frustrated, unable to find a solution to their dilemma.

THEY DISCOVERED the next morning that Lord Burtelen was both a shrewd interrogator and a man of action. He questioned them closely for almost two hours. As his questions finally came to an end, Kuper realized that the nobleman had picked them clean of information.

"Well, I can see that your Will is an energetic and effective leader as well as a gifted strategist," said the lord. "We're going to need those qualities in the days to come. And I'm gratified to learn that the Lady Neave—Anneka as she's known to you—is still alive, albeit in greatly reduced circumstances. The so-called justice carried out against her husband was a mockery. When all of this is over we must see what can be done about her situation."

Kuper stole a glance at Rellan. His brother looked pale and uneasy.

"On a happier note," the nobleman continued, "Erestor and Arvenon—and indeed the entire civilized world—will be a better place without Pisander playing his poisonous games."

He sighed. "But we still need to deal with the Rogandans. It hasn't escaped me that you are more than usually capable, both of you. So I'm going to put you to work. You understand the Rogandans as well as anyone in Erestor. You know the terrain around the Citadel. And you're willing to take risks when necessary to get the job done. I need you to come up with a plan to deal with the Rogandan army camped outside Steffan's Citadel. Go there and assess the situation. To assist you, I will grant you limited authority over my soldiers at the Citadel. You will command twenty men.

"Take your time. Come back to me with a plan in two weeks."

As he spoke he wrote on a parchment, dripped hot wax onto it and stamped it with his seal. Handing them the document, he dismissed them.

Kuper walked from the audience chamber in a state of bewilderment. "How did that just happen?" he asked, holding up the document. Rellan simply shrugged, lost in his thoughts.

They rode out of Maranelle before another hour had passed. As their horses climbed the low hills surrounding the city, Kuper looked back, admiring the colorful pennants waving from the fair towers of the city. Dark clouds were gathering on the horizon, providing a striking contrast to the varied blues of the sea. Tiny fishing boats with white sails dotted the broad bay, sailing home on the tide ahead of the coming storm.

The refined tranquility of the many-hued scene presented a

striking contrast to the deep greens and browns of the rugged forested mountains of his childhood. Something stirred inside him as he gazed upon it. For the first time in his life he wondered what it would be like to leave war and soldiering behind, and to settle down and raise a family. He glanced across at his brother. Was Rellan also harboring such thoughts? Had he truly been foolish enough to surrender his heart to a woman of noble birth?

They crested the ridge above the bay, and Maranelle disappeared from sight. He shook his head, as if to clear it. Lord Burtelen had just set them an impossible task, and granted them two short weeks to achieve it. He turned his face away from peaceful daydreams and set his mind instead to the harsh realities of the road that lay ahead.

"The Rogandans are still sending soldiers into the forest," said Scar. "We kill their scouts, and they send more."

Anneka frowned. "How close to our settlement have they come?" she asked.

"Not very close. Not yet. But it's looking like they will. We need to decide what to do."

She glanced around the clearing, her gaze resting on children and on groups of the old and frail huddling together against the rain and the cold. So even this sanctuary was going to be denied her. She hardened herself and presented them with a face empty of emotion. They needed her to be strong. "How long do we have before they show up in force?"

"Maybe a few days. Maybe less." Scar didn't meet her eyes. "Perhaps we can begin preparations, just in case we need to leave in a hurry."

She shook her head decisively. Delaying the inevitable was pointless. All of them knew what they needed to do. "The very old and the very young won't be able to hurry," she said. "They need to leave now. Today. We can't wait until an army of Rogandans is yapping at their heels. It will take them days to reach the refuge, especially in this weather." She glanced up at the sky, scowling at the dark clouds that blotted out the sun. The rain had been unrelenting over the last few days, and it was going to make their task much more difficult.

"The refuge isn't big enough to accommodate everyone," Scar said. "We never imagined we'd have so many to care for."

She detected a hint of desperation in his voice, and willed herself to remain calm. "The most needy will take the huts. The rest of us will just have to manage as best we can."

She glanced at the men sitting around her, all watching her intently. Every one of them trusted her. The weight of that burden had not crushed her, though, because she in turn had learned to rely on them. The community had survived only thanks to their resourcefulness and sacrifice.

She looked them in the eye, allowing them to see that she was not afraid. "Most of us won't be going to the refuge yet," she told them. "Not while the Rogandans are roaming freely in the forest. Only the weak and helpless will go. They will need a few people to guide and protect them, of course, but no more than absolutely necessary. The rest of us will somehow have to make sure the Rogandans don't go anywhere near the refuge."

She paused, assessing their mood.

"We also need to make sure they don't find a way into Erestor," she added.

Her final statement met with a mixed reaction, as she expected.

"Why should we risk our lives for Erestor?" Scar asked bluntly. "No one there has ever done us any favors."

"We're not doing it for the nobles," she replied, shaking her head. "We'll be doing it for the common people. We already know what the Rogandans will do to them if given the chance." She added some iron to her tone. "You can think whatever you like, but this topic is not up for discussion."

Some of them weren't happy about it, but she could see that they accepted it.

"I have a suggestion," said Yosef.

She didn't hesitate. "Let's hear it." Yosef rarely had much to say, but when he did speak he was always worth listening to.

"Give me half a dozen of our better archers," he said, "and I'll make sure the Rogandans don't find their way to the lake. Scar can take Hender and the rest and keep them away from the refuge. Between us we'll steer them into the valley. They could spend weeks wandering around down there without injuring anyone except themselves."

She glanced around the group. Several others were nodding, including Scar. "That's settled, then. Scar, you'll have most of the men. I'll go with Yosef. All of us can join the others at the refuge whenever it's safe to do so. There will be plenty to do when we get there."

She nodded to another of her veterans. "Wilton, I'm placing you in charge of the women and children. Choose four men to go with you. Take whatever's essential, and leave the rest behind. If we're lucky the Rogandans won't find this place and we can come back later. Don't build your hopes up, though."

ANNEKA STAYED BEHIND to see the women and children off. Scar and Hender and a dozen others followed soon after them. Yosef gathered his small group and left, too, promising to wait for her on the trail beside the fallen redwood.

Her people had followed her, believing for better times. Now she stood in the middle of an empty clearing, surrounded only by silence and abandoned dwellings. So much effort had been spent in establishing this place, in making it a home. Now the Rogandans would find it and put it to the torch. All that they had built together over years would be gone in minutes, consumed in angry red flames.

It was hard, so hard, to lay down everything she had lived for, and to walk away. And not for the first time in her life, either.

She stood unmoving in the stillness and closed her eyes. Only memories remained here now. She remembered the joy of the dispossessed when they saw they had come at last to a place of safety. She thought of the babies born, the loved ones laid to rest beneath the greensward in the little graveyard through the trees.

She remembered, too, dancing in the firelight, intense eyes upon her, burning into her soul. She had been so angry with him. *Don't you torment me with hope. Don't you dare!* She recalled the sleepless night that had followed. And her foolishness the next morning in putting his flowers in her hair and for a fleeting moment allowing herself to feel like a woman again.

She opened her eyes once more. He had left, and it was a good thing. She would never see him again, and that was a good thing, too. Foolish sentiment was a weakness she simply could not afford.

She turned her back on the clearing, mounted her horse, and rode away.

11

King Steffan sat outside the Castelan royal tent, enjoying the warmth of the late afternoon sun in the company of his father-in-law.

"There's a matter I've been wanting to discuss with you," said Steffan.

"Eisgold?"

"Yes. I don't understand why you persevere with him."

His father-in-law looked pained. "These situations are never simple, Steffan. No throne is entirely secure without the support of the nobles—you know that as well as I do. And Eisgold is very well connected. If it proves necessary to push him aside, I'll do it without hesitation. But it's not something I can afford to do lightly. It would unsettle the other nobles, and I need their unqualified support more than ever right now."

"I fully understand your difficulty. Nevertheless, I'm not comfortable leaving Eisgold in charge of so many of your men," Steffan said frankly. "After the debacle at Pinder's Flat, it isn't clear to me that he can be trusted."

"The man is certainly stubborn at times," Istel acknowledged.

"But there can be no question about his loyalty. And I have no doubt that he will follow orders from now on."

"Even if the orders come from Will?"

"Even then."

Steffan frowned. "What makes you so sure?"

Istel sighed. "I was ready to relieve him of command myself after Pinder's Flat, in spite of the complications. But when I went to speak with him, he was most apologetic. Profusely so. He assured me that he now viewed his own actions as unacceptable, and that in future I would see a complete change in his attitude toward Will."

"Why the change?"

"He told me he realized that defeating the Rogandans was more important than any differences between him and Will. He said he understands that only one person can command, and that my choice of commander will have his full support, no matter who it is."

"Do you think he's sincere?"

"I do. Humble is not a word that I would normally associate with Eisgold, but he certainly came across that way."

"I wouldn't call him humble, either. He was singing the praises of his own military prowess when we first attempted to break through the Rogandans blocking Deadman's Pass. We both know how that turned out. We only succeeded thanks to the siege engine, and he opposed that idea vigorously when it was first suggested."

"Yes, he's no military strategist, whatever he might think. But it is possible to lead soldiers well without being a military strategist—Rufe Sarjant has proven that. Eisgold is both capable and effective as a leader. Men are willing to follow him. And there's no suggestion of giving him broader authority. Will is the one with overall command. Eisgold will stand or fall purely on whether he's willing to follow Will's orders."

"Are you completely sure he won't try a repeat of his little game at Pinder's Flat?"

"Yes, I am," Istel replied.

"Very well. You know the man better than I do. Let me make it clear that I still have strong misgivings. Nevertheless, I'm willing to give him an opportunity to prove his sincerity. But I'll be watching him. At the first hint of dissension, we need to replace him. I fully understand the challenges you will face if you remove him, but we cannot go into battle uncertain about how one of our key leaders will behave. There's far too much at stake!"

"I agree completely. I'll be watching him, too. Very closely. He's insisted that his attitude to Will has changed. If he gives the slightest indication that he isn't following through on that, he'll have to go. I won't give him another chance. The other nobles will just have to live with it."

THE LATEST COUNCIL MEETING, hosted for senior leaders of the joint army, had just broken up, and King Steffan and Will found themselves leaving the tent together.

The session had been called to monitor preparation for the next stage of the conflict with the Rogandans. To all outward appearances the meeting had been remarkably smooth. Lord Eisgold certainly seemed to have undergone a complete change of attitude. He still had many differences of opinion with the other leaders, and especially with Will, but he now readily deferred to the commander. He used Will's title sparingly, but said it without any hint of sarcasm.

King Steffan turned to Will. "It would seem that your detractors have finally decided to see reason," he said.

"I trust that it is so, Sire," Will replied noncommittally.

The king directed a thoughtful glance toward him. "People do change, Will. Lord Eisgold says that he has, and I need you to give him an opportunity to demonstrate it. You can be assured that I will not stand idly by if he fails to deliver."

Will nodded his acknowledgment. He didn't know the reason behind the king's request, but he guessed that it probably had as much to do with politics as with second chances. It was obvious to Will that Lord Eisgold had strong support among the Castelan nobility, and it was unlikely that King Istel would find it easy to move the nobleman aside, quietly or otherwise.

For his own part, he wasn't quite sure what to make of Eisgold's sudden transformation. He hadn't forgotten the hatred on Eisgold's face at the meeting after the battle at Pinder's Flat. And yet the nobleman was betraying no hint of animosity now.

Will had seen enough to recognize Eisgold's leadership abilities as well as his broad influence. If he truly had undergone a change of heart, there was no doubt that he would be a useful asset to the allied army.

Had he truly changed, or had he simply decided to mask his hostility?

Time would tell. In the meantime, given King Steffan's direct request, Will had no option but to give Eisgold the chance to prove his sincerity.

BOTTREN SPOTTED Will alone on a ridge not far from Hazelwood Ford. The commander sat astride his horse, reviewing soldiers on exercise. It was too good an opportunity to miss, and the Arvenian nobleman wasted no time in spurring his horse in Will's direction.

"Commander," he said, greeting Will with a nod.

"My Lord," Will replied, bobbing his head respectfully.

The ghost of a welcoming smile crossed Will's lips, causing Bottren's eyes to widen momentarily in surprise. Such a display was rare indeed for the grave young commander, and Bottren took it as a high compliment.

Bottren knew that Will trusted him. Of late he had even wondered if Will might also count him as a friend, in some sense at least. He had no idea how that could possibly work in practice, of course. Friendship simply wasn't possible between nobles and commoners.

He thrust such fancies from his mind to focus on more pressing problems. "What do you make of Eisgold's new mood of cooperation?" he asked.

Will shrugged. "By all appearances he has changed completely. I'm still not entirely sure about it, though," he said candidly. "Perhaps I'm overly skeptical."

"My response is similar," Bottren told him. "I would like to believe in the sincerity of his sudden turnaround. But I'm not fully convinced. Not yet."

He paused for a moment, studying Will carefully. "Let me be direct with you, Will," he said. "I know you have little stomach for intrigue. Internal dissension may well be dying down, and it's obvious that our main attention must be on our real enemy. But when it comes to the motivations and intentions of the Castelan nobles, you can't afford to leave it to guesswork. Not when our last battle so nearly ended in disaster."

Will nodded. "You are right, My Lord. I have come to realize that I need to prepare for internal battles as thoroughly as I prepare to fight the Rogandans. I admit I've been slow to recognize that, but it is very clear to me now."

Bottren raised his eyebrows in surprise. He hadn't expected Will to be so easily convinced. "So what are you planning to do about it?" he asked.

"I've already taken steps," Will replied.

This announcement surprised Bottren even more.

"I asked Nestor to keep his ears open," said Will, "and he's responded energetically. To say the least." A wry smile appeared on his face. "I had no idea how well suited he was to this kind of work."

"Nestor? He came with you from Arnost, didn't he?" asked Bottren. "What has he been doing? Has he learned anything useful?"

"He's woven an extensive spiderweb that's already trapping an impressive amount of information. He seems to have no difficulty finding informants who are sympathetic and willing to help—he has soldiers and even minor Castelan nobles working for him. You are welcome to examine what he's discovered if you're interested. You'd probably make much more sense of it than I can."

"I'll be most interested to look at whatever he's discovered. Has he learned anything that sheds light on the intentions of Eisgold or the other senior Castelan commanders?"

"No. Nothing definite. Perhaps there's nothing worth uncovering about Lord Eisgold anymore. If there is, he's been wise enough to keep his own counsel. Either way, the king has asked me to give Lord Eisgold an opportunity to demonstrate that he now supports my leadership. I'm sure I don't need to tell you that I intend to honor his request."

"I see," said Bottren. "The king's request does not require you to close your eyes, though. And there can be no harm in continuing to keep a watchful eye on King Istel's nobles.

"I must say I'm greatly encouraged to hear about Nestor's initiatives on your behalf. They're a wise precaution, even if they prove unnecessary. And I hope you realize that your information gathering won't be limited to Nestor—you can count on me as well. I will be your eyes and ears among the nobility. My position there gives me opportunity to hear and see things that Nestor's contacts could never be a party to."

"I am grateful to you, My Lord," said Will with a bow.

"You don't need to thank me," Bottren replied. "Both of us are only trying to save the two kingdoms."

"Our resources are extremely limited," said King Steffan. "We can only afford to undertake one campaign at a time. The focus of that campaign needs to be the relief of Arnost." The Arvenian king sat beside his father-in-law in a hastily erected building in the camp at Hazelwood Ford, accompanied by the leaders of the combined army.

"I sympathize with your desire to see your capital freed," said King Istel. "I'm sure I would feel the same way. But should we make that our first priority?"

"I believe we must. For practical reasons—if we don't relieve Arnost now, we run the risk of seeing it fall to the Rogandans. And there are symbolic reasons as well. Taking control of our capital will demonstrate that the Rogandans have lost the initiative."

King Istel nodded an acknowledgment. "I propose we hear all of the alternatives before we decide," he said, glancing across at his fellow sovereign. King Steffan paused before inclining his head reluctantly.

"What was the strategy you were advocating, Eisgold?" King Istel asked.

"Some of us have wondered, Your Majesties, if our goal should be to prevent the Rogandans from making further gains. Rather than taking new risks, we could strengthen what we have. That would give us a base we can use later, to take back what we have lost."

"What do you think, Will?" asked King Steffan.

"I believe, Your Majesty, that there is only one way to end this war, and that is to defeat our enemy. We cannot do that by capturing or holding locations," he replied. "We must draw the Rogandans into battle, on terms favorable only to us. It must be a decisive battle. We must inflict on them a defeat from which they cannot recover."

"But how can we do that?" King Istel asked. "They have so many more men."

"We must choose a battlefield that denies our enemies the benefit of their superior numbers."

"Does such a site exist?" asked Lord Bottren.

"We must search until we find one," Will replied. "If we fail to destroy the Rogandans, sooner or later they will wear us down."

King Istel turned to the nobles. "My Lords?"

"Our combined forces are nowhere near big enough to fight a pitched battle against the Rogandans," said Bottren. "Nevertheless, I believe that Will is right, provided we can somehow lure the Rogandans into a battle that is not of their own choosing."

"To have any hope of winning, conditions would need to favor our forces massively," said Eisgold. "And yet I can't help feeling that our commander is right," he conceded. "We must act decisively. Time is on their side, not ours."

King Istel turned to his ally. "Steffan?"

"Reluctant as I am to delay the relief of Arnost, I can appreciate the good sense of Will's reasoning. I am therefore willing to put my preference aside and agree to pursue Will's strategy," King Steffan replied. "But I would like to know when our anticipated reinforcements will arrive. Has there been any word from Erestor?"

"Not yet," Will replied. "I sent two of my men, Kuper and Rellan, to fetch the army being raised in Erestor. They are good men, but they have been gone longer than I expected and nothing has been heard from them. Lord Bottren has since sent others, but as yet there has not been time for them to reach Erestor and return."

"I will not give up hope of Erestor arriving in time," said King Steffan. "But in the meantime we must make our plans based on the forces we have available to us."

The conference eventually broke up having achieved general agreement on strategy, at least in principle. Detailed planning had not yet begun.

Will's point of view had prevailed, and the man who had previously been his most bitter opponent had openly agreed to put aside his own ideas and support him. Common sense suggested that he ought to have been elated, but he nevertheless left the meeting with a vague sense of unease. Lord Eisgold's new mood of cooperation troubled him for reasons he couldn't readily identify. He told himself that he was probably being unreasonable. Nevertheless, he intended to keep a close eye on the nobleman. Meanwhile, he comforted himself with the awareness that if there was anything sinister to uncover, Nestor would be working hard to expose it.

"I've just received a communication from Count Gordan," Steffan told his father-in-law. The two kings sat alone together in Istel's tent in the late afternoon. They were sipping wine, and enjoying a few moments of respite from the seemingly endless burden of their responsibilities.

"Anything of significance?" Istel asked.

"He relays a request from Essanda. She wishes to visit our encampment at Hazelwood Ford."

"What?" Istel exclaimed, rising from his chair. "This is no place for a girl! What is Gordan thinking?"

"So she's just a girl now, is she?" said Steffan, tilting his head and gazing up at Istel from under a raised eyebrow.

Istel looked at him testily. "You know what I mean! Seriously, Steffan. We have enough battles on our hands—let's not fight that one again."

"You needn't worry," Steffan replied, an ironic smile on his face. "Joining battle with you is not any kind of priority for me."

Istel gradually calmed down and resumed his seat. "Why would she want to come here?" he asked. "I don't understand it."

"She says she is missing her husband. And her father."

Istel looked at him and frowned. "I'm not going to ask you what you think of this foolishness. The look on your face makes it all too obvious."

Steffan made no attempt to hide his grin. "I can't deny that a visit from our 'girl' would make a welcome change for me. I don't doubt that it would lift your spirits, too," he said, raising his eyebrow again.

"But the roads are not safe!" Istel protested. "Do you want to lose your wife before she's even become your wife in more than just name?"

A flush of anger flared on Steffan's face.

"Wait!" Istel cried. "Don't be angry. She's told me nothing! Following your instructions, no doubt," he added with a grumble. "But I know Essanda—don't forget that I'm her father. And I'm not stupid."

He sighed. "You're a good man, Steffan, and I'm grateful that you choose to treat my daughter so well. I dare say I don't deserve you as my son-in-law."

Istel's comments raised issues that were best left for another occasion. Steffan decided to stay with the main point. "There's nothing unsafe about the roads provided she is accompanied by a proper escort," he observed calmly. "It isn't an especially long ride from Castel Citadel, and there are no Rogandans between your capital and Hazelwood Ford."

Istel sighed again. "Very well, then. Have it your own way. She is your wife, after all. But make sure that Gordan leaves nothing to chance."

Steffan set off for his own tent with a new spring in his step, already composing a suitable reply in his mind. A visit wasn't going to be practical for a while. Dealing with the Rogandans was his highest priority, and he could not afford any kind of distraction in the immediate future. He would request Gordan to arrange for her to arrive in one week's time.

"How is your mother, Commander?" Zornath asked, accosting Karevis with one of his irritating smiles.

Karevis frowned. The question caught him completely by surprise, and he was at a loss to know how to even begin to respond. "My mother?" he asked blankly.

"I am told that one of our soldiers met her. In Varacellan. The capital, you understand."

Karevis frowned again, more bemused than ever. Surely Zornath didn't think it was necessary to explain to him that Varacellan was the capital of Varas!

"I have been assured that she is a charming old woman. Very proud of her son, too. As she should be." Zornath flashed another smile at him.

Karevis said nothing, but a chill began to run down his spine as he pondered the possible implications of Rogandan soldiers tracking down his mother.

Zornath eyed him silently for a moment. "I have some very good news," he announced. "Even you will think it is good news. Even you!"

His teeth appeared once again in a grimace that was probably intended as a smile. "Oh, I know what you think, my dear Commander. The opinion of your dear liaison is not enough to sway you. Oh, no!" He wagged a finger at Karevis and smiled conspiratorially.

"King Agon is planning to shower the people of Varas with his special favor. He desires to show the world the great wisdom of cooperating with Rogand instead of resisting. Your people must pay their taxes without complaint, of course. But they will be treated well. Very well, indeed. This truly is good news, is it not?"

Karevis frowned once more. He had no doubt there would be a sting in the tail of this sudden excess of Rogandan bounty. He just wasn't clear about the specific direction it might take.

"You and your soldiers also have a special part to play, of course," Zornath continued mildly.

Here it comes, thought Karevis.

"Lord Drettroth requires very little from the army of Varas. Very little, indeed. He asks only that you take your stand beside your Rogandan allies, defying the enemies of Agon, our mutual king."

Zornath rose to his feet and drew himself to his full height. "You will fight at our side, and together we will crush the Arvenians!" he cried, his face alight and his fists pounding energetically down onto the table before him. Then he sat down once more, his eyes glowing.

"Never!" said Karevis fiercely, his face set hard like granite.

The mood of the Rogandan changed in an instant. Springing from his chair and planting both hands on the table, he thrust his face threateningly toward Karevis, a look of thunder on his brow.

"Do not imagine—even for an instant—my *dear* Commander, that you, or your pitiful little army, can hope to defy me in this."

Karevis drew back in disgust from the stream of spittle that punctuated Zornath's every word. The Rogandan simply leaned forward even further.

"Every one of your soldiers has left behind a sweetheart...a wife...a child. Perhaps even a *mother*." He fixed Karevis with a nasty smile. "I care nothing for them!" He snapped his fingers dismissively. "Nothing! Their safety depends *solely* on your cooperation. Your *enthusiastic* cooperation. Think carefully, Commander. Think very carefully, indeed."

The Rogandan again stood erect, looking down upon Karevis in disdain. "You are DISMISSED!" he roared.

Karevis remained in his seat and glared back at the Rogandan for as long as he dared. Then he rose to his feet and marched defiantly from the tent.

He was beaten, though, and he knew it. He thought of his frail and defenseless mother and began to tremble with suppressed rage. His stomach twisted mercilessly into knots inside of him.

It had always been obvious that foreign occupation would leave the ordinary citizens of Varas vulnerable, but he had stubbornly refused to dwell on that, telling himself he had enough troubles of his own to worry about. He could remain in denial no longer.

He knew that Zornath had about as much human feeling as a viper. He and his kind would not hesitate to trample the helpless women and children of Varas. They would do it eagerly, too, if offered half an opportunity.

Karevis and his entire army were caught in a trap, and the iron jaws were beginning to close tight.

What could he do? How could he find a way to halt this relentless slide into horror and despair?

Such questions had become all too familiar—they plagued him constantly throughout his waking hours. He'd found no answers before, and he could not see any way of escaping now.

12

"Why do you need to hide from the Rogandans, Thomas?" Rubin's question caught Thomas off guard. He had promised himself he would tell Rubin and Elena the truth about his situation, and he intended to do so. But he hadn't been able to figure out how to broach the subject without bringing the stone into it.

"I was staying at a monastery in the mountains, and the Rogandans invaded it. I escaped in a boat, and they apparently decided they wouldn't simply let me go."

It was obvious to Thomas that Rubin was not entirely satisfied with his answer.

"Leave him alone, Father," Elena chided. "We all have our secrets."

Not for the first time, he wished he could see the expression on her face. But in the days he had stayed with them he'd never caught so much as a glimpse of it.

Later that afternoon Thomas squatted by the stream dressing a rabbit he had snared. Elena sat beside him scraping the skin from some vegetables she had picked from the small garden beside the cabin. She chatted away happily, telling him about a brightly colored bird she had seen recently.

Listening to her talk, he remembered her taciturn manner and strange tone of voice when he first met her.

"I like the sound of your voice," he said.

She must have been taken aback by his compliment, because the flow of words dried up immediately.

"Thank you," she eventually managed.

"When we first met, you sounded so gruff. And you hardly said a thing."

She didn't respond.

He hadn't been with them long before he began to suspect that her manner of speaking was forced. Then one day he had surprised her talking to her father without any trace of the rough tones he was used to hearing. She had dropped the pretense after that.

None of them ever talked about it. He knew that Elena and her father had intentionally hidden themselves from the world. So he simply assumed she'd tried to make her voice as unattractive as her appearance to frighten off strangers.

Her father's earlier question emboldened him to pose a question of his own. "Why are you and your father hiding in the forest?" he asked.

She lifted her head and seemed to study him for a while.

She finally responded. "People in our village misunderstood us—misunderstood me, that is. Some of them were very superstitious. I was accused of being a witch."

Thomas remembered his own reaction when he first caught sight of her. It wasn't difficult to imagine why the villagers had feared her. But her appearance truly was misleading. She might be unattractive, but there was nothing evil, or even frightening, about her.

"I'm sorry," he said, and meant it.

"Father decided that I would never be safe until we went somewhere far from other people."

"How did you come to be like...like you are?" he asked. His question was awkward and indelicate, and he instantly regretted asking it.

She didn't seem to mind at all. "I was born the way I am," she said without hesitation. "It didn't become a problem until I started to grow up, though."

"How old are you?"

She paused before answering. "Females dislike being asked that question. Has no one ever told you that?"

Her tone carried a hint of rebuke. He had no idea what to make of it. An obviously insensitive question hadn't bothered her, but what seemed to him a straightforward query had gotten a reaction. How could anyone understand women?

She answered him anyway. "I'm probably a year or two older than you."

That was a surprise. He had already guessed that she wasn't as old as he'd first thought. But he'd still imagined her to be quite a bit older than he was himself.

That night as he lay in bed, he found himself thinking about her deformities. Her hunched back could not be hidden, but why was it necessary to conceal her face? Did she have a hook nose with warts on it? Did she have a mustache? On multiple occasions now he'd caught brief glimpses of her chin and the lower part of her cheek. Angry red splotches were always visible on her skin. Could it be leprosy? He shuddered. There was no sign of the disease on her hands, though. And the splotches did not always seem to be in the same location—they moved around. He didn't think leprosy did that. Did she have some other kind of skin disease?

The more his imagination worked away at it, the more hideous the possibilities became. In the end he called a halt to his creativity. He knew that the reality couldn't possibly match the runaway imaginings of his overactive mind.

Why was it so fascinating to dwell on the gruesome? He enjoyed a good ghost story around the campfire as much as anyone. Maybe it was only truly frightening if the horror was real. In this case he concluded that however monstrous Elena's face might be, as a person she was quite agreeable. He felt very sorry for her.

A part of him still wanted to catch a glimpse of her face, dreadful though the sight might be. The fact that it was out of reach only made it all the more tantalizing.

He sighed. At least he had the decency to feel ashamed of himself for thinking about her in this way. He rolled over and tried to get to sleep.

Elena's father gradually warmed up to Thomas, and it didn't take long before Rubin seemed to very much appreciate having a male companion on hand. Thomas showed him how to make more effective snares, and he quickly became good at it.

Rubin already had a basic ability to ride, so Thomas attempted to teach him more about horses. He soon discovered, though, that mastery of that kind didn't come naturally to the older man. With only a single horse between them, Thomas decided there was no pressing need to pass on such skills anyway.

Rubin in turn began to expand Thomas's skills in building and maintaining dwellings. Thomas was already capable of carrying out small projects, as he had demonstrated following his contentious decision to rebuild the damaged barn for his father. But he still had much to learn. He could not readily account for the discrepancy between his incompetence as a laborer when rebuilding the wall of Arnost and his growing abilities in helping Rubin. He eventually decided that the difference mostly had to do with the overseer. Rubin showed considerable patience when Thomas made mistakes and openly expressed appreciation for his persistence as well as his growing aptitude. Thomas tried hard not to dwell for too long on the contrast between Rubin and his own father.

On a couple of occasions when roof repairs were required, Rubin was very glad to hand the task over to someone younger and more nimble than himself. Spending an hour or two working with Rubin became a regular feature of most days for Thomas.

Elena increasingly became part of his daily routine, too. As the days passed they often found themselves spending time together. She proved to be surprisingly good company.

"You've never told me about your mother," he said on one occasion.

"She died when I was little—not even five years old. She died during childbirth, and the baby died, too. I barely remember her."

"That must have been hard," he said.

"It wasn't so bad," she replied. "My childhood was still a happy one. My father was kind, and he found ways of spending time with me, as well as working hard to provide for us. But what about your childhood?"

He told her about his parents, and his life in Arnost. He didn't think there was a great deal to tell, but her gentle questioning gradually uncovered all manner of detail he wouldn't otherwise have thought to offer. She expressed particular interest in his role as horse master for the king's army, and more than once he had to remind himself not to bask unduly in her obvious admiration.

Over time they developed a pattern of spending time together each afternoon, wandering along the stream or sitting in a meadow talking. He learned a great deal about her life, first growing up in a town and later in the forest. She told him about the gradual process of alienation that caused them to flee to their hideaway. Whispers and little slights had gradually turned into open insults, accusations and finally threats. Thomas became angry on her behalf when he began to understand the full extent of everything she had been forced to endure so unfairly.

He in his turn told her about their flight from Arnost. He never referred to Brother Vangellis by name—the capture of his friend still felt too raw.

He shared nothing at all about Elbruhe. It seemed to him that it would be insensitive to describe his experiences with a normal girl, even one who spoke a different language and was therefore difficult to communicate with. He felt sorry for Elena and had no desire to make her uncomfortable.

"Are you happy here, Thomas?" she asked him one afternoon.

He had no need to consider his answer. "Yes," he said without hesitation, "very happy."

"Do you miss being around other people?"

He thought for a moment. "No," he replied. "I need to hide, too, if I want to avoid the Rogandans. And it isn't as if I'm entirely alone here."

"No," she agreed. "You're not alone."

The more he thought about it, the more it became clear to him that there was nowhere else he would rather be. Arnost had felt like home when his mother had been there. But it had changed for him in so many ways. No other place he had visited in his travels felt even vaguely like home. The monastery was the closest, but he was only ever there as a visitor, and as far as he knew the monastery had been completely destroyed by the Rogandans.

The truth was that as the days went by he felt increasingly detached from the outside world and from his previous life. Elbruhe had gradually slipped away from his conscious mind. He still thought of Brother Vangellis many times every day, but he knew there was no point in worrying about the monk when there was nothing useful to be achieved by it.

Elena became his constant companion, and it gradually became difficult for Thomas to remember what life had been like without her.

In spite of the many challenges she faced, she was calm, considerate, and unfailingly cheerful. He could not imagine why people had ever thought she was a witch. It was true that she was having an effect on him, but not because of any kind of spell she'd cast. Her impact was in no way evil. The monk had taught Thomas to fend for himself, and had begun to instill in him a new appreciation for the value of human life. Elena was helping him to recognize the beauty in a harsh and uncertain world, and to cheerfully embrace the simple joys that life had to offer.

Elena had not been crushed by the burdens of her life; somehow she had managed to rise above them. Bitterness had not taken root in her, and he often marveled at that.

. . .

THOMAS HAD NOW BEEN STAYING at the cabin for several weeks. On a number of occasions he found himself on the brink of telling Elena about the stone. But each time, for reasons he didn't understand, he had decided against it.

When he slept he often dreamed of her. In his dreams she never wore a hood, but even so he never managed to see her features. They talked together, but never face to face. Whenever he looked directly at her, her face was turned away from him.

On one occasion he dreamed they were walking hand in hand by the stream. She chatted away merrily, and his heart felt light. After he woke, though, he felt uncomfortable in her presence for almost an entire day.

Finally, one night he dreamed that they were talking as usual, but this time he turned to her and found that she was facing him. The voice he heard was Elena's, but the face he saw belonged to Elbruhe. He woke with a start to find himself drenched with sweat.

She rarely appeared in his dreams after that, and even then only for brief moments.

"THOMAS, COULD YOU HELP ME, PLEASE?" Elena called.

He joined her at the garden beside the little cabin where she was extending the borders of the cultivated patch.

"What's the problem?"

"This rock is in the way. I'm not strong enough to move it."

"Let me do it," Thomas replied. He bent down and lifted it easily. "Where do you want it?"

"Anywhere out of the way," she replied. "You're so much stronger than me!" she added with a little laugh.

"It's nothing," said Thomas modestly. He dropped the rock beside a tree and shook the dirt from his hands. "Bye," he said with a smile, and headed off into the trees.

"Where are you going?" she called after him.

"To the stream. I want to do some fishing."

"May I join you?"

"Of course," he replied.

Thomas had made himself a couple of thin spears with very sharp points and serrated edges, and hardened the points in the fire. Spearing fish in a river was not straightforward, but he had become quite adept at it. He had acquired these skills, along with so many others, from Brother Vangellis. He collected the spears from a hollow log where he kept them, and they made their way to the stream.

He selected a shallow spot where he had caught trout on previous occasions. Spear in hand, he squatted down at the edge of the stream and began watching for any sign of fish. Elena sat down beside him and dangled her feet in the water.

After a while with no sign of action, she began humming quietly, swishing her feet back and forth in time to the tune.

"Hey, stop it—you'll scare the fish away!" said Thomas.

"What fish?" she asked in a dreamy voice. "I can't see any."

He leaned forward and scooped a handful of cold water over her.

She jumped to her feet with a little shriek. Quickly positioning herself behind him, she gave him a small shove. Squatting as he was on the balls of his feet, he tumbled forward into the stream with a loud splash. He lurched to his feet with water pouring off him, and sprang forward to grab her by the arm. She danced back out of reach, squealing with delighted terror. Once safe, she stood well back from the stream with her hands on her hips, and regarded his sodden state with a merry laugh.

"You'll pay for this!" he promised, prompting a fresh burst of laughter in response.

She tried to keep her distance from him as they headed back to the cabin. As they approached it, though, he sidled up beside her and flung his arm around her waist, managing to drench her in the process. She squealed again, trying to pull away, but he had too tight a grip. They arrived with him growling like a wild animal and her giggling uncontrollably.

Rubin stood waiting for them, and he watched their approach with a guarded look on his face. Seeing his expression, Thomas began to wonder whether he approved. Feeling suddenly awkward, he let her go, and went inside to dry off in front of the fire.

When he came outside again, neither one of them was anywhere to be seen. They didn't appear until the afternoon was spent. Rubin looked serious, and Elena was silent. Thomas didn't know what to say, so he remained mute, feeling very uncomfortable. Their meal together was uncharacteristically subdued. All of them settled down to sleep with scarcely a word being said.

The next day Thomas briefly found himself alone with Elena. "Is your father unhappy with us?" he asked casually.

"It isn't my father," she replied. He had become accustomed to the melodic tone of her voice. Today she sounded surprisingly brusque. "I would be glad if we could avoid being familiar in future."

Her reply shocked him speechless. Eventually he found his voice. "I thought you were having fun," he protested.

"I can see that I was unintentionally leading you in an unhelpful direction, and I apologize for that," she replied, her tone distant. And with that she departed, leaving him gaping after her.

It was obvious that her father had a great deal to do with her change of heart. Thomas still felt hurt by her sudden aloofness toward him, though. The old Thomas might have tried to think up a suitably cutting retort. But he had no desire to be angry with her. He just felt miserable.

He spent the rest of the day off by himself, trying to make sense of Elena's unexpected rebuff. Females could be so unpredictable. Elbruhe's mood could change like the wind, but Elena had never been like that. She had always come across as steady and dependable. And thoughtful and kind, too. What had he done? How had he succeeded in changing her so completely?

She must have decided, no doubt with plenty of help from her father, that he wasn't good for her. No other explanation made sense to him. He tried to see it from her point of view. She'd enjoyed a simple life here with her father before he intruded on them. His arrival had just been a complication.

He'd been a burden to plenty of other people, too. He wouldn't like to hear what his father might have to say on this topic. He'd done nothing useful for Will since they left Arnost—he'd just been a liability. Well, he had taught Brother Vangellis to ride. But that was about the extent of it. And he hadn't done any favors for the monk, either, especially considering what eventually happened to him.

Elena had accepted him at first because she thought he'd healed her father. But now she was finally seeing him as he was. What did he have to recommend him, after all? When he examined himself frankly, he couldn't come up with much that was worth boasting of. The more he thought about it, the more painfully obvious it seemed.

He hadn't even been direct with them. He'd known from the beginning that staying here exposed Elena and her father to major risks, but he had never told them. When he was honest with himself, he knew he'd only been able to enjoy the present so much because he'd pretended the future didn't exist. His life here wasn't sustainable. He couldn't keep going on like he had been.

When dusk came, he found himself very reluctant to return to the cabin. In the end the cold and hunger drove him back. Rubin looked up at him when he came in, but Thomas avoided eye contact. Rubin made a few comments, behaving as though everything was normal, but Thomas couldn't manage more than one word answers and grunts. Elena said not a word.

The next day was little different, and Thomas became increasingly uncomfortable. Now that he felt so ill at ease in Elena's presence, he began to realize how much he'd come to take her company for granted. Maybe she resented that as well.

By the time the afternoon was well advanced, his need to be alone had become pressing. He saddled his horse and stuffed a few things into his saddlebags. The horse nickered and pushed at him with its nose. It was pleased to see him; he knew he'd been neglecting it for far too long.

As he mounted, it occurred to him that he could simply go and not come back. He could see no sign of either Rubin or Elena, and he knew it would be very odd to leave without saying goodbye. But maybe it was better that way, for all of them. It was clear that he wasn't wanted here anymore.

He rode away slowly, a tight knot in his stomach. Several times he looked back over his shoulder, hoping against hope that one of the others would appear and stop him. But no one came.

He departed more downcast than he could ever remember feeling. His life had become a succession of partings, and for reasons he didn't entirely grasp this one felt like the most painful of all. He wasn't sure how he was going to face being alone again. But there didn't seem to be any other option.

He followed the path beside the stream. He had no plan and no idea where to go. Leaving was the last thing he wanted, but he knew he had to put distance between himself and Elena. He had stayed with Brother Vangellis because he needed him, and it had ended very badly for the monk. He told himself he couldn't afford to do the same to Elena and her father.

All of that was true. But there was another reason why he had to separate himself from them now. He had to leave because he had overstayed his welcome, and they wanted him gone. He couldn't dwell on that, though. It was too distressing. At that moment he felt numb, and he needed to stay that way.

He'd been gone for about an hour when he heard faint voices, not too far away. Immediately wary, he dismounted and tied up his horse. Then he crept forward until he noticed the flicker of a fire through the trees. The smells indicated that a meal was being prepared. At any other time it would have made him feel hungry, but he couldn't think of his stomach when it was obvious he was listening to the harsh voices of foreigners. He remained still, watching intently, until he was able to confirm beyond doubt that the men around the campfire were Rogandan soldiers. Even this remote corner of Arvenon was not safe from their endless probing and pillaging. Before long they would discover Elena! They only had to follow the stream. What would they do to her? They would surely kill her on sight if they thought she was a witch.

He slunk away in a panic, his heart racing as he hurried back to his horse. Casting caution aside, he urged the horse at breakneck pace back the way he had come, ignoring the branches that whipped across his face as he galloped along the path.

The minute he reached the cabin, he leaped from the horse's back and ran inside. It was empty. He left the cabin and looked around frantically. Elena was nowhere in sight. Her father wasn't anywhere to be seen either. He searched near the little garden, but he found no sign of them there, either. He tried to calm himself to think. Where could she be?

Then a memory came to his mind, and he thought he might know. Not far downstream was a quiet meadow, quite near to the water. She loved to lie there among the wildflowers, watching the branches of the trees waving overhead.

He rode there with his heart thumping in his chest. She had to be there.

When he reached the spot he launched himself from the saddle and ran into the meadow. There before him was Elena, sitting quietly among the flowers. She turned to him.

"The Rogandans are here! Only an hour away—down the stream." His words tumbled out. "It's me they're looking for. I can't explain now, but you need to go. At once! You don't have a moment to lose. Take your father and find somewhere safe to hide."

She just sat there, her face invisible as ever. "You've decided to leave us, haven't you?" she said calmly.

"Yes. You'll never be safe while I'm with you."

"That's not why you're leaving, though, is it?"

"What does it matter? You need to hide!"

"I have to know the reason."

He frowned. This wasn't going the way he needed it to. How could he make her see the urgency?

"I know I'm not wanted anymore. But that's not the point!"

"Why do you care if the Rogandans find us?" she asked.

He couldn't believe what she was saying. "Why do I care? What on earth are you talking about?"

"Why do you care?" she insisted.

"Why? Because you...because you're more important to me than...than anything!" There. He had said it.

"But I'm deformed."

"What?! What difference does that make?"

"Young men don't care about girls who are deformed."

"Who told you that?!"

"Father told me."

"Well, he's wrong! You can't help being deformed. And it's not the way I think about you, anyway. Your looks don't matter to me. That's just the outside of you. It isn't who you are." He realized as he said it that it was true. He truly didn't care that she was deformed. And she *was* more important to him than anything in the world.

"This is all completely crazy! I have to go. They mustn't capture you. I'd die if anything happened to you! I need to lead them away from here. And you need to hide." He glared at her in frustration. How could he make her understand?

"You really do care, don't you!" she said in wonder.

"Arghhh! What will it take to convince you that you need to go?"

"We'll go," she said with sudden decision. "But there's something you need to know first." She left him and ran to the stream. He looked on bewildered as she stood in the stream with her back to him and her head bowed, water splashing around her. Then she did a little jig and bounced up and down once or twice, shrugging her shoulders.

Finally she faced him. He looked at her stupidly, blinking in bafflement. Her hunched back had disappeared, and her deformed shoulder was completely normal. An oddly shaped bundle lay beside her on the ground, and he realized he was looking at what had been her hump.

As he stared at her, perplexed, she threw back her hood, and for the first time he saw her face. His jaw dropped. He had always imagined that her face was monstrous, but nothing had prepared him for the truth. He stood gaping at her in astonishment.

She wasn't ugly. She was beautiful—beautiful beyond words. Her loveliness took his breath away. Completely confounded, he could find nothing to say.

Blushing faintly, she gazed at him, her face shining. Small drops of faint red trickled down her chin, and he belatedly realized that the splotches on her skin had been stains, probably from some kind of berry. It was all part of the disguise, no doubt intended to make her appear diseased. She had washed the berry stains off in the stream.

He stood there dumbfounded, rooted to the ground.

She came to him shyly, and looked up at him. After a moment's hesitation she took his hands in hers. "I'm sorry I couldn't tell you the truth, Thomas. I've been in disguise for so long it's hard to imagine myself any other way. It was Father's idea. Some people couldn't cope with how I looked—not like you see me now, anyway. He wanted to frighten everyone away so I would be safe. But I don't want to conceal myself anymore. Not from you. I want you to see me as I really am."

Thomas didn't answer. He was still struggling to breathe.

"I did hear what you were saying," she told him seriously. "And we will hide from the Rogandans." She looked at him plaintively. "Do you really need to go?"

He nodded. Reluctantly, but firmly. It had to be done. The Rogandans would find her otherwise.

"I couldn't let you leave without knowing the truth," she continued. "Once I knew for sure that you really do care for me, that is." She gazed up into his eyes. "I've come to care for you, too, Thomas. Very much." Another blush appeared, a delicate shade of pink that spread delightfully across her perfect cheeks. It made her even more beautiful, if that was possible.

"Will you come back for me?" she asked.

The anxious look on her face melted his heart, and helped him recover his voice at last. "I will return—I promise!" he stammered. "As soon as it's safe. Nothing will keep me away."

She walked him to his horse. He turned to her, unable to resist gazing upon her one more time. He wished he could stand there forever, drinking in the sight of her.

She surprised him by stretching up on tiptoes and leaving a soft kiss tingling on his cheek. He felt himself blush a furious red, which made her grin. He finally mounted his horse, but then sat there without moving.

"Weren't you in a big hurry?" she teased.

Another blush flooded his face as the reality of their peril broke through his daze. He'd been acting like a half-wit. He urged his horse forward. "Hide quickly!" he called to Elena. "I'll come back. As soon as I can."

The path beside the stream bent around, and he caught a final glimpse of her waving to him. Then she was gone.

Completely stunned by Elena's revelations, he followed the path without a conscious thought about where he was going. The image of her face after she had thrown back her hood was fixed in his mind, and he wanted to keep it there forever.

What an incredible transformation! He tried to recall his crazy imaginings about how monstrously ugly she must be. All along, her true appearance had been breathtaking, beyond anything he could possibly have dreamed up.

He had supposed that people called her a witch because she was ugly. But he saw now that they had been reacting to her astonishing beauty. *How can she look like that? It can't be natural.* It must have been nothing more than envy for many of them. And yet she had emerged unspoiled. He had never heard her speak a word of hatred or even anger toward the people who persecuted her.

Most amazing of all, though, she cared about him. She hadn't been impatient for him to go—she wanted him to stay.

It wrenched his heart to leave. But he knew he had to do it. It was up to him to draw the Rogandans away. He knew, too, that he had every reason to be afraid. He nevertheless rode away feeling stronger and more self-assured than he had ever felt in his life.

13

Driving rain chased the twins most of the way to Steffan's Citadel. They were long since soaked to the skin by the time they arrived. With too many of their fourteen days already behind them, they presented their credentials to the commander of the citadel and made their way immediately to the battlements, accompanied by one of his men. They gazed out over the plain that lay below the pass. A river ran through the meadows, and the ground on either side of it was covered with tents, campfires, clusters of horses and even a couple of small buildings. The river had begun to rise in the rain, and the Rogandans were busy moving tents further away from its banks.

"What have the Rogandans been doing?" Rellan asked.

"Very little," the soldier replied.

Kuper frowned. "Why are they here, then?"

The man shrugged. "They're not strong enough to take the Citadel. And we're not strong enough to drive them off. Maybe they just want to fence us in. Make sure we don't go anywhere."

"Until enough of them arrive to tilt the balance?" Rellan suggested.

The soldier shrugged again. "Their numbers have certainly

grown," he said. "I heard the commander say that every Rogandan soldier in western Arvenon is down there now." He waved his hand across the sea of tents.

"There is one thing they do," he added. "Every day, before dusk. They drag a few villagers up the slope toward the Citadel. Over there." He pointed to a level piece of ground beside the road that wound its way up to the gates of the fortress. "They slaughter them in front of anyone who's willing to watch."

"Can't you do anything to stop them?"

He shook his head. "They stay just out of bow shot range. We could go out and fight them, I suppose. They'd love to drag us away from the protection of these walls," he said, patting the thick stone of the battlements.

He spat, disgust evident on his face. "They're rabid animals that need to be put down. We just don't have an effective way of doing it."

Kuper left the walls none the wiser about a way of dealing with the Rogandans. The commander arranged dry clothes for them and directed them to a mess where they were served a simple meal.

As they ate, Kuper voiced something that had been on his mind for the last couple of days. "I don't understand why Lord Burtelen is so different from the other nobles," he said. "To start with, he's very impressed with Will. Then he gives us twenty men. Why? Apparently it's just because we're resourceful."

Rellan shrugged. "Lord Burtelen is like the king. If you're good at something, it doesn't seem to bother him if you're a commoner."

"You're right," Kuper replied. "He might not care about us being commoners, but I wish he'd given us a task we could succeed at. He's expecting us to come up with a way of removing an entire army of Rogandans. How are we going to do that? I don't have any clever ideas."

Rellan shrugged again.

With no solution in plain view, they decided to sleep on it.

As they prepared to rest, Kuper turned to his brother. "What's eating you, Rellan? You've barely said a word since we left Maranelle."

With no reply forthcoming, Kuper decided it was time to be more direct. "It's Anneka, isn't it? Or Lady Neave, or whatever her name is."

Rellan just looked back at him with haunted eyes. Knowing his brother well, Kuper waited patiently, saying nothing.

Eventually Rellan found his voice. "When we were in the forest I began to think something might be possible between us," he said. "Even when Yosef told us where she'd come from, I didn't think it needed to make a difference."

He paused for a long time, and Kuper waited him out.

"I was only fooling myself. Lord Burtelen made that clear. She's a noblewoman, and she belongs with her own kind. Once this war is over, the king will put her situation to rights, and that will be an end to it." He fell silent.

Kuper sighed. "I thought it might work out for you at first, too," he said. "I don't think I've ever seen you so alive. But I didn't know about her background then. Knowing about it changes everything. What you're saying is right—people like that don't end up with the likes of us."

THE NEW DAY brought them no insights into an effective way of dealing with the Rogandans. The commander of the citadel arranged for them to meet with the twenty soldiers assigned to them, then they joined him in conference. They were still together when another soldier brought in a report.

"A large band of Rogandans has moved into the forest, Commander," he said.

"What do you think they're doing?" the commander asked.

"Some of the men think they're probably trying to find a way around the Citadel," he replied.

Kuper shot a glance at Rellan. The look on his face reflected the alarm he felt himself.

The brothers excused themselves as soon as they could reasonably do so, and found a quiet place to talk.

"Do you think there's any way they could discover the path around the lake?" Kuper asked.

"It doesn't seem likely," Rellan replied. "If they captured Yosef, though, or someone else who knows the way, they could force it out of them."

"We have to stop that happening," Kuper said. "I wonder if Anneka and her people can prevent them from getting to the lake."

Rellan shook his head. "She doesn't have enough people to pick a fight with a large band of Rogandans."

"We need to find out what's happening."

"I agree. We could take some soldiers with us. Enough to deal with the band of Rogandans."

"No." Kuper shook his head. "The alternative route wouldn't stay a secret for more than a day if we did that. It needs to be one of us." He looked his brother in the eye. "It needs to be you."

"If you think I want to see Anneka again, you're wrong."

Kuper could clearly see the conflict on his brother's face. Rellan wanted to stay away, and he wanted to see her, probably in equal measure. Kuper decided to let his brother come to his own conclusion.

After a long pause, Rellan looked up, his face showing no emotion. "I'll go," he said. "This isn't about Anneka. It's about preventing the Rogandans from getting into Erestor."

Kuper nodded. "In that case," he said, "you might as well leave immediately. I'll brief the commander."

Rellan left to gather his things. "Be careful," Kuper called after him.

Rellan had the lake in sight when the light failed. As the sun set, the rain started again in earnest, and he spent a miserable night huddled under some trees. He tried lighting a fire, but the wood was too wet, and he eventually gave up.

Dawn came without any let up in the downpour. He set off early and soon arrived at the lake. Water was pouring into it from a number of swollen rivers and streams, and the level had risen noticeably in the few days since they left. He set off around the lake, riding as long as it was safe to do so. Once the ground became less firm he dismounted and led his horse on foot.

Yosef's prediction was right. With several days of heavy rain, the slope had become unstable, and forward movement was extremely treacherous. It was very slow going, and he lost his footing more than once. On one occasion the ground broke away beneath him, and he avoided tumbling down the slope to the lake only by hanging on grimly to the reins of his horse. The animal somehow managed to hold its ground and support him as he slipped and slithered his way back up the slope. By the time he finally reached the horse, he was completely covered with mud.

The afternoon was almost spent by the time he reached more solid ground. He found a stream and cleaned off the mud as best he could, then searched out a vaguely sheltered location to spend the night. The rain continued fitfully, and he spent the night soaking wet and shivering. When a stiff breeze sprang up, it chilled him to the bone.

When the new day came, he set off once again, sodden and miserable.

Anneka stood with Yosef under a large overhanging tree. The tree provided some shelter from the rain, but it made little difference since they were wet already. The other men had taken up positions nearby, and everyone had settled down to wait. For all they knew their waiting had no purpose. The Rogandans might never come here.

Since he had the larger group, Scar had agreed to send out a couple of scouts. They would keep him informed about the movements of the Rogandans. The scouts would also seek out Yosef's party from time to time. There should be some warning at least before any of the enemy came their way.

By the time a couple of hours had passed, Anneka was already bored. She suspected that this task would become very tiresome very quickly. Then Yosef drew her attention to one of the other men. He was vigorously waving his arms. They waved back, and he pointed behind them toward the lake. They turned to see a horse and rider heading toward them, coming from the direction of Erestor.

Yosef put an arrow to the string of his bow and waited. As the rider drew near he turned to Anneka. "The rider reminds me of someone. But he doesn't look quite right." After a couple more minutes he laughed. "Of course," he said. "It's Rellan! But he's missing his sling."

Anneka's heart skipped a beat. What was he doing here? Then she took a firm grip on her emotions and let her mind take over. She was very good at it. She'd had years of practice.

When Rellan drew close, Yosef stepped out from under the tree and hailed him. Rellan's immediate response was to reach for his bow, then he recognized Yosef, and called back cheerfully. He dismounted and approached Yosef, greeting him warmly.

Then he noticed Anneka. Glancing into her eyes for a moment, he nodded and said, "Hello," before snatching away his gaze and turning his attention back to Yosef.

"You look like you've been bathing in mud," Yosef told him.

As the two of them exchanged banter, Anneka stared at him in surprise. She'd been bracing herself for a barrage of cheeky flirtations. Instead, he seemed strangely reserved.

She waited for a pause in the conversation. "What brings you back, Rellan?" she asked, keeping her tone level.

Some kind of emotion flashed across his face as he turned to her, then he seemed impassive again. "My brother and I were at the Citadel," he said. "Lord Burtelen sent us there. We learned that the Rogandans had sent a force into the forest, and we were concerned that they might be trying to find a back door into Erestor. I've come to assess the situation." He hesitated. "We also thought your community might be affected." His voice trailed off.

"Nice of you to think of us," she said, a touch of sarcasm in her tone.

Once again an emotion flickered briefly across his face, followed by a faint flush.

Why did I do that?! He hadn't even been trying to annoy her. Well, not this time, anyway. She didn't understand her own reactions at times.

Yosef broke in, clearly trying to steer the conversation somewhere safe. "We're aware of the Rogandans, Rellan. Anneka wanted to prevent them finding the other route into Erestor. That's why we're here."

"Just the two of you?"

"No," Yosef replied with a laugh. Anneka remained silent, not trusting herself to avoid another sarcastic retort.

At that moment Yosef's other men began appearing, apparently unwilling to miss out on whatever might be happening. They greeted Rellan warmly. Seeing him with Anneka, a couple of them gave him a wink.

Anneka broke in on their chatter. "Rellan is just here to find out what the Rogandans are up to. He'll be leaving shortly." She turned to him. "Scar has a couple of scouts out there. Keep an eye open for them, and give them our greetings if you see them."

Her intention had been to bring the conversation to an end, but she hadn't reckoned on her men.

"Do you know what the Rogandans are planning?"

"Have you heard what the king is going to do?"

"Has this rain flooded the Rogandans out yet? I hear they're camped in the meadow below the Citadel."

"Is anyone in Erestor gathering an army to fight them?"

"Wait! Be quiet, all of you!" It was Yosef who cut them off.

They fell silent, looking at him.

"You've just reminded me of something," he said. "Something that might be important. My great uncle—he died in his nineties—told me about a disaster that happened when he was a boy. There was an unusual amount of rain that year, and it triggered a landslide into the lake. A huge amount of water overflowed into the river and swept away everything along both banks of the river. The guards on the Citadel walls saw the whole thing happen before their eyes. Apparently people talked about it for years."

He turned to Rellan. "You've just been there. Could we trigger a landslide?"

"The slopes are very unstable," Rellan replied. "I nearly didn't make it here. But I'm not sure how we could cause a landslide. Especially without ending up in the lake ourselves."

One of the other men spoke up. "It should just be a matter of rolling something down the hill. We used to do it as children where I grew up. One time we managed to create a landslide big enough to block the entire river for hours. Enough water built up that it caused flooding downstream when our little dam burst. We were in big trouble when the adults found out that we caused it."

Rellan raised his eyebrows. "Sounds like it's worth an attempt," he said.

"Let's go do it, then!"

The men would have rushed off to the lake in a group if Anneka hadn't broken in. "Stop! We're not all going to try it. Apart from the fact that it's too risky, it's unnecessary." She pointed to the last speaker. "Jon, you can come with Yosef and me. And him." She jerked her thumb at Rellan. "The rest of you get back to your places."

They grumbled, but followed her orders. It was quite clear to Anneka that if they could arrange it, every one of them would choose vantage points that allowed them to witness the action.

"We'll split into pairs," she instructed. "Yosef, you're with me. Get your horses. We'll meet back here."

She fetched her horse and made her way back to the meeting point. The others hadn't arrived yet, and she found herself alone with Rellan. She busied herself with her saddle.

"Are you angry with me?" he asked.

"Angry with you?" she said. "Why would I be angry with you?"

He shrugged. "You're right. There's no reason for Lady Neave to even notice someone like me."

His reply took her aback. So that's why he was so withdrawn. Well, she could soon set him straight on that.

"There is no Lady Neave. She ceased to exist seven years ago. I'm Anneka. That's all."

She could see he wasn't convinced.

"The king will make it right," he said. "Lord Burtelen is planning to speak to him about it."

"It isn't up to them," she insisted. "That life is over. I don't want it back!"

He said nothing. He just gazed at her. He continued for long enough that she ceased feeling embarrassed and began to feel irritated. What did he think he was doing? And where were the others? Why were they taking so long?

"What are you expecting from me?" she asked him testily.

"I want to dance with you again in the moonlight," he said with a sudden grin, briefly exposing his former self. Then he subsided, his new restraint replacing the old brashness. She decided reluctantly that she preferred the brashness.

"I'm not expecting anything from you," he said. He looked into her eyes. "What about you? What are you expecting from life?"

She didn't bother to respond. The truth was that she expected nothing from life. Not for herself. Nothing at all.

"What about joy?" he persisted. "Do you have room for that?"

His question unsettled her. She thought she saw compassion in his eyes, and she wasn't sure she could cope with that. She set her face. "Don't talk to me about joy," she said stiffly. "I buried it along with my two-year old son."

He looked at her strangely. "Can anyone be truly alive without joy?" he asked. He paused, studying her silently. He spoke again, slowly, apparently trying to find the right words. "You don't have hope, either, do you?"

Hope? she thought dully. *I buried that, too.* Maybe her world lacked color, but she'd trained herself not to think about it. Until he came along, brim full of life and constantly poking and prodding at her.

He smiled sadly. "I wanted to help you find it again. I believed I could do it—that we could do it together. But I was wrong. I'm sorry." He bowed his head, as though he couldn't look at her.

She opened her mouth to speak, then closed it again. She wasn't sure whether to yell at him or to burst into tears. How did he manage to unsettle her so?

She did the only thing she knew how, and pushed her feelings down, deep, where they couldn't distress her.

The arrival of Yosef and Jon saved her further awkwardness. She wondered darkly if they had deliberately delayed their return to give Rellan time with her. They all mounted, and set off for the lake without further comment.

When they arrived and dismounted, Rellan produced a very long coil of rope that he had brought with him, and threw it over his shoulder. Then they left their horses and walked beside the lake, trying to locate a suitable spot.

"A steep slope might work the best," said Jon. "Somewhere with a lot of loose rocks."

"There's a section like that further along the shore," Yosef said, and set off walking carefully.

They reached the location without incident. Yosef pointed. "That's where I slid halfway down the slope," he said.

"And over there is where I slid down yesterday," Rellan added, also pointing.

"It's extremely dangerous," said Yosef. "We'll need to be careful."

Jon found a rock that was a suitable size for him to handle. He hefted it and threw it as far down the slope as he could manage. It didn't roll at all, immediately sinking into the soft earth instead. The soil around it slid down a short distance, but then stopped.

Jon was clearly disappointed. "This isn't going to be easy," he said.

Yosef headed down the slope toward another rock, larger than the one Jon had thrown. "Give me a hand, Jon," he called. Jon joined him, and together they lifted the rock. As they did so, the ground beneath them slowly began to move.

"Get out of there!" Anneka shouted.

They began scrambling up again, but the soil fell away faster than they could climb.

The soil was moving downhill slowly enough that they didn't seem far out of reach. Anneka ran toward them, hoping to grab one of their hands. Then the ground began to slide beneath her as well. She screamed involuntarily.

She looked up to see Rellan running away from them, up the slope. Even at this moment of crisis, a detached part of her mind registered surprise and disappointment at his cowardice. Then he reappeared, trailing rope behind him. He must have found something to secure the rope to. He quickly tied a loop with the other end and slipped it over his shoulders and under his arms. Then he leaped down the slope in her direction.

She began sliding more quickly and screamed again. She looked up to see Rellan skidding down rapidly toward her.

"Grab my legs!" he cried.

She reached out and grasped hold of his legs. The rope pulled tight, and he stopped sliding abruptly, almost shaking loose her grip. She slipped down further until her muddy hands were barely clasping his ankles.

Slowly he began to bend his knees, pulling her up with him. Then he reached down with one hand and grabbed her arm. He clenched her so tightly that she cried out in pain. But he did not loosen his grip. He continued to pull her toward him until she was close enough to wrap her arms around him. He released her arm then, and pulled her in close.

The two of them looked down. The entire slope was flowing away beneath them. Yosef and Jon were nowhere to be seen. A wave created by the landslide traveled slowly across the lake. Eventually it reached the other side and swept up the opposite bank. The ground on the other side in turn fell away into the lake, creating an even bigger wave that slowly but purposefully moved back in their direction. When it hit, it rushed up the slope toward them. She watched in silent horror as it reached their feet, threatening to suck them down into the lake. She clung to Rellan more tightly than ever. His arms enfolded her unwaveringly.

Then the wave was gone. The water in the lake slowly began to ebb away. The top section of the natural dam must have collapsed, because the water level continued to fall until the lake had been half emptied.

As the water receded, Rellan began climbing slowly upward, supported by the rope. Anneka was dragged along with him. Realizing that he must be limited to the full use of only one arm, she began trying to cooperate, scrabbling at the slope with her legs while still clinging fiercely to him with her arms.

Eventually they reached the top, both of them falling down prostrate in utter exhaustion. She clung to him still, and he drew her head gently in to his shoulder.

The enormity of what had happened gradually overwhelmed her, and she began to shake uncontrollably. For so long she had kept her feelings firmly in check. Now the barrier that held them at bay was more fragile than ever, and her emotions welled up overpoweringly. Wrapped securely in Rellan's strong arms, her face buried in his chest, she finally yielded.

She began to weep, quietly at first, then with increasing abandon. She wept for Yosef and Jon. She wept for the loss of their home in the forest. She wept for the pain and suffering in the world, and for the evil and injustice that had made her sanctuary necessary. Finally, a reservoir of tears was released that had never been breached, and she wept long and bitterly for her lost husband and her infant son. She did not weep because she chose to; she wept because her grief could no longer be contained.

In time she became silent. Pain and loss still surrounded her, but somehow a tiny deposit of peace, unexpected and unlooked for, had lodged itself deep within her being.

Eventually they got to their feet. She placed her hand in his, and their fingers intertwined. Then they carefully began to retrace their steps back across the ruined slope.

Kuper leaned on the battlements and looked down over the meadow. The scene was deceptively tranquil. The Rogandan soldiers were responding to a brief break in the incessant rain and had emerged from their tents. They appeared to be enjoying a midday meal.

Kuper wondered where his brother was at that moment. He tried to imagine his reunion with Anneka.

A voice cut across his thoughts. "What's that noise?" One of the soldiers was leaning forward over the battlements, his head cocked to listen.

Kuper heard it, too. A distant rumbling sound was slowly growing in volume.

Activity in the meadow abruptly ceased. All the Rogandans were staring upstream. Suddenly they scattered, frantically trying to get away from the river. Shouts of alarm sounded faintly on the wind, then were blotted out by a deafening roar. A massive wall of water swept into view. Nothing could stand before it. Huge trees were uprooted and swept away like straws in the wind. The mighty wave surged across the meadow, engulfing it in an irresistible flood.

Men ran to the battlements and gaped in awe, rendered speechless by the stupendous scale of the destruction. The peaceful meadow below them had been transformed into a raging sea. Kuper stared down at the maelstrom, completely dumbfounded. The water continued to pour in, unabated and roaring its fury.

Many minutes passed before the raging torrent began at last to show signs of subsiding. The soldiers crowding the battlements still did not move. Dazed and speechless, they stood rooted to the spot.

Kuper was the first to tear himself away. It was clear to him what he needed to do.

He spotted the commander standing on the wall with the rest of his soldiers, so he sought him out and drew him aside. "With your permission, I'm going to gather my men," he said. "As soon as it's safe to ride down there, I will lead them into the forest to hunt down that Rogandan band we heard about."

The commander nodded his approval. "There will be other strays as well. I will see to it that they are dealt with."

"One other request," Kuper added. "Can you send a message to Lord Burtelen? Please inform His Lordship that the way to Castel is now open."

VOLUME 2—THE KNOWING

14

"Our scouts appear to have identified a suitable location for the battle, My Lords." At Will's announcement the persistent murmur of background conversation ceased abruptly. A great deal depended on this choice. Everyone present knew that the fate of two kingdoms would be determined by the looming encounter.

"There are unmistakable signs that the Rogandans have been massing their forces." Will told them. "They clearly want to draw us into a decisive battle. As you all know, the Rogandans outnumber us significantly, and they will be looking to inflict a heavy defeat upon us. They will set out to end our resistance once and for all."

"With the additional levies we have been able to raise from Arvenon and Castel, we have ten thousand men," King Istel said frankly. "How big is their army?"

"Based on the reports of our scouts, Your Majesty, our best estimate is that the Rogandans have nearly three times that number."

An undercurrent of murmuring broke out at Will's words.

He waited until the noise had died down. "Neither side has a substantial contingent of archers," he continued, "so archers are not likely to prove decisive. Cavalry, however, is a different matter. Only four thousand of their men are mounted. Our mounted strength is close to three thousand men, which means we have a cavalry force almost as large as theirs. That fact will have an important bearing on our plans."

"What about the reinforcements from Erestor?" one of the nobles asked.

"We still haven't heard from any of the messengers we sent west," King Steffan replied.

"We do know that a large Rogandan force was sent to Erestor," Will added. "They were almost certainly not strong enough to breach the defenses of Steffan's Citadel, but that may not have been their purpose. Their intent may have simply been to prevent Lord Burtelen from reinforcing us. And even if Erestor somehow found a way of sending us additional men now, it's unlikely they would reach us in time."

King Steffan nodded his agreement, although with obvious reluctance. "Will is right. We have no choice except to work with what we have," he concluded grimly.

"We must never lose heart, though," King Istel said. "Numbers alone do not decide battles."

Will bowed to the Castelan king, acknowledging the wisdom of his comment.

The commander turned to Lord Bottren, who retrieved a large map and approached the table. As Bottren began to spread it out, one of the nobles spoke up. "You say we've found a suitable location," he said. "How do we know the Rogandans will be willing to fight on a battleground they didn't choose?"

"They will come to us wherever we are, My Lord," Will replied. "They want to meet us in battle. And they will like this site. They want us to face them in the open, because they don't believe we have any hope of winning a pitched battle. They won't imagine there is any chance they can lose, given their vast superiority in numbers. So we will be offering them a lure they cannot resist.

"The challenge we face is a simple one," he said. "We need to find a way of ensuring that most of the Rogandan soldiers are not actually able to join the fighting. If we can do that, their advantage in numbers will not help them. This battleground does not guarantee us success. It does allow us to choose a strategy that suits us, though. If our strategy is good, and we execute it well, we have a chance. Once the battle begins, our primary goal will be to maneuver them into a position where most of their forces cannot participate."

He pointed to the map, and the men gathered around the table leaned forward to get a closer look.

"This site features a broad plain, bounded by a tall escarpment on the eastern side known as Torbury Scarp, and a group of low hills on the western side. Both the northern and southern ends of the plain are open. We propose to occupy the northern end.

"The cliff face of Torbury Scarp is steep and inaccessible both to horses and to men—climbing it is not an option. We will place it on our left. The hills across from it on the other side of the plain form a natural boundary for the field of battle on our right flank. The area between these two natural boundaries is broad enough to allow plenty of freedom for battlefield maneuvering. It's also broad enough to encourage the Rogandans to think they can deploy their entire army to full advantage. They will expect to be able to outflank us."

He paused to make sure everyone understood.

"Let me explain the strategy. I am proposing to form up our men three lines deep, facing south, with the escarpment rising above us on our left and the hills away to our right. The Rogandans will enter the battlefield from the south. The obvious place for them to outflank us will be on our right where there is more open space. When the two armies engage, though, we will instead allow them to drive a wedge into our line beside the cliff face of Torbury Scarp. It will appear to them that they have broken through on our left. The left side of our line will fall back rapidly, drawing the Rogandan forces into a stretched out line along the cliff face.

"While this is taking place, half of our cavalry—positioned on our right flank—will engage the Rogandan cavalry. We will be outnumbered more than two to one, but we must nevertheless find a way to drive the Rogandan horsemen from the field. I believe we can do it. I have seen our men, and I have fought the Rogandans. Our mounted soldiers are better trained, better led, and they are better fighters. Our riders must get behind the Rogandan army and drive them further into their new position along the escarpment.

"The rest of our foot soldiers will swing left and stretch out to form a new line opposite them. The Rogandans will now be positioned with the cliff face at their backs, and our men stretched out in front of them. They will be blocked on their left—the southern side—by our cavalry.

"The remainder of our cavalry will be waiting to the north on a ridge that commands an outlook over the whole site. Initially this will be at the rear of our position but as the battle progresses it will become our left flank. As the Rogandans continue to drive their wedge further forward along the cliff face, hoping to spill out around our new position and attack us from the rear, our cavalry will advance down from the ridge and engage them. The result will be that the Rogandans are blocked on the northern side as well. This movement will complete the containment of the Rogandan army.

"By then their soldiers will be spread, many men deep, across the whole length of the escarpment. Most of them will be unable to reach our soldiers, so they won't be able to fight. But they'll get in the way of those who are fighting. The more vigorously we can push their line back toward the cliff face, the more the Rogandans will trip over each other. Their numbers will be of no use to them—the press of men will eventually prevent any of them from fighting effectively."

The minute Will finished speaking, others jumped in energetically with their own comments and questions. Everyone had an opinion, and the debate became heated at times. Many of the lords were very impressed, though, and didn't try to hide it.

The meeting came to an end with a lot of questions still to be answered. There were always risks, of course, but the two kings approved both the site and the battle plan, and they did so enthusiastically.

While King Steffan was bringing the meeting to a conclusion, Will glanced around the table, assessing the expressions on the faces of the nobles. Nothing that he could see revealed open hostility, but he knew that most of the lords were well able to mask their true feelings and intentions.

Thanks to the vigorous efforts of Nestor, though, Will was no longer reduced entirely to guesswork to understand what the nobles around the table were thinking. Apart from his own liaison, Lord Bottren, Will knew that two of the lords had come to this meeting strongly supportive of his leadership while a couple more were largely positive. The remaining four—Lord Eisgold among them—were saying very little, either in public or behind closed doors. They were certainly not speaking negatively, which was something.

Neither Will nor Nestor had been able to discover clear signs that intrigue was still alive and well among the nobles. If it still existed at all, it had gone deep underground.

The only thing that mattered was how the nobles would behave when they found themselves fighting together for their lives and their futures. On that front at least, Will had not been able to detect any obvious cause for alarm.

"Today is the day that Essanda is coming to visit." King Steffan groaned and buried his head in his hands. With a site chosen for the battle and active planning underway, the timing couldn't have been worse. "What was I thinking when I agreed to that?"

King Istel smiled grimly. "You might remember that I thought the idea was absurd from the beginning," he said, shaking his head. "In any event, it's much too late to do anything about it now. And I imagine she'll be as safe here at Hazelwood Ford as she would be in the capital."

When Queen Essanda did arrive at the main camp, Steffan was far too busy to meet her. The best he could manage was to send a warm greeting along with his apology. The message was delivered through Count Gordan, who had accompanied her from the citadel.

It was the early hours of the morning before Steffan was able to return to his tent. He opened the flap and stepped inside to find the tent dimly illuminated by the light of a couple of candles. He had arranged for a separate section of the tent to be set aside for his young wife, behind a canvas partition. Expecting her to be asleep, he moved through the large tent as quietly as he could.

As he headed for his own sleeping quarters at the opposite end of the shelter, he heard a voice softly call his name. He turned to see Essanda's head appear briefly around the flap that partitioned off her room. Her head disappeared again, then a few moments later she emerged with a cloak thrown over her nightgown and a blanket draped loosely around the cloak. Even so, she was shivering slightly in the cold.

"Hello, Steffan," she said, with a sleepy smile. "I am so happy to see you again at last."

"I'm sorry to have woken you, Essanda. But I am delighted to see you, too," he said affectionately.

She gazed across at him with bleary eyes, studying him critically. "You haven't been getting enough sleep."

"You're right. There's been a lot of demand on my time."

She gave him a little frown, shaking her head. Then she yawned hugely.

"It seems that both of us need some sleep," he told her, stifling a yawn of his own.

She nodded. "I will not distract you," she said determinedly. "We can talk tomorrow." She gave him another drowsy smile before heading back to her room.

"Sleep well," he called softly after her.

He waited until she had disappeared, then he made his way to his own sleeping quarters. Too tired to properly undress, he shed his cloak, pulled off his shoes, and climbed onto his bed as he was, covering himself with a mixed assortment of blankets and coats. He lay there for a moment thinking about Essanda. She had managed to show care and concern for him, young as she was. He resolved sleepily that he would not allow her to outdo him.

Rolling onto his side, he closed his eyes. He was so tired that he drifted off to sleep at once.

Steffan woke to full daylight. He jumped up from the bed in alarm—there were things he should have been doing instead of sleeping the morning away. Hurrying outside the tent, he found a table laden with food and drink waiting for him. He stood there squinting at it in the bright daylight.

A servant was on hand ready to offer assistance.

"Where did the food come from?" Steffan asked.

"Her Majesty arranged for it, Sire. She also insisted that you not be disturbed before you woke up."

He groaned. He glanced down at the meal spread out before him. It did look appealing, and he was hungry. He shrugged and sat down. Before long he was attacking the food energetically.

"Where is my wife?" he asked.

"I do not know, Sire. She left quite early."

He raised an eyebrow curiously—he couldn't help wondering what she was doing. He turned his attention once more to eating.

He left when he had arranged for dinner to be served for the two of them in his tent.

As he returned at the end of the day, Steffan found himself uncertain about what to say to Essanda. He spent his days preparing for war. But she wouldn't be interested in that. He realized how much he still had to learn about her—they'd had so little opportunity to spend relaxed time together. What did she do with her days back at the capital? He arrived feeling uncharacteristically apprehensive and unsure of himself.

He need not have worried.

When he entered the tent, she rose and greeted him warmly, giving him an affectionate kiss on the cheek.

"Did you have a good day?" she asked, appraising him with her searching look.

"All things considered, it was good enough," he said. "Thank you for asking. How was your day?"

She smiled, pausing to pour him a drink before replying. "It was very enlightening."

He looked at her quizzically. What did that mean?

She giggled when she saw his face. "You look so serious," she said.

"I'm sorry," he said. "Preparing for war is serious business. But tell me how your day was enlightening."

"Some of my father's nobles are not excited about having a commoner as their commander," she began.

He looked at her sharply. "Who have you been talking to?" he asked, more brusquely than he intended.

She looked a little offended, and he quickly apologized for his tone of voice.

"I haven't been *talking* to many people at all," she told him. "I've been doing a great deal of listening."

He was not surprised. He already had a high regard for her ability to ferret things out. "What have you discovered?" he asked.

"That the nobles will follow the agreed plan of battle. But Lord Eisgold might have a plan of his own in store."

He waved his hand dismissively. "That rumor has been around for a while. But your father knows him better than anyone, and he doesn't believe it. I've been keeping a close eye on Eisgold myself, and he gives every indication that's he very supportive of Will."

"Has he always been supportive?" she asked.

"No, not at first. But he's changed."

"What was the reason for the change?"

"Your father wasn't willing to put up with his previous obstructiveness, and he clearly realized that. The man isn't stupid. And it's not impossible that he simply decided that Will's ideas were worthy of his support."

She offered him an innocent smile but said nothing.

Then she changed the subject. "Where will you be during the battle?" she asked, a frown of concern creasing her young brow.

"You needn't worry," he told her. "Istel and I have promised Will that we will stay well away from the fighting."

She sighed with relief.

"Will was concerned that the need to ensure our safety could prove to be a distraction at critical moments. This battle will be challenging enough—none of our fighters can afford distractions. It's galling, but I know he's right."

He adopted a look of reluctant resignation, winning him a pleased grin from Essanda.

They ended up speaking of many things. Later, when he reflected on the conversation, he realized that they hadn't talked at all about the kind of things most noblewomen seemed fixated upon. He'd done most of the talking, and she had listened. In fact, almost all of her contributions had been gentle questions that teased out a considerable amount of information from him.

THE ARMY OF ERESTOR, finally on its way east, now stretched out for miles. It had taken far too long to get the soldiers through the pass at Steffan's Citadel and over the soggy mire that had once been the road below it. Huge sections of the countryside below the citadel had been swept away by the torrent, leaving behind a swamp that now made travel of any kind extremely difficult. Getting a few thousand men and horses through this quagmire had proven to be a logistical nightmare. The last of the men were finally traveling on solid ground, but it had taken far longer than Kuper could ever have imagined.

Kuper and Rellan had been busy, not least because they had acquired new responsibilities. In view of their service to the Duchy, a grateful Lord Burtelen had extended to them a considerable degree of authority over the army that was now on the march. Neither of them were required to command men directly, but they had been granted unfettered access to the senior commanders and given a voice into both the tactics and the overall strategy of the force.

"We need to find a way to pick up the pace," Kuper said to his twin as they rode together near the front of the column.

"Yes," Rellan agreed. "The sooner we go, the sooner we can get back."

Kuper laughed. "The forest life seems to have acquired a new appeal for you," he said with a grin.

Rellan looked pained. "Anneka wasn't at all happy with me when I left."

"So the two of you had another of your raging arguments, did you?"

A resigned look flashed across Rellan's face. "We have had one or two. Life certainly hasn't been boring since I met Anneka."

"No. And I can't imagine that's likely to change any time soon," Kuper said.

"I hope not," Rellan replied with energy. "She certainly is a lively one," he added, a wry grin appearing on his face.

"You have yourself to thank for that. By all accounts you're the one who's brought her back to life," Kuper told him.

Rellan replied with a wink.

Both of them fell silent for a time. When Kuper next glanced across at his brother he saw a faraway look in his eyes. "What are you thinking about?" he asked.

"Anneka, of course. She was furious with me when I was about to leave. She wouldn't speak to me. Then when I mounted my horse she burst into tears and stormed off. I couldn't figure out what was going on."

Kuper looked at him in disbelief. "Are you serious? You really don't know? It's perfectly obvious to everyone else."

"What do you mean?"

"She's worried about losing you! She took years to get over the loss of her husband and son. She eventually managed to do it, but only after you arrived on the scene. Finally she's started to think she might have a future worth living for. Now you're going, too. Off to war! There's nothing at all complicated about it."

Rellan was frowning. "I thought it must have been something I said."

Kuper shook his head. "You're hopeless."

"Sounds like it should be easy to resolve, then," said Rellan, his face brightening. "I'll send her a message."

"There's only one way you can resolve it," Kuper told him. "And that's by returning alive and in one piece."

"Let's get on with it, then," Rellan replied. "Time to get them moving." He kicked in his heels and headed back down the column.

Kuper rolled his eyes. Rellan's intentions were wonderful, but impossibly unrealistic. You couldn't simply decide to ride off, win a war, and come back again. There was never any certainty about anything when you were a soldier.

Kuper looked back at the line of men and horses stretching away into the distance and sighed. The coming days promised to be more than usually challenging.

15

Brother Vangellis groaned. He opened his eyes and strained once again to see around him in the dark. It was futile, and he quickly gave it up. The cold seemed to penetrate through to his bones, and his hunger gnawed at him constantly. *O God, Father of all, whose Son commanded us to love our enemies...*

The incessant drip-drip-dripping of water frayed at his nerves, but it was better than the cries of pain and wails of despair that otherwise punctuated the stillness from time to time. He decided to close his eyes again and wait for the morning. *Deliver them, and deliver us, from hatred, cruelty, and revenge...*

He'd lost count of the days since they had brought him here and thrown him into the dungeon. Cold and alone in the dark, his sole comfort was the liturgy, fixed in his memory, that he used to mark his passage through each day. He greeted the new day with morning prayers, marked the arrival of noon with matins, and ended the day with vespers. The familiar ritual remained impervious to circumstances, in stark contrast to his emotions. The litany remained fixed and unchanging, unlike any hopes he might have entertained for a future that now seemed doubtful in the extreme.

With no window to the outside world, he didn't exactly know

when the sun rose and set, much less the actual moment of noon. But a tiny amount of dim light did penetrate his cell during daylight hours, and he was given a little bread and water at what seemed to be the start of each day. He marked this meal with special thankfulness.

Only once had he been called before the master of this stronghold. He had been quite literally dragged into the presence of Lord Drettroth and dumped on the stone floor.

He remained where he had been deposited, staring up at the Rogandan commander with considerable curiosity. His captor was tall, and simply clad in a black cloak. He might have been fifty years old—his black hair showed tinges of gray at the temples—but he was lean and muscular.

Many long minutes had passed before the Rogandan leader even bothered to notice his presence. He finally glanced down at his prisoner, fixing him in a piercing gaze. The monk saw intelligence in his face, and also sensed that a cold animal cunning lurked behind his calm demeanor. If the eyes offered any indication, the dark-clad nobleman had no acquaintance whatsoever with compassion. Brother Vangellis shivered involuntarily.

"Ah. The monk," the Rogandan had said, speaking smoothly in the language of Arvenon. "Are you missing your young friend? You will be reunited soon, I promise. Do you think he will enjoy the accommodations?" Drettroth had smiled broadly, apparently pleased with his own sense of humor.

And that was it. After those few words the Rogandan had dismissed him summarily. Brother Vangellis was bemused, unable to fathom the purpose of the visit, if indeed there had been a purpose.

As the guards dragged him away, Drettroth had spoken to the guards in their own language. "We might be able to find a use for him. Make sure you keep him alive."

Did Drettroth assume that his captive could not speak Rogandan? Or had he intended Brother Vangellis to understand his comment? The monk couldn't decide.

Nor could he guess how Drettroth might be planning to use him.

Perhaps his jailer thought he could induce him to put pressure on Thomas to hand over the stone.

Brother Vangellis didn't find it difficult to imagine the kind of inducements that Drettroth had in mind—he could threaten torture if the monk refused to cooperate, or hold out the offer of freedom if he did. He smiled grimly to himself. The Rogandan would discover that he was wasting his time.

Still, it was nice to know that they weren't planning to dispose of him. Not yet, anyway. And Drettroth's plans were entirely dependent on his men catching Thomas first. It was gratifying to know that they still hadn't managed to do so. That was another thing well worth being thankful for.

Brother Vangellis kept his eyes open as they dragged him back to his cell, and he made a couple of discoveries as a result. He noted first that prisoners were being held on other levels above the dungeon. They passed a large and surprisingly well-furnished cell occupied by what appeared to be a young nobleman. The prisoner peered out curiously at the monk as he was towed along behind the guards.

He also spotted a youth wandering around freely, if furtively. He looked a little younger than Thomas, and he appeared to be Arvenian, if his clothing and demeanor offered any indication. On impulse, the monk called out a friendly "Hello," but either the youth didn't understand him, or he chose not to respond. He slipped away instead into the shadows, leaving Brother Vangellis to wonder who he was and what he was doing there.

The guards didn't return the monk to the lower dungeon. They dumped him instead in a cell on the level below the nobleman. Perhaps the change was a response to Lord Drettroth's instruction to keep him alive. The cell with its stone floor and stone walls felt almost as cold as the dungeon, but a single torch flickered somewhere down the passageway, so it wasn't entirely dark. After bolting the iron door, they abandoned him once more to the loneliness of total isolation.

He wondered briefly what was going on outside in the wide world. That made him think of Thomas again, and prompted him to offer up a prayer of gratitude that his friend was apparently still enjoying his freedom.

His stomach rumbled, causing him to smile wistfully to himself. Going without food might not have been voluntary, but it nevertheless brought his observances to mind—it was almost time for his prayers. They could deprive him of food and warmth and companionship, but at least they couldn't take away the dependable familiarity of his disciplines or separate him from God.

THOMAS PEERED out warily from his vantage point behind a tree. The horses of the Rogandans stood close at hand, stamping restlessly.

He had resolved to release and scatter the horses before revealing himself. That would force the Rogandans to chase him on foot. His own horse was tied near the stream, hidden from plain sight but still within easy reach of the path. He should be able to flee quickly when the moment arrived.

He crept forward until the Rogandan soldiers were in sight. Wisps of mist were beginning to swirl slowly through the trees, but he was still able to see well enough. The soldiers had finished their meal and were sitting around drinking. If their boisterous talk and loud laughter offered any indication, they were not expecting trouble. Sentries were nowhere to be seen—to all appearances they had not bothered to post any.

Thomas took a deep breath to steady himself. He knew it was necessary to place himself at great risk if he was going to draw the Rogandans away from Elena and her father. But that didn't mean he had to let them capture him. He fully intended to make a clean escape.

Acts of daring seemed to come easily to Will, but Thomas was not like his friend. Will had embarked upon a surprising number of audacious exploits, even in the time Thomas had known him. But no one thought for a moment that Will was foolhardy. Thomas knew that if he had attempted the same things, he would rightly be seen as crazy.

And yet he was about to do something extremely reckless. And, strangely enough, although he knew he ought to be terrified, he found himself filled with unexpected resolve. Even the risk to the stone did not deter him.

He eyed the horses more closely. They appeared to be unguarded. He watched quietly for a few minutes more, looking nervously this way and that. Then he made his move.

Crouching low, he hurried to the horses. The animals became even more restless when he suddenly appeared among them. He did his best to calm them, but without a lot of success—there were simply too many of them, and he was too nervous to be able to give his full attention to the task.

He was about to begin untying the horses when he heard a sound. A soldier was heading in his direction! If it was a sentry come to check on the horses, he was lost. He was certain to be discovered. He shrank down fearfully among the horses, hoping the soldier would pass by without stopping.

The man seemed to be mumbling to himself. Thomas risked a glance in his direction and saw the soldier swaying unsteadily as he walked. He was clearly drunk. It soon became apparent that he had left the campfire to relieve himself. Everything depended on whether he would decide to check on the horses while he was there.

Thomas stayed low. His heart was racing, and he had begun to sweat. The horses became more restless than ever. Surely the soldier would come to investigate.

The Rogandan wasn't leaving. He stood there mumbling out loud. Thomas would have given a lot to be able to understand what he was saying. What should be do? He could run for it, but the soldier would be certain to see him. Drunk as he was, he would surely raise the alarm. Anything might happen after that.

Everything went quiet. Thomas hadn't heard the soldier leave, so he must still be there. The youth continued to wait, his anxiety increasing by the minute. What was the Rogandan doing? Had something alerted him? Was he creeping toward the horses right at that moment to investigate?

The pressure built until Thomas could stand it no longer. Anything would be better than just crouching there. He slowly began to stand, peering out anxiously to catch a glimpse of the Rogandan. He couldn't see him anywhere. Then a wave of horror washed over him as he realized that the man might be standing behind him, right this minute! Thomas broke out into a cold sweat. Overcome with dread, he spun slowly around.

No one was there. He gazed around in bewilderment. Finally he spotted the soldier. The man lay on the ground, right beside the horses. He appeared to have collapsed in a drunken stupor.

Thomas stood silently, watching for any sign of movement. The soldier didn't stir.

What should he do? Releasing the horses could not be done quietly. There was every chance it would wake the man up.

The Rogandan began to snore loudly. That decided it for Thomas. He would do what he came here to do, and if the man woke up, he would decide how to deal with it then.

The animals wore halters, and their ropes had been tied to the branches of trees. It was slow and tedious work for one person to release them all. He couldn't afford to let them wander, either. Before long someone would notice if horses began wandering around freely.

As he untied a horse, he looped its rope over his left arm. There must have been twenty of the animals, though, and it simply wasn't possible to manage that many at once. After freeing half of the horses, he tied their halters loosely to a branch. As soon as he was ready, he would do something to startle them—they should easily be able to pull free.

He began untying the remaining horses. After a while he moved almost without thinking from horse to horse, calming the animal, untying it, securing its rope to his arm, then on to the next one. He had two horses to go when he realized that something felt different. He paused, trying to make sense of his unease. Then it hit him—the soldier wasn't snoring.

He looked across to where the soldier was lying and discovered he wasn't there. He looked around and found himself looking into the startled eyes of the Rogandan. The man stared uncomprehendingly for a moment. Then his eyes went wide, and he opened his mouth and bellowed.

Everything happened at once after that. The first group of horses whinnied in fright and began pulling at their ropes. In a moment they were free and galloping away. His left shoulder was wrenched violently as the horses still tethered to his arm pulled in different directions. Wincing with pain, he somehow managed to slide the ropes from his arm.

The horses he had been holding were gone in a moment. One of them, wide eyed and screaming, turned blindly and crashed into the Rogandan soldier, knocking him to the ground. He didn't get up.

Thomas ran for it, clutching his injured shoulder. He dashed back to his horse and untied it. The horse was spooked and difficult to manage. Somehow he clambered into the saddle. He was about to gallop away when he remembered that he needed to reveal himself so that his pursuers would set off in the right direction.

By the time he headed along the path the Rogandan camp was in an uproar. Men were running around, trying to catch horses. A couple of voices appeared to be shouting orders. Two men were already in the saddle, no doubt riding the horses he had been unable to release.

Someone spotted him, and a cry went up. He kicked his heels into his horse and set off along the path, bending down to avoid low hanging branches. He glanced back over his shoulder and saw through the thickening fog that both mounted soldiers were already in close pursuit. Other men were faintly visible running after them along the path.

His plan was not at all working out as he had expected. The pain in his shoulder had become excruciating now that he was bouncing along on horseback. He began to feel faint. He gritted his teeth and willed himself to stay in the saddle. He was determined to lead the Rogandans far away from Elena. Nothing else mattered.

The path wound its way into a denser region of the forest. The trees seemed to be closing in around him. The fog had also thickened considerably, and he could barely see further ahead than a couple of horse lengths. The chase became a confused blur, galloping blindly through the haze and somehow clinging to consciousness, in stubborn denial of his suffering.

Then abruptly a large branch appeared from out of the gloom. Rigid and unyielding, it knocked him from his horse. He fell heavily and rolled onto his injured shoulder. Everything went black, and he knew no more.

16

"Ah, Mr. Nestor! Please, take a seat."

Nestor bowed deeply. "Your Majesty." He joined Queen Essanda at the table, and they sat quietly for a few minutes gazing across the grassland that stretched out before them. Soldiers on exercise moved endlessly back and forth, conveying a sense of restless energy.

The battle scarred veteran stole a glance at the young queen. One of his contacts had arranged for them to meet on her first day at Hazelwood Ford, and he had quickly taken a liking to her.

Queen Essanda was remarkable for her age. He himself was a man of few words, but his taciturn nature hid his real strength—he was an unusually shrewd listener. He had a sharp memory, unending patience, and he knew how to ask the right question at the right time. He had rarely met his equal at this game. This little queen showed considerable promise, though. He had quickly discovered that her pretty young face masked a keen ear and an unusually perceptive mind.

"Are you well, Mr. Nestor?"

"I am, Your Majesty. Thank you for asking. But please, call me Nes. All my friends do."

That earned him a smile. "Mr. Nes, then," she said cheerfully.

He smiled back. He had the feeling that she liked him, too.

At their first meeting she had shown considerable curiosity about the attitude of the nobles, especially toward Will. Nestor had been reluctant at first to say anything that might be seen as disparaging toward the nobility. But he had soon realized that her real concern was for the good of the two kingdoms. She didn't seem invested in showing respect for people who didn't deserve it, whether or not they were highborn. Like her new husband, she apparently valued people more for their integrity than for their social status.

"Have you been enjoying your visit to Hazelwood Ford, Your Majesty?" he asked.

She smiled briefly. "It's been interesting." Then she looked at him seriously. "I've heard something, and I'm hoping you can help me to understand it," she said.

"I would be glad to, if I can."

"It was something Lord Eisgold said," she continued.

He raised his eyebrows in surprise. "He said it to you?"

"No," she said, shaking her head. "He said it to some of our other nobles. But I was there as well."

"They talk openly, with you there listening?" He didn't try to hide his surprise.

She shrugged. "They talk in riddles. And they think I'm simple. That's probably why they don't mind talking when I'm around."

He shook his head at the magnitude of their miscalculation. Anyone who thought she was a simpleton was making a big mistake. "Where did this happen, Your Majesty?"

"In a large barn. They go there to drink together. I went with some of their younger sons."

"If you were there with others your own age, I'm surprised you got any chance to hear what the nobles were saying."

"The sons don't have much to say. I think they're scared of me." She giggled bashfully.

"So what was it you heard, Your Majesty?"

"Lord Eisgold said something strange. He said, 'Even when every move of a game is played strictly by the rules, an apprentice might struggle to master the timing.' Some of the other nobles wanted him to say more, but he wouldn't. He didn't say anything else. They all left soon after that."

"You're sure that's what he said? Exactly that?"

"Yes, I'm certain. I have a very good memory," she told him proudly.

He sat there quietly, thinking. After a while he turned to her. "I've learned that the nobles refer to Will as the 'apprentice'. But what does he mean by the 'game'? I'm not sure," he said.

"I've been wondering about that, too. Do you think it might be the battle plan?" she asked.

He paused for a few minutes, deep in thought. "I believe you may be right," he said finally.

He leaned forward and lowered his voice. "You know from our last conversation that there have been vague rumors about the Castelan nobles, and about Lord Eisgold in particular. The rumors suggest that he might be planning a surprise for Will.

"The worst possible interpretation of what you've just told me is that Lord Eisgold intends to deploy his soldiers when it suits him, not when Will needs them. When the commander orders the Castelan soldiers into action at a crucial point in the battle, Lord Eisgold might decide to hold them back. The commander would be forced to join the battle personally in an attempt to save the day, just like he did last time. This time, though, he might not be so lucky. Once Will is out of the way, Lord Eisgold could throw the full weight of the Castelan army into the battle, and take the credit for the resulting victory."

He sat back in his chair. "That may not be what he meant at all, though. There are other less sinister ways of interpreting it. Lord Eisgold might simply mean that even if a battle plan is followed carefully, success will depend on how well the commander executes the timing of each move. That is undeniably true."

She didn't comment.

"I'm not at all sure that either King Steffan or your father would find this information incriminating," he continued. "I suspect that any alarming interpretation would be seen by them as far fetched. If I understand them rightly, they're convinced that Lord Eisgold had a change of heart, and now fully supports Will."

She nodded, confirming his view. "Would Lord Eisgold take the risk of doing something that might cause us to lose the battle?" she asked.

"Not intentionally. But it's possible he thinks he's smarter than he really is. He might believe he can get away with making a few changes to the battle plan without affecting the final outcome."

"Could someone try to talk him out of it?"

"I could ask Lord Bottren to speak to him. But if Lord Eisgold does have plans of his own, he'd simply deny it. And once he knew we were aware of his intentions, he'd make adjustments. Then none of us would be any the wiser."

She nodded slowly.

"And even if the worst reading of this is correct," Nestor pointed out, "Lord Eisgold may not actually deviate from the battle plan once the fighting starts. As it happens, I've recently learned something that supports that view."

She looked at him inquiringly.

"A servant overheard two of the Castelan nobles talking—two of the nobles most closely aligned with Lord Eisgold. One of them claimed that he's just talk. He said Lord Eisgold might like to give the impression that he's an independent thinker, but that he'll follow orders when it comes to the battle. The other nobleman agreed with him.

"That makes sense to me. It isn't just Arvenon's future that's at stake—Castel has just as much to lose. Lord Eisgold understands that as well as we do."

A thoughtful look came over her face. "Are you planning to tell Will any of this?" she asked.

He shook his head slowly. "We have nothing solid to tell him, Your Majesty. I'm not sure it would be responsible to distract him with vague uncertainties. How can a commander lead effectively if he doubts his own allies? Would it be responsible of us to suggest that in the heat of battle he might need to outmaneuver his friends as well as his foes? Will's task is difficult enough already." He raised his hands helplessly.

The two of them sat there for some time without speaking.

Finally the queen turned to him. "What are you going to do, Mr. Nes?" she asked quietly.

He shrugged. "Nothing, Your Majesty. It's hard for me to believe that Lord Eisgold really is planning to repeat exactly the same tactic he used at Pinder's Flat. He might be proud and stubborn, but I don't think of him as a fool."

She didn't look entirely satisfied. She sat staring off into the distance, a thoughtful look on her face.

There was nothing more he could say. He asked for permission to withdraw, and she granted it with a nod and a word of thanks. He left wishing that he had solid evidence, one way or the other. The signs were confusing, and he'd rarely felt so uncertain about how to read them clearly.

"What are you up to, Essanda?" Steffan had stepped into his tent to find his young wife parading herself in front of a mirror. She'd never shown any inclination to do that before. And she was wearing armor.

She didn't answer, but her deep blush confirmed that he'd surprised her at something.

"Where did you get the cuirass?" She was wearing a breastplate and backplate fastened together by leather straps. It fitted her surprisingly well. And it actually looked quite fetching.

"Do you like it?" she asked shyly.

"It makes you look much older," he said admiringly.

She fixed him with a mock frown. "I'm still just a girl, however old I might look. I hope you won't forget that."

He laughed. Coming closer, he took her by the shoulders and pulled her to him. But he contented himself with a kiss on her forehead.

"So why the armor?" he asked.

"We're at war, and I think that royals should dress appropriately. Do you like it?"

"I do. Although I'm not sure about the purple gown. I think white might suit the look better."

She looked down at her dress with a little frown of concentration.

"Putting on armor is well and good," he told her. "But don't imagine you'll be coming any closer to the fighting than this mirror."

She responded with a deep curtsy and a humble bow of her pretty head. Then she straightened and stood there silently, a delicate blush on her cheeks, basking in his obvious admiration.

She would make a queen worth waiting for. Assuming he still had a kingdom when the coming encounter was over.

THE ROGANDAN SOLDIERS huddled together in the early morning light as a biting wind blew through the camp. Haldek stood among them, chilled to the bone, wondering once again what he had done to deserve this particular fate. How did he come to be here in this strange land battling foreigners who fought like demons? He simply didn't understand the reasons behind it all.

The soldiers had been rounded up once again so the leader of their army could harangue them. The recently appointed Kulzeike had already earned himself a terrifying reputation. The previous commander, Luzik, now seemed positively genial by comparison. Where did Lord Drettroth find these monsters?

Haldek looked around him. Only Rogandan soldiers were present. Once again no Varasan soldiers had been rounded up. He was not sorry. The Varasans were savages who could not be trusted. They were supposed to be allies, but they had nasty tempers and seemed all too ready to pick fights with his countrymen. They had quickly built reputations as fierce fighters, too. Haldek made sure he stayed far away from them.

When Kulzeike arrived he mounted a platform erected for the

occasion. He surveyed the crowd before him, then spat contemptuously onto the ground. Apparently he did not like what he saw. "Are you soldiers, or are you WORMS?" the new commander roared.

Haldek kept his head down fearfully, anxious to remain as inconspicuous as possible. He wondered who would be singled out this time so that Kulzeike could make his point. But the commander showed no immediate inclination to satisfy his seemingly endless blood lust. For once it appeared that he had come here just to talk.

"Soon you will fight. Soon we will WIN!" Kulzeike looked out over them with a horrible grimace on his face that might have been intended as a grin.

The gathered throng gradually realized that something was expected of them, and a belated and very half-hearted cheer greeted their commander's pronouncement. His face grew ever more wrathful, and soon the men were cheering wildly. Haldek screamed with them, howling at the top of his lungs. Kulzeike seemed satisfied, and the din gradually abated.

"The fight—the real fight—will begin soon," Kulzeike told them. "Just this once, puny mice, you must fight like tigers. Then your job will be done. No more fighting. Just the spoils of VICTORY!"

He paused again. The necessary shrieking arose without any prompting this time. He waited for it to die down.

"These Arvenian fools believe they have our measure. But they are in for a surprise. A BIG surprise. Already we have a mighty army. But another army is on the march and will join us in the battle. Our enemies will be caught like fish in a net! We will squeeze the life from them."

The men delivered another obligatory roar, and then Kulzeike abruptly dismissed them. Haldek had never seen the commander in such a good mood.

He pondered the coming battle as they all shuffled away. Perhaps Kulzeike was telling the truth. Perhaps if they could just defeat the Arvenians this time, the fighting would finally come to an end. Then maybe he would be free at last.

That would finally be something worth fighting for.

The scout pulled his horse to a halt beside Lord Burtelen and his aides. "A large body of soldiers is approaching from the south, My Lord," he said. "If they hold to their current path, they will intersect with us in two or three hours."

"Are they Rogandans?" the nobleman asked.

"They don't appear to be," the scout replied.

Lord Burtelen turned to his commander. "Alert the men just in case," he ordered. "I don't want us taken by surprise." The commander acknowledged the order and rode back down the column.

The nobleman directed his attention to Kuper and Rellan. "Go with the scout, and find out what we're dealing with," he told them.

They left immediately.

As they rode away Kuper drew his mount alongside the scout. "How many men are we talking about?" he asked.

"Hundreds, at least," the scout replied. "Probably fewer than a thousand."

Kuper raised an eyebrow. "Enough to make it worth avoiding a fight, then," he observed. "Can you take us someplace where we can observe their approach?"

"Certainly," the scout replied.

They rode for some time before the scout signaled to them that they needed to proceed more cautiously.

After a few minutes Rellan called softly to the others. "We're being watched," he said, nodding toward a lone rider off to one side.

"Let's just keep going," Kuper replied. "There are only three of us —we're not likely to cause them too much concern. We'll need to keep our wits about us, though, just in case we have to leave in a hurry."

They rode on, wary and alert, until they caught sight of the column of soldiers in the distance. They reined in their horses and observed the soldiers silently. After a time several men detached themselves from the column and rode purposefully toward them. Long before they arrived it was clear that they were not Rogandans.

The three of them decided to stay where they were.

"That's Ranauld!" exclaimed Rellan as they drew closer.

Kuper frowned. "I wonder what he's doing here." He didn't say it, but his first thought was that Arnost must have fallen.

The riders challenged them as soon as they came within hailing distance. "Who are you, and what is your business?"

"Greetings, Count Ranauld. We were sent by Lord Burtelen to ask you the same questions."

"I don't know you," the count replied. "Have we met before?"

"No, My Lord. My name is Kuper. My brother, Rellan, and I were part of the small group that accompanied Will when he left Arnost. Our other companion here is one of Lord Burtelen's scouts."

"Are you still traveling with Will?"

"No, My Lord. He sent us to Erestor for reinforcements. We are marching to join him, although we don't know exactly where he is."

"Is Lord Burtelen nearby?"

"Yes, your column will join his if you continue in the same direction for another hour or two."

Count Ranauld nodded. He gave a rapid series of instructions to his second-in-command, and then addressed Kuper. "Take me to Lord Burtelen."

They retraced their steps, riding fast, accompanied by the count and a couple of his senior men.

When they reached Lord Burtelen they found him in conference with another rider. The newcomer's horse was covered with lather from hard riding, and everything about him conveyed a sense of urgency.

"Ranauld!" Lord Burtelen called. "Well met. I hope you bring good tidings from the capital."

"Arnost still stands, I am glad to say," Ranauld replied.

"Turn aside with me, Ranauld," the lord said. "I've instructed my column to continue—it's time they picked up their pace significantly.

But we need to carefully consider our next steps. Kuper, Rellan, I want you with us."

The select group rode a short distance from the column and dismounted.

"I'm bringing three and a half thousand men from Erestor," Lord Burtelen began. "About one thousand of them are mounted. We've been planning to join Will Prentis to strengthen his army. What's your situation?"

"I have about a thousand men with me, two hundred of them mounted," Count Ranauld replied. "As you know, we have been besieged in Arnost from the beginning of this war. A few days ago we became aware that the Rogandans had lifted the siege. Their army simply melted away. At first we wondered if that meant that the war was over, but it seemed more likely that they'd just been ordered elsewhere.

"I saw no value in leaving twenty-five hundred good fighting men locked up in Arnost if a decisive battle was about to be fought. The regent agreed with me. We left fifteen hundred men behind to defend the capital, and I set off after the Rogandans with the rest. We've been trailing them ever since."

"How many men do the Rogandans have, and how far ahead of you are they?"

"They were more than a day ahead of us, but we've gained on them. They're still a good few hours away, though. Most of them are on foot, but they've been moving fast.

"It's hard to be certain about their numbers. They were joined by another army after they set out—we passed the place where the tracks merged a couple of days ago. I suspect that Drettroth is drawing all of his forces together for one big push. There may be as many as ten thousand of them."

Kuper gave out a low whistle.

The newcomer could restrain himself no longer. "May I speak, My Lord?" he asked Lord Burtelen. The nobleman nodded. "Will sent out a number of us in different directions in case reinforcements were in the area. A major battle is about to be fought. I expect it to begin tomorrow. As far as I'm aware, though, the commander has no knowledge of this new Rogandan army. It's very likely they will take him entirely by surprise."

"Do you know the planned site of the battle?" Lord Burtelen asked him.

"Yes, My Lord. The location is Torbury Scarp. I can lead you there. It is many hours away, though."

"Clearly there is considerable urgency about this," Lord Burtelen said. "Ranauld, I propose that you take control of the cavalry. I will place the mounted men from my column under your command, and you can send for your mounted soldiers as well. I suggest you set out immediately. Ride for as long as you have light, then continue as soon as the sun rises. If the battle is already in progress, you'll have to do as you see fit. If not, you can receive instructions from Will when you join him. I will follow as soon as is practicable with the remainder of our combined force."

Ranauld readily agreed to this proposal.

Lord Burtelen turned to Will's messenger. "You can accompany Count Ranauld to the battle site. But you'll need to give us clear directions first. Whenever possible, of course, we'll simply follow your trail." The messenger nodded his acknowledgment.

The messenger gave detailed directions to Kuper, Rellan, and some of Lord Burtelen's scouts while Ranauld was assembling the mounted soldiers. The cavalry departed without further delay. They were soon out of sight.

While the column continued to file past, Lord Burtelen gathered his commanders, along with Kuper and Rellan. "If we continue at this rate, we won't get there in time," he said. "The men can march until sunset. We'll feed them as soon as they stop. Then we'll empty the supply wagons. All of them. Each of the men can carry enough food for tomorrow morning. The rest of the supplies can stay where we dump them.

"In the meantime, send men into the countryside, one hour's ride in every direction. Requisition any wagons you find and bring them back.

"Once the men have been fed, we'll load as many of them as we can fit into the wagons. The ground ahead is supposed to be even, so the wagons can be driven slowly all night. It will be uncomfortable for the men, but it will have to do. They can sleep sitting up if necessary. We'll resume marching at first light."

"I have a suggestion, My Lord," Kuper said.

"Speak freely," the lord replied.

"The horses pulling the wagons will be working hard through the night. But we have a good few packhorses as well," Kuper said. "When we unload the men from the wagons, we could give the packhorses to any soldiers who can ride. Most of them won't want to fight on horseback, but the horses will get them there much faster and in better condition than if they march."

"Make it happen," Lord Burtelen said. "You and your brother can lead the group on the packhorses. Get the burdens off those horses now. You'll need them as fresh as possible in the morning.

"The rest of my men and Ranauld's men will follow on foot. It will be a forced march, but it has to be done."

Kuper spent the next couple of hours counting packhorses and finding soldiers capable of riding them. Rellan rode to Ranauld's column and did the same there. Very few of the packhorses had saddles, so the search was restricted to men who could ride bareback. In the end, they located three hundred packhorses. They stopped their search as soon as they identified the same number of competent riders.

Ranauld's men joined the main column, and Lord Burtelen urged them forward as fast as they could go. Together they marched into the east, destiny before them, and the sun setting at their backs.

17

Unknown faces swam fuzzily into view as Thomas struggled to return to consciousness. Intense pain assaulted him. The universe shrank to his shoulder and the agony radiating from it.

Strange voices sounded in his ear, speaking words he couldn't comprehend. Someone pressed a flask to his lips, and a bitter liquid spilled into his mouth. He coughed and sputtered. The liquid went down, mocking his feeble attempts to avoid swallowing it.

Someone stood over him and pressed down hard on his shoulder. A new wave of suffering crashed over him, pulling him down into blackness.

THE TORCH in the passageway sputtered on as Brother Vangellis sat in the semi-dark, uncomfortable on the cold stone floor. He closed his eyes, trying to remember the sights and sounds and smells of the outside world. It was too difficult.

Instead he began to sing. Apart from the guard who brought his daily ration of food and water, he had neither seen nor heard any sign of another person since being placed in his new cell, so he sang without restraint or self-consciousness.

After a while he realized he had strayed into the song he used to serenade the bear on his way to the monastery with Thomas. Momentarily transported in his memory back to that moment, he flicked open his eyes, half expecting to find a bear listening patiently nearby.

Instead he was startled to discover a person staring at him through the metal bars of his cell door. It was the youth he had seen wandering the passageways previously. The monk stopped his singing abruptly, halfway through a line.

"Hello," he said warmly.

The youth stared at him, a faint look of distaste on his face. "Are you insane?" he asked.

"That's a curious question," the monk exclaimed. "What makes you ask it?"

"Prisoners don't sing," the youth told him frankly. "Not unless they've gone soft in the head."

"I see," he replied with a smile. "I like to sing. So perhaps I am insane."

He gazed at the youth. The eyes that stared back at him revealed no appetite for life—it was almost as if their owner had aged prematurely. It disturbed him to see one so young in such a state.

"I am Brother Vangellis," he said. "What are you doing here, in a place like this?"

The youth paused, as if deciding whether or not to answer. "I am the food taster for Lord Drettroth," he finally replied.

The monk raised his eyebrows. "An important role. He must regard you as a trusted friend," he said.

"I hate him," the youth replied with sudden passion. "I hate everything about him!"

His response took Brother Vangellis by surprise. The monk's brows furrowed thoughtfully. "I suppose that makes sense," he finally concluded. "It wouldn't be fitting to ask a real friend to take that kind of a risk on your behalf."

"He is not my friend! He has no friends."

"How did you come to be here?" Brother Vangellis asked.

A look of pain—or perhaps shame—passed over the face of the youth. "I made a mistake. Now my life is over."

The monk shook his head in denial. "Your life doesn't have to be over because of your mistakes," he asserted.

"You're a monk. You wouldn't understand."

"I understand much better than you could imagine. I once thought like you do."

The youth looked at him skeptically. Then he shrugged. "It makes no difference," he said. "There is nothing I can do about my situation."

The monk shook his head again. "There is always something you can do. The choices before us may not seem obvious at times. But we always have choices."

They talked on, the imprisoned man calm and earnest, the one at liberty restless and unhappy. Eventually the youth left.

He came again, though, repeatedly, over the next couple of days. Slowly he began to thaw, and the monk's astonishment grew as the history laid out by the youth slowly took shape in his mind. The most important thing to Brother Vangellis, though, was the spark of life that gradually began to appear in the youth's eyes. Seeing it, he was content.

Hope did not naturally thrive in the stronghold of despair that was Drettroth's fortress. But, like a glimmer of light in a dark place, its presence was unmistakable once it appeared. Hope is as unpredictable as it is potent, and the effects of even a tiny dose of it can be far reaching, just as the fall of a single drop of water spreads ripples well beyond its point of entry.

THOMAS AWOKE SLOWLY to flashes of light playing across his face and a constant jarring and bumping. He dimly became aware that he was in a moving carriage. He squinted, trying to adjust his eyes to the light so he could see where he was. His shoulder ached—a dull throb intensified by each new jolt of the carriage.

He moved his head to look around him. Two men sat opposite him, one a soldier and the other in a blue cloak. Seeing that he was awake, the man in the blue cloak immediately reached into a bag. A small flask appeared in his hand.

Thomas's eyes grew wide as the man approached and firmly placed a restraining hand on his chest. Thomas twisted his head away, but the man forced the flask between his lips. Once again he tasted the remembered bitterness of fluid on his tongue. Once again he was pulled down into blackness.

HOPE CAME VISITING the young nobleman one morning as he sat in his comfortable but cheerless cell. It called so unexpectedly and came so well disguised that the nobleman was unable to recognize it for what it was.

It appeared in the form of a youth creeping furtively to his door.

"What would you do if you were set free?" the youth asked him quietly.

The nobleman had glimpsed the youth from time to time without ever having spoken to him, and he saw no reason to take either the question or the inquirer seriously. His reply was therefore terse and dismissive.

"Set free? From this prison? That hardly seems likely."

The visitor ignored his disregard. "I've heard you in the night," he told him. "Muttering. About your regrets."

Taken aback, the prisoner offered no response.

"What would you do if you were set free?" the youth repeated.

"Look, I don't know who you are, or why you've been spying on me," the nobleman replied testily, "but it's none of your business what I would do."

"If you had another chance, you'd act differently. I've heard you say so. Is it true?"

"Why are you asking me these questions!?"

The youth's mouth snapped shut. It was apparent he could see he was getting nowhere, and it clearly frustrated him.

And then he was gone.

The nobleman spent the rest of the morning trying to decide if he should have responded differently. He prided himself on his ability to read people, and in the end he concluded reluctantly that the youth, in spite of his blunt questions and his unusual manner, was probably genuine. He also acknowledged to himself that he had been unnecessarily discourteous.

As the hours passed, the youth's question began to haunt him. What *would* he do if he was set free? He was still pondering the matter when he finally drifted off to sleep.

The hours dragged by without any further sign of his visitor. Then, a full twenty-four hours after his first appearance, the youth abruptly emerged again.

The nobleman decided to aim for a new start on a different footing. "I apologize for my rudeness yesterday," he said.

The youth ignored his attempt at civility, instead going straight to the point. "Would you try to repair your mistakes if you were freed?" he asked.

The nobleman frowned.

"Would you make the attempt?" his inquisitor insisted.

"Of course!" he hissed.

The youth nodded to himself, apparently satisfied. "Do you have anything of value?" he asked.

The nobleman hesitated, then removed an armlet of silver from his upper arm and held it up.

"It will do." The youth reached out a hand for it.

The nobleman hesitated again. Then, deciding on impulse to trust his instincts, he shrugged and handed it over.

The youth slipped away without a further word, leaving as silently as he had come.

The day passed slowly, and the nobleman saw and heard nothing more of his strange visitor. He reluctantly began to conclude that he had been taken for a fool. His only consolation was the knowledge that here, imprisoned in this cell, he had no possible use for the armlet.

Each day in the late afternoon he was served a light meal. It was never enough to fully satisfy his hunger, but he didn't doubt that other prisoners fared much worse. Today his food was brought by a guard he had never seen before. The guard put down the food and departed without locking the cell door behind him. As he walked away down the passage, his hooded cloak fell from his shoulders. He left it lying where it had fallen.

The nobleman looked on, wide eyed. Freedom beckoned. Could it really be that easy, though? Were guards lurking out of sight down the passageway, eagerly anticipating an excuse to begin mistreating him? He sat unmoving, paralyzed in an agony of indecision.

Finally the face of the youth appeared around his door, his brows furrowed in exasperation. "What are you waiting for?" he whispered fiercely.

His challenge stung the nobleman into action. He pushed at the door, wincing as it squeaked and groaned in protest. Then he slipped out of the cell, forcing the door shut behind him. Finally, he scooped up the cloak discarded by the guard and swung it across his shoulders, pulling the hood down low over his head to hide his face.

The youth beckoned, and he set off after him into the dark.

THE NOBLEMAN STOOD at a small postern door, staring out into the slowly fading light of dusk. The sun had only just set. The youth had led him on a winding route through an endless succession of dark passages until finally he felt the cool evening air on his face. Impossibly, he stood on the brink of freedom.

He turned to the youth. "Why are you doing this?"

In the dim light the expression on the face of his rescuer could not be discerned. "I can't mend my mistake," the youth replied. "Perhaps I can give you a chance to mend yours. That would be worth something to me."

For a moment setting aside his rank, the nobleman bowed low in honor of the youth.

"You need to go!" the youth insisted.

"You haven't told me your name."

"My name is Simon," he whispered back. Then he stepped inside without further comment, pulling the postern door closed behind him.

The nobleman stepped away from the walls, bending low as he ran toward the drawbridge that crossed the moat. He was relieved to see that the drawbridge was down.

His legs responded stiffly to the unaccustomed exercise, but he pushed on, not willing to lose even a minute. He needed to get across the bridge undetected, and he needed to do it quickly. He had no idea how long it might be before his absence was discovered. Perhaps not until the morning. But he couldn't take any chances. He thought about his mysterious rescuer, and hoped fervently that Simon's role in his escape would not be exposed.

As soon as he reached the bridge he stopped. Torches were positioned at various points across the bridge, but fortunately for him they had not yet been lit. Peering around him in the semi-darkness, he could see no one in sight. Taking a deep breath, he set out walking briskly across the bridge, his back straight and his head held high.

He passed the halfway mark without incident. Then he heard the sound of approaching hoof beats. Someone was riding toward the fortress. He looked quickly about him—there was nowhere to hide. The hoof beats grew closer, then he heard voices behind him, men shouting words he didn't understand.

He did the only thing he could do—he kept walking.

Two horsemen rode into view. He hugged the side of the bridge as he went and kept his head down. They rode past him without a second glance. He quickly looked behind him and saw men striding out onto the bridge, lighting the torches. He hastened forward, increasing his stride until he was all but running.

Finally reaching the end of the bridge, he followed the road a short distance until he came to a thick stand of trees. Then he moved off the road and peered out, watching for any signs of a pursuit.

None came.

The men finished lighting the torches and returned to the fortress. It was becoming clear that they hadn't even seen him.

What would you do if you were set free? Prompted by Simon's searching question, he knew exactly what he wanted to do. All he needed was a horse.

He poked around in the dark among the trees until he found a suitable fallen branch. Then he selected a place where the branches of a great tree overhung the road. Taking the lump of wood with him, he climbed onto a low hanging limb and settled down to wait. It didn't take long before a lone rider approached, coming from the fortress. As the horse passed below, he swung the piece of wood with all the force he could muster, aiming to knock the rider from his horse. The branch struck the horseman on the helmet, and he went down hard. Still armed with his tree branch, the nobleman scrambled down from the tree ready to do battle. But it was not necessary. The rider lay dead on the ground, his neck apparently broken by the fall.

The nobleman stripped the soldier of his weapons then dragged his body from the road and hid it among the trees. The horse had been spooked by his actions, and it took him a while to catch it. Once he did, he drew it aside under the trees and settled down once again to wait.

He needed to find the Rogandan army. Lord Drettroth was certain to be in constant communication with his army, which meant that he would be sending and receiving dispatches frequently. The nobleman's plan was to wait for the next outgoing dispatch rider, and simply follow him at a safe distance. The prospect of traveling through the night didn't trouble him at all; he was eager to get there as soon as he possibly could.

In the end almost an hour went by before another rider emerged from the fortress. The nobleman waited until he had passed, then swung in behind him. The challenge was to stay far enough away that he wasn't seen, but close enough that he didn't lose him.

The rider followed the road for some time before heading cross country over even ground. By then the moon had appeared low over the horizon, providing enough light for him to keep the silhouette of the rider comfortably in sight. The night wore on, each hour bringing him closer to his goal.

"THOMAS...THOMAS!...CAN YOU HEAR ME?"

The insistent voice that nagged at him was somehow vaguely familiar, but he couldn't place it. His head was swimming, rolling around groggily, not readily cooperating with his attempts to clear it. As self-awareness slowly returned he discovered that his left shoulder ached, and his head was thumping from somewhere behind his eyes.

Very reluctantly, he opened his eyes.

A dimly lit room lay before him. He was sitting almost in a corner of the room with a wall at his back. Along the adjoining wall sat the owner of the voice he had heard. It was Brother Vangellis. At the sight of the monk his eyes bulged, and his jaw sagged with surprise. His friend was chained to the wall by his ankles, although his hands were free. He had fallen silent, but he was looking at Thomas intently.

Thomas looked down and discovered that his own ankles had been chained and secured to the wall behind him. His left arm was strapped across his body in a sling, and his right arm was also chained to the wall.

Then he remembered the stone, and his heart skipped a beat. A hurried glance showed his leather pouch still secured to the belt around his waist. He strained his right hand toward it. But the chain was not long enough to allow him to reach it, and he gave up in frustration.

"Are you injured, Thomas?"

It all came back to him in a rush—releasing the Rogandans'

horses and injuring his shoulder, fleeing on horseback, a tree limb knocking him to the ground. Then he thought of Elena. He groaned.

"Thomas?!" The monk sounded thoroughly alarmed.

He looked up at his friend and shook his head. "I injured my shoulder. But I don't think I'm badly hurt." He peered around him and frowned. "Where are we?"

"We are guests of Lord Drettroth; this is his fortress. I don't exactly know where it is, though."

"How long have we been here?"

"I have been in this fortress since I was captured a few weeks ago. I was only brought to this room today, though. They brought you in here soon after."

Thomas took a closer look at the monk. "You look very thin."

His friend gave him a wry smile. "Perhaps you thought our fare was meager in the wilderness. Compared to the food here, we were feasting like kings."

Thomas closed his eyes and leaned back. It was impossible to get comfortable.

"I want to hear what's happened to you since we parted, Thomas. But there's something you should know first. Something I need to prepare you for."

The monk never had a chance to say what was on his mind. Both of them turned their heads at the sound of voices, doors opening, and footsteps approaching. Thomas felt his stomach begin to churn. He had no idea what was about to happen, but it surely couldn't be good.

18

Will stood alone on a hillside near Torbury Scarp, staring up at the blaze of stars in the cloudless sky. He knew that any further attempt at sleep was pointless.

So much would be decided on the day that was about to dawn. His men were in place, and everything had been done that needed to be done. Everything he knew to do, anyway.

His mind wandered back over the journey that had led him to this place at this time, with the armies of two kingdoms awaiting his word. Was it destiny that brought him here? Did something other than fate determine the rise and fall of kingdoms? He shook his head as if to clear it. Such matters were beyond his comprehension.

Will was a practical person, and he knew that even before the sun rose there was much that would require his attention. Taking a deep breath and pausing to settle his thoughts, he left the hillside and set off to find Lord Bottren.

THE SENTRY SAT BROODING by the fire, staring mindlessly out into the dark. His vigil seemed pointless. The Varasan camp was surrounded on both sides by the countless hordes of Rogand—it hardly needed him to be guarding it.

Try as he might, he couldn't manage to prevent himself from thinking about the pending battle. He was no different from most of his comrades—the very notion of fighting for the Rogandans left him cold. But they had no choice. He knew it as well as they all did.

He spat into the fire. A satisfying image came to his mind of Zornath roasting over the flames on a slow spit. Such a fate would be too good for that snake! He spat again.

All of a sudden a dark and hooded figure appeared at the edge of the firelight, almost startling the sentry out of his wits. The apparition became a man in a dark cloak, and the sentry leaped to his feet, reaching clumsily for his sword.

The man showed him a pair of empty hands before slowly squatting down beside the fire. The stranger greeted him quietly in the sentry's own language, then put a finger significantly to his lips. The sentry remained standing, sword in hand, staring wide eyed at the cloaked figure and trying to decide whether to call out or not.

"I need to speak with Lord Karevis urgently," the man said quietly. The sentry still didn't move, so he added, "I have a message for him."

"A message?"

"For Lord Karevis," the stranger said patiently.

The sentry remained rooted to the ground, apparently too bemused to speak.

The newcomer sighed. "I've traveled all night to get here, and I'm very weary," he said testily. "I need to see Lord Karevis. Now!"

The stranger was clearly a nobleman accustomed to being obeyed, and the sentry responded involuntarily to his air of authority. "Come with me," he said apologetically.

Still watching the newcomer warily, the sentry led him past a seemingly endless succession of campfires, weaving his way among the huddled forms of sleeping men. Finally he came to a small tent.

A pair of soldiers stood guard outside.

"This man has a message for Lord Karevis—it's urgent!" the sentry told them.

The guards looked doubtful, but after a moment's pause one of them slipped into the tent. He soon emerged with the Varasan commander.

Karevis looked tired and drawn, but he clearly hadn't been asleep. He approached the stranger and peered into his hood. His eyes grew wide.

Once again the stranger put a finger to his lips. Karevis nodded, and immediately ushered him into the tent.

Then he gave an order to the sentry. "Find my second-in-command and bring him here right now. If he's asleep, then wake him up!"

Before he disappeared into the tent himself, the commander turned to the guards. "Do not allow us to be disturbed before dawn. Not under any circumstances!"

As the sun rose above the hills on the day of the battle, Essanda turned her horse off the road. She guided it southward onto a grassy plain that stretched away toward the horizon on one side, and ended in a series of low foothills on the other. Her destination was a distant ridge where she knew a major part of the cavalry of Castel waited to join battle. She glanced up at the sun, and urged her horse forward. She knew far more than she should have known about Will's battle plan, and she was keenly aware that timing was crucial—she couldn't afford to waste a minute.

She was supposed to be leaving Hazelwood Ford with Count Gordan that very day to return to Castel Citadel, and before long her escort was going to discover that she was missing. He would be horrified when he found out what she was actually doing. As for her husband...she decided not to think about that. Neither consideration swayed her, though, not even for a moment.

She called to her page boy, ordering him to pick up his pace. He looked hesitant and pale, and she experienced a brief pang of remorse for badgering him into joining her in this mad scheme. Not wanting to travel alone, and knowing she could expect no support from those she knew and trusted, Essanda had pressed him into her service. She had insisted that she needed him to protect her. But the terrified look on his face made it obvious that he felt the need for protection much more than she did.

If she was honest with herself, she was terrified, too. She was stepping into the inferno without any clear idea about how she might find her way out again. But given what she knew—or thought she knew—she had to do something. She would never be able to live with herself if she sat back and waited for the battle to end in disaster.

She put her head down and concentrated on the plain before her. She had allowed herself two hours to reach the ridge. A lot of hard riding lay ahead of them.

IN THE HALF light before dawn, away to the west, throngs of bleary eyed men tumbled down out of Lord Burtelen's wagons. The men were allowed to stretch their cramped legs while they broke their fast. Then they were loaded back into the wagons.

Lord Burtelen had realized that the men could be transported faster than they could march, and he therefore decided to abandon the wagons only when the terrain made it necessary. With the light growing steadily stronger, they were driven forward again, and at a much faster pace than had been possible during the night.

Meanwhile, Kuper and Rellan hastily gathered their riders. They mounted the packhorses and set off, following the trail of Ranauld's cavalry. Kuper kept the riders together. He had no more idea than any of them what awaited them on the battlefield. He knew only that they needed to travel fast.

As the sun cleared the horizon, he glanced across at his brother. Whatever was going through Rellan's mind in that moment, Kuper knew that his heart was far away, in a forest refuge on the border of Erestor.

There was never any point thinking about the future when you were heading into battle. Nevertheless, Kuper sent a silent prayer into the heavens. He asked nothing for himself. All he wanted was for his brother to be safely returned to Anneka.

He turned his full attention back to the task ahead. The sun was up, and they still had a long ride ahead of them. Unable to shake off the feeling that every minute counted, he urged his horse forward. Three hundred horsemen followed hard behind him.

THE SUN HAD BARELY RISEN over the battlefield when the distant beating of drums sounded faintly in the still morning air. The army of Rogand was on the march. Every head turned to the south, squinting into the distance, watching for the first sign of the enemy. The drum beat grew steadily louder as a formless lump wriggled into view. The blot on the horizon slowly took shape and became a solid line, then a wall of moving figures crowned by the tips of thousands of glistening spears. A dense cluster of horsemen covered the Rogandan left flank, but otherwise an endless wave of men had begun to flood the even ground between Torbury Scarp on the east and the low hills to the west.

"Hold steady, men," Rufe called. He managed to keep his voice level, even though his insides were roiling. He reminded himself that he only needed to deal with the enemy soldiers within reach of his sword. He didn't have to worry about how to stem this mighty tide— Will would be working on that.

He knew that the commander stood with Lord Bottren on a low hill behind Rufe's position to the right, almost in the northwest corner of the battlefield. He would be calmly assessing the enemy, deciding where best to move his pieces on the board spread out before him.

The wall of enemy soldiers drew closer. Rufe could guess what was going on in the minds of his men. Plenty of knees would be starting to feel weak. In the brief calm before the clash of weapons, he bellowed out a challenge to his men. "These men have come to burn our homes and butcher our women and children. WHEN are we going to let them do that?"

The men roared back their answer. "NEVER!"

The Rogandans were shouting now, and his men were shouting as well. Then the two lines met, and his world narrowed to thrust, block, twist, turn, thrust again. He heard a voice roaring above the din and realized it was his own. Faces came and went before him—sculptures of fear, anger, bewilderment. It soon became little more than a confused blur.

WILL PEERED through the dust at the battle raging before him. Rufe was holding the center as he knew he would. The left flank was beginning to yield, exactly as planned. On the right wing, his horsemen had already pushed back the Rogandan cavalry. The lines shifted back and forward, as men fought and men died.

Then he spotted movement on the right flank. The Rogandans had so many soldiers milling around, there was nowhere for most of them to go. The removal of the horsemen had opened up a gap and already Rogandan soldiers were spilling into it.

Will had anticipated this outcome, and a small cavalry unit had been held in reserve to deal with it. The reserve needed to be deployed immediately. If it wasn't done quickly, his entire right flank would be surrounded. The only possible outcome would be disaster.

He turned urgently to Lord Bottren. "Our right flank, My Lord—we've got to reinforce it. Now!"

His second-in-command peered intently down into the chaos below. "I see it," he said. He moved swiftly, barking orders as he went, with no trace of panic. Within minutes the cavalry reserve unit—the only reserve unit—had closed the gap, and the line had stabilized.

Bottren reappeared, and Will dipped his head in silent acknowledgment of his quick action. The nobleman quickly turned away, apparently to hide the smile of satisfaction that had flashed across his face. Will returned his attention to the conflict.

The Rogandans were beginning to pour into the breach on the allied left flank, spreading out along the cliff face. Will's men were pivoting left to accommodate them. The enemy had so many soldiers that the new allied front line was forced backward, reforming further away from the escarpment.

Will's men made space as the Rogandans surged forward across the base of the escarpment. The Rogandan force was beginning to resemble a long stretched out wineskin. Will was planning to cork it at each end with his horsemen—the riders already in the field would seal off the far end, and Lord Eisgold's cavalry, waiting on a ridge to the rear, would seal off the near end.

The Rogandan cavalry must have been driven away, because some of Will's mounted soldiers had begun to reappear on the battlefield. They were attempting to plug the far end of the wineskin, away to the south.

The first Rogandan soldiers had reached the near end, to the north, and were already pushing hard at the thin line that held them in. There were so many of them that if they ever succeeded in escaping the containment they would quickly begin to swarm around the allied position. There was no time to lose—Lord Eisgold's horsemen must charge down to seal the northern end of the line, and they must do it immediately.

Will sent a dispatch rider hurrying to Eisgold with the directive. He did so with an acute awareness that the moment of truth had arrived. Would Eisgold follow orders, or would he withhold his forces at the crucial moment as he had done at Pinder's Flat? The pressure was growing by the minute—the position was deteriorating much more rapidly than Will could ever have anticipated. A wave of anxiety overwhelmed him for the first time on this momentous day, as the fate of kingdoms hung in the balance.

THE RIDGE WAS at last within reach, and the ground began to slope upward noticeably. For some time Essanda had been able to see

Castelan horsemen massed at its summit. None of the soldiers had noticed her or her companion, though. The two of them had almost reached the steeper slopes of the hill before they were finally spotted. The moment they were seen, a rider detached himself from the ridge and rode swiftly to intercept them.

Essanda understood the distraction of the soldiers. The distant sounds of battle—the cries of men and horses and the clash of metal on metal—were penetrating faintly even to her current position.

"Your Majesty! What are you doing here?" She didn't know the soldier, but he had clearly recognized her.

"Take me to Lord Eisgold!" she commanded, feigning a confidence she didn't feel. The soldier bowed his head respectfully and swung his horse in beside her. She turned to her page boy. "Wait for me here," she instructed him.

The soldier guided her to the crest of the ridge, and they soon found themselves among the men. He took her to the middle of the line, and led her forward.

She steered her horse between the last of the riders into an open space before the waiting ranks. After taking a deep breath to steady herself, she turned to face them. Every head turned in her direction. She reached up and removed her helm, then she tossed her head to free her long unbound tresses. Her hair streamed out behind her as the wind caught it. The rays of the sun lit up her burnished breastplate, and the crisp white gown beneath it billowed softly about her in the breeze. A collective gasp escaped from the lips of the soldiers as they gazed upon her and realized who she was.

She exerted every ounce of her self control, presenting them with a stern and determined face. Inwardly, though, she glowed with satisfaction. She knew she was dazzling—she could see it in their faces. The men were giving her exactly the reception she had been hoping for.

Lord Eisgold rode up, his face red and his brows furrowed. "Essanda, Your Majesty! What on earth are you doing?" he demanded. "Who brought you here? This is no place for a girl!"

"I have come to salute my men," she replied, loudly enough that all could hear. They raised a cheer in response.

She was Princess of Castel, and Queen of Arvenon, and in that moment she knew that she had been born and raised for such a time as this. Young as she was, she understood what she needed to say and how to say it. She turned calmly toward the gathered ranks.

"Today you face great danger for king and country," she called, her young voice ringing out strong and clear. "Some of you may not return. You fight to defend those you hold dear, and we love you for it! I have come here now, on the eve of battle, to honor your courage and your sacrifice."

She fell silent, raising an arm high in salute. The men rose in their stirrups and cheered, banging their spears against their shields. The noise was deafening. She dipped her head low in acknowledgment.

Lord Eisgold stared at her in astonishment. His eyes flicked from her, to his men, then back to her again. The enraptured response of his soldiers was not lost on him. She smiled to herself, knowing that she had placed him in a difficult position. Her presence was good for the morale of his men. Even a fool could see that. But Eisgold did not want her there.

"My Lord, I know I must leave soon," she said, preempting him. "I do not wish to interfere with you carrying out your duty. I trust you will indulge me for a few minutes longer, though."

"Your Majesty," he acknowledged with a dip of his head. He cast an eye once again toward his men, then back to her. "Perhaps a moment more," he conceded. "Then one of my men will escort you to safety."

For the first time she allowed her attention to be drawn down to the battle raging below her. From this vantage point it was plainly evident that Will and his men were impossibly outnumbered. Surely the commander must call upon his Castelan allies soon!

As if in response to her thoughts, a dispatch rider galloped up, his horse in a lather. "The commander sends his respects," he said, addressing himself to Lord Eisgold. "His orders are for you to proceed with your attack as planned."

A ripple of nervous expectancy went through the waiting ranks.

"Was that the commander's message? Did you convey it exactly?" Lord Eisgold asked haughtily.

"Yes, My Lord," the rider confirmed.

"When is our attack expected, then?" Eisgold asked.

"Now, of course!" replied the messenger, a baffled look on his face.

"The message said *nothing* about timing," Eisgold insisted.

The rider stared back at him in bewilderment. A few of the Castelan soldiers murmured openly.

"Well, don't just sit there!" Eisgold shouted at him. "Return to your commander and clarify the order!"

Wide eyed, the dispatch rider spurred his horse and galloped back toward the beleaguered captain of Arvenon.

So her instincts had been right—all of it was true. She hadn't come all this way for no reason.

Essanda turned to Eisgold, holding her anger in check with difficulty. "By the time he returns, My Lord, it may be too late," she said pointedly, once again speaking loudly.

Eisgold rounded on her. "With respect, Your Majesty," he said curtly, "military strategy is not the province of girls." He turned to one of his aides. "Escort Her Majesty to the rear," he ordered.

"Not before I honor our flag," she replied sharply, raising herself up in her stirrups and lifting a hand commandingly. The aide faltered. Eisgold frowned, and she moved swiftly before he could speak again.

Riding to the young man bearing the standard, she stretched out her hand and beckoned for the flag. The standard bearer lowered it to her, and she grasped it in both hands, kissing it reverently. Her action drew another cheer from the watching throngs. Once more she had their full attention.

Moving suddenly, she snatched the flag from the hand of the startled standard bearer. She separated herself from him and raised the standard high. "You have been called to battle," she cried in her clear high voice. "Now is the time for deeds of renown! For the king! For Castel! For your commander!"

Spinning her horse around, she raced away down the hill toward the fighting. A mighty roar rose from fifteen hundred throats as a sea of mounted warriors surged down behind her from the ridge. Essanda saw the young standard bearer riding beside her, and thrust the flag back into his hands. He raised it high, adding his voice to the din.

Slowing her pace, she allowed the tide of men and horses to sweep by her. Once she found herself alone, she turned her horse and headed back up the hill. Lord Eisgold remained on the ridge astride his stallion, alone apart from a handful of his aides. Moments later, though, he galloped down the hill in pursuit of his men, his aides close behind him. He turned toward her as he rode past, and she plainly saw the fury on his face.

Lord Eisgold had followed through with his plan. And she had followed through with hers. She permitted herself a grim little smile of satisfaction.

Essanda rode alone up onto the empty ridge.

THE SUN HAD PASSED its zenith, and the battle was moving into a new and dangerous phase. Will's soldiers had been pressing hard on the Rogandans all along the line, forcing them back inch by inch toward Torbury Scarp, attempting to pack them in so densely they would be unable to fight effectively. But the enemy had shown plenty of spirit, and Will's men had been gaining ground more slowly than he had hoped. His battle plan was intact, but unless the allies could force the Rogandans back more decisively, they risked losing the initiative. Before long Will's soldiers must surely be worn down by sheer weight of numbers. The allied armies had already sustained fearful losses.

Will himself had become increasingly testy, and on occasion Lord Bottren had only restrained him with difficulty from charging down and lending his own weight to the fighting. In spite of his reckless impulses, though, the commander did not fail to recognize that he was needed where he was.

Then, slowly and inexorably, the tides of war began to turn, and Will found himself struggling to find a way to prevent the complete collapse of the armies he commanded.

A throbbing boom-boom-boom pounded ominously in the distance, growing slowly in volume. Marching steadily to the drumbeat, an entire Rogandan army appeared at the southern extremity of the battlefield, unexpected and unwelcome, promising a bitter end to the hopes of Arvenon and Castel. The horde was so vast that Will did not even attempt to guess at their numbers.

Responding swiftly, he sent dispatch riders scurrying down to the right flank of the allies, at the far end of the battlefield. He watched on in nervous tension as the riders arrived, and the men sealing off the southern end of the Rogandan containment abandoned their previous strategy and swung around awkwardly to face the new threat. The enemy soldiers approaching from the south were so numerous that Will knew that his fighters would quickly be swept away before the coming onslaught.

Then the Rogandan commander struck his final blow. Behind the new Rogandan horde, Will and the watchers at his position could dimly glimpse the banners of the Varasan army. Together, the two new armies far exceeded the size of Will's entire force. Introducing the Varasans to the battle seemed to be little more than an idle boast, because the Rogandan advantage was overwhelming even without them.

The armies of four kingdoms had now crowded onto the field. Will stood and watched, and waited for the onslaught. He had no further reserves to commit, and no possible rearrangement of his armies offered any hope of defeating the forces now arrayed against him.

19

The door to the prison room swung open. Two guards marched in and positioned themselves near Brother Vangellis and Thomas. Nothing about their appearance or manner offered the faintest whiff of encouragement to Thomas. His stomach twisted tighter.

Another man walked in, tall and dark haired. Something indefinable about his bearing said he was a man accustomed to power. Thomas didn't need to be told that he wielded power ruthlessly and without mercy.

Nor did the man need any introduction. Without any possibility of doubt, Thomas was now face to face with the one man he had tried for so long to avoid.

Lord Drettroth glanced across at them and nodded, a smile of casual satisfaction on his face.

One last person walked into the room, and Thomas gasped in shock and disbelief. It was Simon. The youth's brows were furrowed, and his face wore a defiant frown.

A number of mysteries instantly resolved themselves for Thomas. He no longer had to guess how the Rogandan lord knew he had the stone—Simon must have betrayed him. Thomas had told Brother

Vangellis that no one else other than Will knew about the stone. But he realized belatedly that he had been mistaken. Simon had, of course, briefly held the stone as well. At the time Simon almost certainly had no awareness of what the stone was capable of. But he must have heard whispers from the Council meeting where Pisander was exposed, and put the pieces together. And so he had somehow slipped away from Arnost and found Drettroth.

The spitefulness behind Simon's actions was beyond comprehension. Thomas had witnessed so much suffering. The sacking of the monastery, the capture and mistreatment of Brother Vangellis, and now his own capture—all of it had come about simply because Simon hated him and wanted to see him suffer. Thomas wondered if he was satisfied. He certainly didn't look happy.

Drettroth broke in on his dark wanderings. "What a merry reunion this is!" he said, a humorless smile twisting his face. He turned to Brother Vangellis. "I did promise that you would soon be reunited with your companion, did I not? And here he is."

Drettroth turned to Simon. "I understand you've become acquainted with the monk as well, my Simon. You seem to have been spending a lot of time with him lately," he said. He watched their faces closely, before tipping back his head and laughing harshly. "Surely you're not surprised. I make sure I know what's going on in my own fortress."

He addressed Simon again. "You've been playing some little games with another of my guests, too. Don't imagine there will not be consequences. I take it personally when people decide to cross me."

The Rogandan licked his lips, and Thomas shuddered. He had no sympathy at all for Simon after his betrayal, but the Rogandan lord filled him with horror.

Drettroth turned his attention to Thomas. "It must have been quite some time since you last saw Simon," he said with an ironic smile. "You must be delighted to find yourself reunited with him once again."

It was clear that no response was expected of Thomas, and he offered none. The angry scowl on his face said all he wanted to say.

"I'm sure that's more than enough of pleasantries, though," said Drettroth. He turned to the guards and spoke to them rapidly in Rogandan. They left the room, closing the door behind them.

The Rogandan lord turned back to his prisoners. "We're all here for one reason. Simon, fetch the stone from Thomas."

Simon walked over to Thomas and knelt down, reaching out to his pouch. Thomas reacted violently, thrashing around in a vain attempt to deny him access to it. All he succeeded in doing was to make his shoulder hurt even more. In final frustration he used the only weapon available to him—he leaned swiftly forward and head butted Simon.

The younger boy cried out in pain and reeled back, rubbing his head vigorously and wincing. He approached again, more carefully this time, staying out of range as he opened the pouch and reached in for the stone.

Thomas yelled his frustration out loud, but he was unable to prevent Simon from emerging with the stone in his hand. Simon stood gazing at him for a moment, his face revealing more regret than triumph, then spun on his heel and headed over to Drettroth.

Drettroth watched the progress of the stone with an expression revealing both longing and gratification. When Simon reached him he stretched out a hand. "Give it to me!" he commanded.

Simon hesitated for a lingering moment, then handed it over. Drettroth twirled it slowly around and around in his hand, consuming it hungrily with his eyes. Then he permitted himself a smug nod. "There can be no doubt about it," he said with satisfaction. "It is the Stone of Knowing, as I expected. It has come to me at last!"

He turned to Thomas. "Perhaps you will be surprised," he said, "but I have no intention of keeping the stone. I will not be taking the slightest risk with this prize. I will not take it by force. It will remain with you. It will be yours until you freely decide to give it to me."

He gave Thomas an indulgent smirk. "You may find it difficult to imagine yourself giving me the stone, young man. The truth is that you will not just be willing to hand it over—you will be frenzied in your eagerness. After the proper encouragement, of course."

He returned it to Simon, then jabbed a finger in the direction of Thomas. The youth retraced his steps and restored the stone to Thomas's pouch, much more warily this time. Drettroth approached Thomas himself, and after a warning glare to discourage any repeat of the prisoner's earlier aggressive behavior, satisfied himself that the stone was indeed safely back in the pouch.

"You should understand how generous I have been in my treatment of you, young Thomas," Drettroth told him, "especially considering the amount of trouble you have put me to. It seems you had a dislocated shoulder. My men have reset it, and it will heal in time, provided you are careful," he promised. "And also assuming you live long enough," he added with another mirthless smile.

"You need to understand—all of you—that your future is entirely in my hands," he continued. "Perhaps you have hopes that your friends will somehow prevail against my armies, but that is no more than an idle fancy.

"Arvenon and Castel have capable soldiers—I am the first to acknowledge it. But between them they have proven incapable of assembling an army with any hope of defeating my forces. Even if reinforcements from Erestor had been able to reach them in time, and even if they had persuaded the troublesome Varasans to join them as allies, they still would not have enough men." He paused to let his words sink in.

Thomas wasn't convinced. Will and Rufe had defeated much larger forces before, and he was certain they would somehow find a way to do so again.

Drettroth saw his reaction and offered him a condescending smile. "You have no way of knowing it, Thomas, but a battle is being fought today. Right now, in fact. And I'm sorry to be the bearer of bad tidings, but by now your friends will have discovered the little surprise I have prepared for them. They know they are facing a much bigger army today, and they know it is not the entire Rogandan force. But they think the rest of my men are spread far and wide throughout every corner of Arvenon and Varas. They are so very wrong.

"I have long planned this battle, and I have secretly gathered together every one of my soldiers stationed throughout the whole of Arvenon—from everywhere except Erestor.

"I have even withdrawn the bulk of my occupying force from Varas. I will send them back as soon as their job here is done." He paused, sighing with contentment. It was becoming obvious to Thomas that the Rogandan liked the sound of his own voice.

"The end result is that I have assembled a second Rogandan army, one that is bigger in its own right than the combined forces of Arvenon and Castel." Drettroth's face glowed with pride, and he swelled with self-satisfaction. "That army has just arrived at the battlefield and is even now joining the fight.

"Your friends will have been very busy making plans. But all of it is for naught. There are simply too few of them. They will be overwhelmed. Even their much vaunted commander will not be able to rescue the situation this time.

"No, by the time the sun sets, the armies of Arvenon and Castel will be finished. The two kingdoms will be finished as well—they will be ripe for the plucking."

Thomas tried desperately to believe that it wasn't true, that Drettroth was lying, or at least exaggerating in his conceit. But he was not able to convince himself.

"None of this makes any difference to you, though, Thomas," the Rogandan continued. "I intend to get the stone, and the only question that matters is whether you are going to make it easy or difficult.

"The hard way will not be pleasant. Not for any of us. Look at our monk here, for example. I have a feeling that a man like him might take a very long time to die. The screams can go on and on. It's all very distasteful.

"And what about you? If, at the very last, you refuse to save yourself, I cannot in all conscience simply allow you to expire—I'm sorry to say I will need to make life unbearable for you. You will long for death, but it will be denied you. I must actively encourage you to rid yourself of the burdensome encumbrance of the stone. Prolonging your suffering will be the only way I can extend your opportunity to do that.

"By the time you do eventually yield—and I promise that you will!—you will beg and plead with me to end your life. By then, your death will be inevitable, of course. It will only be a matter of timing. As a reward, I may decide to be merciful and grant you a quick release from your suffering. Once I have used the stone to pick your mind clean of information, that is."

He shrugged, and spread his hands wide. "None of this is necessary, though. The easy way is for you to simply give it to me. If you do that, the monk doesn't have to die. And, more importantly as far as you're concerned, you don't need to die, either.

"I'm sure I can find a use for you both should you choose the path of common sense." He nodded in the direction of Simon and sighed eloquently. "Simon here has been doing a fine job as my food taster. I suspect that sooner or later I will need a replacement, though. I seem to have acquired so many enemies. I simply cannot understand the reason why." He raised his arms in a gesture of helplessness.

Thomas was already learning to loathe Drettroth as much as he feared him—he had no difficulty at all understanding why the man had enemies.

"A man like myself needs the protection offered by this stone. I can trust Simon to devote himself to ensuring that my food and drink are safe, because I know he is a coward at heart—he has already demonstrated that he will go to extreme lengths to preserve his miserable life. But not everyone is so reliable, and the stone will remove any possible doubt about the motives of every person I am forced to rely upon."

The idea of Drettroth having the power to read minds was the stuff of nightmares. Thomas refused to even imagine the implications.

Drettroth's eyes were alight, his face creased in a triumphant grin. "I have it at last!" He laughed, an evil cackle that inspired nothing but horror.

The Rogandan returned his attention to Thomas. "I have told you that a great battle is being fought, at this very moment. Perhaps you are wondering why I am not with my army. I care nothing for battles!"

he said, waving an arm dismissively. "Battles are a means to an end, nothing more. And I have mustered such an overwhelming force that my soldiers cannot fail to win. Even without me there to drive them forward.

"No, I care for one thing only—I must have this stone!

"It should have been mine long ago. I once entrusted one of my servants with the task of retrieving it and bringing it to me. Instead, the fool kept it for himself and fled. I hunted him for years, and learned eventually that he had made his way to Arvenon. Since that time I have taken a very special interest in your kingdom."

So it was true—the stone *was* the reason for the war. That possibility had occurred to Thomas, but he had never believed it could actually be true.

"Perhaps the timing has proven fortuitous—my understanding of the stone was incomplete at that time. Now I am fully prepared, and more in need of it than ever.

"How the stone came to be in your possession, Thomas, I do not know and don't care. But it was only thanks to Simon that I learned you were the one who had it, and even then not until after you had fled your capital. You have led me a merry chase since that time. Your paltry efforts to hide from me were always doomed to futility, though." He gave Thomas a contemptuous smile. "You were a fool if you thought you could escape me. Once I put my hand to a task, I never give up. Never!"

Thomas turned his head away, unable to endure the gloating look on the Rogandan's face.

Drettroth continued. "You may not be aware, Thomas, but there are other stones, too, offering virtues of their own. I have certain knowledge of them, and I will not rest until all of them are in my possession! I will bring these virtues together to ensure the security and longevity of my rule. I intend to create an empire that will last beyond your wildest imaginings.

"I have worked unstintingly to arrive in this place at this time. Perhaps you will begin to see that your hopes and dreams are insignificant in comparison with the great tasks that I am undertaking. You cannot stand in the way of destiny. I will not allow it!"

A look of unshakable resolve commanded Drettroth's face. The Rogandan lord stood silent for a moment, his feet firmly planted and his arms folded.

"I will leave you now. Consider your options carefully, Thomas. If you are planning to refuse me, you need to take this one opportunity to explain to the monk why his life means nothing to you.

"I will return in one hour for your answer. Don't imagine that you can stall me—I am not a patient man."

Drettroth directed a penetrating look at Thomas. Then he left, pushing Simon out ahead of him. The door closed behind them.

Thomas turned to Brother Vangellis. "What am I going to do? Drettroth is evil, pure evil! If he gets the stone, there'll be no hope for anyone."

"You can't give him the stone, Thomas. Don't be fooled, even for a moment, into doing what he wants. And certainly don't give it to him because you think it will save me. He's the kind of man who would kill me anyway, just for the pleasure of it."

Thomas squeezed his eyes shut and shook his head in denial. It was beyond understanding. Why did the balance have to be tilted so strongly against people who simply wanted to live quietly and in peace—people who were just trying to do what was right?

He opened his eyes again, and narrowed them in anger. "This is Simon's fault! All of it. The miserable toad doesn't deserve to live."

"Don't be too harsh on him, Thomas. He is sorry for what he did. I believe he would take it back if he could."

"How can you excuse him? You've suffered as much as anyone, and it's all thanks to him!"

The monk held his peace.

Thomas shook his head hopelessly. "We did everything we could to hide from Drettroth," he said, "but it was useless—he caught us anyway. Pretty soon there won't be anyone left who's free.

"King Steffan doesn't want to control every other kingdom! And Will might be a great commander, but he isn't fighting just for the sake of it. Now that our kingdom has been invaded, he has no other choice.

"I don't understand it. Why do people like Drettroth have to win all the time?"

The monk did not reply.

"We can't even trust our own people," said Thomas. "Elbruhe died because Baron Rudungen betrayed us. Now Simon's betrayed us. Meanwhile, Drettroth has huge armies just waiting to do whatever he says. How can anyone possibly stand against him?"

"Why can't good people have the power for once?" Thomas fell silent, hanging his head in misery.

After a long delay, Brother Vangellis finally spoke. "These are big questions, Thomas. I don't have simple answers for you. All I know is that we always have choices, whatever situation we're facing. We can choose to do what's right, or we can try to find excuses to justify doing what we know deep down is wrong. We can decide to act with integrity, even if we know it won't change the outcome. Even if it seems completely pointless, and everyone else around us has chosen the easy way."

"Does that mean the two of us have to decide to be tortured and to die?" Thomas asked, unable to keep the dismay from his voice.

"Perhaps it does," the monk replied. "But at least we won't be dying for nothing. Drettroth can't control the stone unless you give it to him."

"I know what the right choice is," Thomas said. "But how can I just sit here and watch them torture you? And what if I'm not strong enough when my turn comes?"

"God will give you the strength you need, if you ask him," was all the monk offered.

They both fell silent.

Thomas, distressed and restless, squirmed uncomfortably in his chains. He wasn't at all ready to die. He wanted to live.

In spite of his own convictions about what was right, he began to cast about in his mind, searching for any possible rationale that might permit him to simply hand over the stone and be done with it.

He began to question all of his assumptions. What made him think it was his responsibility to decide who should possess the Stone of Knowing? Surely that was arrogance on his part. The stone had only come to him in the first place because of pure chance. It was obvious that Drettroth had known about it for years.

And why was it his place to deal with Drettroth? There were plenty of people in the world much more important—and more capable—than a lowly stable hand. Surely it was up to them to decide what to do about Drettroth, whether or not the Rogandan had the stone.

His mind churned on and on. In the end, though, he knew that the monk was right, and that he was only looking for excuses. He was unable to shake off one simple fact—however it had come about, he was the one with the stone. That made it his responsibility.

Two things finally helped to settle him. One was Brother Vangellis. The monk had no say at all in what was about to happen, and it was almost certainly going to end very badly for him. Yet he was facing it with remarkable grace. Thomas had known for a long time how much he had to learn from Brother Vangellis. He was seeing it more clearly than ever in this desperate situation.

The other thing that helped him was the memory of Elena. She might be far away, but he had not forgotten her and all that she meant to him, and he was in no doubt about what she would encourage him to do, much as she wouldn't want to lose him.

His decision was made. He was not going to cooperate with Drettroth. Whatever the consequences.

Anxious and afraid, he watched the door, hoping against hope that Drettroth's return would for some reason be long delayed.

20

From her vantage point, Essanda could see the horsemen of Castel locked in a furious struggle for survival. Until now she had failed utterly to grasp the immensity of the task that lay before Steffan and his allies. The army of her enemies was vast beyond comprehending.

Nor had she understood at all the horror of war. She herself had called her soldiers to battle. She wondered now if any of them would live to see another dawn. She had no misgivings about her actions. She had done what needed to be done—of that she was certain. But in that moment the stark reality of the conflict below was too awful for her to bear, and she was left feeling ill and weak. A single tear escaped her eye and rolled down her cheek.

Alone on the ridge with a battle raging below her, she recognized that Lord Eisgold had been right about one thing—this was no place for a girl. Dizzy and anxious, and oppressed by the weight of the burden of responsibility she had taken upon herself, she crested the rise and headed her horse down toward the page boy who still waited below.

As soon as she rejoined him, they set off quickly, returning along the way they had come. No more than a few minutes had passed before a small group of riders appeared in the distance, racing toward them at full gallop from the direction of Hazelwood Ford. Long before she recognized the leading horseman, she knew who it must be.

The rider pulled his steaming horse to a halt before her. He said nothing, but his wide, reproachful eyes conveyed far more than words could ever have done.

A new teardrop emerged, quickly followed by another. Her tears threatened to become a torrent. The bold young queen had vanished, leaving behind a pale and frightened girl.

"I'm tired, and I'm worried, Gordy," she said, her voice trembling. "Please take me away from here."

THE ROGANDAN CAMP had long since emptied and the sun had passed its highest point in the heavens before Zornath sent for Karevis. "Our commander has reserved a little role for the army of Varas," the Rogandan told him condescendingly. "You will be privileged to witness the annihilation that must be visited upon the enemies of Rogand. And, as favored vassals and allies, you will be allowed to twist the knife into the Arvenians before they meet their final end. As a reward you will be granted a small share in the spoils of victory. The greatest reward will, of course, come from doing your duty." He flashed his teeth.

Karevis offered no response.

The Varasan army soon marched out in full battle array. They followed a much larger contingent of Rogandan soldiers—at least twice their number—onto the battlefield.

Zornath rode at their head, with Karevis close behind. If Zornath noticed a new aide riding beside the Varasan commander, he chose not to comment on it.

Soon the fighting could be seen and heard ahead. It was immediately obvious that the Arvenians and Castelans were already massively outnumbered.

Zornath turned to Karevis. "Now your men will join the fight. On to victory!"

Karevis drew his sword. He turned to his men. "You've heard what the Rogandans want from us. Now hear from your KING!"

The new aide accompanying Karevis spun around to face the men. Throwing off his helm, he raised himself in his stirrups. "I am Delmar, your king!" he shouted. "DEATH to the Rogandans!"

An astonished silence greeted him. Time seemed to stand still for a long moment as the soldiers of Varas stood frozen in a state of shock. For so long they had been threatened and manipulated. For so long they had endured humiliation and frustration. Now, as if by magic, their sovereign had reappeared, commanding them to turn on their oppressors. He was suddenly and unexpectedly offering them the fitting outlet for their pent up rage. Recovering abruptly from their surprise, they found their voices. A deafening roar erupted from their throats.

Everything happened very quickly after that. The first to die were the small number of informants in the Varasan ranks. The Rogandan liaisons followed swiftly after them.

Zornath, howling with fury, raised his sword and charged at Delmar. Karevis thrust his horse into the Rogandan's path, his own weapon lifted high. The horses screamed as they collided, and Zornath turned his wrath upon the commander. Raw hatred covered the face of the Rogandan as he aimed a vicious blow at his former subordinate. Steel rang on steel as Karevis blocked the thrust.

Shouting their battle cry, the army of Varas surged forward, their king at their head. Impatient to engage the enemy, the ranks parted and flowed around the two combatants. The men knew how much their commander despised Zornath, and were more than content to leave it to him to deal with the hated Rogandan serpent. None of them doubted the outcome for a moment, and none felt any need to remain behind to witness the contest apart from two of Karevis's senior aides. The aides waited patiently to one side, keeping well clear to allow their commander plenty of room.

Having lorded it over the Varasan soldiers for so long, Zornath found himself utterly ignored by them. This loss of face was the final indignity for the Rogandan. Incandescent with fury, he began raining blows upon Karevis until the air rang with the sound of their clashes.

The Varasan commander was not dismayed at all. How could he be, when this very contest had been the unwavering theme of his favorite daydreams? He had never dared to hope that it could actually happen. As the two of them traded blows, he felt an idiot grin of pure delight spreading slowly across his face.

Zornath's energetic sallies proved entirely ineffective, and he soon began to visibly tire. As his fury cooled, a look first of alarm, then of panic, began to distort his face. The smile on Karevis grew broader, and he began in his turn to press in relentlessly on his enemy.

The former tyrant began to glance frantically around him, no doubt seeking a way to break free. He could ill afford the lapse in concentration, though, because it led swiftly to his downfall. Karevis saw an opening and lunged forward, his sweeping stroke slipping through the guard of his hated enemy. Bearing a jagged wound to his neck, Zornath slid from the saddle and slumped to the ground.

Karevis only paused long enough to satisfy himself that Zornath would trouble his countrymen no more. Then, followed closely by his aides, he turned his horse toward the battle and set off after his king and his army.

The Rogandans had been taken by surprise when Delmar and his army smashed into them from the rear. The Varasans quickly thrust deeply into the Rogandan lines, and the battle had moved away from Karevis. As he rode forward he was forced to pick his way around piles of Rogandan dead. He was not at all surprised by the ferocity with which his countrymen had attacked their overlords, and he noted with satisfaction that few of his own soldiers lay among the slain.

Karevis knew he should be thinking about the strategic situation, but at that moment he did not care. There was just one thing he wanted, and so badly it almost felt like physical pain. He wanted to make the Rogandans pay.

THE TIDE HAD TURNED AGAIN with the defection of Varas. Nevertheless, victory was far from Will's grasp.

The Rogandan position now resembled a bent arm, with the forearm stretched along the escarpment, and a thick upper arm at right angles to it across the southern end of the battlefield. The upper arm was bordered by the Varasans to the south, and a thin line of Arvenians and Castelans to the north.

Bottren stood beside his commander, looking dispirited. "This battle is not turning out at all as we expected," he said. "The Varasans are doing a lot of damage to the Rogandans, though," he added, awe in his voice.

"They're doing their job a bit too well," Will replied. "Our men opposite them are struggling to hold their positions. They've been fighting since early this morning, and the Varasans are starting to force too many Rogandans onto them." He scanned the flanks once again. "Our biggest risk is over there," he said, pointing to the western side of the position.

"You're worried about the Rogandans breaking out?" Bottren replied.

Will nodded. "Their sheer numbers pose a huge problem for us. If they manage to burst out, they'll spill into the area behind our lines. Our men right along the escarpment will be surrounded."

"That would mean a complete collapse!" Bottren said.

Will nodded grimly. "We have a difficult choice to make, and almost no time to decide," he said. "We can hold our current positions. If the Rogandans break out, though, it will lead to disaster. The battle will be over." He peered across the battlefield. "There's another option that will buy us some time. But we'll have to reform our line completely. It's extremely risky. And we'll be saying goodbye to any hope of forcing a victory."

As they watched, the Rogandans broke through the defenders at the very top of the arm. The lines slowly bent and twisted to seal the breach. The breach was repaired, but even from this distance it was clearly achieved with considerable difficulty. Will didn't want to think about the cost.

"The decision has just been made for us," Will said. "It isn't a question of whether the Rogandans will break out. It's just a matter of time."

Will turned aside and rapidly issued orders. Dispatch riders were soon racing to every section of the allied lines.

"What are you doing?" Bottren asked him anxiously.

"I'm pulling our men back. We need to form a new line. Down here." He swept his arm left to right below their position. "The Varasans are already holding a similar line, across the southern end. I'm instructing our men nearest to their line to join the Varasans." He pointed away to the far end of the battlefield where the Varasans were fighting.

"We need to do it right now. We won't get another opportunity."

ANDER HAD QUICKLY EMERGED as a key leader in the thin Arvenian line that had swung around to face the second Rogandan army. He and his men had survived only because of the vicious Varasan assault on the rear of the new Rogandan force. Having now received Will's orders to push through the Rogandans and join the Varasans, Ander was eager to carry out these instructions as soon as possible. His men, vastly outnumbered and in continuous action for far too long, were perilously close to collapse. And the relative safety of the Varasan line lay near at hand—tantalizingly so.

"One more push, men. After me!" Ander bellowed. Willing himself to summon up a new burst of energy, he threw himself at the enemy soldiers before him. The men facing him saw what was coming and fell back to avoid him. They were keeping an anxious eye on the Varasans fighting behind them, though, and their caution quickly dissolved into confusion. A fighting wedge formed behind Ander, and together they carved their way deeply through the Rogandan line.

The men opposing them thinned considerably, then disappeared entirely as the Varasans stepped forward and attacked them vigorously from the rear. They were through!

Ander turned, determined to keep the gap in the Rogandan line open. He soon realized that he was not alone—a solid wedge of Varasans had quickly formed on either side of him. Seeing them, the Rogandans melted away, and the last of his men stumbled wearily forward to safety.

The Varasans stepped around him, and he found himself behind the front line. He leaned wearily on his sword, sucking in great gulps of air.

A Varasan leader appeared before him. The dust, sweat, and blood that covered the man could not mask the unmistakable air of authority about him.

"Well met!" he said with a grim smile. "I am Karevis. I command these men."

"I am Ander. My thanks to you, Commander!" Ander replied. "Your help was timely indeed. We were ordered to push through to your lines. Some others might need your help, too."

"Your line bunched into four groups," Karevis replied, speaking rapidly. "Yours was the first through, thanks to your own efforts. Two other groups have also made it through with our help. The fourth is in trouble. Can you come with me?"

Ander readily agreed. The commander led him swiftly to the left flank of the Varasan position where a large pocket of Ander's comrades fought desperately behind enemy lines. They stood back to back, surrounded entirely by Rogandan soldiers. The Varasan line was driving forward toward them, but the pocket was slowly being pushed further away.

Karevis wasted no time. Barking orders rapidly, he drew together a sizable group of his soldiers. With a newly energized Ander at his side, Karevis led a vicious attack on the Rogandan line to the right of the stranded men. Such was their ferocity that they drove clean through the enemy line. The rescued soldiers raised a ragged cheer as the two forces merged.

Now the tables were turned. Their swift action had left a cluster of Rogandans cut off from their main force. About one hundred men on the extreme end of the flank were now stranded, and the Varasans surrounded them and pressed in hard against them. Fighting side by side, Karevis and Ander drew the combined line tight. They forced their way back toward the main Varasan force, driving the trapped men before them. The rate of their forward movement kept the Rogandans constantly off balance. None of them escaped.

"Take your men out of the battle line and let them rest briefly," Karevis told him. "My men are fresher. And you've been having all the excitement."

"We're in your debt, Commander!" Ander told him gratefully, at once moving to follow his suggestion.

"Never fear," said Karevis. "There will still be plenty of them left once your men are ready for another round." Then he was gone, no doubt searching out the place where he was needed the most.

Rufe Sarjant commanded the main body of men facing the Rogandans along the face of Torbury Scarp. Will had ordered a pivot backward to form a new line—at right angles to their current position—that would seal off the northern end of the battlefield immediately below Will's command post. The entire battle line, currently stretched out in front of the cliff face, would need to swing back in a sweeping arc. The men fighting at the leftmost, northern, end of the line would scarcely need to move at all. Those at the far southern end would have to retreat diagonally across almost the entire battlefield, fighting every step of the way.

Rufe knew he was in trouble as soon as Will's order had been relayed to him. He trusted his commander implicitly, and he didn't doubt that Will was fully aware of the risks attending this new maneuver. Will must have a compelling reason to issue such an order. He also knew that no help would be forthcoming to assist his men as they pulled away from the escarpment. They could not protect their right flank, either—Will would need to worry about that.

Rufe ran along the line, splitting his men into two parallel groups running the length of the battle line. The first group would need to stand and fight while the second group swung back a short distance. Then the second group would turn to cover the first group while they did the same. The pattern would need to be repeated until they reached their new position.

Such a maneuver would challenge the most disciplined of soldiers when they were fresh. Rufe's men had already been fighting for hours, as well as being heavily outnumbered. If some of the men moved too fast or too slow, holes would open up in the line. There was nothing he could do to prevent that, though. Will would notice the problem if it began to develop. He would have to deal with it.

Rufe issued orders for the movement to begin. Then without delay he set out toward the right of the line, where his men came nearest to the Varasans. These men would need the most support, because they had the furthest distance to travel.

The maneuver began. His men immediately came under intense pressure as the Rogandans spilled out from their containment and moved to the attack. As the previously solid battle line began to dissolve, Rufe was forced to call upon all of his skill as well as his indomitable spirit to keep his men alive and moving. At first, every minute that passed saw his men inch closer to their goal. But before long the rate of progress slowed dramatically. The men were soon reduced to fighting for their lives.

Rufe fought on with all of his considerable might. Strong as he was, though, he knew he could not keep the entire Rogandan army at bay.

WILL WAS KEENLY aware of the need to protect his right flank. Both ends of the original position had been sealed with cavalry, but now Torbury Scarp was becoming the left flank of the new position. That meant that the bulk of the men originally positioned on that flank—led by Lord Eisgold—could be redeployed. Many of the mounted soldiers had long since reverted to fighting on foot. Will therefore sent immediate orders to Lord Eisgold to remount as many of his men as possible, and lead them in support of the protruding right flank. The outer extremities of the right flank were already hanging dangerously out into blank space.

The efforts of the Varasans in support of his men to the south was not lost on Will. Witnessing the effective way they had been absorbed into the Varasan line was a source of immense gratification to him. As the day wore on, the debt owed by the allies to the Varasans only continued to increase.

However, it was immediately apparent to Will that Rufe's men were facing very serious problems. He could see that they would not be able to reach the new position assigned to them. Dangerous rents were already developing in the front line as different groups of men moved at different rates. If Will could not find an answer, and find it soon, his men would be engulfed.

21

As the door opened once again, Thomas began to tremble uncontrollably, completely incapable of mastering his anxiety. He glanced across at Brother Vangellis. How did he manage to stay so calm?

Lord Drettroth walked in, Simon trailing along behind him.

The Rogandan stood facing them, hands on his hips. "The moment of truth has arrived for you, Thomas." He held up a bunch of keys. "You can both be free in a matter of minutes. Or I can call in my team of assistants." He gave them another of his nasty smiles.

"Before we begin, though, the stone needs to be secured. Simon, bring it to me."

Simon approached Thomas and retrieved the stone. This time Thomas did not attempt to resist him. Simon brought the stone to the Rogandan and handed it over.

Drettroth grasped it with a gloating smile. "What is your decision, Thomas?" he asked. "Have you chosen common sense, or would you prefer for me to arrange painful and lingering deaths for the two of you?"

Thomas shook his head, unable to trust himself to speak.

"I will make it easy for you," Drettroth told him. "Just nod your head if you have decided to relieve yourself of this burden."

His face set stubbornly, Thomas shook his head firmly once again.

"I told you I am not a patient man," the Rogandan said, an angry scowl appearing on his face. "I will offer you one last chance. Take it while you can, or things will become very unpleasant. When your turn comes, you will beg for death, Thomas, but it will be denied you."

Thomas finally managed to bring his shaking under control. "I will NEVER give you the stone!" he replied defiantly.

Drettroth glowered at him. "We shall see, young man. We shall see. Simon, call for my assistants!"

Simon did not leave the room. Instead, he leaned closer to the Rogandan and whispered something into his ear. Then he drew back swiftly, putting distance between the two of them.

A look of utter astonishment came over Drettroth's face. Then he went purple with fury. "What have you done?" he screamed. He drew his sword, and strode menacingly toward Simon. The youth closed his eyes, but held his ground without flinching.

The Rogandan raised his sword high, ready to strike. Then abruptly he began to convulse, his body bending and twisting repeatedly, until his backbone began to arch, snapping backward and forward. He fell writhing to the floor, wracked with continuous spasms.

Simon stepped up to Drettroth and placed a foot firmly on his wildly twitching sword arm. Then he reached down for the sword. Prizing it from the Rogandan's fingers, he took a deep breath in an attempt to steady himself, then raised the sword and ran him through. Drettroth gasped a few choking breaths, then released a final rattling sigh. His body slumped, then lay still.

Thomas watched it all with mouth agape, too agitated to make a sound.

Simon flung the sword away as if it had stung him. It skidded across the room, coming to a halt not far from the monk. Then, apparently remembering his audience, Simon turned toward them. "He was going to have both of you killed," he told them passionately. "Whatever you decided. You do realize that, don't you?"

He stared down at the body of the late tyrant. "It's only fifteen minutes since he had his goblet of wine," he said, his voice beginning to tremble. "He swallowed a large dose of poison with it. It was his own poison—I took it from his collection. He told me that it came from the seeds of a tree with some weird name." He tore his eyes from Drettroth and looked at them once again. "His death would have been extremely painful if I hadn't finished him. I showed him more mercy than he ever showed to anyone else."

Neither Thomas nor the monk could find a word to say.

Simon passed an unsteady hand across his brow. "As his wine taster, I prepared his wine. He trusted me not to tamper with it because he always made me drink it first. I had to drink it this time, too, of course." He smiled weakly. "So I don't have long myself. Once the spasms start I need to make sure I go quickly as well."

The fingers of Drettroth's left hand were still clasped around the stone, and the youth unbent them until the stone tumbled out. He retrieved it, then hunted for the keys, which Drettroth had dropped when he unsheathed his sword.

Simon went to Brother Vangellis and bent over him, speaking quietly into his ear as he fumbled with the locks. The monk looked across at Thomas, and his eyes grew wide with surprise. What was Simon telling him? Thomas couldn't think of any secrets he'd kept from his friend.

Finally Simon managed to release the chains. Freed at last, the monk stood up and stretched his limbs, wincing as he moved back and forth. Thomas felt cramped and uncomfortable; no doubt the monk's muscles were in even worse condition given his long imprisonment.

Simon stood up and turned toward Thomas. The effort seemed to trigger a reaction, and he began to convulse. As the spasms intensified he urgently wrestled a small wineskin from his belt. He unstopped it and began to swallow noisily, fluid spilling around him as he hastened to get it down. A bitter almond smell tainted the air.

The effect was immediate. All at once his breathing became very rapid. He convulsed one more time, then he collapsed.

The monk hurried to him and bent low over his prostrate form. Then he straightened and turned to Thomas with a tear in his eye. "He's gone," he said.

Brother Vangellis stood respectfully before Simon's body for a few moments more, then he brought the keys to Thomas and worked at his manacled right hand until he managed to unchain it.

Then the monk stretched out his own left hand. On his open palm sat the stone. "Take it, Thomas. It's yours. I give it to you gladly and freely."

Thomas frowned, puzzled by his words and surprised by the look on his face. He slowly reached out his freed right hand and took the stone.

The impact was staggering. He was entirely unprepared for the unrelenting onslaught that assailed his senses as the stone blazed into life in his hand. The intensity of it rivaled anything he remembered from his early experiences with the stone.

His mind reeled as he struggled to bring order to the chaos of thoughts, impressions, and memories that flooded to him from the monk. Even so, many things at last became clear—baffling oddities that for so long had completely bewildered him. He closed his eyes, desperate for a pause in the flow, at least for a moment.

Chains rattled as the monk unsuccessfully tried one key after another in his attempt to remove the ankle irons from Thomas. Then a knock sounded at the door of the room, tentative at first, then with more force. Thomas snapped his eyes open in alarm. The monk froze.

With no response forthcoming to the knocks, the door opened a crack, and a head appeared. With the stone in his hand, Thomas immediately saw that it was a dispatch rider with information from the battlefield. He sensed that the overall report wasn't bad, but something had nevertheless gone wrong, and the messenger was presenting himself in mortal fear of the possible reaction of his master.

The door opened wider, and a cloaked figure came in. The messenger was immediately confronted with the body of the Rogandan lord sprawled on the floor before him. He stood there paralyzed with shock, a jumble of emotions washing over him as he stared down at his former lord. Wavering between relief and indignation, he looked up and saw first the body of Simon, then the discarded sword. Finally, he looked across at the monk, still kneeling over Thomas.

Thomas watched with mounting anxiety as the messenger drew the obvious conclusion that the monk had killed both Drettroth and his food taster, and was now attempting to free the prisoner. Thanks to the stone, Thomas knew the messenger's intent as soon as the man knew it himself—he would satisfy his growing outrage by taking revenge on his lord's murderer. He would first kill the monk, then forever frustrate his attempts to liberate the prisoner by killing him as well. The dispatch rider drew his sword and stepped toward them.

Thomas whispered an urgent warning to Brother Vangellis, who dropped the keys and stood to face the Rogandan. Thomas saw his friend glance across at the sword lying nearby beside Simon. Then a memory flashed into the mind of the monk: a memory of a young girl fleeing, glancing back over her shoulder as she ran. Of a lecherous nobleman turning his back on the younger Brother Vangellis, who immediately reached down for a rock.

His friend turned his face away from the sword, rejecting it emphatically. Instead he began speaking to the Rogandan in his own language.

Thomas could not focus on what was happening, though. The face of the young girl had filled his mind and was haunting his thoughts. Her beauty stamped her unmistakably. The monk's long, slow slide into despair had been triggered by his act of violence in defense of a young Elena. Thomas knew beyond doubt that it was her, that he had not somehow managed to substitute a younger version of her face into the story.

"Thomas, free yourself!"

Brother Vangellis's hissed warning snapped him out of his reverie. His friend's attempt to talk the Rogandan out of his intention was apparently proving futile. Thomas put down the stone and grabbed the key. Fumbling in his haste, he began trying keys in the lock on his left ankle iron. He found the correct key on his third attempt and released the lock.

"Run, Thomas." The words came to him as a whispered sigh.

Thomas looked up in alarm as the monk's knees began to buckle. Blood was seeping through the back of his robe, and he saw him grasp hold of the Rogandan as he fell. Frantically returning his attention to the final ankle iron, Thomas tried the same key. It didn't work! In a panic he began poking keys randomly into the lock. Would he never find the correct one? At last, after innumerable attempts, the lock clicked open.

Pushing aside the chain, he threw down the keys and grabbed the stone. He launched himself upward even as the Rogandan tossed the monk aside and thrust forward his sword for a killing blow on his final victim. Thomas scrambled aside with barely a moment to spare as the sword struck the wall where he had been sitting.

Before the Rogandan could attempt a second blow, Thomas darted past him and out the door. Energized by his terror, the escapee flew blindly down a passageway, darting down side passages whenever they presented themselves. He encountered no one, and eventually hid himself in a dark room filled with large barrels. If the dust around him offered any indication, this room rarely saw a visitor.

He was still alive. But at what a cost. Brother Vangellis was dead.

The rush of energy that propelled him from the room had dissipated, and his pent up emotions were finally granted release. His whole body quivered with shock. Overwhelmed by the devastating impact of the death of his friend, along with his own close encounter with death, he silently began to sob.

He struggled to comprehend what had just happened. By some kind of a miracle the monk had escaped torture and death at the hands of Drettroth, only to be struck down by a nameless dispatch rider. Why did it have to end this way?

Brother Vangellis was a man who had touched the lives of so many. Now he was gone, his passing unmarked and unheralded. The onus of mourning his loss had fallen entirely to a solitary fugitive huddling fearfully in the dark in an enemy fortress.

The stone had at least allowed him a glimpse of the monk's final moments. The last lingering impression as he slipped away was one of peace. In his journey through life Brother Vangellis had clambered toward the light, had slipped and fallen hard, but had found his way forward once again. He had run the race, and finished it at last without lingering regret.

It was true that Thomas had only known him for a relatively short time. But the significance of everything that had happened in that brief period, along with the key role that the monk had played in so much of it, gave the friendship an importance far beyond any reckoning based on the length of time.

Thomas allowed his memory to wander freely over the pathways he had traveled with Brother Vangellis since they had met on a dark night at the Monastery of St. Rodrig the Martyr. He recalled teaching him to ride, the monk's brush with death as a result of withdrawals, his intercession on behalf of the villagers, his healing of Ander. He remembered the encounter with the bear and their visit to the monastery, the flight down the river, and the monk's easy companionship and careful instruction in the wilderness. Most of all he remembered the patient smile and quiet wisdom of a selfless and trustworthy friend.

His bitter tears flowed unchecked as he grieved without restraint for Brother Vangellis, giving honor to his friend and mentor in the only way that remained to him.

IN TIME his mind began to wander in different directions. The stone had revealed a great deal in the short period of time after the monk returned it to him. He began now to try to piece it together.

Brother Vangellis had been granted a great many insights by the stone as soon as Simon handed it to him. The monk had gained brief but unfettered access to Simon's mind. The same information became available to Thomas through Brother Vangellis once the monk had given him the stone.

The first thing Thomas recognized was that the stone had never truly belonged to him since the day he lost it so long ago. For all the intense pressure applied by Drettroth to coerce him into handing over the stone, it hadn't even been his to give. Back in the capital, once he had forcibly regained possession of the stone, it had allowed him to use it on rare occasions. But it was obvious now that its full virtue had passed to its finder: Simon. The youth had possessed it only for a few short minutes in the stables at Arnost before Thomas violently wrenched it away from him. It had granted Simon brief revelation about Thomas—the only person he had seen while it was in his possession—but the younger youth had not understood at the time that these insights were connected with the stone.

Simon had finally experienced its unrestrained power when he took the stone from Thomas at Drettroth's command. For the first time the secret ambitions of the Rogandan had been laid bare, and in plumbing the depths of his evil, Simon had understood at last the true nature of Drettroth's purpose. The Rogandan had freely acknowledged that he was actively seeking to bring together the three stones, and had claimed to have definite knowledge of them. Simon now saw that Drettroth intended to unite in his own person the power of good health and long life, authority over men and unlimited insight into the thoughts and intents of others.

But to his horror Simon had also glimpsed a darker purpose. Drettroth lusted to extend his own life indefinitely and was willing to go to any lengths to achieve that goal. He had secretly invested much of his energy pursuing a special understanding with his Dark Gods. Whether such a covenant had any meaning, and whether it could have delivered on his expectations, no one would ever know. But Drettroth had believed in its power, and he had been actively working to secure an unending supply of human sacrifice to establish and maintain the pact. His insatiable appetite for conquest could only be properly understood in light of this information.

For Arvenon, Castel, and Varas, a final Rogandan victory would have resulted in far more than a change of masters. The extent of the terror awaiting the ordinary people of the three kingdoms was more than Simon could take in. He knew enough about Drettroth, though, to be certain that the self-serving Rogandan lord would follow through on his plans without hesitation and entirely without consideration for his victims.

What the old Simon would have done with this knowledge was hard to guess. But everything had changed for the youth when he met Brother Vangellis. The unlikely friendship had stirred in him a desire for a new beginning, while at the same time bringing him unexpected hope. The first stirrings of change had caused him to arrange the escape of the young nobleman, who proved to be King Delmar of Varas. Once in brief possession of the stone, though, its disturbing revelations had brought Simon a new clarity of purpose. He immediately concluded that ending Drettroth's life must assume far greater importance than continuing to preserve his own.

Instead of calling for the torturers as instructed, Simon had gifted the stone to Drettroth, who at that moment had it in his hand. In a moment of supreme irony, the Rogandan lord had at last achieved his greatest desire only to discover that he had been betrayed. His life was about to end, and in excruciating agony. Far from cheating Malzakh, he realized he was imminently about to fall into the ravenous clutches of his insatiable god.

Having killed Drettroth, Simon could not reclaim the stone. But he handed it to Brother Vangellis who was able to learn a great deal from Simon, even though the opportunity was frustratingly brief.

The monk's surprise when looking at Thomas was not due to anything Simon was whispering to him. With sudden access to the mind and memories of Thomas, the monk had been startled to recognize Elena in the forefront of his consciousness. Although the monk never had an opportunity to express it in words, Thomas had been able to discern that Brother Vangellis took great delight in knowing they had found each other.

Thinking of his friend in this way triggered a fresh round of anguish in Thomas. He was aware that the monk could so easily have run for his life, as Thomas himself had later done. Brother Vangellis probably would have survived if he had fled. Instead he willingly chose to buy time for Thomas, and paid for that choice with his life.

Eventually Thomas was able to think calmly again. He pondered the monk's gift of the stone. His friend had told the truth when he assured Thomas that he had no desire for the burden of the stone's gifts. In turning it over to Thomas, though, he was ensuring that crucial knowledge and insights passed along from multiple people would not be lost.

Provided that Thomas, alone and defenseless in an enemy fortress, could somehow find a way to survive.

22

The men in Rufe's battle line had little time to think of anything beyond survival. A soldier beside Rufe took a blow to his helmet and went down hard, stunned. Two Rogandans rushed in eagerly to finish him off.

Rufe was not willing to give him up, though. Yelling a challenge, the giant leader thrust himself sideways into the gap, attacking both of them at once. Seeing his size and his determination, they hastily backed away. Rufe brought one of them down, causing the other to trip. Another Arvenian came to his support and dealt with the second man.

Rufe stretched an arm down to the fallen Arvenian soldier. He grasped it, and Rufe pulled him to his feet. The soldier shook his head a couple of times, but didn't hesitate before resuming his place in the line.

As the battle wore on, it became obvious that neither Rufe's role as leader nor his effectiveness in battle were lost on his enemies. The fight immediately became very dangerous for Rufe as the Rogandans began to specifically target him. Two men came at him at once. They went down, but three others quickly replaced them. Rufe knew he could not continue at this pace for long.

His men saw what was happening and moved vigorously to his aid. Soon Rufe stood at the center of a knot of men weaving back and forth, fighting frenetically. Rogandan soldiers crowded in, trying to bring him down. His own men threw themselves into the fight in his defense.

In the heat of battle Rufe stepped backward, stumbled over a body, and fell flat on his back. Sensing an opportunity, the Rogandans roared at the top of their voices and pressed in recklessly to the attack. One of them, a huge brute wearing a manic grimace on his face, stood over him and raised his sword high for the kill. Two of Rufe's men crashed into him from the side, knocking him from his feet. Scrambling up, one of Rufe's comrades thrust the Rogandan through. His companion, though, was cut down before he could find his feet.

Another Arvenian helped Rufe up. The big man immediately repaid him by blocking an enemy soldier who rushed in while he was distracted. More soldiers came at them both, and the fighting resumed its frantic rhythm. Rufe rushed to the defense of two more of his men and in turn was defended by two others.

In the melee the soldier immediately to Rufe's left went down. Rufe, already fending off another determined attack, could do nothing to help. The Rogandan attacker, instead of finishing off the soldier at Rufe's side, joined the assault on Rufe, drawing back his sword for a killing thrust. Exposed and distracted as Rufe was, the blow should have finished him. But another Arvenian, unable to impede the Rogandan in any other way, leaped forward and took the sword thrust himself.

Several frenzied minutes passed before Rufe could even turn to his rescuer. When he finally did, he found the man lying dead on the ground. Rufe didn't even know his name. Not for the first time that day, he owed another man his life. But there was no way for him ever to repay the debt. No chance even to thank him.

More attackers moved in against Rufe. He would not even be granted a moment to grieve.

Rufe plunged back into the battle with fresh determination,

though. There was a purpose behind the unselfish sacrifice of these nameless soldiers. All of them fought to end a pitiless invasion, a ruthless violation that left their land ravaged and their people murdered. They fought for the defenseless, for those who could not fight for themselves.

And beyond that deeper purpose lay a more elemental impulse. Rufe and the men beside him fought that day for their brothers, for men who had forged a kinship with their own blood. More than once today other men had laid down their lives for Rufe. More than once today he had very nearly done the same in return. He would not shrink from doing so again for the sake of those who remained.

Pain and suffering and bitter loss surrounded him on all sides. But it was a soldier's duty to fight, and, if necessary, to die. Rufe took his place in the battle line once more, shoulder to shoulder with his brothers in arms, ready to face whatever might come. In that moment, standing erect with them at his side, he was content.

FEW ARMIES COULD HOPE to retain cohesion under such conditions, and a lump came to Will's throat as he looked out over his men and witnessed again their quality, their fighting spirit and their sacrifice. It had become apparent that they were about to be overwhelmed in spite of everything they had worked so hard to achieve. He resolved that he would not stand by and allow them to face it alone.

"I'm going down there," he told Bottren decisively.

"But you can't!" Bottren retorted in dismay.

"I'm needed there. Much more than I'm needed here," Will told him. "You're in charge. If it comes to the worst, try to extract as many of the men as you can. I don't doubt that the Varasans will retreat in good order, and a good few of our men are with them now."

Bottren was opening his mouth to argue when a warning shout rang out behind them.

Will swung around to see a body of men riding in swiftly, skirting the low hills to the west.

Then another voice called, "They're ours!"

Unforeseen and unlooked for, and at the very threshold of disaster, a seemingly endless stream of riders poured onto the plain. Ranauld had arrived. Many of his horsemen carried hunting horns from Erestor, and with the battlefield before them at last, they raised the horns to their lips and blew. Wild and discordant, the sound swelled as it echoed back insistently from the escarpment.

Every head turned, across the entire battlefield. Rufe's men, embattled and almost overwhelmed, stood taller and gripped their weapons more tightly.

New hope awoke in Will. "Get their leaders up here urgently!" he called.

His dispatch riders raced like the wind to the column. They spurred their horses back up the hill with two men following close behind.

The leader dismounted and strode up the hill to Will and Bottren.

"Ranauld! It is good to see you," cried Bottren. Then his face fell. "Has Arnost fallen, then?"

"No! Arnost still stands!" Ranauld replied. "I've brought only a part of our strength. I'm sorry we couldn't get here sooner."

"Your help is timely beyond words!" Will told him. "You must have a thousand men down there. How did you find mounts for so many?"

"I have twelve hundred. These are mainly Burtelen's riders, though. Most of my men are on foot."

"Lord Burtelen is nearby? How many more men? When will they get here?"

"He has another three thousand, including my men. They are on foot, though. I cannot see how they could arrive today."

Will's brows bristled. He needed those three thousand, so badly. But he must work with what he had. "I need you to secure our right wing and stabilize our line," he told Ranauld. He quickly explained, and Ranauld set off without delay.

Will watched with awe as twelve hundred fresh soldiers poured onto the battlefield. Their impact was immediate. The right flank dangled no longer, and the Rogandans fell back rapidly as the horsemen swept across their line. Finding themselves free to disengage, Rufe's harassed soldiers turned their backs on the fighting and scurried back to their new assigned positions below Will. Their wounded, previously behind the line, now found themselves exposed. Rufe came last with a small group of soldiers, shepherding the wounded men.

The Rogandans now commanded most of the battlefield, and their weight of numbers soon began to be felt. Heavily outnumbered, Ranauld's men were driven back steadily toward the newly formed line behind them. The men in the battle line stepped aside and let the riders through, and most of the horsemen dismounted and rushed forward to strengthen the line.

The afternoon began to wear away. The Rogandans were far too numerous to be overcome. And Will's army was too stubborn to yield.

THE ROGANDAN COMMANDER, Kulzeike, was present on the battlefield. He himself had stayed out of the fighting, though. He harbored no doubts about the outcome, and he saw no reason to expose himself to the ever-willing clutches of Malzakh when he could leave it to his men to do the dying for him.

He had given his army everything it could possibly need to deliver a crushing defeat to the combined Arvenian and Castelan forces. Not least was their overwhelming superiority in numbers. And yet, in spite of everything, the fools had so far failed to bring their enemies to their knees.

The treachery of the Varasans at a critical moment was especially infuriating. It had plunged a knife into the back of his second army. Kulzeike was livid when he thought of their betrayal. The entire Varasan nation would pay in blood!

He still had more than enough men. But it was becoming clear to him that he was going to have to win the victory himself. Frustrating as that notion seemed at first, the more he thought about it, the more attractive it became. Being able to claim the glory personally offered considerable appeal to the commander. He was still new to this appointment. What better way to entrench himself as Drettroth's favorite?

The personal bodyguard of Kulzeike consisted of one hundred of the biggest, strongest, and most brutal men in the Rogandan army. None of them had seen any fighting today. He gathered them together and yelled at them for five solid minutes. Then he led them to what he deemed to be the weakest point in Will's northern battle line, near the western flank of the Rogandan position.

The men in Will's battle line had been in action all day. Kulzeike's attack smashed into them like a tidal wave. The defenders were unable to withstand the ferocity of the attack, and Kulzeike's assault quickly punched a gaping hole in the allied line. In those first frantic moments, the outcome of the entire battle hung in the balance.

IN A DAY OF SURPRISES, though, another unexpected twist was developing. Even as Will prepared once more to hurry down to the fighting in an attempt to stem the tide by his own efforts, a new group of horsemen swung around the hills to the northwest and streamed unheralded onto the battlefield.

Will was not expecting their arrival. Even Ranauld had no knowledge of their movements.

The packhorses commandeered by Kuper and Rellan and their men were not sprinters, but they had more stamina than their swifter cousins, and they had plodded on steadily. The horsemen, riding bareback, were mostly hardy men from the mountains of Erestor. They were well accustomed to rough conditions and had been honed for war in Lord Burtelen's training camps. They were spoiling for a fight.

Kuper did not wait to find Will. He led his men directly into battle. His three hundred threw themselves into the struggle, right at the point where Kulzeike was rampaging unchecked with his bodyguard. Some of Kuper's men literally leaped from their horses straight onto their startled enemies.

In the heat of battle, Rellan spotted Kulzeike and recognized him as the key to the struggle. He plunged immediately into the attack. Kulzeike's bodyguards rallied around their commander, and Rellan was soon surrounded and in trouble.

The soldiers who had ridden to the battle with Rellan had no previous connection with him and no personal reason to specially look out for him. None of them stood ready to defend him with their lives. None except his twin.

Having dealt with an opponent of his own, Kuper looked up and recognized his brother's peril. Bellowing for support, he raced to Rellan's defense and threw himself at Kulzeike. He crashed into the Rogandan and bore him to the ground, his thrusting sword carving a brutal slice across Kulzeike's neck. Kulzeike did not get up.

The Rogandan commander's bodyguards reacted instinctively, several of them hacking mercilessly at Kuper while he was down and defenseless. For a moment Kuper struggled to rise. Then he slumped back down onto the ground, subsiding helplessly as his life ebbed away.

Rellan, his mouth agape, looked on with horror and disbelief. Then he exploded into action, attacking his brother's killers with deadly wrath. Unsettled by the sudden loss of their leader, none of the Rogandans were willing to abide his fury.

Having scattered his enemies, Rellan returned to his brother and stood trembling by his side. Numbed at the enormity of his loss, he struggled to accept what had occurred. All his life Kuper had been at his side. He was without doubt the best man that Rellan had ever known. And he had just saved Rellan's life, with never a moment's thought for his own safety. Why did he have to die?

Rellan's eyes brimmed with tears as he gazed down in anguish at his brother's body. He began to weep unashamedly, heedless of the battle raging nearby.

Finally, noticing the fighting drawing closer again, he recovered himself and called for help. Recognizing Rellan, another horseman came to his aid, and together they bore his brother from the field.

Costly as it proved to be, Kuper and Rellan's attack had restored the balance between the armies. It appeared that the day was set to end without either side able to force a decisive result. The Rogandans retained an overwhelming advantage in numbers, but the position of the battle lines, combined with the geography of the site, ensured that most of their soldiers were unable to reach their enemies. They were therefore reduced to milling around in the middle of the battlefield waiting their turn in the battle line.

Of the rival armies, Will's forces were in the most precarious position. The allies still had the Rogandans boxed in, which placed the initiative for any withdrawal with Will. He reluctantly began to consider the logistical challenges of pulling back from the battlefield. His difficulty was that any such action would immediately release the Rogandans. If they pursued his men with sufficient vigor, a retreat could easily turn into a rout. And if the Rogandans chose to surround Will's forces, they had the numbers to destroy them.

The tide was about to turn one last time, though, with none of the combatants able to foresee what was about to happen.

Lord Burtelen's wagons had done their job. Having rolled his soldiers forward steadily through the night and then more rapidly throughout the whole of the following morning and into the afternoon, the nobleman formed the men up and marched them on at a relentless pace, permitting only brief and infrequent breaks. The forced march continued for the remainder of the afternoon. It brought them to the battlefield late in the day, but far sooner than Ranauld could ever have imagined.

A final barrier lay in their path: the series of low hills that formed Will's right flank. Instead of following the trail of the horsemen and marching around them, the men took the most direct route and tramped up and over the hills. The sun was less than an hour above the horizon when the first of them began to appear on the western fringes of the battlefield.

The earliest to arrive were the archers. They had traveled light, carrying nothing except their longbows and large clusters of arrows strapped to their backs. The hill face that fronted the plain was steep enough to discourage easy access from below, but the approach from the western side was more gentle, and the archers traversed it easily.

No horn or drum beat heralded their arrival. They moved silently into position, just over the crest of the final hill, and calmly began laying out their arrows. The entire Rogandan army lay spread out thickly before them across the battlefield, contained by the Varasans to the south and Will's men to the north. For the archers, the targets that blotted out the plain were abundant beyond their wildest imagining.

Thus far they had remained largely undetected. For most of the soldiers on the battlefield, the first hint of the archers' presence was the eerie whistle-whoosh of the arrows that soon poured, volley after volley, into the Rogandan ranks.

The effect was catastrophic. Men began to fall by the hundreds. The Rogandans immediately sent every available rider against them. Having no ready access up the slope of the hills, the horsemen milled around uselessly at the bottom of the hill face. The archers simply lowered their aim and sent the riders crashing from their saddles.

A sizable Rogandan force set out on foot, urgently sprinting toward the archers. There were far too many of them for the bowmen to deal with, but there was little need for concern. Before the Rogandans could begin clambering up the hill face, further elements of Lord Burtelen's thousands swarmed across the hills and took up defensive positions below the bowmen. These reinforcements were soon engaged in heavy fighting as they fended off the Rogandan attackers.

Some of the new arrivals had carried spare arrows, and they laid the bundles down beside the archers as they passed. With barely a break, the archers renewed their relentless destruction. The setting sun stained the clouds blood red in the west, and darts of death poured without pause out of the glowering horizon onto the battlefield. The human toll became staggering.

Will's men and the Varasans now fought with sudden hope and renewed energy.

All day the Rogandans had witnessed how thin the lines were that faced them, and they had never doubted that victory would eventually belong to them. Now, for the first time, doubt assailed them. A collective shudder ran through the thousands milling around on the plain. The fighting spirit of the army of Rogand began to crumble.

Men cast about desperately, searching for a haven from the deadly rain. The eastern end of the battlefield beside the cliff face of Torbury Scarp was out of range of the arrows, and Rogandan soldiers flooded into the area, pushing and shoving each other in an attempt to position themselves as close to the cliff face as possible.

Seeing this exodus, most of the archers gathered up their unspent shafts and scrambled down onto the plain, taking up positions behind the northern Arvenian battle line below Will, or behind the Varasan line to the south. The lethal hail resumed as the bowmen began firing over the heads of their fighting comrades.

Almost the entire battlefield was now within reach of the archers. The Rogandans, blocked by their enemies on three sides and by a sheer cliff on the fourth, had nowhere to go. No safe haven remained, apart from the established battle lines that ran across the northern and southern boundaries of the battlefield, and the new battle line to the west, below the original position of the bowmen. The archers avoided these areas for fear of hitting their own men, so Rogandan soldiers not in the battle line crowded together as near to the combat as they could. They achieved nothing except to hinder those of their countrymen doing the fighting.

WITH THE OTHER observers at his command post, Will watched stupefied as the archers methodically set about their demolition of the Rogandan army. Such an outcome was the sole purpose of his battle plan, but the nature and the scale of the carnage nevertheless numbed his senses.

It was obvious to Will that a decisive opportunity had finally arrived, and he immediately issued orders for an advance along the entire line. This time Bottren was unable to restrain him. No longer willing to remain an observer even for another minute, Will found his horse and set out to join Rufe. Cheers followed him as he rode along the line, and the men erupted the minute they realized that their commander would be joining them in the fighting.

As soon as he located Rufe, he dismounted. Seeing his friend still standing, Will greeted him with joy and relief. Rufe's face was grimed with sweat and dust and flecked with blood. His every movement betrayed his exhaustion.

"Were the archers another of your little surprises?" Rufe asked him with a weary smile.

"No. We will win today, and we have the archers to thank for it. But none of that credit belongs to me."

"We're still here and we're still fighting. You deserve credit for that," Rufe said.

Will shook his head. "The credit will go to all of you. But it's too early yet for anyone to claim credit. We need to finish this!"

For the first time that day, Will personally led his men to the attack, and in response they dug deep to dredge up a final reserve of strength. The entire line lurched forward. Slowly at first, then with growing momentum, they drove the Rogandans back.

The invaders had been told that overwhelming numbers would bring them an easy victory. Instead they had fought all day without prevailing. They had lost their leader, and with him much of their impetus to fight. Then they had endured death raining down mercilessly from the skies. Now, pressed back by an enemy that refused to yield, and jostled and crowded from behind by their own men, the Rogandan line began to totter.

Seeing the movement to the north, the Varasans began to force their way forward from the south with equal vigor. The last rays of sunlight illuminated the death throes of the army of Rogand, as the jaws of destruction slowly closed and ground it to pieces.

In the darkness and the confusion, a good few Rogandan soldiers managed to slip away from the battlefield. Nevertheless, as a fighting force the Rogandan army ceased to exist.

23

Thirst eventually drove Thomas from his hiding place. By then, several hours had passed during which he heard nothing, apart from a brief period of confused shouting two or three hours earlier.

He crept aimlessly through the empty passageways, having no idea at all where he was in the castle. At one time he passed a window that looked out onto a sky filled with stars, so he knew it was evening. Perhaps most of the inhabitants of the fortress were sleeping.

Eventually he decided to head downward whenever the opportunity arose. By this means he somehow found his way to the kitchens. Everything looked cold and abandoned, but he found water aplenty and drank until he was satisfied. After a brief hunt he found half a loaf of stale bread and an onion; he was so hungry that it seemed like a feast. He searched out a quiet corner and ate the food.

While foraging he was delighted to find an empty wineskin. After again slaking his thirst, he filled the wineskin with water and departed with it. He found himself a new hiding place and sat down to wait out the night.

With the coming of the dawn, he emerged once again, restless and weary after a night without sleep. He still saw no sign of any other person in the castle. The state of the kitchen finally convinced him that the fortress had been abandoned, and he eventually found the courage to explore the stronghold boldly from top to bottom as well as inside and out. No horses had been left in the stables. Even the dungeons had been emptied. The gates of the fortress stood wide open, and the drawbridge was down over the moat.

Behind the fortress stood a single tall tree in a broad meadow covered with green grass and dotted with white snowdrop anemones. Thomas hunted around until he found a metal spade, and he took it to the meadow. He began to dig two graves near the tree. The ground was soft, and he dug as well as he could with his single good arm. After what must have been hours, he felt confident the holes were deep enough to discourage wild animals.

He found a small cart behind the kitchens and wheeled it to the room where he had been imprisoned. Somehow he bundled Simon's body into the cart. Wincing with pain at every bump, he wheeled him awkwardly along the passageways, down the flights of steps, and over to the graveside. Then he carefully rolled him into the smaller of the two graves.

He anticipated more difficulty when he went back for Brother Vangellis, but the monk had become very thin during his imprisonment, and he was surprisingly light.

Drettroth he left lying where he had fallen.

By the time the light was fading, Thomas was bone weary, and his shoulder throbbed painfully. He had filled in both graves and gathered together a small pile of rocks to form a cairn between them. He managed to fashion a single crude cross, and he pushed it into the ground at the head of the mound where he had laid Brother Vangellis.

Perhaps no one in the world would truly miss Simon apart from Axel Stablehand, Thomas's father. But Thomas, at least, fully understood the magnitude of the debt owed by the people of Arvenon and Castel to Simon, and he spoke aloud a few halting words to honor him and to acknowledge his sacrifice. He also voiced his own remorse for the ways he had failed the youth. He said nothing of Simon's betrayal. In light of all the youth had done since, it seemed to Thomas that his earlier mistakes ought to be readily forgiven and quietly forgotten.

Finally he stood at the foot of the grave of Brother Vangellis. He paused, silent for a moment, eyes lightly shut and his thoughts drifting with the cool breeze that brushed at his hair. Then he opened his eyes and repeated aloud whatever words he could remember from the things Brother Vangellis had said at the funeral in the village and later by the graveside of Elbruhe. Finally, tears rolling freely down his cheeks, he spoke from the heart, honoring a man who had expressed his compassion unstintingly and without consideration for rank or status, one who had finally poured himself out in the most pragmatic way possible, by laying down his life for a friend.

WILL's scouts found Thomas sitting alone at the gateway to the empty fortress. A horse was found for him, and he rode back with them to the camp at Hazelwood Ford.

He was greeted with genuine delight, especially by Will and Rufe, and they soon arranged for a reunion of the small party that had ridden away together from Arnost. Pleased as they were to find themselves together again after all that had happened, it was nevertheless a somber gathering. None of them had remained unchanged by the tide in which they had been swept along.

Thomas was grieved to learn that Kuper had not survived the battle. He was also disappointed to have missed seeing Rellan, who, after supervising the burial of his brother, had hurried back to Erestor at the earliest possible opportunity. Nevertheless, the review of the Battle of Torbury Scarp laid out solely for the benefit of Thomas scarcely had an equal anywhere, even among the kings and their nobles.

He listened with a mixture of awe and horror as Will, Rufe, Ander, and Nestor each took up the tale in their turn. None of them had any illusions about the reasons for the decisive victory. The battle had been won only thanks to a combination of circumstances entirely beyond their control. Yet it was also obvious to Thomas that no victory could have been won at all without their extraordinary efforts. He also rejoiced—and greatly marveled—that each of them had somehow survived when so many other brave men had fallen.

When the story was told, Thomas still had many questions.

"What was it like when the reinforcements from Erestor arrived on the battlefield?" Thomas asked.

"Watching Count Ranauld's riders pouring onto the battlefield—it seemed like an endless stream—was one of the most stirring sights I have ever seen," said Will. "Especially in light of what was happening at the time. And the arrival of Kuper and Rellan with their horsemen was no less significant. Neither group could have arrived at a more critical moment."

"For me it was the impact of the archers," said Rufe. "When the arrows first started coming in, fighting completely stopped for a few moments. Even the Rogandans paused to watch it. None of us could help ourselves.

"We were barely hanging on. And suddenly Rogandan soldiers behind the battle line started going down, far too many to count. Then it became chaos, with Rogandans running everywhere in a panic. The effect on their morale was ruinous. That's when I truly began to hope again."

"And none of it could have happened without Kuper and Rellan and their friends!" said Thomas. "What did you all say when Rellan first told you about the way they managed to remove the Rogandan army in Erestor?"

"We were completely dumbfounded," said Rufe.

Will was clearly still astonished by it. "The avalanche was a stroke of genius!" he said. "I've never heard of anything like it—an entire army destroyed in minutes, and with so little loss to ourselves."

They talked for some time in awed tones about the timely arrival of the soldiers from Erestor—entirely unexpected by either side—and how it had completely transformed the outcome of the battle.

"And what about Queen Essanda?" Thomas asked. "Is she safe? She seems to be a truly remarkable girl—or is she a woman?"

"She is remarkable. And thankfully she is safe as well," said Will. "She's little more than a girl, but without her intervention the battle would certainly have been lost not long after it started. Her efforts, assisted by some canny guidance from our Nes, completely unraveled the plans of Lord Eisgold."

"What's become of Lord Eisgold?" Thomas asked.

"He has been banished by King Istel," Will replied. "After the way he blatantly ignored orders at the critical moment early in the battle, he almost certainly would have forfeited his life if he hadn't fought so bravely later. After he actually committed himself to the fighting, he did all that was asked of him and more, and that is undoubtedly what saved him."

"And what about the Varasans?" asked Thomas.

"We couldn't have won without them, either," Ander told him. "They are ferocious fighters."

"They lost many men at Torbury Scarp," said Will. "So King Steffan lent King Delmar a large contingent from Erestor—over a thousand men—since they had seen very little of the fighting. The combined force has marched on Varas to retake it from the Rogandans."

"That shouldn't prove too difficult," said Thomas. "Drettroth withdrew most of the Rogandan army from Varas for the battle."

"So that's where the extra men came from!" Nestor exclaimed.

"From Varas, and from elsewhere throughout Arvenon," Thomas replied. "Drettroth secretly pulled together almost his entire occupying army. He intended to take you by surprise."

"He certainly succeeded in doing that," said Will. "But it's becoming clear you have a lot to tell us, Thomas. Start from the beginning, from the moment you and Brother Vangellis left us after the passing of Elbruhe."

The hours slipped away as Thomas related the full story of all that had happened, interrupted by a great many questions on the way through. His friends did not conceal their amazement as the tale unfolded. All of them were stirred when he told them of Simon's resolve in bringing down Drettroth. And, hardened soldiers though they were, none were unmoved when he related the willing sacrifice of Brother Vangellis on his behalf.

He omitted nothing from his account except Elena and the stone, and if it seemed remarkable that Drettroth should have pursued Thomas and the monk so tenaciously, none of them commented on it.

"So now I finally understand how King Delmar managed to appear on the battlefield at such a critical moment," Nestor remarked. "None of my sources could account for it at all."

"The thing I don't understand is why the Rogandans abandoned the fortress," said Thomas.

"Word must have reached them about the outcome of the battle," said Will. "It's surprising how quickly news travels, especially bad news. They probably all packed up and headed for Rogand. Our scouts have been reporting a constant stream of refugees heading east."

"I doubt they'll receive a warm welcome from King Agon," said Nestor.

"No," Will replied. "Drettroth is gone, but Agon remains. We now have an alliance with Varas as well as with Castel. All of us will need to strengthen our borders and rebuild our armies."

King Steffan paced back and forth impatiently, waiting to be informed of the arrival of Essanda.

Steffan had heard nothing about her exploits until after the battle. By then she had been escorted to Castel Citadel by Count Gordan as originally planned, even if her departure was somewhat belated. Steffan had been almost frantic with alarm when he first heard the story. He still felt agitated now, even though he knew she was safe and unharmed.

He had been entirely preoccupied with an endless round of official duties since the battle at Torbury Scarp, with no possibility whatsoever of traveling to the citadel to see her. Unable to speak with her, his frustration had grown until he felt like he was almost at breaking point.

In the end King Istel had decided he could bear it no longer. Taking matters into his own hands, he arranged for Gordan to bring her back to the camp at Hazelwood Ford. He held off telling his son-in-law until a few hours before she was due to arrive. Istel had been more than a little apprehensive about Steffan's reaction, but Steffan was delighted, to Istel's obvious relief.

Essanda was now due any minute.

"As far as I'm concerned she can't get here soon enough," said Istel. "You've been like a bear with a sore tooth from the moment I told you she was on her way!"

Steffan said nothing, but he managed a self-conscious smile.

A head finally appeared at the entrance of the tent where the two of them were waiting. "They've arrived, Sire."

Steffan burst out of the tent, almost colliding with Count Gordan. "I'll have words with you later!" he promised the nobleman fiercely. "Where is she?"

Essanda had just been helped from her horse, her face looking flushed after the ride. His protective instincts rose up at his first glimpse of her—to him she seemed both beautiful and fragile. And infinitely precious.

He ran to her and swept her into his arms. An overpowering jumble of emotions—brimming pride, intense relief, firm reproach—totally engulfed him, and tears flooded his eyes. He drew her away from his chest and pressed her forehead firmly to his lips.

"Essanda, I couldn't *bear* to lose you! It would destroy me."

She buried herself in his chest once more, her eyes overflowing.

"I'm so sorry, Steffan," she managed through her tears. "I never wanted you to worry about me. I just felt I couldn't let him do it—I couldn't let him destroy Will and everything you'd worked for."

"You wonderful girl. I'm not angry with you! I was very distressed, but I'm so proud of you. You're incredibly brave! And you saw the truth when I was blind to it."

"I didn't feel very brave. Seeing our men fighting and dying before my eyes—it was too much for me. I hadn't understood how terrible war is."

"It is terrible. But it's over now. And I'm so glad you're safe!"

She sighed her relief at his words, and hugged him tighter. "Please don't be angry with Gordy," she pleaded. "He feels so guilty, but it wasn't his fault."

"Hmmm. I'll have to see about that," he said with a half-hearted grumble. "Good did come of it in the end, I suppose."

He held her at arm's length and gazed seriously into her eyes. "No more escapades without discussing it with me first. Promise?"

"I promise," she said meekly, smiling as she wiped away her tears.

He tucked her under his arm and turned her toward the tent. "Come and see your father," he said with a happy smile.

THE NEXT DAY Will found Thomas sitting alone eating some food.

"What are your plans now, Thomas?" he asked.

"I'm planning to leave Hazelwood Ford as soon as I can. There were some pieces of the story that I left out," he said, a little shamefacedly.

"I thought as much," Will replied with a smile. "The stone?"

"Yes. I still have it. And it is working reliably again. There's quite a story behind that, too."

"I'll look forward to hearing it."

"And there's someone waiting for me, too."

Will raised his eyebrows. "Oh," he said. "That sounds like a tale worth hearing."

"The problem is that I'm not sure how to find her again."

"Tell me more," said Will.

Thomas briefly described his time in the forest. If he was vague in his description of Elena and her father, it was only because he felt at a loss to know how best to describe them.

Will listened for a while, then he smiled again. "This girl living alone with her father in the wilderness—did she appear at first glance to be an old hunchback dressed in black?"

Thomas was too astonished to reply. But he nodded his agreement.

"In that case, I think I can help you find them, because I suspect I met them myself when I was traveling to Stantony," Will told him. "In fact, I can do better than that. I will accompany you. I need to visit somewhere very near there myself. I should warn you, though—it will be a few days before I'll be able to leave."

He explained his own connection with the mysterious pair. Thomas could only shake his head in amazement.

Will clearly had many demands on his time. Thomas was overwhelmed with gratitude for the help that his friend had promised, and told him so many times.

IN THE END a full week went by before Will was ready to set out. To the delight of Thomas, Rufe had announced he would be traveling with them as well.

A large party of mounted soldiers would also be accompanying them at the insistence of King Steffan. Will had tried to talk him out of it, but the king was unbending. He was not willing to take any risks with his two key leaders, for all that they were commoners.

On the last day before their departure from Hazelwood Ford, Nestor hosted a final farewell for the travelers. They ate their evening meal together, then relaxed in the cold evening air appreciating a magnificent sunset.

"I've decided to become a monk," said Ander.

A loud guffaw immediately exploded from Nestor. He guffawed again, and before long all of them were laughing, Ander included. The mood of the moment took complete hold, and every one of them was soon held fast in the grip of uproarious merriment, weeping with laughter. Thomas knew it was excessive, but there had been so little to laugh about in recent days.

Finally they were able to calm themselves. Nestor shook his head. "You had me for a moment," he told Ander, a new chuckle rising up to threaten his equanimity once more.

"You've more than proven your mettle as a soldier and a leader," said Will. "We'll miss you."

Rufe nodded. "You'll be a huge loss to the army. But the world needs men like Brother Vangellis a lot more than it needs soldiers."

"Please don't compare me with Brother Vangellis," Ander protested. "I can't do more than aspire to be like him."

Nestor looked back and forth between them, a bewildered look on his face. "You're actually serious?" he asked.

"Of course," said Ander.

"But I don't get it."

Ander looked at him thoughtfully. "Do you understand what made him like he was?" he asked.

Nestor paused for a moment, then shook his head.

"Neither do I," said Ander. "But I intend to try to find out."

"Brother Vangellis would be pleased if he knew," said Thomas.

"He would," agreed Rufe.

THEY SET off from Hazelwood Ford early the next morning. King Steffan was there to see them off, with Queen Essanda at his side. Young as she was, she had already made a name for herself. It was the first glimpse for Thomas of his new queen, and he was impressed.

"Safe travels, Will! Take care of him, Rufe!" she called out in her clear high voice, a shy smile on her face.

Will bowed deeply in response. Thomas could see from his ready smile that she had won his affection as well as his admiration.

Once they were underway, Thomas looked back to see the young queen sending a final wave. Feeling unusually bold, he waved back.

They traveled along established roads whenever they could, and only set off across the fields when they needed to. They spent their first night under the stars. It was bitingly cold, but thankfully the worst of the winter weather was not upon them yet.

On the second day their scouts surprised a small group of men, who ran from them in fear. The soldiers spread out and rounded them up, bringing them to Will.

They were clearly Rogandan soldiers, and a miserable looking lot. The real question was whether they were defeated soldiers fleeing back to Rogand, or an armed rabble roaming the countryside looking for trouble. None of them were armed, but they might well have discarded their weapons when they were first discovered.

Will looked at them searchingly. Then he saw something that seemed to startle him. He pointed to one of the men, who shuffled forward unhappily. Will spoke to him in Rogandan. The man replied, and a long interaction ensued.

Will left the men and rode up to Thomas. He leaned forward, speaking in a low voice. "I need you to take a look at these men, Thomas. They claim they are simply on their way back to Rogand. I would like some verification."

Thomas surreptitiously reached for the stone, and surveyed the group. "They're harmless," he told Will.

"Including that one?" Will pointed out one of the men.

"He's weary and discouraged," Thomas told him. "He seems to have little to look forward to, and he certainly doesn't want to be a soldier. But there's nothing sinister about him at all."

Will nodded. He spoke to the men sternly before sending them on their way. He did, however, detain the one he had pointed out to Thomas.

He apparently asked the man his name.

"Haldek," was the reply.

Further conversation took place between them. Then Will asked for a spare horse. "This man will be joining us," he said.

The soldiers were clearly taken aback by Will's announcement. Rufe, who knew his commander too well to be surprised by anything he did, simply smiled.

Will swung Haldek in beside Thomas, asking him to keep an eye out for the Rogandan, and the column set off again. From the occasional glances Thomas directed at his new companion, the man seemed anxious and unhappy.

Thomas knew there was no reason to fear him, and he found himself recalling Elbruhe's initial reaction when she first joined them. The memory brought him a wave of compassion for his new companion. When Haldek next looked in his direction, he presented him with a friendly smile. The Rogandan looked slightly less miserable, and Thomas was willing to claim that as a success.

Over the next few days the two of them began teaching each other words in their own languages. Haldek proved the more able student. With little else to do as they rode, he concentrated hard on learning vocabulary, and soon was able to attempt very simple conversations. Thomas gradually discovered that he had a kind heart and an easy manner. Thomas could also see that Haldek was warming to him.

On one occasion Thomas found himself briefly alone with Will. "Why did you single out Haldek to join us?" he asked.

"He doesn't realize it, but he's saved me twice," Will replied.

"Another story for another time?" asked Thomas.

Will nodded, grinning.

SEVERAL DAYS HAD PASSED when Will finally drew Thomas aside. "We will soon be nearing the location where I expect to find your friend and her father," he told him.

Thomas felt his heart skip a beat. A flush flooded over his face. He had been so eager to see Elena, but now he felt unexpectedly shy. How should he behave when he saw her again? What if she had lost interest in him?

Will smiled at his confusion, but chose not to comment. "We don't need to take all of the soldiers with us," he said. "We can rejoin them later. I suggest we just take Rufe and Haldek."

Thomas was surprised at Will's inclusion of Haldek, but he decided not to question it. Will undoubtedly had his reasons.

When they set up camp that night Will told the soldiers that they should expect to be there for two or three days at the least. The smaller party set off in the morning after Will issued instructions for the soldiers to wait for his return.

Thomas did not recognize any landmarks, and Will could not identify the precise location of the cabin by the stream, either. So their search began without any clear idea of where to look.

Mid afternoon arrived with no apparent progress toward reaching their goal, and Thomas began to despair of ever finding Elena again. Then Rufe found a stream with a path beside it. Nothing about it was familiar to Thomas, but they decided to follow the path in one direction until it became dark. Will chose the direction, and they set off.

After a while Thomas began to suspect that they were retracing his path as he fled from the Rogandans. His excitement grew even as the light was failing. He became certain they were heading in the right direction. They picked up their pace and reached the cabin as the darkness deepened around them.

Thomas ran to the cabin and went in. It was deserted.

There was nothing they could do except wait until daylight came. They tethered their horses and bedded down near the cabin.

Thomas lay there in the dark, wide awake and deeply troubled. Where were Elena and Rubin? Had they been taken after all, in spite of his warning and his efforts to lead the Rogandans away?

He hadn't forgotten that he advised Elena to hide, though. Maybe she and her father had taken his advice and removed themselves to a different location. But she had asked him if he would come back for her. That made no sense if she wasn't going to be here anymore.

The night was far advanced before he finally surrendered to exhaustion and drifted off to sleep.

He woke with a start to bright sunlight. The others were up already. Rufe spotted him and came to speak with him.

"Is this the right location, Thomas? The cabin hasn't been lived in for some time."

"Yes. This is where they were living. Where could they have gone?"

Will appeared from the direction of the stream. "I've found animal snares in the forest nearby—I'd say they were set not too long ago. And the garden beside the cabin appears to have been tended in the recent past."

Will's report restored a glimmer of hope to Thomas. There and then he decided that he would stay and wait, however long it took. He would remain there on his own if necessary.

His patience wasn't put to much of a test in the end. In the early afternoon a voice sounded tentatively from nearby. "Thomas, is that you?"

He looked up to see Rubin peering out cautiously from behind a tree.

Thomas ran to him with a joyful cry. "Rubin! Is Elena safe? Are you both well?"

"Yes, we are both safe and well."

Thomas's relief knew no bounds. "Where is she? Can I go to her?"

Hearing voices, the others gathered, and Rubin looked around him uncertainly.

Taking a deep breath, Thomas tried hard to calm himself. "Let me introduce my friends," he said. Restraining his eagerness with difficulty, he formally presented Will, Rufe, and Haldek to Rubin.

When the introductions were over, Rubin turned to Thomas. "I know you are anxious to see Elena, but I think it would be best if I break the news to her. It will be a very happy surprise, but still a shock. She understood why you needed to leave, but she has taken it hard as the days have gone by. She has greatly feared for your safety." He glanced around him. "I think, too, that she will be shy with so many people here."

Thomas was crestfallen, but he accepted that Rubin knew best.

"The Rogandans have been defeated," Will told Rubin. "They're leaving Arvenon. I think it is safe for the two of you to return to your cabin now."

Rubin nodded gratefully. "I don't know you," he said with a puzzled look on his face, "but there is something familiar about you."

Will smiled. "I once accepted your hospitality for the night," he replied. "It feels like a long time ago. I probably looked a little different back then as well."

"Of course," said Rubin, his face lighting up. "Elena told me that you faced some trouble after you left. I am glad you found a way through it."

"That is largely why I am here," Will replied. "It is time to end the folly that has forced you and your daughter into isolation from the world. The trouble has spread well beyond the two of you. You can continue to choose to live apart from other people if you wish, but the persecution must end."

Rubin looked hesitant, but he nodded his understanding.

Will nodded toward Thomas. "My friend here seems barely able to contain himself," he said with a smile. "Perhaps you could fetch your daughter."

Rubin readily agreed and disappeared into the forest.

Little more than thirty minutes passed before Rubin reappeared, this time with a radiant Elena. Ignoring everyone else, she flew to Thomas and embraced him joyfully, tears of gladness flooding her cheeks.

After a few moments she drew back, noticing his arm bound tightly in the sling. "You're hurt!" she cried, alarm in her voice.

"It's nothing," he told her happily, pulling her in once more with his good arm.

Will had been conferring quietly with Rubin, and he now called the others together. "We will spend the night here," he said. "But in the morning we will travel together into Tallesford, a town that lies not far from here."

Elena looked anxiously to her father, who gave her a nod and a reassuring smile.

Haldek took upon himself the task of preparing a meal. When he came to serve it, he bustled about cheerfully, paying special attention to Elena. It was very obvious that he had taken quite a shine to her.

Will taught him the Arvenian word for uncle, and he embraced it with a nod and a ready smile, speaking it aloud to practice his pronunciation.

Once they had eaten, they all lay down to sleep. Elena and her father re-established themselves in the cabin again, for this one night at least.

As Thomas lay quietly, waiting to drift off, he remembered his anxiety about how he should respond to Elena, and his uncertainty about whether she still cared for him. He smiled to himself, more amused than embarrassed at his own insecurity.

He did not think he had ever felt so content in his entire life.

24

The column of soldiers trooped into the town of Tallesford with Will and Rufe at their head. Rubin rode in the middle of the column, with Elena perched in front of him. Thomas had positioned his horse beside them.

As soon as it became known that the commander of the king's army had arrived, after defeating the Rogandans in a great battle, a large and enthusiastic crowd gathered to cheer them in. Hearing that the local baron had been sent for, and that he was on his way to greet them, they came to a halt in the market square.

Thomas knew that neither Rubin nor Elena felt at all comfortable in a crowd, and he hovered near them protectively.

The baron rode up and greeted them graciously, welcoming them officially to Tallesford. The nobleman was tall and dark and looked every inch a warrior. Thomas was gratified to see that he paid appropriate deference to Will, given his status as commander. Surprisingly, Will seemed uncharacteristically restless and distracted.

The baron invited them to join him and led them to a large building on the edge of the square. The soldiers remained outside with Haldek. The others began to file inside.

As they went in, a harsh voice called from the crowd, "The witch! The witch is with them."

A couple of others took up the cry.

Will came to a halt and surveyed the crowd. It was impossible to tell who had spoken. Calling for the captain, he turned to Thomas. "Can you identify the people who said that?" he asked him quietly.

Thomas took the stone and scanned the crowd. The mental din was almost overwhelming, but he narrowed his focus and was soon able to pick out two women and an old man who still radiated hatred. Thomas pointed them out to the captain, and he disappeared into the crowd with several of his men.

Thomas followed the others inside, Will entering last of all.

Refreshments were being served, and Rufe was responding to the questions of the baron, delivering news of the king and the recent battle at Torbury Scarp. Pleasantries were exchanged, and the baron expressed gratification that no further incursions were to be expected from Rogandan invaders.

He explained that for many weeks he had been able to protect his lands from their scourge only with great difficulty and considerable loss of life. Then the Rogandans had all mysteriously disappeared. With the news of the recent battle, the reason for their exodus was now clear.

When the conversation slowed a little, Will addressed the nobleman. "My Lord Baron, could I please speak with you in private?"

The baron nodded his acquiescence, and ushered him into a small chamber off to one side of the main hall. Thomas watched them go with considerable interest. He suspected it had something to do with Elena, but he resisted the temptation to use the stone to discover Will's intent in calling for the discussion.

"I HAVE two reasons for wishing to speak with you, My Lord."

The baron nodded his permission to speak, all the while regarding him with obvious curiosity.

"The first concerns the young lady, Elena, who is traveling with us."

"She is very striking, to say the least," the baron acknowledged. "Does she live in this region? I wonder that I have not seen her before."

Will felt his eyes narrow. "She is spoken for, by another of my companions, the young man called Thomas. He also stands high in the king's regard, having played a key role in bringing down Lord Drettroth, the High Commander of the Rogandan army."

"Please, do not misunderstand my inquisitiveness!" protested the baron. "I have no interest in her for myself. I simply feel great sympathy for her father. It cannot be comfortable to have responsibility for a daughter with such beauty. I have a daughter myself, and I have more than once congratulated myself that she is merely attractive." He gave Will a rueful smile.

The nobleman seemed sincere. Will promised himself he would ask Thomas to confirm it.

"It is uncomfortable," Will continued, "and great harm has come from it already, thanks to superstitious minds and idle tongues. The truth, though, is that nothing about her or her father is at all unusual, apart from her remarkable appearance. They are common people who want nothing more than to live a quiet life. And they have already done great service to their king—I can attest to it personally.

"I wish to make a request on their behalf that they would never ask for themselves. I beg you to extend your protection over them. Even as we entered this hall some people in the crowd called her a witch. My men were able to identify those involved, and they have taken them aside in case you would like to examine their reasons for making such an accusation."

The baron frowned. "I will deal with this, and firmly." He pulled a cord, and a servant entered. He issued instructions to the man, and sent him away.

"I thank you," said Will, with a bow.

"You said that great harm has already come from this superstitious talk. Are you referring to some other wrong that has been done?"

Will felt himself color. "It is my turn to feel uncomfortable, My Lord. You and I have met before."

The baron looked surprised. "I have no memory of it."

"You were calling down curses on me as I rode away from you. I am the person who killed your son."

The nobleman's brows bristled.

"I was heading to Stantony on urgent business for the king. Elena and her father had sheltered me overnight and she gave me directions. Your son saw us parting, and tried to intercept me, believing that I had conspired with a witch. My business could not be delayed, even for an hour. I was forced to defend myself. To my lasting regret, I killed him. That was never my intention."

Will paused in an attempt to calm himself. "This is the second reason why I wished to speak with you. I felt it only right to give you the opportunity to confront your son's killer, and to take whatever action you deem necessary."

The baron regarded him silently for what seemed like an eternity. Then he spoke.

"I honor you, Will Prentis. You are a different kind of commander from anything I expected. I don't doubt that the king greatly values your obvious integrity. It cannot have been easy to face me in this way —I doubt that one man in a hundred would have been willing to attempt it.

"But you have punished yourself for no reason. My son is indeed dead, but you are not responsible for his passing. Yes, you did leave him gravely wounded. But he recovered. And I believe the encounter left him with a new appreciation for the value of a cool head and an even temper.

"My son died bravely, just three weeks ago, in battle against the Rogandans."

The eyes of the baron misted over, and he did not speak for a time. Finally he stood to his feet. "Your face is scarred, and you walk with a limp. No doubt you acquired these tokens in service to your king. I also carry a limp, and for the same reason. My face may not carry scars, but my heart certainly does. Will you walk with me?"

Will nodded, and he accompanied the baron out of a side door. Shoulder to shoulder the two veterans hobbled to a peaceful graveyard beside a large stone church. They stood together, silent before a cold stone tomb, mourning the death of a beloved son and grieving the departure of innocence from the world.

THOMAS HAD no need of the stone to discern the new sense of peace that radiated from Will when he returned with the baron. He followed his friend from the building as the baron led them to a different corner of the square where a crowd had gathered and hecklers could be heard calling loudly. The crowd parted as they approached to reveal two women and a man constrained in the stocks. It was obvious from the reaction of the bystanders that they were not popular.

The baron faced the crowd. "I will not tolerate accusations against this young woman," he said, pointing to Elena. "I am satisfied that she is no witch! If others of you are unable to control your envy, then keep your slurs to yourselves or pay the penalty."

Elena stood before the accused with a look of grief on her face. "I cannot bear for anyone to be punished on my account, My Lord," she said to the baron quietly. "Please release them! I forgive them freely."

"I will honor your request for mercy," he replied. "But they can bear their punishment for a while longer." He turned to his servants. "Release them before the sun goes down," he ordered.

The town no longer felt comfortable to Thomas, and he was relieved to learn that they were leaving immediately. The baron clasped hands warmly with Will, then bade them all farewell, and they departed.

Once clear of the town, Will drew his horse alongside Thomas. "Rufe and I have promised to return without unnecessary delay to rejoin the king. I am sure you will want to stay with Elena, though, Thomas."

"Yes, I have been planning to remain here," Thomas replied, trying not to sound too eager.

Will nodded. "After all that has happened, I suspect that such a course will be safest for you anyway.

"I have a request to make of you, though. Would you be willing to welcome Haldek among you? He has rescued me, twice, as I have told you, and you know better than anyone that there is no great harm in him.

"He has no family and no future back in Rogand. But I believe he might be helpful to you here. I have already spoken to Rubin and Elena, and they have given their consent. But I would not leave him here without your approval as well."

Thomas readily agreed, and Will went to Haldek to extend their offer. The Rogandan rode first to Rubin and Elena and then to Thomas to express his thanks. He probably could not have concealed his delight if he had tried, and even in his halting Arvenian he managed to be effusive.

The company parted well before they reached the forest refuge. Thomas had learned to value solitude almost as much as Elena and her father, and he looked forward eagerly to passing his time with them in the days to come. He nevertheless had a lump in his throat as he farewelled Will and Rufe and watched them ride away. It was hard to imagine a future devoid of them.

THE SMALLER GROUP of four reached the cabin before nightfall. After eating a simple meal they somehow all managed to stretch out on the floor inside, and in that way they spent their first night together as a small community.

In the morning Haldek was full of ideas for extending the cabin, and building a second beside it. He squatted down in the dirt and began drawing up rough plans, drawing a chuckle of appreciation from Rubin.

Thomas had lain awake for several hours, thinking about the future. He knew there were many things that he needed to tell Elena, so he sought and received Rubin's permission to spend the whole day with her.

They wandered slowly along the stream, remembering many previous happy afternoons spent in similar fashion. Then they sat down in Elena's favorite meadow, and Thomas made a beginning. The sun rose in the sky and passed its zenith as he laid out before her the whole of his history with the stone, hiding nothing, not even the most shameful of his memories. She remembered Brother Vangellis fondly from her earlier years, and she hung on every word as Thomas told her all they had experienced together. Her eagerness turned to shock when he revealed what the monk had done to protect her, and she became deeply distressed as he described the terrible consequences that had followed for him. Her discomfort began to ease as Thomas unfolded the events through which Brother Vangellis had found redemption. With great reluctance he relived the hours in Drettroth's prison room, and they wept together as he recounted the monk's final moments.

The daylight had almost faded by the time he finally finished. They returned to the cabin. Thomas was silent, lost in his memories. Elena had a faraway look in her eyes.

The following afternoon they set off together again.

Thomas was beginning to feel like a new person. His life in recent months had degenerated into a seemingly endless succession of crises, but he was daring to hope that the upheavals of the past might finally be behind him.

Elena had been thoughtful since his revelations, and it soon became clear that their conversation the previous day had left her with many questions. "Thomas, you said that for much of the time you had the stone it actually belonged to Simon."

"Yes. The stone didn't belong to me anymore once I lost it, although I didn't realize that at the time. Simon was the one who found it, so after that it belonged to him."

"If it belonged to him, why did it still occasionally work for you after you took it back?"

"I don't know."

"Didn't the scroll say that the stone would stop working if someone took it by force?"

"Yes, it did. I don't understand that, either. Maybe it was different in this case because the stone wasn't new to me. Perhaps I had adapted to it somehow. I'm only guessing, though. The scroll gave no hints about what might happen in that situation. There might have been answers in the section that was missing."

Elena nodded. "But it worked properly for Simon as soon as he had it in his hand again," she said. "So he suddenly understood all of Lord Drettroth's secrets. What about when he handed it to Lord Drettroth the first time, though? Why didn't the ownership change?"

"He put it into Drettroth's hand, but that's not the same as giving it to him." Thomas took out the stone and passed it to Elena. She examined it closely for a while with considerable interest, then returned it. He put it back in his pouch immediately. "The stone was still mine while you had it just then," Thomas told her, "because I was only letting you hold it and examine it. I didn't give it to you."

"Well, I'm glad you didn't give it to me, because I don't want it!" she said decidedly.

He wasn't surprised. In light of everything she now knew about the stone, he understood her reaction completely.

"I noticed you didn't look at me while you had the stone in your hand," she said.

"No. I've never used the stone to see into your mind, apart from the first time we met, when I thought you might be dangerous. You know about that already. And it wasn't working fully at the time, anyway. But I've never tried it on you or your father since, and I promise that I never will."

"Thank you, Thomas," she said with a smile and the faintest of blushes. "It would give you an unfair advantage."

Elena became thoughtful once again. "You said that Simon whispered something in Lord Drettroth's ear when he told Simon to call for the torturers," she continued. "What did Simon say to him? Was he telling Lord Drettroth he'd been poisoned?"

"No. He told Drettroth that he was freely and willingly giving him the stone. Simon could do that, because it was his to give away. And once he had the stone in his hand, he was soon able to get the full picture of how it worked from Drettroth and from me, especially since the stone was uppermost in both of our minds."

"Oh. So Simon gave Lord Drettroth the stone, and he was immediately able to read Simon's thoughts. Is that how he knew he'd been poisoned and was about to die?"

"Yes," said Thomas. "It must have been a huge shock to finally get what he wanted, only to discover it was all for nothing."

"And then Simon took the stone back after he'd killed Lord Drettroth. Did that make it his again?"

"No, he couldn't just take it back from Drettroth. He couldn't claim the stone after killing him. It didn't belong to anyone until Simon handed it to Brother Vangellis. As the next person who 'found' it, he became the new owner."

"Until he gave it to you again."

"Yes. And it's been mine since then."

"There's another thing I've been curious about," Elena said. "You told me that the scroll mentioned three stones, and that Lord Drettroth said he had knowledge of them. Where are the other two stones now?"

"I don't know," Thomas replied. "There's something I didn't tell you, and I wouldn't have mentioned it if you hadn't asked about the other stones. It occurred to me that Drettroth might already have the Stone of Authority, considering how powerful he had become. So I searched him before I left. Thoroughly, too.

"It wasn't because I wanted the other stones for myself. I didn't think it was safe to just leave them there. I thought the Stone of Authority would be safe with King Steffan. Or with Will, except that I don't think he needs it!

"Anyway, there was no sign of another stone. Either he didn't actually have the other stones yet, or one of his men had already searched him before abandoning the fortress. We'll probably never know."

Thomas became quiet for a moment, caught up in his memories.

"I also wondered if he might have had another copy of the scroll there with him," he continued. "Maybe even a complete copy, with a full description of all three stones and a more complete history of what has happened with them. I did see a few scrolls in one of the rooms in the fortress. But I couldn't tell what they said," he admitted. "I can't read."

"I can't read, either," she said. "Nor can my father."

"Perhaps I should have brought the scrolls with me, just in case. Will could have read them." He shrugged. "It's too late now, though."

They sat together quietly, absorbed in their thoughts.

Elena was first to break the silence, steering the conversation in a different direction. "What about your parents, Thomas?"

"Will expects to return to Arnost soon," he replied, "and he promised to let my father know that I'm safe. And now that the Rogandans have gone, I expect my mother will return to Arnost. So she'll find out the news as well."

"Do you want to go back to Arnost, to be with your parents?"

Thomas shook his head emphatically.

"Don't you think your mother would want to see you again?" she prodded gently.

"Yes, she would," he said. "I can't simply decide to move back to Arnost, though. I need to escape attention, even more than you do. After the Council meeting where Pisander was exposed, some of the nobles have probably guessed about the stone. It isn't safe for me there anymore."

He gazed at her earnestly. "But I very much want my mother to meet you. My father, too."

Thomas became thoughtful. "I learned something about my father from the stone. It came to me through Brother Vangellis, who caught a glimpse of Simon's thoughts, as you know. Simon seemed to think that my father was missing me. And that he blamed himself for driving me away. I didn't expect that." He fell silent, staring off into the distance.

"I know you and your father clashed at times," Elena said. "But from everything you've told me, I'm sure that he truly cares about you."

Thomas nodded. "I think you're right, although it's taken me a while to see that. I need to talk with him. I don't want things to stay the way they've been between us."

Elena nodded approvingly.

"This is my home now," he concluded, "and a part of me wishes I could just stay here and hide away from the world. But I know it's important to see my parents again. I'll find a way to do it somehow."

He paused, looking intently at Elena with a frown of concern. "I've been hoping I'll be safe here. But it does worry me to think that trouble might come to you because of me."

"I wish there was a way to escape trouble completely," she said with a wistful smile. "But it doesn't seem possible. I think what matters is how we behave when trouble comes."

She gazed up at him. "I'm so proud of you, Thomas!" she said.

"Why?" Her remark took him by surprise.

"Because of the way you stood up to Lord Drettroth. You thought it would lead to a horrible death, but you stood strong anyway."

Thomas would have been willing to bask in her esteem, but he wasn't entirely sure that he deserved it. He had defied Drettroth. But she didn't know how sorely tempted he had been to take the easy way out.

"I'm sure you've faced more trouble in the last few months than most people face in their entire lives. And you've been so brave!" She looked up at him, her face shining. "You risked your life to lead the Rogandans away from us. That was very selfless of you. And you were prepared to do it for a girl that you thought was deformed."

That at least was true. He knew he wasn't the same person who had left Arnost.

"I don't know if my father has told you, Thomas, but he missed you while you were away. He's come to depend on you in so many ways. Both of us have." A faint blush tinged her lovely cheeks.

Elena's words were gratifying. Nevertheless, Thomas couldn't manage to convince himself he was especially worthy of admiration.

He couldn't count the number of times in the last few months when he'd felt awkward or embarrassed. Or even completely out of his depth.

He thought about Brother Vangellis, and Will, and Rufe, and the other men he had come to know and respect. They were adults, and he knew he wasn't entirely there yet. He aspired to be like them, but he didn't know how to make it happen.

"Maybe trouble is behind us now. Maybe not," Elena continued. "But I'm not going to worry about what might happen in the future. There's so much to be grateful for, right here and right now." She got to her feet and spun slowly around with arms raised, taking in the peaceful meadow dotted with wildflowers, the sky with its flecks of blue among billowing white and gray clouds, and the deep greens and browns of the trees. The merry sound of the nearby stream provided a fitting accompaniment to her graceful movements.

He nodded slowly. She was right. He remembered Brother Vangellis saying that sometimes you had to let the future worry about itself.

Trouble would undoubtedly come calling again, sooner or later. But it didn't need to consume his thoughts or energy now. Every moment deserved to be lived to the full. And he felt like his life was only just beginning.

EPILOGUE

A face appeared tentatively in the opening among the rubble. "It's safe to come out," Brother Dannel called. "They're gone."

The first of the monks emerged into the ruins of what had been the library, squinting and shielding his eyes from the bright sunlight. Another followed, and then another. Soon the ruined library building was dotted with robed figures picking their way through the rubble. Others stood motionless, dazed at the extent of the destruction. Brother Erastus sat on the remains of a wall, his head bent low and his hands covering his face.

The monks had huddled together in their bolt hole below the library for almost two days, while the Rogandans continued their rampage above. When everything had finally gone quiet, they waited another full day. Then Brother Dannel sent all of them except Brother Erastus to safety at the bottom of the winding stairway, while he went out through the secret entrance to explore the monastery. Once he was certain that the Rogandans had abandoned the plateau, he sent Brother Erastus down the stairs to fetch the others.

Brother Dannel called them together. "I found Brother Beneface over there," he said, pointing toward the fallen gates of the monastery. The monks followed him to a white-clad figure lying spreadeagled on the ground. Brother Dannel had known there was very little chance they would find their leader alive. Nevertheless, it had still been a source of great dismay to him when he discovered his body.

As they gathered around the earthly remains of their beloved abbot, Brother Dannel saw his own grief mirrored on the faces of others. The burden of leadership had fallen to him now, though, and he knew he needed to be strong for them all. He led the monks to a grassy meadow beyond the shattered outer wall of the monastery, and set them to work preparing a grave. They buried Brother Beneface there, in sight of the place that had been his home for so long.

When it was over Brother Dannel sent them out to see what could be retrieved from the ruins.

Lord Drettroth's men had been thorough. Everything had been destroyed. Not a single building remained standing. The piggery and goat pens had been broken down, and the ground around the pens was littered with the carcasses of goats, pigs, and chickens. Every single fruit tree had fallen to the ax, and even the plants in the cultivated strips of farm land had been torn up.

Late in the afternoon they gathered together outside the broken walls. It was a somber gathering. Brother Dannel led them in prayers. Then he invited questions.

"What will we do?" asked one of the monks in despair.

"We will rebuild," Brother Dannel replied. "If the Rogandans have been defeated and left Arvenon," he added.

"So we won't rebuild the monastery if they're still around?"

Brother Dannel shook his head. "No. If the Rogandans haven't gone, we'll be needed out there, among the people." He swept an arm across the lowlands surrounding the plateau. "And even if they are gone, people will still need our help for a while. Many other people will have been killed or injured, and farms and buildings destroyed."

He turned toward the shell of their home. "Tonight we will shelter here as best we can. Then tomorrow we will leave this place. If it is God's purpose, we will return in the spring and make a new beginning."

"What did you think about the conference, Essanda?" Steffan asked. His young wife had just accompanied him for the first time to a key meeting of the nobles, where plans and priorities for the future were under discussion.

Given the widespread destruction caused by the Rogandans, men had been sent throughout Arvenon to assess the state of the towns and villages and the preparedness of the people for winter. The first reports were just beginning to come in. Thankfully the weather had been unseasonably mild, and the first bitterly cold weather had yet to make an appearance.

Steffan had sent Ranauld back to Arnost with a strong contingent of soldiers. The Lords Dongan and Burtelen were about to head south and west, each with their own squads of soldiers. All of them were under instruction to provide assistance wherever it was needed.

Steffan would soon be returning to Arnost himself. His leadership was needed more than ever in the aftermath of a brutal invasion. Essanda would remain at the citadel for the moment, at least until Arnost had returned to some semblance of normality.

Inviting Essanda to the meeting was unconventional, but Steffan wanted sympathetic eyes and ears in the room, and he knew he would be able to debrief with her frankly.

She didn't respond immediately to his question. "It was interesting," she finally replied, a hesitant look on her face.

"What does that mean?"

"I don't think all of them were happy about having me there."

"Nonsense!" he exclaimed.

Her face fell, and she looked away.

"I'm sorry!" he said repentantly. "That came out much more harshly than I intended."

Her big round eyes reappeared slowly.

He sighed, raising his arms in resignation. "You're probably right, Essanda. When it comes to these things, you usually seem to be."

That won him the hint of a smile.

"As for you attending the meeting, I don't care what anyone else thinks," he told her. "I needed you there! And you've earned the right. You did far more to save our kingdoms than most of the self-important peacocks around the table."

Steffan paused long enough to regain his composure. Then he slowly reassessed the key points of the discussion, inviting her to comment. As usual, she asked thoughtful questions while offering few opinions. But she nevertheless managed to steer him in the direction of important insights he otherwise might have missed. He knew he was much too easily distracted by his annoyance at the blindness —sometimes the sheer stupidity—of many among the nobility.

Essanda had said nothing at all in the meeting, and most of the nobles probably thought that including her was a complete waste of time. They had no idea how keenly she had been observing them.

"I like Lord Burtelen," she told him. "He seems very wise. And he worked hard to get the archers—as well as Kuper and Rellan and Count Ranauld—to the battle on time."

"Yes. I'll have great need of Burtelen when I get back to Arnost. Capable and reliable noblemen like him are all too rare."

"I like Lord Karevis, too. I'm glad the Varasans are on our side now."

"I agree. Karevis impresses me. I'm pleased that he's able to remain in Castel for a while, now that he's returned the men we lent to Delmar. It was gratifying to hear him confirm that his country is firmly back under Varasan control again.

"Thankfully, neither Delmar nor Karevis has any illusions about the potential threat that Agon is likely to pose in the future, either. I'm willing to go to considerable lengths to strengthen our ties with Varas."

Essanda nodded. "That seems like a good idea."

She gazed up at him uncertainly. "It's nice that you wanted me at the meeting, Steffan. I didn't understand a lot of the things you were discussing, though. Have you thought about inviting Nestor instead? He has a lot more experience than me, and he's good at understanding why people behave the way they do. His opinions would be much more useful than mine."

He shook his head. "Impossible, I'm afraid. He's a commoner."

"Will is a commoner, and he was there."

"That's different."

She didn't look convinced. "Do the other nobles think it's different?"

"We just fought the greatest battle in Arvenon's history, and he was the commander who won it for us!"

She nodded. "That's the way I see it, too." She was silent for a moment. "Does everyone believe that he won it for us, though? In the meeting Will told everyone he doesn't deserve the credit. It looked like some of the nobles agreed with him."

Steffan felt his hackles rise at this latest reminder of the stubborn stupidity of the nobles, but he managed to keep himself in check. "Will was just being modest. There were other reasons for our victory, of course. We couldn't have won without Ranauld, and Kuper and Rellan, and especially the archers. Or without you, for that matter. But Torbury Scarp was fought against a vastly stronger enemy. No one else could have held the army together for so long in the way he did. None of the nobles with any military understanding—like Ranauld or Bottren—harbor any doubts about that. Nor anyone with common sense, like Burtelen!"

Essanda looked thoughtful again. "If it's such a problem that Will is a commoner, can't you make him a nobleman?" she asked.

Steffan was too surprised to respond immediately. "I'm not sure it would satisfy the nobles," he finally replied. "It might even make them more annoyed."

"It's been done before, in Castel at least. Did you know that Lord Eisgold's grandfather was born a commoner?"

"No, I didn't know! That's curious. Unfortunately, Eisgold isn't exactly an ideal example at the moment. But when I return to Arnost,

I will take a close look at Arvenian heraldry. There might be other precedents."

Steffan smiled warmly down at her, and she returned a smile of her own.

She was full of surprises, and had been from the beginning. Since his initial distress at discovering he had been deceived about her age, the surprises had been uniformly agreeable, serving only to highlight the astonishing depth of her character and her qualities. And the tiny seed of affection and respect planted at their first meeting had sprouted and grown prolifically. The truth was that she had won him over completely.

Essanda's presence at the conference had more than fulfilled Steffan's expectations. She had attended for his sake, and he decided to return the favor.

"Would you care to stroll with me, My Lady?"

She took the arm he offered with a pleased smile, and Steffan led her down to a sheltered garden just beyond the walls of the citadel. He looked on affectionately as she wandered among the winter blossoms—bright yellow pansies, carnations clad in white or dark red, and perfumed pink roses. Seeing the elegant grace of her movements, it might have been possible to mistake her for a woman.

But she was not a woman.

Steffan had married a bride who could not become his wife in full measure for a few more years at least. That had led to very real frustrations. He was a normal man with normal desires, and he couldn't pretend otherwise.

Even so, he valued her greatly, and he had high hopes for a future with her at his side. And in spite of his impatience, one thing had become clear to him. Even if he could magically revisit his decision to marry Essanda, he would not choose differently.

Whatever his frustrations in the short term, Steffan never doubted he would be thoroughly delighted with Essanda when she finally emerged into womanhood. He also recognized that it was no one's responsibility but his own to ensure that she emerged equally delighted with him.

Winter was well advanced, and a chill was in the air. A fresh layer of snow had dusted white the hut and everything that surrounded it. Nevertheless, each afternoon Thomas and Elena made their way to the meadow as they had done before.

They chatted happily about many things, but they didn't return to the past. By some kind of unspoken agreement, they had decided to make their home in the present.

Thomas had never felt so much at peace with the world. He was finding endless delight simply from being in Elena's presence. "There's nothing I want more than to be with you," he told her. "If I had to choose between the stone and you, I would give it up without a second thought."

He gazed into her face, a face that had been so long hidden from his sight. "I...I love you, Elena." He felt like he could drown in her eyes, and die happy. A sudden boldness filled him, and he spoke the words that rose unbidden to his tongue. "Would you marry me?"

Having said it, his heart skipped a beat. His own audacity took his breath away—even in his daydreams he had never dared to hope he could find the courage to ask her that question. If he had come to the meadow with any such plan, he knew he'd have frozen up long before he found a way to push the words past his lips. Somehow it had just happened, seemingly of its own accord.

How could he expect her to take such a question seriously, though? It wasn't unusual to marry at his age, and he didn't doubt that Elena was ready for such a step. But to seriously imagine that he was good enough for her? He felt a flush begin to creep up his forehead.

She gazed back at him. Slowly the smile faded from her face, and she regarded him seriously. "Yes, Thomas, I will marry you. I choose you, and I will bind myself to you. Whatever comes, for good or for ill, we will walk the journey together."

He felt dizzy with joy. Perhaps he didn't deserve her, but he was willing to spend a lifetime trying.

His heart overflowing, he took her hand, and they ran together back to the cabin to tell Rubin and Haldek.

The End

THE SAGA CONTINUES in *The Stone of Authority* (Book Three of *The Stone Cycle*).

SOME QUESTIONS REMAIN unanswered in the story so far. For example, how did Simon find his way to Lord Drettroth, and what took place at Drettroth's fortress before Brother Vangellis arrived?

To satisfy any who might be curious, I am including below a bonus novelette—*The Gamble*—that presents Simon's perspective.

Does the novelette also introduce a spoiler or two for the story that follows? You can judge for yourself.

The Gamble traces Simon's story from the period following the departure of Thomas from Arnost…

PART II

BONUS NOVELETTE—THE GAMBLE

1

Simon stood motionless, hidden in the shadows near the gates of Arnost. The walls towered above him—thick, strong, and so far impervious to the Rogandan army besieging the capital of Arvenon.

As soon as night fell he had crept silently to the walls and taken up a concealed position near the gate, just as he had done every night for the past week. In all that time he had come no closer to finding an answer to his central problem—how to find a way out of the city.

From the moment he decided to leave Arnost, all of his attention had been focused on getting outside the walls, undetected and in one piece. He was no closer to a solution. In a siege the gates stayed shut. No one entered, and no one left. It was as simple as that.

As he watched in continued frustration, the guards emerged from the gatehouses on either side of the gates. The gatehouses held a dozen guards, more than enough to rouse the soldiers stationed nearby in case of an attack. Simon knew all this from close observation. The guards milled around, talking and laughing. He wasn't quite close enough to hear what they were saying. Then most of them looked around warily before heading off at a trot away from the walls. They obviously had plans—plans that didn't involve guard duties.

He frowned. Surely such behavior would be regarded as irresponsible at any time. It was reckless and dangerous in a siege.

Only two of their number remained. Once the others had left, these two began peering around them in the darkness. They appeared restless and impatient.

Before long he heard the sound of a horse approaching, and he shrank deeper into the shadows to stay out of sight. A rider approached the gate, and the pair of guards stepped forward to challenge him. The rider bent down and spoke to them in a low voice, before slipping off the horse's back and handing the reins to one of the guards. All three of them stepped back into the shadows on the far side of the gates and stood there quietly. If anything, they appeared even more anxious than before.

What could they be doing? Their behavior seemed very suspicious. His curiosity aroused, Simon crept closer, careful to stay out of sight, until he was standing immediately beside the left gate.

It occurred to him to wonder if he should be alerting someone in authority. Then he thought about the questions that might be asked. *Who are you, and what were you doing snooping around near the gates? What business did you have there?* With the kingdom at war, the city gates were off limits to anyone except the guards. He decided to take the sensible approach and stay where he was. Protecting the Arvenian capital was someone else's problem—he wasn't planning to be in the city for long anyway.

As he stood there wondering whether to retrace his steps and just slip away into the night, he heard the sound of footfalls. Someone was approaching, and at a rapid pace. He'd heard nothing until the person was almost upon him, giving him no opportunity at all to escape. Heart pounding, he crouched down in the shadows beside the gates, desperately trying to remain inconspicuous.

A figure hurried past him, and he caught a brief glimpse of a richly dressed man in late middle age, red in the face from exertion. Whoever it was had clearly not noticed him.

As the red faced man appeared at the gates, the three hidden figures stepped forward. A mumbled conversation took place. A bag, small but bulging, appeared in the hand of the newcomer. Simon heard the dull clink of coins as the bag was handed over to the person who had brought the horse. The reins of the horse were yielded up in exchange.

The man who had arrived with the horse climbed up onto the wall and peered out into the darkness. After a couple of minutes he called down softly to the men below. The two guards moved to the gates. They were so close to Simon that he didn't dare breathe. One by one the heavy bars were removed from the gates, the guards panting with the effort. Then the gates were pulled open.

The gates swung slowly inward until a wide gap had appeared. Hoof beats sounded as the horse raced abruptly through the opening, with the richly dressed man in the saddle. Once clear of the gates the horseman was soon out of sight.

"Hurry up!" a rough voice hissed. "There'll be hell to pay if these gates are still open when the others get back. Especially once the duke discovers that Pisander's gone missing!"

The Earl of Pisander? He was the red faced horseman? He must have somehow bribed his way out of the dungeons.

Simon had become very familiar with Pisander's name in recent days. Endless gossip had swirled around the disgraced nobleman after his treason had been laid bare. The information that leaked out had changed everything for Simon.

The two guards hurried into position and slowly began pushing the heavy gates shut. Simon stared wide eyed at the steadily narrowing gap. His opportunity had arrived at last, if he could only find the courage to grasp it. With the opening continuing to shrink, Simon abandoned his agonizing and thrust aside his caution. Heart pounding, he darted forward into the gap.

The guards were taken completely by surprise. Before they could react he had sprinted through the gates and disappeared into the darkness.

"Hey! Come back!"

He ignored the soft call from the guards—he knew there was nothing they could do about his escape. They couldn't afford to waste time chasing him. And even if they had known who he was, they could hardly report him missing. That would require them to explain why the gates were open in the first place.

He could scarcely believe it—he was outside the walls.

Simon heard the sound of the bars being slid back into place. Then all went quiet.

He moved quickly away from the city, gradually putting distance between himself and the gates. Then he stopped and remained motionless, fully alert and listening for the slightest sound.

Everything was still and quiet. He crept on cautiously, not pausing until he was well out of bowshot range. A dip in the terrain appeared ahead of him. Once he reached it, he eased himself down into a sitting position. He was confident that he was no longer visible from the city walls.

He had done it. He was clear of the city.

What was he going to do now? He realized that all of his thinking and planning had been bent on finding a way out of Arnost undetected. He had expected that the next step would be obvious if he could achieve that. Now he wasn't so sure.

He shivered a little in the crisp night air, only partly because of the cold.

Huddling in the dark, an uncertain future before him, Simon thought back over the journey that had brought him here. So much had changed since the days in the stables when he had been happy. Even the faint recollection of that time—it seemed so long ago—caused a wave of anger to flood over him again.

It had felt like such a brief period. Years of humiliation and suffering had preceded it, and the experience of belonging had been exhilarating when it came. His jubilation had been short lived, though. It had all come crashing down when Thomas Stablehand—for reasons he still couldn't comprehend—had decided to make an enemy of him.

He hardened himself. He couldn't afford to be weak. Not now. Not tonight.

He began creeping forward, heading away from the city and

toward the Rogandan camp. He knew that his next move was extremely risky. Any Rogandan soldiers who stumbled upon him might simply decide to kill him.

His thoughts tumbled over each other, and he began to sweat. He tried to calm himself. He had a plan. He would demand to see Lord Drettroth. He couldn't speak Rogandan, but he had carefully memorized the name of the Rogandan army commander, and he felt certain it would carry weight.

He tried to remind himself that he had no reason for alarm. The reports he had heard about the letter found on the Earl of Pisander might have been fourth-hand, but they were surely close to the mark. If they were even vaguely accurate, Lord Drettroth would want to hear what he had to say. He would want to know about Thomas Stablehand. He would want to know everything Simon could tell him.

The very thought of his rival was enough to bring Simon back down to earth and renew his determination. He was doing this for a reason. After the Council meeting where the Earl of Pisander had been exposed, the news had spread like wildfire, but most of the attention had been focused on Pisander's treachery. It had taken Simon a while to piece together the information about the stone, and longer still to fully grasp what it meant.

Then his anger had slowly mounted as he began to realize that Thomas had used the stone—the same stone he had violently wrested from Simon in the stables—to selfishly carve out a reputation for himself. His use of the stone had allowed Thomas to mix with the likes of Will Prentis, the army commander, and the Duke of Erestor, who in the absence of King Steffan was the regent of the kingdom.

According to Pisander's letter, though, the stone actually belonged to the Rogandan lord.

Simon was doing the honorable thing by letting Lord Drettroth know who had his stone. He felt no compunction at all about exposing Thomas—the much vaunted army horse master fully deserved it.

It was unlikely that anything much would come of it, unfortunately. Thomas had long since left the city, and it was hard to imagine what the Rogandan lord could do to retrieve the stone. That wasn't Simon's problem, though. And it might give Thomas pause if he ever learned that the Rogandans were onto him.

Satisfying as it would be to avenge himself on Thomas, another matter had been working away in the back of his mind as he planned his escape from the city. The letter from Lord Drettroth had promised gold in return for the stone. Surely there would be some kind of reward for information. Maybe even a rich reward. He was, after all, able to identify the person who had the stone.

He had always been ignored and undervalued. Why should Thomas be the only one to benefit? He licked his lips involuntarily.

Simon peered ahead into the darkness. Campfires dimly flickered in the distance. He began to feel nervous again. He took another tentative step forward.

All of a sudden a dark figure loomed before him, and a harsh voice barked out words he could not understand. Then he heard a movement behind him. He opened his mouth to speak, but a sharp blow to the back of his head stunned him into silence. Pain flooded his consciousness. Then everything went dark.

A pounding headache greeted Simon when he woke. He opened his eyes to dazzling daylight, and immediately shut them again, trying to ease the pain in his head. His efforts were in vain. After a moment he cautiously squeezed his eyes open again and squinted around him. He was in some kind of animal pen with a few other men who looked like Arvenian farmers. He peered at them curiously. All of them looked thoroughly cowed—he could see no hope in their eyes. Rogandan soldiers surrounded them on every side, although they ignored their captives.

He groaned. The other prisoners turned to him, alarm on their faces. One of them put a finger to his lips.

So it wasn't safe to speak. Simon realized that he was thirsty and glanced around him. A small water trough sat within the enclosure, but he began wondering whether the water was fit to drink. He was even less certain if the prisoners were allowed to use the water without permission. He decided it was safest to wait and see.

His thirst became increasingly difficult to bear as the hours dragged slowly by. No one spoke, and the others barely moved. As the sun began to set, though, his fellow prisoners became visibly agitated. They watched the Rogandans anxiously, although Simon had no idea why. Clearly they were expecting something—something that filled them with dread.

Then two burly soldiers approached the enclosure. A few of his fellow captives began trembling uncontrollably, and Simon broke out in a cold sweat himself. The new arrivals barked orders that Simon could not understand, and other soldiers hurried to the enclosure. Pulling open a gate, they pushed into the enclosure and grabbed the first two prisoners who caught their eye.

One of the captives began struggling and crying out for mercy. They backhanded him, and he subsided to a fearful whimpering. The other man remained silent as they dragged him into the open. The soldiers closed the gate and bustled the two captives out of sight.

"Looks like we get to stay alive for another day," one of the other prisoners muttered. The words were spoken so quietly that Simon could barely make them out. The comment appeared to be addressed to no one in particular.

A soldier arrived and threw some stale bread into the enclosure. One of the captives retrieved it. He broke it into pieces and handed them around. He didn't hesitate before giving Simon a share as well. The men all ate. The portions were small, and it didn't take long. Then each of them shuffled over to the water trough and knelt, scooping up water in their open hands and bending down to drink it. Simon copied them. The water tasted foul, but by then he was so thirsty that he didn't care.

As soon as darkness fell, Simon moved quietly to the person who had muttered aloud. "What's going to happen to us?" He spoke as quietly as he could.

The other man turned to him and shrugged. "Each day they come and take two of us," he whispered. "No one has ever come back, so it isn't hard to guess what happens."

"How did they capture you?" Simon asked.

"The filthy Rogandans stole my goats. I was trying to take one of them back. I have youngsters who need the milk. I would have gotten away with it, too, if the goat hadn't made such an infernal racket." He paused. "What about you?"

Simon didn't know what to say. It was already abundantly clear to him that he had made a colossal mistake. "I guess I was in the wrong place at the wrong time," he eventually managed.

The other man accepted his reply at face value. He nodded. "My name is Lennard. What's yours?"

"Simon."

Lennard studied him with a frown. "Someone as young as you shouldn't be in here. Maybe they'll take pity on you." He sounded doubtful.

Dusk finally heralded the end of another anxious day. The soldiers came as before, and Simon cowered down, desperate to avoid their attention. His efforts proved futile. One of the soldiers headed straight for him, grabbing his arm and pulling him to his feet. As they dragged him outside he called out in desperation, "Drettroth! I must see Lord Drettroth!"

The soldiers paused, frowning. They exchanged a few words, then they both laughed—a cruel sound that filled Simon with fear. Calling to another soldier, they thrust Simon toward him. Then one of them re-entered the enclosure and to Simon's horror emerged with Lennard.

As he was dragged past Simon, the farmer aimed a look of surprise and disappointment at the youth. Simon opened his mouth to call out, to tell the farmer it wasn't as it appeared, that he had good reasons for his appeal to the Rogandan lord. But the words stuck in his throat.

Simon was held outside the enclosure in sight of his former

fellow captives. They said nothing, but they peered at him grimly through the gloom. Darkness couldn't come soon enough for the youth. He sat in utter dejection, head in his hands, unable to think of anything except the farmer who had taken his place. Lennard's hungry children would never see their father again.

The sun was rising when a Rogandan soldier arrived who spoke a little Arvenian. "You seek Lord Drettroth? Why?" he asked bluntly.

Simon answered quietly, hoping the other captives wouldn't overhear their conversation. "He is looking for something—an heirloom. I have information about it."

"You want reward, no?" The soldier had an ugly smile on his face. "Maybe you lucky. Maybe he let you die quick."

The soldier looked critically at him for a long moment. Then he barked some commands, and the youth was bustled away toward some horses.

Simon had plenty of time to berate himself as the leagues rolled by under the hooves of their horses. What had possessed him to leave the safety of Arnost? He had thought to avenge himself against Thomas and enrich himself in the bargain. Having now experienced Arvenon's enemies up close for himself, his intentions seemed petty and absurd.

2

Simon's journey eventually ended at a stone fortress somewhere within Arvenon that the Rogandan commander had made his base. The youth was almost paralyzed with fear by the time he finally found himself in the presence of Lord Drettroth. The commander was tall with close cropped dark hair and an indefinable air of authority. Something about him radiated malice.

The Rogandan lord calmly looked him up and down. He didn't seem at all impressed with what he saw. Simon did not have the slightest doubt that his life would be over the instant that Drettroth lost interest in him. He began shivering uncontrollably.

"I am told you have information that might interest me." The nobleman spoke excellent Arvenian. He sounded bored.

"Y...y...yes. It's about your heirloom."

Lord Drettroth raised an eyebrow, then turned his head and gestured sharply to the guards who had brought Simon in. They bowed quickly and left the room, closing the door behind them.

"What do you know about this heirloom?"

"I heard about it," Simon said nervously. "From the letter you wrote to the Earl of Pisander."

The brow of Lord Drettroth darkened, and Simon belatedly regretted revealing that the letter had become public.

"I know who has the stone!" the youth blurted.

The Rogandan leaned close and narrowed his eyes. "Tell me everything you know," he said in a threatening growl. "Leave nothing out! I might even let you live if I decide your information is useful to me."

Simon swallowed convulsively. "Thomas Stablehand has it!"

"How do you know?"

Simon, thoroughly frightened, was on the brink of blurting out his entire history with Thomas and the stone. Then it occurred to him that it might not be wise to tell the whole story. Things might end badly for him if he appeared to be laying any kind of claim of his own to the stone.

A stream of answers spilled out. "I saw him with it once. I worked with him—in the royal stables. I didn't realize what it was. Not until later. Not until I heard the stories. About the meeting—where the Earl of Pisander was arrested." All of that was true enough.

"This Thomas Stablehand. Is he in Arnost?"

"No." He shook his head rapidly. "He left. Some time ago."

"On his own?"

"No. He went with some others."

"Where did he go?"

"I don't know."

"And he took the stone with him?"

"I think so." Then he nodded, vigorously, hoping to appear certain. "He wouldn't have left it behind."

The nobleman questioned Simon very closely. He gradually extracted everything the youth knew about the stone. The only thing Simon concealed was his fight with Thomas in the stables—he gave Drettroth no hint at all that the stone had ever been in his possession.

The Rogandan came away with a very detailed description of Thomas. To his shame, Simon also revealed that Will Prentis had departed Arnost with Thomas. He hadn't intended to say anything that might compromise the security of the capital. But Drettroth's questioning was relentless. Once the youth began answering questions, he couldn't find a way of stopping.

"So why have you told me all this? No doubt you heard about the reward I was offering."

He shook his head energetically. "No. I heard that the stone belonged to you. It seemed only right...to let you know what had become of it."

"So you abandoned your countrymen and sought out the commander of your enemies, all because of a moral obligation? Come now, Simon. Do you really think I am that naive? If you were so intent on doing the right thing, why have you turned so eagerly on the son of your mentor? And why have you willingly betrayed the commander of your own army?"

Drettroth stood tall, hands on his hips. "Perhaps you've invented this story because you're a coward. You'd do or say anything to save your skin, wouldn't you? Yes, I'm well aware of how eager you were for someone else to be taken away in your place after you were captured. A poor farmer, I'm told."

He gazed down at Simon with a condescending smile. Simon couldn't meet his eyes.

"Perhaps you think I should be grateful to you. But the truth is that you've told me little more than an entertaining tale. You claim that a Thomas Stablehand has the stone, but you offer no proof. You tell me he's left Arnost, but you can't say where he's gone. You don't even know if he took this supposed stone with him. You've given me no way to verify your fairy tale.

"It's obvious that you see this Thomas as an enemy. Perhaps you're simply making all this up in the hope that I will seek him out and kill him for you."

"No! I'm telling you the truth!"

"I think you were caught by my guards. You'd heard some rumors, about an heirloom I supposedly lost. So you thought of a clever way to save yourself. I'm impressed, Simon, really I am."

"That isn't how it happened! I came here by choice—to tell you about the stone!"

"So you chose to leave the safety of your city. And you decided to just walk up to my soldiers and give yourself up. Do you think I'm stupid?" Drettroth's eyes flashed dangerously.

The Rogandan commander called for the guards and spoke rapidly to them in their own language. "I will decide about you tomorrow," he told Simon in an offhand tone. "In the meantime, I hope you find your new accommodations to your liking." He aimed a mocking sneer at the youth, then turned away.

The guards dragged Simon out of the room. They led him for several minutes through a series of passageways and down multiple flights of steps. Eventually they came to a halt in front of a dank and gloomy cell. They shoved him inside and locked the door. No natural light penetrated into this dark place. The only illumination came from a single torch burning dimly somewhere down the passageway.

The cell held nothing except a hard bed with a single thin blanket. Simon sat down on the bed and buried his head in his hands.

FIVE SEEMINGLY ENDLESS days passed before Lord Drettroth called for Simon again. The youth had been fed once each day, and he felt certain that his ration could not sustain life for long. He was never given enough to drink, either. He was accustomed to cruelty growing up in the home of his uncle, but he had never gone hungry or thirsty. Now, hunger gnawed at him constantly throughout his waking hours, competing for attention with his thirst. He couldn't sleep for the cold, either. His mind churned over and over, the same thoughts spinning through his head as he constantly berated himself.

Simon could not summon up the resources to cope with his situation, and he soon began to abandon any hope of surviving his imprisonment.

When he was brought once again before Lord Drettroth, the nobleman assessed him critically for a long moment before speaking.

"You look tired, Simon. Haven't you found your quarters comfortable?" His words were accompanied by an ironic smile.

Simon didn't answer. Their previous interaction had drained his confidence as well as extinguishing his hope. He had delivered up the best information he had to offer, and it had failed to impress the Rogandan lord even a whit. He had nothing more to give.

"I have some good news for you. It seems I might be able to find a use for you after all."

Simon looked dully at his captor, unable to guess what might be coming next.

"You look hungry. Here, have some food and wine." The Rogandan nodded to a guard, who led the youth to a table laden with food.

The youth looked suspiciously at the food, then back at Drettroth.

"Go on," the Rogandan insisted, "help yourself! No need to hurry. Take your time."

Simon decided he had nothing to lose. And he was starving. He stretched out a trembling hand for some food, brought it to his mouth, and took a bite. He was convinced he had never eaten food that tasted so good. He ignored the wine and drank from an earthen cup filled with water, closing his eyes to fully savor the simple pleasure of slaking his thirst.

He stole a glance at Lord Drettroth. The Rogandan stood with arms folded across his chest, a self-satisfied smile playing across his lips. "Does it taste good?" he asked.

Simon nodded, stuffing more food into his mouth. He had no idea how long the nobleman's indulgence might last, and he decided to make the most of it.

"Try some of the wine. I insist! I'm told it's excellent."

He hesitated for a moment, then obediently sipped the wine. He had no doubt that it was the most expensive liquid he had ever glimpsed, much less consumed.

"Any strange aftertaste?" he was asked.

The youth stopped chewing, frowning in puzzlement.

"This food was prepared for me," Drettroth told him. "I'm interested to know if someone poisoned it."

Simon almost choked, gagging involuntarily. He felt the blood drain from his face, and he began to sweat.

Drettroth laughed contemptuously at his discomposure.

"My food taster always samples my food and drink before I eat," said the Rogandan. "He plays an important role—just yesterday he was able to save my life. It was, of course, necessary for him to sacrifice his own life to do so.

"But you'll be glad to know that he has been avenged. I personally supervised an investigation to find the fools responsible, and two of the kitchen hands along with one of my guards were executed early this morning. So I doubt that you need to concern yourself too much about being poisoned. Not on this occasion, at least.

"One can never be certain, though. For obvious reasons, I cannot afford to take any risks. So I find myself needing a new food taster.

"I pride myself on being a reliable judge of character, and it seems to me that you'll do very nicely," his captor concluded brightly. "You will oversee the preparation of my meals. Whenever food and drink are brought to me, I will select portions for you to eat. It will be strongly in your own interests to ensure that no one interferes with the food."

Simon wasn't asked if he was willing—he was not offered a choice. He began the job immediately.

The very first time he presented a meal to Drettroth, the Rogandan sniffed suspiciously at it before turning to Simon with fury on his face. "You spat in my food! Don't try to deny it! I'll have you strung up on the nearest tree!" He approached Simon threateningly, his eyes bulging wildly.

Simon was so taken aback he couldn't speak. He shrank back trembling with fear, his mouth agape.

Then Drettroth chortled, bursting into uproarious laughter. "Simon, you are invaluable! The village imbecile could not look more idiotic."

From that moment on, the nobleman went out of his way to devise creative ways of belittling his new food taster. Simon was familiar with abuse, but he had never been mocked so relentlessly. Nor did the Rogandan limit himself to verbal abuse. Whenever Drettroth was in a foul mood, he took it out on Simon. It was not uncommon for him to strike the youth multiple times each day for his supposed stupidity.

Simon's new job was not without its own set of risks, either. The quality of the food served to Drettroth was outstanding—uniformly so. No cook lived long enough to serve substandard food twice to his master. Quality made no difference if the food was poisoned, though.

On one occasion, sampling a truly delicious meal, Simon began to feel extremely ill. He was soon throwing up violently, feeling utterly miserable. Worst of all, he was convinced that he was about to die, certain that the food must have been poisoned.

His master stood by laughing raucously, apparently deriving considerable amusement from Simon's discomfort. "Absolutely delightful! You never disappoint me, my Simon." Drettroth belted him heartily on the back, prompting a further bout of vomiting.

Simon could not remember ever feeling so wretched.

"There's no need for alarm," Drettroth told him. "This isn't a surprise attack. I poisoned the food myself. Just a little joke of mine—not enough to kill you." He looked thoughtful for a moment. "At least I don't think it was enough to kill you. We'll have to wait and see." Then he burst out laughing again.

However good the food might be, Simon was never able to enjoy it again. He could never be sure that Drettroth hadn't arranged for it to be poisoned, simply to satisfy his depraved sense of humor.

Simon soon doubted that it was possible to loathe a person more than he did Drettroth. The Rogandan lord was at least evenhanded—he endlessly invented new ways of inflicting his brutishness on anyone unlucky enough to be around him. As his frequent companion, though, more often than not Simon bore the brunt of his petty hatefulness. The youth began to wonder if his predecessor might have welcomed death by poisoning.

IN SPITE of the bleakness of his situation, there were periods of time when Simon was almost happy. The food taster was not expected to accompany Lord Drettroth when he traveled beyond his fortress—

the nobleman apparently had other arrangements—so Simon occasionally enjoyed a temporary release from the torment visited upon him by his new master.

And he was not alone in his relief. When the commander departed, it almost felt as if the entire fortress heaved a sigh of contentment.

A senior Rogandan army officer was left in charge. The officer was terrifying, and Simon stayed well clear of him. But even so, Lord Drettroth's deputy seemed almost genial compared to the commander himself.

In this more relaxed environment, Simon was able to form a friendship with two of the kitchen maids. They were fluent in both Arvenian and Rogandan due to a mixed heritage.

Svea was quiet and gentle, a hard worker who rarely spoke, even when spoken to.

Ines, by contrast, was intense and passionate. Simon hadn't known her long before discovering that her waking hours were consumed with wild schemes and imaginings concerning the demise of her lord and master.

Hating the Rogandan overlord was one thing; talking about it openly in his own fortress was another, even using a foreign language. Simon didn't need to speak Rogandan to see that everyone around him hated Lord Drettroth almost as much as he did. But that didn't make it safe to be blatant about it in the way that Ines was. Most others rightly feared the nobleman even more than they hated him.

Simon worried at times that he might be putting himself at risk by associating with Ines. But it was hard to resist the gratification of hearing someone say openly what everyone else only dared to think.

Lord Drettroth had left the fortress that morning, and no one seemed to have any idea when he might return. Simon took the opportunity to sit outside with the two maids, enjoying the afternoon sunshine.

Of late his secret thoughts had increasingly been wandering in the direction of Svea. Such idle fancies were by no means disagreeable, but they were still sufficiently unfamiliar to leave him feeling awkward. At that moment he sat quietly, trying not to be too obvious as he stole glances in her direction.

"I have a plan to get rid of Drettroth," Ines announced, tossing the hair restlessly from her face.

Simon looked at her skeptically.

"The plan depends on you," she told him.

He snorted, not feeling any need to take her seriously.

"Come with me," she said. "I have something to show you."

Simon wasn't sure whether to laugh at her or to be worried. He sat unmoving for a moment, then shrugged and got to his feet. Following Ines, he headed back into the castle. Svea trailed along quietly behind them.

Ines led the way to a small room adjacent to Drettroth's quarters. Normally it was guarded, but today the guards were nowhere to be seen. With their master absent, they were undoubtedly also appreciating the opportunity for a break.

The three of them slipped inside, and Ines pulled the door closed. The room, dimly lit from a high window, was filled with shelves covered with jars and pots, all labeled in Rogandan.

"These are all poisons collected by Drettroth," Ines told them. "I overheard some of the guards talking about it." She pointed to a particular jar. "This is the one we need."

"You're planning to poison him?" Simon couldn't believe she was serious. "You know what happened last time."

"The plan only failed last time because the food taster wasn't involved."

"How do you know that? No one can say for certain what went wrong. None of the plotters are still alive to ask!"

She tossed her head again. "We don't need to ask them. It's obvious."

He shook his head. "If you're planning to poison him, don't expect any help from me. Have you forgotten that I'm expected to eat and drink a portion of anything that's served to him?"

"Don't you want to see him gone?"

"Of course I do. But that doesn't mean I'm ready to poison myself."

"You won't need to. We won't poison all of his food. He loves leeks, so we'll poison them. When you sample his food, just make sure you don't eat any leeks."

Simon was aghast. "That's your plan? There's no way I'm going to be involved!"

"There's nothing to worry about! All you need to do is avoid eating the leeks."

Simon desperately wanted to be rid of Drettroth. But this wasn't the way.

The next few days were going to be extremely challenging. He knew from experience that once Ines got an idea in her head, she would never let it go.

3

"What's the matter, Simon? Is it possible that you're not pleased to have me back again?" Drettroth wore a condescending smile. He seemed to be watching Simon with unusual interest.

Simon's heart was racing, and he began to sweat. He said nothing, not trusting himself to respond.

"This food looks and smells delicious. Sadly, though, I find that I'm not at all hungry," Drettroth told him. "It would be a pity to waste such a fine meal. You can eat it, Simon." His eyes narrowed, and his voice took on a threatening tone. "All of it!" he commanded.

Simon began to shake uncontrollably.

The Rogandan lord began to smile, a pitiless leer that filled Simon with dread. He called in his guards and spoke to them rapidly in Rogandan. They left the room immediately.

"I have invited our cooks to join us," the nobleman explained. "The ones who prepared the meal."

Simon couldn't hide his dismay.

Soon Ines was dragged into the room, followed by Svea.

"I'm not hungry, and Simon seems to have lost his appetite as well. The two of you can eat the meal."

Ines shook her head.

"Eat it!" Drettroth roared.

The guards forced the two girls toward the plate. After a moment's hesitation, Ines grabbed the plate and began shoveling the food into her mouth, swallowing it whole without bothering to chew it.

When she had entirely consumed the food, she sat back, aiming a look of disdain at Simon. Then she turned her full attention to Lord Drettroth, making no attempt to hide the hatred on her face.

Svea watched on, pale and trembling.

Drettroth nodded in the direction of Ines. "She shows courage," he said, with reluctant admiration. He turned to his food taster. "Thankfully you are not equally bold, my Simon, or we might have been facing a different outcome." He fixed the youth with a look somewhere between a smile and a sneer. "Don't think I'm ungrateful, though. I can read you like a scroll. You're everything I hoped for in a food taster."

Drettroth fell silent, apparently content simply to wait. The minutes dragged painfully by. Then Ines abruptly began to spasm, her head snapping back and forth. Soon her entire body was convulsing violently. Lord Drettroth seemed to enjoy the spectacle, standing with arms folded across his chest and a tight smile of satisfaction on his face. Svea buried her face in her hands, unable to watch. Simon stood rooted to the spot, filled with horror.

After a few minutes even Drettroth seemed to have had enough. He spoke to his guards, and they carried Ines, still writhing, from the room. One of them grabbed Svea by the arm and bustled her out with them.

The Rogandan nobleman turned to Simon. "In recognition of the courage of your friend, I've decided to be more generous to her than she deserves. She will be executed immediately, along with her companion." Seeing the look of anguish on Simon's face, he growled, "Be grateful I didn't insist that all three of you take the same medicine."

FOR SIMON, the execution of his friends signaled the passing of any remaining hope he might have had. From that hour, he plodded through life in a daze.

Once long ago he had caught a glimpse of a wind-swept hilltop where a twisted tree stood alone, bent and blasted by the elements. His life now seemed like that tree, stunted and shattered, solitary in the midst of a barren wasteland.

He no longer spent his free minutes with the kitchen hands. He felt too ashamed to show his face there now. He avoided human companionship entirely. Instead he haunted the deserted passageways of the fortress, passing through the shadows as silent as a ghost.

On one occasion Drettroth took him into the room with the poisons, pointing out the various substances and expanding on their origins.

"I've found these substances to be extremely useful at times," Drettroth boasted. "I've never made a secret of my research into poisons, and my enemies in Rogand have quickly learned to employ food tasters of their own. I've simply taken that as an encouragement to become more creative."

It was obvious that the Rogandan enjoyed any opportunity to gloat with an audience. Simon said nothing.

"You understand better than most," he continued. "You have some small experience of my prowess yourself." He laughed, a jarring sound that sent shivers down Simon's spine.

"You might wonder why I'm showing you this, Simon. I'm not at all concerned that you'll use these poisons against me. It should be obvious to you by now that I'll know immediately if you do. But I thought you might one day decide you need to take some of this yourself."

He lifted one of the jars from the shelf. "This is the poison that your friend tried to use on me. It's very effective—you witnessed the results first hand." He pointed to another jar. "This one is a better choice for you. Take some of this, and all your troubles will be over in a few short minutes."

Drettroth looked at him condescendingly. "Come and help yourself. Any time. I've already instructed my guards to let you in."

He gave Simon another of his mirthless smiles. "Taking poison would first require you to stop being a coward, of course. I simply can't imagine that ever happening." He threw his head back, and a harsh and mocking laugh echoed around the tiny space.

Simon was too dispirited to reply. He was aware that Drettroth was goading him, but he had no fight left in him. He was entirely powerless against Drettroth now. The Rogandan knew it, and he knew it as well.

IT WAS on one of his wanderings that Simon first became aware that a monk was being held in the prison. The robed figure was being taken somewhere by the guards, and he spotted Simon and called out a greeting, using the language of Arvenon. Simon slipped out of sight without offering a response.

The youth could not easily put the monk out of his mind, though. Since the demise of his two friends, only Lord Drettroth was able to speak to him in his own language. And every minute Simon spent in the company of the nobleman felt like a punishment.

It wasn't long before a pressing need for less vicious human companionship led him to the cell of the monk. His first impressions were not encouraging. He quickly concluded that the prisoner had gone mad when he found him singing. And not just singing, but sounding forth with cheerful abandon.

The monk, who introduced himself as Brother Vangellis, wasn't crazy, though. It took no more than a brief conversation to confirm that.

"How did you come to be here?" Brother Vangellis had asked.

Simon squirmed inside. Every day he risked his life in service to a man that he hated and feared. Every day he endured countless humiliations, great and small. Yet none of it was necessary. He had left the safety of Arnost by his own choice. And for what purpose? He had long since abandoned any pretense that he had acted out of noble motives.

He knew now that he could never be free from the consequences of his folly. He had watched as Lennard was led away in his place. He had refused out of cowardice to eat Drettroth's poisoned food, then stood by while Ines ate it instead. He had witnessed silently the horror of the death throes of his friend, and made no protest as Svea was led away to be executed. His shame haunted his waking thoughts and tortured his dreams.

No one could be blamed but himself. His lot in life was to grovel each day before his master, and it was no more than he deserved.

"I made a mistake. Now my life is over."

The monk had shaken his head in denial. "Your life doesn't have to be over because of your mistakes."

No one who made such a statement could possibly fathom the ugly realities of life. "You're a monk. You wouldn't understand."

"I understand much better than you could imagine. I once thought like you do."

Simon had simply shrugged. How could a monk begin to understand the depths to which he had sunk? And even if he could somehow comprehend it, what use would that be?

"It makes no difference," he had said. "There is nothing I can do about my situation."

"There is always something you can do," the monk had insisted. "The choices before us may not seem obvious at times. But we always have choices."

Simon had not come to the cell with any intention of holding a serious conversation with this stranger. But he unexpectedly found himself engaging with someone who not only spoke the same language, but was a willing listener. He was soon drawn in, in spite of himself.

It didn't take long for his feelings about Drettroth to emerge. The stranger was Drettroth's prisoner, so it hadn't been difficult to believe he might be sympathetic. And as Simon's story began to spill out, the monk did not disappoint him.

Simon related the early part of his life, and how he had found his way to the royal stables at Arnost. "I was happy, working alongside Thomas Stablehand. For a while. But then he turned on me. I still don't know why."

"That must have been hard to take," the monk offered.

"It felt like a dagger to my heart. I was angry and upset, and I decided to get him back. I'd always been the victim before. This time I decided it was someone else's turn. My anger woke something in me—a burning desire for revenge; a passion I didn't know was there. I began scheming. I could see that the timing needed to be right, and somehow I found the patience to bide my time. I prepared my revenge, and when it came I savored it to the full."

"What did you do?"

"My first target was Ben, a mastiff that belonged to Thomas. That dog was the delight of his life. I convinced his father that the animal was dangerous and needed to be put down. Thomas didn't even see it coming.

"That was only the beginning, though. My main achievement—if you could call it that—was finding ways to get between Thomas and his father. That didn't turn out to be too difficult. Neither of them needed a lot of encouragement—they were already good at misunderstanding each other. His father eventually lost patience entirely with Thomas and preferred to work with me instead.

"But it was all for nothing in the end. After Thomas left Arnost, his father berated himself incessantly for driving his only son away, and became preoccupied with how upset Thomas's mother would be. He couldn't forgive himself for not doing things differently. It became obvious he cared very little about me."

"That must have upset you."

Simon nodded. "At the time I found it very frustrating. It's what finally convinced me to leave. Whether or not the Rogandans managed to capture the city, it was clear to me that I had no future in Arnost.

"I suppose I knew deep down that I deserved it, though. Maybe Thomas was entitled to some payback, but my revenge eventually went way beyond anything he'd done to me. When I look back now, I can see that I'd finally discovered something I was good at. Unfortunately for all of us, it wasn't anything useful or productive."

"Are you still angry with Thomas?"

"Yes, of course I am! I wouldn't be here now if he hadn't turned on me. But I know I can't blame him for my own responses. I did when I left Arnost. But not now. Drettroth constantly tells me that I'm worthless. And when I look back on everything I've done, I know he's right."

Brother Vangellis shook his head firmly. "You're not a hopeless case, Simon. Any more than I was."

The conversation ended soon after that. Simon knew he'd shown himself in a very bad light, and it was obvious that the monk had been distressed by what he'd heard. Yet for some reason Simon didn't feel judged by him.

It wasn't long before the youth was back, drawn almost compulsively to the cell of the monk.

Brother Vangellis began to unfold his own story, and Simon was quickly captivated. He listened intently as the monk told him about his early life, his fall and his slide into oblivion, and his eventual rehabilitation. He began to understand why the monk had been reluctant to pass judgment on him.

"There's something you need to know, Simon. You talked about Thomas, and, as it happens, I know him myself. We traveled together after he left Arnost. In fact, we were hiding together from the Rogandans at the time I was captured."

Simon couldn't hide his astonishment.

"And that's not all. Thomas talked to me about his history with you. You might be surprised to hear that he feels ashamed about the way he treated you. He largely blames himself for everything that happened as a result."

The monk's revelation astounded Simon. The youth said very little in response; he needed time to ponder this information.

BROTHER VANGELLIS MADE no mention of the stone as the days passed. Nevertheless, Simon guessed that he must know something of it. He imagined that the monk had his own reasons for choosing not to talk about it. The youth didn't care. The stone had loomed large in his thinking at the time he left Arnost, but it now seemed little more than a distraction to him. The stone wasn't his story. There were more important things he needed to think about.

The truth was that Simon's time with Brother Vangellis had increasingly unsettled him. He wasn't being dragged down further into despair. He wasn't exactly becoming more content, either. Something deep inside him was struggling to gain a foothold, and it refused to give up. The process left him feeling restless and troubled.

Brother Vangellis might not be crazy, but there was something very unusual about him. A mysterious quality oozed out of him, one that left him calm and peaceful in spite of his imprisonment and his uncertain future. It wasn't normal. Simon couldn't readily identify what this quality was, but it had begun to call to him. He increasingly caught himself longing for it, almost to the point of desperation.

He finally found a name for it—joyfulness. Given the monk's circumstances, both in the past and now in his prison cell, insanity might have seemed entirely understandable. It was much harder to account for him being joyful. Perhaps it had to do with Brother Vangellis successfully emerging from the depths of his own guilt and shame. And, strangest of all, the monk had said that in breaking free he encountered God as liberator, not as accuser. Simon was both baffled and intrigued.

Although the youth could not fully comprehend what he was experiencing, he eventually sought an opportunity to express in a practical way the changes stirring inside him. He had discovered another prisoner in the fortress—a nobleman who turned out to be King Delmar of Varas. Simon decided to free him.

He fully understood the risk he was taking, and he was in no doubt about the likely consequences once Lord Drettroth became aware of his actions. Nevertheless, he was eager for some kind of outlet.

Given the seismic shifts taking place within him, releasing the royal prisoner seemed to Simon little more than a token gesture. But his act of defiance proved to be more significant than he expected. It solidified what had been happening within him, and it also demonstrated that his master's hold over him was beginning to weaken.

His actions required a boldness that he would not previously have believed himself capable of. Yet he did it without hesitating.

He was rediscovering a quality he thought was lost to him forever—hope.

If Lord Drettroth had perceived the tiniest portion of what was happening in the prison cells of his own fortress, he would have instantly disposed of both his food taster and the monk. As yet, though, the Rogandan lord was not privy to the secret thoughts of others. Without the Stone of Knowing he had no way to pry loose the hidden intents and imaginings of those around him.

4

"Come with me, Simon. I have a surprise for you." Lord Drettroth bared his teeth in a self-satisfied smirk.

Simon followed his master with considerable trepidation, a frown creasing his brow. Drettroth's surprises had never been pleasant, and he couldn't think of any possible reason why that might ever change.

Trailing along in the nobleman's wake, he entered a room where, to his intense alarm, he glimpsed Brother Vangellis chained to the wall. His friend did not appear to be injured, but attracting Lord Drettroth's close attention signaled extreme danger. It amounted to a death knell.

Then he saw Thomas Stablehand. He felt the blood drain from his face as he absorbed the shock. He had never imagined for a moment that they would meet again. But for it to happen here, under these circumstances?

His first emotion was one of overwhelming shame. Then he fully grasped the implications of Thomas's presence, and the completeness of Drettroth's victory began to dawn on him. Would his master's triumphs never end? An angry frown covered his face as he contemplated this latest setback for anything good in the world.

Thomas was chained not far from the monk, and he appeared to have injured his arm. He was clearly not at all pleased to see Simon.

"What a merry reunion this is!" said Drettroth. He turned to the monk. "I did promise that you would soon be reunited with your companion, did I not? And here he is."

Then he addressed Simon. "I understand you've become acquainted with the monk as well, my Simon. You seem to have been spending a lot of time with him lately." He watched their faces closely, then he laughed. "Surely you're not surprised. I make sure I know what's going on in my own fortress."

He scowled at Simon. "You've been playing some little games with another of my guests, too. Don't imagine there will not be consequences. I take it personally when people decide to cross me."

Simon did not flinch. He wasn't sure why, but the Rogandan lord no longer had the same hold over him.

Drettroth swung around to face Thomas. "It must have been quite some time since you last saw Simon. You must be delighted to find yourself reunited with him once again." Thomas did not speak, but the look on his face said plenty.

"I'm sure that's more than enough of pleasantries, though," said Drettroth, dismissing his guards. "We're all here for one reason. Simon, fetch the stone from Thomas."

Thomas resisted fiercely as Simon retrieved the stone, head butting him violently and screaming his rage. He inflicted pain on his former friend, but he was unable to prevent the removal of the stone from his pouch.

Simon squinted and rubbed his head, trying to ease the throbbing. Then, as he glanced down at Thomas with the stone in his hand, his eyes were opened.

He stood there, stupefied.

Thomas's fury battered him silently, washing over him with invisible force. Simon suddenly witnessed the extent of the damage his actions had caused. He saw the evidence of the Rogandans spreading out across Arvenon in their search for Thomas, leaving death and destruction in their wake. He saw the monks cowering beneath the ground while Drettroth's men demolished their beloved monastery. He saw Thomas fleeing downriver with his friend, and watched as a bound and helpless Brother Vangellis was beaten to the ground, felled by a heavy blow. He saw Thomas leading the Rogandans away from Elena and her father, and his injury and capture that had followed as a result.

Simon was responsible—for all of it. Lord Drettroth had not known who had the stone before Simon abandoned the safety and security of his life in Arnost to reveal it to him. The youth had acted out of a petty desire to wound Thomas, and the enormity of the consequences overwhelmed him.

Nor was that all. He glimpsed the origins of his quarrel with Thomas and perceived it to be little more than foolish immaturity on the part of the older youth. He saw that the monk had been right, and that Thomas regretted his behavior. And Simon witnessed for himself the magnitude by which his revenge had exceeded the wrongs that prompted it.

Now, experiencing the raw power of the stone, he immediately understood why Thomas had tried so desperately to keep it from Drettroth.

All this he grasped in no more than a few heartbeats. Seeking relief from the intensity of it, he spun on his heel and headed to Drettroth.

The moment his eyes fell upon the Rogandan nobleman, though, he was plunged into the vile turmoil of his master's inner being. He knew what Drettroth was like—every single day he had found himself on the sharp end of the nobleman's viciousness—but nothing prepared him for the assault on his own sanity that came with unrestricted access to Drettroth's mind. He blinked, and it all faded momentarily, then it flooded inexorably over him again.

Drettroth's full strategy for acquiring the stone was laid bare; his plans for Brother Vangellis and Thomas were instantly apparent. Simon inwardly recoiled from the horror of it. The barbarity planned for them was just the beginning, though. Once Drettroth commanded the Stone of Knowing, the world as Simon had known it would end.

He learned that there were other stones, too, and saw that the Rogandan would not rest until he possessed them all. Simon glimpsed, but could not entirely grasp, his machinations around securing a covenant with his Dark Gods. But he saw that Drettroth believed he could bargain with them to secure his longevity, and that he expected a heavy obligation in return. He would expunge this debt by means of human sacrifice on a grand scale. Tens of thousands of his captives would die—as many as it might take to achieve his purpose.

Simon was aware that he himself would not long survive. With the stone in the hand of his master, there would be little further need for a food taster. But the youth was not dismayed. He had no desire to live in the kind of world that Drettroth wanted to create.

Curiously, the recent infusion of hope into Simon's life had not come unaccompanied. Other qualities, arriving unannounced, had settled in at the same time. One of them was the willingness—whatever the cost—to take a stand when it genuinely mattered. Simon was not the same person who had hidden in the shadows when Brother Vangellis first called a greeting. He did not fully realize it yet, but he was no longer a coward.

Drettroth demanded the stone, and Simon briefly handed it over, before later returning it to Thomas's pouch. While Drettroth gloated aloud about the imminent glory of his future and the pointless futility of opposing him, the food taster's mind was working furiously. The youth only half heard the nobleman as he droned on. Before he was pushed from the room before his master, he knew exactly what he needed to do.

As the door closed behind them, the Rogandan lord strode off down the passageway, positively oozing with glee. "Wine, boy," he called back over his shoulder, "and be quick about it! All this talking is thirsty work."

Simon hurried away. He intended to do his master's bidding. But he had a twist of his own in store. First he went to his room and retrieved two small leather pouches, upending them to make sure they were empty. Then he set off for the poison room. His heart began to race as he saw the two guards standing alert in their usual position, but they made no attempt to interfere as he pushed past them into the room. They smirked knowingly at him, and he ignored them, closing the door behind him. Lifting down the two jars identified by Drettroth, he carefully emptied a generous amount of each poison into his pouches.

Scurrying down to the kitchen, he retrieved two silver chalices before making his way to the cellar. He knew the habits of his master well enough to anticipate that Drettroth would drain one chalice immediately, then demand the second later, most likely a few minutes before rejoining his prisoners. He filled the chalices with wine from the Rogandan commander's favorite barrel.

Finally, he returned to his room. Opening the pouches carefully, he chose the poison originally used by Ines. He had no idea how much would be needed, so he tipped a liberal dose into one of the cups. Then he glanced around the room, looking for something to stir it with.

A small piece of metal caught his eye—part of a horse's snaffle bit. To anyone else it was a useless piece of junk, but to him it was precious. He had been no more than a child, wide eyed and eager at the stables, when the stable master had given it to him and told him he could keep it. The broken snaffle bit had been his most treasured possession ever since. It had traveled with him all the way from Arnost.

He picked it up and gazed at it for a long moment, allowing his mind to wander freely back to a simpler, happier time. Those days had vanished, like mist before the noonday sun. Soon even the memory of them would be gone forever.

For a moment his eyes brimmed, and the welling tears overflowed and rolled down his cheeks. Then he frowned, unwilling to allow himself the distraction of self indulgence. He wiped away the tears, choosing instead to embrace the starkness of his present reality.

Dipping the metal into the chalice, he slowly stirred the wine until all trace of the poison had disappeared.

Beside his bed lay a small wineskin, half filled with wine. He unstopped the wineskin and tipped the other pouch of poison into the opening—the entire dose. Sealing it again, he shook the wineskin vigorously before securing it under his belt.

He grasped the tainted chalice in his left hand and the normal chalice in his right hand, and set off to find Lord Drettroth.

Simon arrived flushed and agitated, working hard at trying to stay calm, and willing himself not to tremble. His master paced back and forth, awash with nervous energy. He failed even to spare a glance for his food taster.

Drettroth finally noticed him. "Where have you been? Give me my wine!"

Simon knew he had the opportunity to end it—once and for all—right here, right now. But he steadied himself. Brother Vangellis and Thomas should be allowed to witness the demise of their tormentor.

Sampling a generous portion from the untainted chalice, he passed it to his master. The nobleman drank greedily, wine spilling out around his cheeks. Having drained the cup, he cast it heedlessly aside, ignoring the clatter as it fell to the floor.

Drettroth seemed to forget that Simon was there. He continued to pace around the room, muttering loudly to himself in his own language.

Simon had set his course, and the pieces were all in place. He relaxed, finally allowing his thoughts to be drawn back to the stone. In spite of the overwhelming jumble of thoughts and impressions, so much now made sense. He felt that he understood Thomas for the first time. Even Lord Drettroth's single-mindedness no longer baffled him.

He wondered briefly what his life might have been like if Thomas had not wrested the stone away from him. But he had now seen the havoc wreaked by the stone on Thomas's life. What might it have done to his own? Simon had managed to do immense harm without the stone—he could only imagine the damage he might have unleashed if he had retained it. He quickly decided that he had been better off as he was.

"Wine, Simon!" Drettroth had snapped out of his reverie. The Rogandan lord had given Thomas one hour to make his decision, and soon the hour would be up.

The fateful moment had arrived.

Simon's heart began to thump. Bitter though his life had become, he didn't want to die. His hopes and dreams had been reawakened, and the greater part of his experiences and memories were still precious to him.

Everything would end with a single mouthful of the liquid. Could he bear it?

Simon blinked slowly and sucked in a breath.

He stood tall. *Ines, this is for you.*

Raising the chalice, he drank deeply from the poisoned wine.

Then he handed the cup to his master.

Lord Drettroth took it and drank.

The Rogandan grimaced briefly once, but continued swallowing until the chalice had been drained.

WHEN THEY RETURNED to the room, Drettroth called for the stone once again. Simon retrieved it, trying to ignore the overwhelming deluge that inundated his senses whenever he glanced at anyone. He handed it over with considerable relief.

The Rogandan overlord began talking again, but Simon had become restless, unable to concentrate. It was hard to believe that everything was about to end. He tried to remind himself that it was all for good reasons, but he couldn't seem to think straight.

Then Drettroth turned to him with a command, "Simon, call for my assistants!"

Simon snapped abruptly back to reality. The stone belonged to him—the unrestrained exhibition of its power confirmed it—and he had uncovered the principles that governed the way it worked. Everything he needed to know he had learned from the thoughts of both

Drettroth and Thomas. Instead of obeying the command, he leaned over to the nobleman and whispered in his ear. "The stone is yours—I'm giving it to you. Enjoy it while you can!" Then he stepped back, away from his tormentor.

Simon saw on the face of the Rogandan lord the dawning of full comprehension at last, as Drettroth finally attained his greatest prize. It was too late. "What have you done?" the overlord screamed, apoplectic with fury.

When Drettroth drew his sword and came for Simon, the youth made no attempt to flee. Knowing his end could not be long delayed anyway, he closed his eyes and waited for the blow to fall. It never happened. The Rogandan commander had instead triggered his own death throes.

Simon, unwilling to witness another agonizing death by poison, even if the victim was Drettroth, surprised himself by managing to dispatch the Rogandan with his own sword. Then he flung the weapon away.

He spoke to Brother Vangellis and Thomas in a detached way, explaining what had happened. But only part of his mind was engaged. The rest of his thoughts drifted aimlessly, remembering what had been, and imagining what might have been.

The monk and Thomas were still chained to the wall, and Simon had just enough presence of mind to retrieve both the stone and Drettroth's keys and to take them to Brother Vangellis. As he freed the monk, a profound sense of gratitude welled up within him. Leaning forward, he quietly whispered his heartfelt thanks. He dimly wondered how his life might have been if he had met the monk sooner. He handed Brother Vangellis the stone, and saw in his face the telltale signs of its revelations.

Then he turned to Thomas, intending to free him as well.

The poison got to him first, and he began to convulse. He tugged frantically at the wineskin under his belt, struggling to free it. Fumbling anxiously, he unstopped it, raised it to his lips, and gulped down the poisoned liquid.

As his life faded steadily away, his final thought was of something

Brother Vangellis had told him. He grasped hold of it tightly, just as a drowning man might snatch at a branch that floats unexpectedly within reach.

The end, when it came, found him at peace.

The saga will continue in
The Stone of Authority
the next installment in Allan N. Packer's
The Stone Cycle

LIST OF CHARACTERS

- *Agon* - king of Rogand
- *Ander* - Arvenian soldier from Erestor; skilled swordsman and archer; healed of severe wounds by Brother Vangellis
- *Anneka* - former noblewoman, Lady Neave; leader of a forest community near Erestor
- *Axel Stablehand* - master of the Arvenian royal stables at Arnost, and the father of Thomas
- *Beneface* - abbot of a high plateau monastery in Arvenon boasting an extensive library
- *Bottren* - high-ranking Arvenian nobleman and close confidante of King Steffan
- *Burtelen* - high-ranking Arvenian nobleman from Erestor and close confidante of King Steffan
- *Dannel* - monk at a high plateau monastery in Arvenon boasting an extensive library
- *Delmar* - king of Varas, a neighboring kingdom to Arvenon
- *Drettroth* - high-ranking Rogandan nobleman; commander of the Rogandan army
- *Duke of Erestor* - The uncle of King Steffan of Arvenon, and

List of Characters

the regent during the king's absence; the senior member of the nobility in Erestor
- *Eisgold* - influential Castelan nobleman; senior commander of the Castelan army
- *Elbruhe* - young Rogandan woman; runaway slave
- *Elena* - young woman living in hiding with her father Rubin in the forests of Arvenon
- *Erastus* - librarian at a high plateau monastery in Arvenon
- *Essanda* - Princess of Castel who marries King Steffan, becoming queen of Arvenon
- *Gordan* - Castelan nobleman; confidante of King Istel and Essanda
- *Grunsetz* - Rogandan ambassador to Varas
- *Haldek* - Rogandan soldier; stronghold guard
- *Hann* - young monk at a high plateau monastery in Arvenon
- *Hender* - young bowman living in Anneka's forest community
- *Istel* - king of Castel, a neighboring kingdom to Arvenon
- *Karevis* - Varasan nobleman; commander of the Varasan army
- *Kulzeike* - commander of the Rogandan army
- *Kuper* - Arvenian soldier from Erestor; skilled swordsman and archer and twin brother to Rellan
- *Luzik* - former Rogandan army commander
- *Marya* - wife of Axel Stablehand and mother of Thomas
- *Nestor* - Arvenian soldier from Arnost
- *Pisander* - Arvenian earl and head of King Steffan's foreign spy network; member of the nobility from Erestor
- *Ranauld* - Arvenian count; a confidante of King Steffan
- *Randolf of Clerbon* - author of an ancient scroll
- *Rellan* - Arvenian soldier from Erestor; skilled swordsman and archer and twin brother to Kuper
- *Rubin* - father of Elena
- *Rudungen* - a minor Arvenian baron

- *Rufe Sarjant* - respected and physically imposing Arvenian soldier; a close friend of Will Prentis
- *Simon* - boy who helped in the Arvenian royal stables
- *Steffan the Second* - king of Arvenon
- *Tarestel* - wealthy and influential Varasan nobleman
- *Thomas Stablehand* - possessor of the Stone of Knowing; son of Axel, the Arvenian royal stable master, and Marya
- *Vangellis* - widely traveled Arvenian monk
- *Will Prentis* - young, ambitious, and unusually capable Arvenian soldier; fluent in Rogandan and widely traveled
- *Yosef* - respected member of Anneka's forest community
- *Zornath* - senior Rogandan army liaison

NOTE FROM THE AUTHOR

Thank you for reading *The Cost of Knowing*—I hope you enjoyed it. Please consider leaving a review on Amazon for the benefit of other readers.

The Stone Cycle saga continues in *The Stone of Authority*.

A prequel to *The Stone of Knowing*, called *The Seer*, is also available, revealing how the stone came to be where Thomas found it. Details below.

To be kept up to date on new releases, sign up to my mailing list at www.allanpacker.com. New subscribers will receive an exclusive bonus novelette, available in ebook and audiobook format. The novelette, *The Rending*, is described below.

But first, *The Stone of Authority*.

The invasion is over, and the shattered Rogandan army has straggled home. The people of Arvenon and the surrounding kingdoms are at peace. Or so they believe.

Little do they know that a new stone of power has emerged, controlled by a cruel tyrant bent on destruction. But King Agon of

Rogand lusts after much more than conquest. He will settle for nothing less than unending power.

No armies are massing at the border. The threat to the kingdom comes from within.

As chaos spreads, Will, Steffan, Essanda, and Arvenon's other key defenders are each confronted with crisis. If any one of them stumbles, the kingdom will fall.

How did the stone come to be where Thomas found it? The answer can be found in a new prequel to *The Stone of Knowing*.

The Seer is a novelette, 5 chapters (13,500 words) in length. It is a standalone story, and as such can be read independently of other books in *The Stone Cycle* series. The novelette is described below.

Eyes see no more than a glimpse

Sheylha is a seer—a woman with unique and extraordinary abilities. Powerful men want to control her, to use her to dominate others.

Kalvor is a warrior of unusual tenacity, a hunter who never gives up. Driven by his past, he has become a dangerous enemy.

When Kalvor is sent to find and capture the seer, each of them will be tested in ways they could never have imagined.

In time the outcome will determine the fate of kingdoms.

The Seer is available at Amazon's Kindle store.

To be kept up to date on new releases, sign up to my mailing list at *allanpacker.com*. New subscribers will receive an exclusive bonus novelette—a prequel to *The Cost of Knowing*. The novelette, *The Rending*, is a complete story four chapters (13,000 words) in length. It provides additional context to one of the story threads from *The Cost of Knowing* without introducing spoilers for other books in *The Stone Cycle* series. The novelette is described below.

Endings may be beginnings in disguise

Anneka is comfortable and confident, a noblewoman of consequence living a life of privilege. Until the day her world is torn apart.

After losing everything she most cares about, she must abandon her home and her way of life in an attempt to secure the future of those who depend on her.

No one, least of all Anneka, could anticipate a deeper significance to her struggle. Yet her journey will one day influence the fate of kingdoms.

RESEARCH NOTES

Spoiler Alert!

The reader is advised to avoid this section before finishing *The Cost of Knowing*.

Poisons

Strychnine, ingested by both Lord Drettroth and Simon, has been used as a poison since ancient times. Its effects are described at:

https://en.wikipedia.org/wiki/Strychnine_poisoning.

Cyanide, used by Simon at the end, is another poison of long standing. It is said to have been the preferred poison of the Roman Emperor Nero. The effects of acute exposure to cyanide are described at:

https://en.wikipedia.org/wiki/Cyanide_poisoning.

ACKNOWLEDGMENTS

Once again, I need to thank my wife and children for their encouragement throughout the journey. My wife, Merilyn, deserves special credit for being the first to follow the story to its conclusion. She patiently provided invaluable feedback at every stage of the process and always managed to be encouraging even when pointing out weaknesses.

My son-in-law Ray has been an enthusiastic supporter in recent years, and I have found his feedback particularly insightful. My son-in-law Marc also provided valuable feedback of his own on the manuscript. I have dedicated this story to them both. I admire and appreciate their cheerful engagement with the inescapable flow of words, both written and verbal, that emanates from our family.

Special thanks to my beta readers, Merilyn, Stephen, Jen Neal, Ray, Deborah, Brian Plush, Francie Hardy, Marc, Cherilyn White, and Ali. Their feedback and suggestions led to improvements in a number of areas.

My grateful thanks go to Brian Plush for the awesome map.

I have very much appreciated the help of my editors. My developmental editor, Mary Novak, provided useful constructive criticism.

The story is better for it. And the final copy benefited once again from Deborah's careful proofreading.

The responsibility for remaining flaws lies solely with me.

Thanks, again, to my daughter, Melanie Cellier, for ongoing advice and feedback around presentation and release practicalities.

I wrote this novel as I was emerging from a period of grief and loss. So final thanks go to God, who sustains and nurtures me through the ongoing joys and trials of life.

ABOUT THE AUTHOR

Allan Packer is an emerging author of epic fantasy. *The Cost of Knowing* is his second novel.

Allan grew up surrounded by books and became an avid reader during his childhood. In his university years fantasy displaced science fiction as his favorite genre, thanks primarily to J. R. R. Tolkien. He later shared this love with his four children by reading *The Lord of the Rings* to them aloud—a three-month marathon he completed twice during their formative years.

Born in Australia, Allan has lived and worked on three continents, and spent one quarter of his working years abroad. Having worked as an IT professional throughout his career, he was first published as a technical author.

Today he lives with his wife in Adelaide, South Australia, near their children and a small but growing band of grandchildren.

Allan is currently working on the next installment in his series *The Stone Cycle*.

CPSIA information can be obtained
at www.ICGtesting.com
Printed in the USA
BVHW030818280820
587541BV00001B/5

9 781925 898019